ELLEN GODFREY

Murder Behind Locked Doors

Published by VIRAGO PRESS Limited 1989
20–23 Mandela Street, Camden Town, London NW1 0HQ

Copyright © Ellen Godfrey 1988

First published by Penguin Books Canada Limited 1988

A CIP catalogue record of this book
is available from the British Library

Printed in Great Britain by Cox & Wyman Ltd, Reading, Berkshire

To my Wednesday friends, without whom
I would never have written any books.
Especially the founders: Sarah Bowser,
Betty Ferguson, Diane Rotstein,
Sylvia Tyson and Kristine Wookey.

Acknowledgements

My thanks to friends and business associates who read and advised on the manuscript including John Kernick, Peter Newman, Adam Vereshak and Paul Williams. Thanks also to Softwords software engineers Campbell Good and Grant Kratofil for helping with the computer programming bits. No doubt any mistakes come from disregarding their advice.

And therefore think him as a serpent's egg
which hatched, would as his kind grow mischievous,
and kill him in his shell.

Julius Caesar, II.i.32

MURDER BEHIND LOCKED DOORS

THE TORONTO DAILY NEWS

Report on Business   *November 21, 1985*

Cautious Risk-Taking Wins Award for Software Firm

Twenty awards were given out last night at a gala banquet hosted by the Canadian Computer Industry Association (CCIA) in Ottawa. On hand to present the awards was Gerald McMaster, Minister of Industry and Small Business, who praised the winning firms for their contributions to Canadian industry and to the country's export picture.

The big winner, as it has been for the past five years, was Brian Taylor Systems Inc. (BTS), the fast-growing, Toronto-based software firm. In his acceptance speech, founder and chief executive officer, and president Brian Taylor said that the awards were won by the entire firm, not by himself. "It's the management team that has built this firm and earned this recognition."

BTS has been a trail-blazer in using the latest in management techniques to achieve excellence. A team of six senior managers runs a firm of 100 employees with constant input *from all levels. Revenues in 1984 were $40-million with profits of more than 20 percent.*

As we have said many times in this column, there is no magic formula for ensuring excellence, but those who wish to emulate the rapid growth, high profitability and sound management of BTS would do well to note the following themes from Brian Taylor's acceptance speech:

* Top-level commitment. Senior management must have a vision about the company's future and corporate culture and convey it clearly to the employees.

* Technological innovations. The company's "applications generators" — software programs that automatically "write" other software programs — were developed by a concerted effort at all levels of the company. Analysts credit these generators with the continual high-profit margins achieved by BTS in an extremely competitive industry.

* Willingness to change. From its founding as a small data-processing company to its current leading position as both a software developer for sectors of the business community and a data-processing service supplier to major Canadian firms, BTS has gone through constant and rapid change. Yet staff turnover has been low. "We have basically the same management we started with when we began our growth," Brian Taylor says. "We chose carefully and got the best people. We selected managers who like constant change, growth and risk. We like to think of ourselves as cautious risk-takers."

These winning themes can help virtually any company in any industry achieve success. The initiative must come from the top executive officer. Top management too must commit themselves wholly to the task.

Jane Tregar was surrounded by men. She hadn't noticed it on the flight coming in from Vancouver, but now, waiting for her luggage, pressed in by all the large bodies, she was uncomfortably aware of her vulnerability. Feeling at a disadvantage always made Jane aggressive. She stepped on someone's large brogue, putting all her weight on the stacked heel of her high boot, at the same time pressing her elbow back into the paunch that was edging her away from the carousel. This allowed her to push in close to the moving belt. Standing on her toes, she peered between shoulders trying to get a glimpse of her baggage. "Excuse me, excuse me," she said, pressing her elbow deep into the tweed jacket that had staked out a claim in front of her making it impossible to see if her suitcase was coming. A small space appeared to the left of the tweed-jacket owner's bristly red neck. Jane stared into the dull light, down the belt and through smeary Plexiglas at the bags moving toward her. They marched forward, emerging from a small doorway like a procession of tightly held secrets.

It's the attaché flight, she thought, straining to see. That's why it's all men on the flight. Is the coddling and extra space worth this fight for the baggage? A body pressed up against her from behind, and cigarette smoke filled her nostrils so that she felt slightly nauseous. Maybe I wouldn't hate it so much if I weren't so tired, she thought, or if I'd done better in Vancouver. Although she had been one of the top performers for the past two years at Orloff Associates, an executive-search firm, lately Jane had begun to think her boss wanted to get rid of her. There was nothing overt, nothing Jane could put her finger on, but she felt sure something was not right.

"Jane, Jane Tregar! What luck! I'm really glad to see you."

Jane looked up to see a spare, fair-haired man smiling down at her. His dark blue, perfectly tailored suit and red tie looked immaculate, not as if he had just emerged from the four-and-a-half-hour flight from Vancouver, though as she looked closer she saw that his face looked strained and tired in the harsh, white airport light. He had a flight bag slung over his shoulder and was pulling a large cardboard box from the carousel. "I bought a Chinese vase for my wife in Vancouver," he said. "I hope to God it isn't in a thousand pieces. How are you, Jane? You're looking well. What luck to meet *you* here.

"Could I give you a lift into town?" he said, as she pulled her bag off the carousel. "I had a meeting near here just before I left, so I've got my car. It's great to see you, Jane."

It was true what they said, she thought to herself, being in the right place, making contacts. I'll leave my car at the airport parking lot, she decided, pick it up tomorrow.

Brian didn't offer to help her with her suitcase, so Jane found a cart and they walked together toward the doors, Jane pushing ahead. But the sliding glass door didn't open. Annoyed, Jane wheeled the cart backward, then forward again over the rubber mat. Nothing happened. Brian came up behind her, and taking her elbow, gently steered her to the next door. "Even Jane Tregar can't go out the in door," he said.

There were three briefcases in the trunk of Brian's Mercedes 360SL. With Jane's suitcase and his flight bag, there didn't appear to be enough space for his large cardboard box. Jane shivered in the cold of the parking lot, but Brian did not open the passenger door for her until he had found a way to pack everything in.

"It's like solving a jigsaw puzzle," Jane said, as she watched him.

"I like puzzles," he said smiling up at her for a moment then turning back to the car, rocking it gently to test if the box was wedged in tightly enough.

"I don't," Jane said.

He unlocked the driver's door, leaned over and opened her side, and then began revving the engine while she slid her briefcase into the back and climbed in. "Funny," Brian said. "I thought you'd be the puzzle-liking type. You've got a very logical mind."

The car sped out of the parking lot, barely stopping at the Stop signs, along the airport access roads to the 401, and then they were sweeping down Highway 427. Jane was tense. Brian was driving very fast. He changed from one lane to another, accelerating suddenly to shoot into a stream of traffic where Jane saw no opening at all. Several times she put her foot down hard on an imaginary brake as the car in front seemed to her to fill the windshield. His was a bad way to drive, in Jane's opinion. He manoeuvred between the cars, judging that they would maintain their speed and direction, without giving them any warning, without signalling. If someone speeded up or slowed down unexpectedly, or behaved erratically in any way, what would happen then?

"You have a lot of accidents?" Jane asked, gripping the door handle as they swerved between two cars and into the right lane to take the ramp onto the Queen Elizabeth Way.

Brian laughed. "I have a perfect driving record," he said. "It's hesitating that gets you into trouble."

"But what if somebody does something really stupid?"

"You've got a point there," Brian said. His smile disappeared, and his face set into the strained expression she had seen at the airport. "I suppose you've heard what happened at BTS?"

"You mean that you won another CCIA award this year?"

"No. I mean that Gary Levin is dead."

"Oh, Brian, I'm sorry. No, I hadn't heard anything about it."

"Well, it's true. And beyond being a friend, someone who's been with us from the beginning, beyond the fact that he's a big shareholder . . . the company is in the middle of a very tricky deal with a U.S. firm — and with no vice-president of finance. We've got to get a replacement as soon as possible, and I think you're just the person to help us."

Jane just stopped herself from saying aloud, hey, fantastic. Finding a vice-president of finance for BTS systems would be a plum job. It would mean a big commission for her and was exactly the sort of business her boss expected her to bring in. Her disappointment over the Vancouver trip was cancelled out by the potential in what Brian Taylor was now telling her. Major placements in high-profile firms were the best kind of business. This would surely keep Eddie Orloff happy.

And what Jane really liked about it was that she already knew Brian's company. She knew the people, and she knew Brian Taylor. I ought to do a good job on this, she thought. When Brian was ready to go public and I found him his management team, we worked together really well. I know he's always said good things about me to people in the industry. It's a fine company. Maybe for once, she thought, I won't have to worry about screwing up. This time she would be in known and familiar territory — no unexpected booby traps.

"I'd enjoy working on it for you, Brian," Jane said happily. "You know how much I like you and all the people at BTS."

"We're a public company now, Jane. That makes a difference. When you helped me before, that was just before we went public. We were smaller then."

"Don't worry, Brian. I've grown up a lot since then myself. I've handled work for plenty of public companies."

He looked sideways at her, a measuring look. "It's that instinct for good people I want, Jane. I'll never forget your thumbnails of the candidates, and your predictions. Everybody I hired whom you warned me against is gone. The ones you really pushed for turned out the best."

Jane tried to keep the anxious feeling his words gave her out of her voice. "There's always some luck in that, Brian. And whatever it is that I do, please don't call it instinct. It's not instinct."

They turned onto Jarvis Street. Jane looked out at the greasy fish-and-chip take-outs, discount clothing outlets, and the dingy variety stores. The stores were shuttered, locked tight, but their lights were on, and the merchandise glittered as if it had real value. After the clean mists of Vancouver, the smears of salt like flyspecks on the windows reminded Jane that she was back in the grime of late fall in Toronto.

Jane couldn't help but wish Brian would be more realistic. It bothered her when people got it into their heads that she had a magic instinct about people. Because there was no way to be certain about such judgments; she never really understood how she came to them. It was ironic; maybe it was because most people in her business were men, or women who hadn't lived through much. But the average middle-aged woman who had seen a bit of the world would be better than I am at sizing up people, Jane thought. I go wrong so often. If he only knew.

"Anyway," Brian went on, "there are just a few things I want to get clear. One is, I want *you* on this job. I'm not hiring Orloff Associates. I want you to tell your boss as little about the job as you can. You'll have to sign a non-disclosure agreement about some of the details we discuss. Okay?"

"Sure." Jane had always trusted Brian Taylor. She was sure he was a good person. But now she felt a slight uneasiness. Perhaps it was the way his hands tightened on the wheel, and his eyes, which from time to time during the drive had sought hers, now stared straight ahead.

"How old are you, Jane?" Brian asked.

Jane was surprised at the question, at the suddenness of it. "I'm thirty-four."

"I guess that's old enough," Brian said, not smiling. "I sure hope so. You're going to have to be very tough for this one."

Jane turned toward him, catching hold of the car door as he swung onto Bloor Street. "What's it all about, Brian? There's something you're not telling me."

His tense face stretched into a quick hard smile, which seemed to acknowledge that she had scored a point against him in some game they were playing, a game she had not yet recognized. Then he said, "You'll just have to trust me."

"Do I have to, Brian?" she said, meaning to tease him a little, hoping he would open up to her.

But this time he didn't smile, didn't make any attempt to charm. "Yes," he said, "you'll have to trust me. That's how I want to play this."

Jane said nothing, as they turned into Rosedale.

Brian took his eyes off the road, and turned toward Jane, looking directly at her. "Jane. Do we have a deal?"

Jane nodded. Now she wasn't smiling either.

2

THE TORONTO DAILY NEWS

Report on Business   *November 28, 1985*

Brian Taylor Systems Inc., one of the fastest-growing companies in the software industry, announced today the death of its chief financial officer, Gary Levin, of an apparent heart attack. Founder and chief executive officer (CEO) Brian Taylor said the search was already under way for a replacement.

BTS was founded 10 years ago by Taylor, as a data-processing company specializing in the financial sector. Since that time it has become an industry leader, providing both services and software packages. Sales last year were over $40-million.

Five years ago Taylor and Levin took the company public, in an eagerly sought-after issue that was sold in record time and immediately became one of the most actively traded stocks in the Toronto Stock Exchange. The stock opened at $2.50 and is now trading at $14.75.

At the time of his death, Levin was reputed to be about to close a lucrative joint-marketing deal with an American data-processing firm in a business closely related to that of BTS. Although unwilling to talk about the U.S. deal, Taylor said that

9

> *it was "business as usual" at BTS and that current plans were*
> *going "full steam ahead." He added: "Levin is a great loss to*
> *the firm, but we have a top-flight management team here, re-*
> *sponsible for all strategic planning. We don't feel that this*
> *tragedy will affect our growth, or our plans for the future."*
> *Taylor had no comment on his U.S. plans.*

It was typical of Brian to ask Jane to meet him at seven
o'clock for breakfast. And typical too, that she should arrive
at his fitness club and find that he was still swimming, and
that she was watching him from the observation balcony, as
he stroked steadily, faster than all the other swimmers, as if
he were timing himself against them.

Watching him swim brought back memories. Perhaps it
was the smell of the chlorine, wafting up from the pool,
mixing with the steam that condensed on the windows of
the pool room to create an atmosphere that was so familiar,
and so evocative of other mornings she had waited for him.
Remembering, she thought that all during the time she had
worked for him five years ago, she had really been studying him, trying to learn from him. She had believed that
somehow he was going to reveal the secrets of success in
business to her. That perhaps, some morning, listening to
him talk in the relaxed mood that seemed, briefly, to come
over him after his swim, she was going to get the hang
of it.

Now, her optimism of five years ago seemed extremely
naïve. But maybe she felt that way because she was so tired.
Seven A.M. was, after all, four in the morning, Vancouver
time, and that no doubt was the time her reluctant body still
thought it was. Where did Brian get his energy? It had
taken what she regarded as a truly heroic effort to tumble
out of bed at six-thirty and get herself into a taxi and up
to North York. Her car, of course, was still at the airport,

which was perhaps just as well, considering how thick-headed she felt. And there was Brian, doing his laps, up as usual at six, out of his house before his wife, Dahlia, was awake.

Brian got out of the pool and waved to her, and she left the balcony and went into the dining room, where she found a buffet of fresh fruit, pots of coffee and baskets of hot rolls. She took a cup of coffee to a table near the window and waited for Brian to join her.

"Sorry, I'm behind schedule," he said as he sat down across from her. He frowned at his watch. "It must be jet lag. It took me ten minutes longer to do my fifty laps than it usually does."

"It felt like old times watching you. I was remembering how often you used to keep me waiting when we worked together before."

He smiled at her, digging his spoon into his grapefruit. "I'm sure we'll get along as well as we did before, and be just as successful."

"Well, tell me about Levin," she said, meaning tell me about his job, so I can get on with mine.

Brian looked thoughtful, and Jane realized he was thinking of something else. "I'm under a great deal of pressure, Jane. The Blumbergs of Vancouver have a large investment in BTS, and Gary was their man. They want him replaced with someone they trust, and they want him replaced fast."

"Their man?" Jane said. "He reported to you, didn't he? You're the major shareholder."

"Oh, BTS is my company, and on the organization charts I was his boss," said Brian, digging his spoon viciously into the grapefruit again. "Yes, it's my company, there's no doubt about that. No doubt whatsoever." He swallowed a section of fruit, sighed and put down his spoon. "But Levin was the financial brain; I let him handle that side of things. That's the way I wanted it, and that's the way the Blumbergs wanted it. I've talked to them over the past few days, and we see eye to eye on the fundamentals, but they'll be a hell of a lot happier when they have a real financial person to deal with."

He looked up at her. "And another thing. Gary was my friend and I miss him. You remember him, don't you? You must have met him."

"I did, of course. . . ." Jane said, trying to bring Levin's appearance, personality into focus.

"Well, he was a terrific guy. For all his flaws, the fact is that for years we worked together beautifully. I did the technical side of things. I know where our technology is going, where the company has to go . . . and Gary helped to make it happen. I couldn't have done it without him. Everything I built, in building the business itself, he was part of it. His death feels like. . . ." He gestured with his spoon. "It's like I've got a rib missing, a hole in my side."

"You two used to fight, though," Jane said smiling, "I seem to remember. . . ."

"God, those fights," said Brian, smiling too. "That was his style, not mine. I'd tell him what I wanted done, and usually he'd do it, but sometimes he'd go his own way, not exactly by the rules, you know, and I'd find out, face him with it, and then he'd start to shout, and we'd have a hell of a row. I'm not like that with anyone else — shouting, arguing. But, who knows, maybe that's why we got along so well."

"And you'd win those arguments?"

"Usually. But of course, it had to be that way. Sometimes, I guess, he thought because he had a piece of the company, because the Blumbergs have a fair chunk — and because they saw him as their man — he thought he had the right to direct the company financially. Of course, sometimes he was right; then I'd listen to him. Even if he was wrong, I'd sometimes give in. You can't go to the mat for every little thing. But when it really counted I'd get my way — that's how it had to be. Though, God knows —" his voice trailed off — "what he thought he was getting up to in those last few weeks." He ate his roll in silence for a minute, waiting while a waitress refilled his cup.

"It was a heart attack?" Jane asked.

"It must have been." Jane noticed Brian avoided her eyes as he said this. "Maybe stress. He smoked too much — those little cigars of his, you remember? He chain-smoked them, non-stop. I never saw him without one. And then, his marriage broke up. . . ."

"I didn't know that."

"His wife found out about the screwing around and just threw him out. He was heartbroken."

Now Jane was remembering Levin. A small man, full of energy, with a great deal of charm. She had met him once, perhaps twice. He had already been a part of BTS when Brian hired her to build his new, expanded management group.

Brian was reminiscing about Levin, talking to her with that easy confidence and trust that had marked their working relationship from the start. She knew that he didn't confide in others the way he did in her; she'd thought, after their conversation the night before, that that aspect of their relationship hadn't survived the five years since they'd seen one another. But now, it seemed, they were back to the way they'd been. She had never really understood the rapport they felt when they were working together before; had just been glad of it, as it made the job easier. She felt the same now.

"I never could figure out Gary's love life," Brian was saying. "Can you understand it?"

She shook her head.

"His wife is a very nice woman, he had three teenage kids, a beautiful house. Yet he'd have affairs with these young girls, one after the other, and each time it was like he'd fallen in love for the first time. His eyes would get bright, he'd be on the prowl, he'd be full of this manic energy. And his wife had to know, that's what I always thought — had to. But I guess she didn't. And when she found out and broke up the marriage, he just couldn't understand it. That's what he told me."

"Well if she just found out he'd been chronically unfaithful, you'd think it would be pretty clear why she ended the marriage," Jane said.

"That's what I thought. But he didn't see it that way. He told me everybody fools around. What could I say? I just looked at him. I couldn't say, *I* don't do it; lots of people don't. You don't say things like that to friends. It doesn't do any good. And he wouldn't have believed me, probably. I felt awfully sorry for his wife, for both of them."

"But in a way he was right, you know that, Brian. Lots of men are unfaithful."

"Sure, but you can't call it the best way to keep your marriage going. You wouldn't expect your wife to accept it if she found out. Anyway, I could never figure out where he got the time. Or why it was worth risking his marriage. Just because you want to do something doesn't mean you always do it. Well —" he smiled slightly "— maybe I did understand a little; it's not as if I'm not human." He looked at Jane, and for a moment she thought she saw something in his expression — desire? lust? — but it passed so quickly she was sure she had imagined it. "It's not as if I haven't fancied some woman or other from time to time. But I'm married, and anyway I. . . ." He looked at his watch. "Why are we talking about this? It must be your fault, Jane." He smiled at her. "The fact is, Gary is dead. I've got to get the Blumbergs calmed down, and this big U.S. deal we're trying to do has to be brought back on track. And it all has to be done fast. If it isn't, our stock will fall too much, and it will make the troubles we have now look like a birthday party."

He reached into a briefcase he had set down on the seat beside him and took out a sheaf of papers. "We'll go over things in general this morning, I'll fill people in today, and then I'll want you to come to BTS tomorrow to meet our management team. They have to be kept on side at all times during the search for Levin's replacement so they feel they've been a part of the final decision. Do you understand?"

"Okay."

"Now this is the kind of a person I want you to find for me, Jane, and this is what I'm prepared to offer him."

They dropped their eyes from one another and looked down at the papers in front of them. Brian was no longer smiling.

"Without a financial vice-president to get things back on track, I'm out on a long limb. We haven't got a lot of time. This limb isn't going to hold us for much longer."

3

The rain came down so heavily that the windshield wipers could not keep the windshield clear. Jane pushed her head forward, trying to see beyond the grey curtain, and felt a trickle of water down the back of her neck. The all-weather top of her Triumph had never fit properly; the woman she'd bought it from said it needed "just a little adjusting." Cold came in through the joints around the windows, too, and Jane wondered if she should have worn her fur coat. Then she wondered if she should have bought a fur coat. There were times when she feared it was all a game of make-believe, and even the props failed to convince.

People thought she was successful, Jane knew. She thought about it often, trying to get the sense of it. Because of her size she knew she still had to fight to get people to take her seriously. Was it success to hear yourself described as the "dynamite little Ms Tregar?" Not to Jane. She didn't have enough money, maybe that was it. Sometimes she thought a lot more money would help overcome being five-foot-two and less than a hundred pounds. Knowing this was absurd didn't make her stop feeling that way. She knew she was making good money at Orloff Associates, but maybe she was on a lucky streak. For sure, it wasn't something she could count on. Maybe by the time she was forty she would know what was skill and what was luck. Maybe if she were earning, say $150,000 a year. . . . Is that what it would take? At thirty-four, $50,000 wasn't that great. Not good enough. Lots of things she wanted and couldn't have. The life she wanted to lead was still beyond her. Plenty of people her age earned much more. And always that feeling of performing a dance on cold, thin ice, never knowing when it might crack and she would fall through into the dark water underneath.

The rain lightened and Jane steeled herself to change lanes in the fast-moving traffic. (Although it was almost seven in the morning, it was close to the nadir of the year and not yet sunrise.) It was no harder driving in this morning from the airport than it would have been two nights before, when Brian had done it as he seemed to do everything, without apparent effort. He was probably at work already, not having to worry about his kids who would be having a proper breakfast with his wife. Maybe having a private life would give a person some balance to her life, a feeling of wholeness. It hadn't worked out that way for her.

She'd given up on all that; given up trying to have a private life. She'd lost the kids when she lost Bernie. Now Bernie and his wife and the boys lived in King City, just outside Toronto, and Bernie made it difficult for her to see them. She knew it was better not to think about it, since there was nothing to be done. Eight years had passed since he left, and took them. Seven since he'd remarried. Their sons had been so little; her life had been so different then: married, kids, finishing university. A rough start, a false start. Or so it seemed afterward, when she realized Bernie had taken it all. Could you call your own kids a false start? It was better not to think about it. She and Bernie had been married three years, apart for eight. How could something so short hurt so much? She hadn't stopped feeling angry. Maybe she didn't want to. Maybe there was good reason to be angry. No, there wasn't. If I could only just despise him, not hate him, that would be an improvement, she thought.

But friends, that was different. Friends you could count on, and they could count on you. They didn't secretly expect what wasn't there. They couldn't take away from you the things you valued most. Why had she thought that she had no private life when she had good friends? Because private life meant a sex life?

Jane thought about sex a great deal, but thinking about it was the easy part. She worked mostly with men; she was interested in them. They could be friends, business-type friends. But men's and women's notions of sex didn't fit. Sad but true. "Little women" got hurt. Love affairs took too much time, were too risky; work was more rewarding. Sexual relationships repeated themselves, and it was hard to learn from them without getting damaged. Anyway, it wasn't as if she had made a decision to give up on sex: it seemed to have given up on her. The love affairs she'd had after her marriage ended had started out with romance and excitement and tapered off into disappointment and boredom. Sometimes she saw too much, and it hurt; sometimes she saw too little, and that hurt too.

For a while she thought the hunger that precipitated her into these affairs was a part of her that would never go away. Then one day, she realized it was gone. It was as if she had been ravenously hungry for a piece of rich chocolate cake. Gooey cake with lots of frosting. When you finally got the cake you were hungry for, you bit into it eagerly and the first few bites were delicious, just as you had imagined. Perhaps if you stopped there, recognized you'd had enough. . . . But who could do that? Instead, you kept on eating, driven by the energy of the first obsessive desire. Suddenly, the cake tastes like sawdust, dry and tasteless, and your tongue sticks to the inside of your mouth. Yet you finish the cake, the memory of your hunger for it driving you to eat every last crumb.

After an experience like that you might easily say you hated chocolate cake, that you couldn't look at a piece without being overcome by the sense of disappointment you had felt as the sweetness dried in your mouth and obsession drove you to fill yourself with sawdust. But if she was no longer hungry, why did she think about it so much?

Jane turned off the 401 and drove into Don Mills. She looked at her watch. She was early. That was bad. She wondered if she had time for a cup of coffee and a doughnut; as usual she hadn't eaten any breakfast, and a doughnut would fill the time until the eight-thirty meeting.

BTS was in an industrial park in North York. The area was filled with doughnut shops, and Jane found one she remembered from years before, when she had helped Brian Taylor recruit his management team. They'd had good talks then, sitting hunched in the back booth, arguing about what qualities it took to survive in an atmosphere of uncertainty and controlled chaos, what kind of person could manage the complexities of the software business.

Jane got gratefully out of the little Triumph, wiping the back of her neck. The cold rain had stopped, but the air was damp and chilly, and when she breathed, it penetrated her lungs as if someone were pressing a cold compress on her chest. Inside, the windows of the doughnut shop were steamy and the smell of the fresh-baked doughnuts and coffee pleased her. She got her order, and as she walked toward a table she recognized the man in the next booth. Jane didn't forget faces or names, perhaps because she found people so interesting.

"It's Martin Kaplan, isn't it?" she said going over to his table. He put down his newspaper and looked up at her, smiling.

Even sitting down, Martin Kaplan was a big man. He wore a brown three-piece suit, a cream-coloured shirt, and a brown-and-green striped tie, carelessly knotted around a collar too tight for his neck. He had two chins, round pink cheeks like a fresh-faced baby and round glasses with clear plastic rims. Jane returned his smile, remembering him from five years before. He had less hair now, but the top of his head was a shiny healthy pink, and his hazel eyes, the whites shot with yellow, looked up at her with the same warmth she remembered. "Hey, it's Jane Tregar, the blazing ball of fire, right? Sit down and tell me how life's been treating you since you sent me spinning down the fast lane. Good to see you, Jane." He shook her hand vigorously, ignoring the powdered sugar left from his doughnut, which floured up between them.

Jane set down her coffee and doughnut and slid into the seat opposite him. "So how is it in the fast lane, Martin?" she asked him. "As good as I promised you when I tempted you to leave Systemhouse?"

"Well I wouldn't go that far," Martin said, "but you are a damned good promiser. And it's been fun and well. . . ." He trailed off, his smile fading. "It's *been* fun."

"Actually, I'm here to meet with all the management people at BTS this morning, did you know that?"

"I knew we were going to meet some headhunter. I never thought of you . . . but hey, it's great stuff that it's you. How's business been for you?"

"Fine. Listen, Martin . . ."

"If you're going to ask me some questions about Gary, save your breath," Martin said. "I don't want to talk about it. Hell, nobody wants to talk about it."

Jane tilted her head and looked at Martin without saying anything.

He shifted in his seat and took a large, angry bite out of a jelly-filled doughnut. Jelly dripped over his fingers and he licked them off, one by one. "What's the use of worrying ourselves into a snitfit? We don't know how he died, and there it is."

"How he died?" Jane repeated softly. She watched Martin's face, saw his eyes narrow, saw the way he swallowed his pastry too quickly, gulped down his coffee.

"It's the damned, locked computer room that's got us all a bit uptight. But hell, why should that be? Anybody can kick the bucket in a locked room, right?"

Jane just looked at him, her silence inviting him to continue.

"Heart attack, must have been. Gary sure was a candidate for one. High blood pressure and a chain-smoker. Always pushing himself and everybody else to their limits and beyond. And we pushed back, no doubt about that. He was under pressure, you know. We were going to put the screws to him and he knew it . . . but that's the way the crumble cookies, right?" Kaplan wasn't looking at her.

"Put the screws to him? I don't understand. Gary couldn't have been fired, could he? I mean, he had a rather big minority share in BTS and the Blumbergs —"

"Fired? Who said anything about being fired? I'm talking about what you might call a strong difference of opinion between him and the rest of us. We were going to have it out with him, that's all." Martin finished his doughnut and began wiping his sticky fingers with a thick wad of paper napkins.

"A difference with Brian too? Martin," Jane said slowly, looking directly at him, holding his unwilling glance in hers, "what's bothering you about Gary's death? I'm on the team now, so you can tell me; I'll hear soon enough."

Martin looked at her steadily for a minute, then reached for his coat, lying crumpled on the banquette beside him. "Time to hit the road if we're not going to be late; you know how that pisses Brian off. You'll find out what's bugging me soon enough, you can count on that. You'll probably find out a hell of a lot more than I know. Or want to know," he muttered, half to himself, as he struggled into his overcoat. "Want a suggestion, love? Go slow in all this, and go careful. There's a lot that doesn't make sense. Maybe you'll make sense of it. Because I sure as hell can't."

They walked outside together, and Jane saw that it had begun to rain again. It was dark and cold and she shivered.

4

The ambient lighting at BTS was dim. It bathed everyone in a rosy glow, smoothing the lines in their faces, and blurring away marks of tension, stress or anxiety. Wearing her identity badge, Jane was escorted by a secretary along carpeted corridors to a large windowless meeting room. It had a big whiteboard, a long table with an overhead projector sitting at one end, and along the far wall, a floor-to-ceiling bookcase full of computer magazines. The meeting room made Jane feel very small, despite the fact that she had dressed in her biggest, bulkiest suit. Everyone standing when she entered only exacerbated the feeling.

There were five people around the table, and Brian introduced her to them. Martin had combed his hair and knotted his tie more carefully; Brian looked calm and neat as usual in a dark suit and yellow tie, but he seemed larger in this room than Jane remembered him.

"This is Martin Kaplan, director of customer support. I'm sure you remember him," Brian was saying. Martin leaned over and took her hand in both of his. "Long time no see," he said, winking at her.

"And I'm sure you remember Tom Henege?" Brian said.

"Vice-president of sales and marketing? As I recall he was the one who took the most persuading to join us."

Jane nodded, shaking Henege's hand. She did remember him. He was a sharp-featured man, medium height, in his late thirties, serious looking, his tanned face intense and ambitious with a square, hard jaw. Dark, curly hair, thin on top, a quick smile showing slightly crooked teeth. He made Jane feel wary and tense, and she wondered if the feeling was mutual. Such feelings usually were.

He sat back in his chair and studied her with a small smile; it was a steady, measuring look and Jane turned away from it.

Martha Gruen leaned over the table and took Jane's hand, and the two women smiled at one another. Jane had known and respected Martha for a long time. She had been determined that there would be a woman hired for the management team at BTS, and had worked hard to convince Martha to come in. "Martha is our vice-president of human resources," Brian was saying. "That's overall people management and she handles project management as well."

"That's kind of a mixed bag, isn't it?" Jane said.

"She's good at it, so she got volunteered," Tom Henege said, smiling at Martha, his crooked teeth showing white in his dark face. It's the tan that makes him so attractive, Jane thought. Too bad I can't like the man.

"Titles don't mean that much around here anyway," Martha said. "But speaking of that, Brian, why don't we think about Martin being made a vice-president, rather than a director? I could never understand why Gary was against it. We all know how important the customer-service division is. Right now making Martin a vice-president could send a signal to our customers when they're feeling uneasy because of Gary's death."

"Right on, right on," Martin Kaplan said.

Jane admired Martha. She liked the commitment in her voice, and she liked the disinterested loyalty Martha was showing to her colleague. Martha was a tall, good-looking woman, with a soft, low, authoritative voice. She looked very businesslike; perhaps it was her straight, short, dark hair and tortoiseshell glasses. She was wearing a navy-blue, double-breasted suit and a very expensive-looking string of pearls. The collar of her grey silk blouse was fastened with a diamond stick-pin. Now she looked at Brian without smiling.

"You're right, Martha," Brian said. "Good point. But today I want you all to meet Jane and understand where she and I are going with finding Gary's replacement. Jane, I don't think you know Robert McDonnell, our comptroller." Brian waved almost dismissively toward a very tall, very thin, pale-looking blond man, who now sat slouched back in his chair at the end of the table, his chin resting against his chest. McDonnell was wearing a light grey suit, a white, oxfordcloth button-down shirt, and a blue-and-grey striped tie. His pale blue eyes were blurred by his thick, gold-rimmed spectacles. "You wouldn't know Robert; he wasn't one of the people you found for us. The fellow I hired despite your advice left, and Gary recruited Robert himself."

Jane went around the table, shook hands with McDonnell, leaned her briefcase and purse against the wall, and took out a pad and her gold Cross pen. Brian, over at the whiteboard, was drawing a neat organization chart. He put a big square at the top, which he labelled CEO/PRES. — BT. "That's me," he said. He drew a vertical line down and intersected it with a horizontal. Changing markers, he drew four red boxes suspended from the horizontal. The marker squeaked on the board, and the acrid smell of marker ink filled the room as he labelled each of the boxes. Jane found the order in which he filled them in interesting; it must have been how he ranked them in his mind. "Alan Bates, vice-president of research and development, he's away for a month, so let's forget about him for a minute; Martin Kaplan, customer support; Tom Henege, sales and marketing; Martha Gruen, human resources.

"Now here's where I see the vice-president of finance." He picked up a green marker and drew another, shorter vertical line from his own box, which he stopped with a box that sat above all the others; he labelled it vp finance. From it he suspended one final box, parallel to the four that hung from the other vertical. In this one he wrote comptroller, Robert McDonnell.

Everyone stared at the green box, which rested, alone, above all the other vice-presidents.

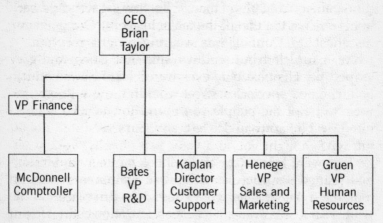

There was a silence. Finally Martha said, "Well, that explains a lot."

"I've never seen a bloody organizational diagram around here before," Martin said, "and I don't like this one."

"I want to be perfectly clear about this," Brian said. "The

VP of finance is not just a numbers man. Gary was more than that, and the new man will be more than that."

"He was also much less, I'm sorry to say," Martha said. "I suggest we don't try to replace him. The problems are obvious from your chart. It seems to me it would make more sense to rethink the whole thing, rethink this attitude about growth — about getting another high-powered, dollar-obsessed person around here."

Martha had always been very articulate, but Jane did not remember her being so tough.

"I'm not sure I see where you're going with this, Brian," Henege said, his voice diplomatic. "Why should finance wag the dog? Getting into the U.S. shouldn't change the kind of company we are." Jane looked for a minute at the wall opposite her side of the table. There was a series of framed prints by Canadian artists, abstracts that seemed to be unconnected pieces of machinery floating weightless in space; reflected in the glass she could see McDonnell's expression. It was stiff, withdrawn, his lips a narrow line.

"We can't afford to plateau; we're not going to," said Brian. "We've got things we have to do. Either we go into the U.S. or they come and get us. I thought we were all agreed on that. The simple question is how to make it happen. That's what we need the right man for."

"But I thought you and Gary had already worked all that out," said Jane. "To play devil's advocate for a minute, doesn't it seem that you might need a 'numbers man' to implement the strategy you've already got in place?"

"Let's not be naïve, Jane," Brian said. "Negotiating a deal like the one we've been working on in the States is not an easy thing and it's not for beginners. None of us has the experience for it. You have to find us someone we like, who can work with us, whom we respect. Someone who's our kind of person, who can go down there and not get chewed to pieces. You've been in too many negotiations yourself to think any different."

Jane looked at Robert McDonnell. He had sucked in his lower lip so that his mouth made a thin, lipless slit, like a faint pencil line. "Would Robert, as comptroller, report to this new vice-president, as he did to Gary Levin?" she asked. The unspoken question was clear to everyone. Why wasn't Robert being considered for the position, being promoted to it?

"That right — that's what we're planning," Brian said. Jane could see that she had annoyed him, but there was a tension in the meeting she didn't understand, and she wanted to poke a little to see if stirring things up would bring something to the surface.

A secretary came in with a tray of coffee cups and a silver carafe. There was a silence as she set down the tray and the carafe, poured the coffee and handed it around. Brian thanked her by name, but he seemed hardly to see her. He had what appeared to Jane a barely controlled impatience, as if he were badly behind schedule and everything at the meeting was a waste of time, preventing him from being somewhere more important, doing something else, something that really mattered. She watched Robert McDonnell pour cream into his coffee, and then carefully measure out three spoonsful of sugar, making sure that each was exactly level before gently sifting the sugar into his cup. Then he stirred, concentrating carefully on what he was doing, not looking at anyone. As he took his first sip, he caught Jane's eye and realized that she was watching him. He looked away, and Jane saw the rims of his ears and the back of neck flush red.

He turned back to her and spoke, his voice flat, without expression, and a little too loud. "I'm not in line for the vice-president of finance." He frowned. "I've got enough on my plate as comptroller, more than enough. I'm perfectly happy with the way things are."

Jane looked quickly around the table, catching a wisp of a mocking smile on Tom Henege's face. Perhaps McDonnell caught it too. He looked at Henege.

"There's no way I want the headaches that go with that job; no way I want to have a heart attack before I'm forty-five," he said. There was a silence, and he repeated, a little louder, a little more forcefully. "No way. I've got the job I want, not like some others I could name."

Henege spoke quickly. "I don't blame Robert. It's a killer of a job, VP of finance, in a company growing as fast as this one."

"Are you saying the *job* killed him?" Kaplan said. "If that's what did it, it's a wonder all the rest of our bodies aren't festooned around the computer room then, and you'd think all the other financial vice-presidents in town would be dropping like flies. But, last time I looked most of 'em were flourishing. It's not the job that's lethal."

"We're getting off topic —" Brian began, but everyone began speaking at once, as if Kaplan's words had opened a pressure valve.

"Wait a minute, nobody knows what killed him —" Henege began.

"Levin's death is not the issue," McDonnell said in his flat, monotonous voice.

But Martha Gruen, her voice higher than the men's, with less timbre, rode over all of them, silencing them by the intensity of her conviction. "We have to stop all this bullshitting for Jane. We have to be honest with her. We owe it to her."

"Oh God, not now, Martha, don't get on that again," Martin Kaplan said. "Give it a break, why don't you?"

Jane knew she had poked up what she was looking

for, and she didn't intend to let go. "What do you mean, Martha?" she asked.

"I think we would be well advised to —" McDonnell began, but Jane interrupted him.

"Brian?" Jane said.

"I'll tell her if none of the rest of you will," Martha said, when Brian didn't speak. She turned to Jane. "You have a right to know, Jane, considering what you are here to do. What we're talking about, what's got our teeth on edge. No use beating around the bush. The real question we have to face is, which one of us murdered Gary Levin? And how in God's name did he do it?"

5

The big problem with North York, from a business point of view, was not the transportation — it was easily accessible by the Don Valley Parkway, which swept northward from downtown Toronto, and by the highways stretching out to the newer suburbs to the north and east, and the older ones to the west; nor was it the real-estate prices, which were attractive enough to appeal to rising firms in the service sector. For the people who worked there, or at least for those who cared about that sort of thing, it was the restaurants. North York restaurants where business people ate seemed to be stuck in a sixties' time warp. Downtown Toronto had entertained its expense-account diners with a succession of trendy restaurants, beginning with the heavy French and Italian cuisine of the sixties and seventies, to the wave of quiche, white wine and fern restaurants of the late seventies, followed by successive waves of pasta, nouvelle cuisine, *nuovo cuicina*, fresh fish on mesquite grills, and then by the emergence of "California cuisine" and restaurants run by chefs as individual, eccentric, creative and uneven as *auteur* film directors.

However, in North York, only half an hour away,

business people still were obliged to lunch on prime rib, shepherd's pie or Caesar salad. They chose from one large restaurant or another, most installed in shopping centres, decorated in maroon, mahogany, and loud-patterned broadloom, and drank from thick pebbly coloured glasses while shielded from the daylight by heavy, dark, dusty curtains.

"How about ordering a bottle of wine, and getting down to it?" Jane suggested, as she, Brian and Martha settled into a table against the wall. Ranks of white-covered tables stretched out in all directions, lit here and there by Tiffany lamps and protected from the grey daylight by garish, stained-glass windows. The waitress, a cheerful-looking woman with a worn middle-aged face, handed them large menus, much of which were taken up with mixed drinks like Rob Roys and Pink Ladies.

Brian ordered a bottle of something white, dry and imported, then said to Jane, "Okay, let's get down to it."

"Let's do the easy part first," Jane said, taking out some printed sheets from her briefcase. She handed them to Brian and Martha, and within ten minutes the overall duties, responsibilities, base salary and benefits were clear in her mind.

"Jane, I think you, Robert and I should have another meeting with our lawyer to discuss different ways to structure what we'll be offering this guy," Brian said. "So, you'll have some room to manoeuvre."

"You keep saying 'guy', 'man'," Martha said. "Does that mean you won't consider a woman?"

"I'm only being realistic. Jane won't find a woman qualified for this position, not in Canada anyway."

"Will you look in the States, Jane?" Martha asked.

"How do you feel about that?" Jane said, turning to Brian.

"I think it's a good idea. In fact, I'd almost prefer it. Someone who has experience doing business in the U.S. would be a real help to us. Do you know people down there, though? I've been hoping we could find someone you know, Jane. This is going to be very tricky, especially the early negotiations. We can't tell the candidate too much before they're on board; but if we don't tell them enough we're not going to get them."

Jane looked across the restaurant. They had arrived early, but now the tables were filling up. Most of the diners were dark-suited men. They wore red or striped ties, they were clean shaven, and they even seemed all the same size. It's probably the light, she thought, and indeed, when she looked closer she saw it was an illusion; here and there she saw sports jackets, jeans, a beard or two, and even a few women. She wondered if the restaurant attracted a homogeneous clientele. Were women still such an alien species in upper and middle management? She was glad for Martha's presence; sometimes working all day with men tired her in the same way as the constant speaking of a foreign language did.

"I've done this kind of thing before," Jane said. "We'll just have to play it by ear. In theory, no problem about finding someone from the U.S.; I know quite a few people. But have we time to go through the hassle of getting them a work permit?" Brian shook his head.

"Then I suggest we try for a Canadian who's worked down there, or is working down there now, or an American who already has a work permit up here."

They discussed it for a while, until the waitress took away their plates, and brought them coffee. The wine was gone, and Jane felt that the tensions from the morning's meeting at BTS had dissipated. If she had annoyed Brian by stirring up the management group, there was no sign of it.

Nor had he shown, either at the meeting or later, any concern over Martha's disclosures.

"I'm going to the ladies'," Martha said, picking up her handbag. "Jane?"

Jane shook her head. She wore very little makeup, so that didn't need attending to, and having trained herself not to leave a meeting if it could be at all avoided, she had planned all along to use Martha's first absence from the table to speak privately to Brian. So now she smiled at Martha, and as soon as she was out of earshot, she turned back to Brian, who was stuffing papers into his briefcase.

They chatted for a few minutes, then she said, "Brian, you'll have to tell me what Martha meant. I can see you don't want to, but you must see it's crucial I know."

He ran his hand up his nose and across his forehead, as if to smooth out the lines of stress that formed there.

"The plain facts are that Gary died in the computer room. It was locked and no one knows how he died."

They looked at each other so intently that they did not see Martha, coming up behind them. "No, Brian," she said, "tell her all of it."

Martha sat down and reached for a sugar cube. There was a silence while she carefully unwrapped it, slitting the paper open with a long, perfectly manicured fingernail.

"I signed everything conceivable for you this morning, Brian. I'd probably be locked up for a century if I even repeated something one secretary said to another," Jane said. "And in any case, you know me well enough to know that I know what and what not to say to whom, and when."

"I don't think secrets are the issue," Martha said. "It's probably too late for that anyway. Our stock was down forty cents this morning."

"That's not the point," Brian said. "The flutter is natural.

We report once a year; we can take our lumps. It's the long view we have to keep in mind."

"I don't agree," Martha said. "We've learned that the price of our shares affects everybody, inside and out. It's a kind of barometer we ignore at our peril." She turned to Jane. "The problem is, Jane, that Gary was working on something quite big: a joint-marketing agreement with a large firm in the States. It's a firm we had reason to believe was about to come up here and slug it out with us. Some of the BTS management team think the joint-marketing agreement will be much better for both firms. It will open up new American markets for our software, give us more products up here, and make us less vulnerable to American competition. Gary believed that, I know. So does Brian. But the problem is, not all of us are in favour of it, and you know how we work here. We speak our minds, and we fight for what we think is best for BTS. Some of us thought that in the long term this agreement could be bad for us. The night of Gary's death we decided to meet and put our concerns on the table, thrash it out and try to reach a consensus."

"Brian?" Jane said.

Brian nodded. He was stirring his coffee with a distant, distracted expression.

"But Gary never showed up at that meeting," Martha said. "The rest of us were there — except for Alan Bates, and his research-and-development division wouldn't have been affected. He's on a six-month leave in any case — burnt out. We hashed it over till two or three in the morning at Brian's house — Brian, Martin Kaplan, Robert McDonnell, Tom Henege and me."

"It wasn't the sort of meeting Gary liked, or thought he ought to attend," Brian said. "We should have guessed that he wouldn't show up for it. I put forward his point of view; on this issue I shared it completely."

"Gary tended to lose his temper," Martha said, "so he'd avoid meetings like that one. Brian is a much better salesman when the troops get restless and need to be brought back in line."

Brian smiled, but Jane thought he wasn't amused.

"We didn't reach the kind of consensus that night we'd all hoped for," Martha went on. "There was disagreement over the figures and Gary's projections. I came in early the next morning, thinking to work out some ideas of my own. I'm usually one of the first to arrive in the morning anyway. People come to see me all day with their problems, so I like to be in by six to have a few quiet hours to get some work done.

"But when I got there, I found that the mini-computer was down. I had to go into the computer room to boot it up, to restart it. I found Gary there. Dead."

Brian was no longer smiling. "The room was locked, as it's supposed to be," he said. "We have a very sophisticated system; our information is our lifeblood. We have an outer door that locks with a key, which very few people have. That door is always locked at night. Then there's an inner door with a card lock. The card lock controls who has access and when. As far as I know, as far as anybody knows, the only people who could get in there at night without special authorization were the six of us, and Sandy Tsu, the systems manager. He was sick that night and his wife took him to the emergency room at the hospital. So there's no way that he came down and let anybody in. Gary died, in the computer room, sometime between eleven at night and two in the morning. The rest of us were at the meeting at my house then. So Gary had to have been alone when he died; he had to have died a natural death."

"I opened up the computer room," Martha said. Her voice was suddenly very cold, very formal. "There he was, lying there. And here's the part Brian feels is not relevant . . ."

"Martha —"

"Look Brian. I trust Jane. You trust Jane. If we replace Gary and the new person goes right on, everything as before. . . ."

Jane had a feeling of foreboding, of things going beyond her, of getting in over her head. It was a dangerous feeling, one that often made her push on when she ought to draw back. A feeling of sick excitement that both stimulated and frightened her.

"I booted up the computer," Martha went on. "The console printer came on and printed a message. The message said, 'That will teach the son of a bitch.' The message was from superuser."

"And that means?" Jane asked. Her voice sounded very high and faint.

"You know our system, Jane," Brian said. "It's part of how we do things. Only eight people can get access to our system as superuser. Only eight people could have sent that message. Seven were nowhere near BTS that night, and the eighth was unlikely to have sent it about himself."

"The eighth being Gary?"

"The eighth being Gary."

"Now here's where I made a decision I've had to live with," Martha said. "One that I'm getting more and more nervous about. I booted up the computer and saw that message. And of course, when the computer came up, it started spewing out messages the way it does when you re-boot; piles of computer paper came racketing out of the console printer right after the message. I read them; I didn't touch them. There was nothing to help explain Gary's death in them. The message 'That will teach the son of a bitch' was lost in the pile of printouts. It's there, waiting like a timebomb, for the police to find. Because I didn't say anything about it to them."

"You did the right thing, Martha. Absolutely," Brian said.

Jane said, "I'm not sure I understand. Why didn't you tell the police about the message?"

"Martha and I have worked together so long and so well, she knows what I want without my saying," said Brian. He smiled, but the smile was very small, rather sad. "Let's get it out on the table — that message made it seem Gary was murdered. I guess Martha still believes that's what happened. I don't. For a company like ours, a murder investigation would be very harmful." His voice was calm. "And why start that hare? The seven other people who had the superuser password and the keys and night passcard access could not have been there that night. Murder is an impossibility."

Jane spoke very slowly. "It's not that simple, is it?"

Martha smiled. "You can't have it both ways, Brian. You wanted Jane to work with us because she knows our business; she knows our field. She's not a naïve user who doesn't understand how computer programming works. You have to trust her."

"I do trust her," Brian said.

"The whole thing was programmed," Jane said suddenly.

The waitress came with the cheque and refilled their coffee cups. They were silent, waiting until she was gone. Jane looked around them. The room was empty now. Busboys were collecting the last cups and saucers and stacking them on the service carts. Others were taking off the white tablecloths, revealing fresh, new, white ones underneath. How many layers do they have? Jane wondered.

"Somebody programmed the computer to go down,

somebody programmed it to send that message to the console. And if the message came from superuser, it had to be one of the eight people with the superuser password," Jane said.

"That much is obvious," Brian said. She saw that he was angry. His jaw was tight and he had an intensity she found unnerving. "But it doesn't prove that Gary was murdered."

"How did he die?" she asked.

"Congestive heart failure," Martha said. "But there are no signs of his having had a heart attack. His lungs showed signs of cyanosis — that's a low level of oxygen in the blood, like a person might have if they suffocated. But nobody knows what caused it in this case."

"How horrible." Jane tried not to shudder.

"I found him," Martha said. "I panicked. It *was* horrible."

"But any way you slice it, it couldn't be murder," Brian insisted.

"I don't agree," Martha said. "And Brian, I don't think you believe that either. You're trying not to think about it, because if it's true there'll be big problems. But it isn't going to go away. You can't talk to Jane about filling this position, unless you face the fact that you may be setting her up."

"Setting her up? How?"

"You can't ask Jane to hire someone else to be murdered, Brian. Surely you can see that."

Jane looked from one to the other as they argued, their voices rising. "Brian," Martha said, "if someone murdered Gary — one of us — because they didn't want this U.S. deal to go through, how do you think they'll feel about a new person brought in to do the same job?"

"That's absolutely absurd, Martha." Brian's tone held complete conviction. "Put it out of your head. It's a flat, out-and-out impossibility. Look at it this way," he said, turning to Jane. "This is a company you helped build. And it helped build you. You know what your success in putting together the management group at BTS when you were just starting out has meant to you. I know I don't have to go into that.

"We're a public company. We're in a service industry. We sell a product our clients can't see and hardly any of them really understand. They come to us and stay with us because they trust us. They trust us to give them what we promise; they trust us that it will be good quality. And they trust us, most of all, year after year, to maintain those systems, to enhance them, to support them. What do you think would happen to our business if the idea got out that one of the management team murdered the number-two man?" Brian was intent now. He leaned toward Jane, fixing her with his compelling, gentle gaze.

"But Brian," Jane said anxiously, "you can't just ignore it. Go on working, wondering. . . ."

"No, of course not." He got up, taking his overcoat off the chair, and began putting it on. "I'd never do that. I'm not saying that. But what we do have to do is get a new man in quickly. Someone people trust, someone who can take over the joint-marketing agreement before it goes sour. Then we'll be in a strong position to deal with these problems."

"The joint-marketing agreement. . . . Where is your sense of perspective, Brian?" Martha was pale with anger.

"Don't shout at me, Martha," Brian said calmly. They were walking toward the door. "It's not as simple as you want it to be. The deal Gary and I were in control of was one thing. If this thing drifts, it could turn into something else. Especially if we look weak at the top. A lot of information has been exchanged; we're a long way into this. We've aroused the kind of interest in the firm that could mean trouble, unless we stay in control."

Jane, walking beside Martha, heard her sudden, surprised intake of breath.

"And I don't intend to lose control of my company," Brian said as they reached the restaurant entryway. He pushed hard on the door, opening it to a cold gust of wind. "I don't intend to. It's as simple as that."

6

Driving back downtown along the Don Valley Parkway, Jane worried. Brian Taylor had been telling the simple truth when he said she owed a great deal to BTS, yet it was almost as if she were being blackmailed. There's no threat, she thought, but Brian is calling in a debt. And its a debt I owe. I really do owe it. Brian trusted me and gave me my first really big job. There's no doubt that it was his influence that got me promoted from research assistant to associate at Orloff's. If it hadn't been for Brian's insistence on hiring me to put together his executive group, Eddie Orloff would have kept stalling, kept promising to make me an associate and never doing it. I would have been just another of that pool of young women he hires promising to promote, who wait and wait and it's always "next year." That's probably what Orloff intended when he hired me. It's only due to Brian that I escaped that fate.

Why *had* Brian trusted her from the time he first met her, when she was just getting started at Orloff Associates? Maybe because of a kind of rapport that made it easy for them to work together, a respect they had felt for one another from the first time they met.

Jane knew what Brian had been saying to her over lunch. The debt she owed him was not the kind that could be written off or forgotten when it was convenient. It was compelling, and to her unavoidable. She knew she had no choice but to honour it.

In the past, during the six months she had helped him find the key additional staff for BTS's big jump in size, Jane had wondered once or twice if there might be something else behind the ease they felt with one another. She had been twenty-nine then, Brian thirty-eight. She knew he was married, but he rarely mentioned his wife or children. In fact, he hardly ever talked about his personal life, even when they had travelled together, interviewing people. There had been that one time, she remembered . . . What had happened? A noisy disco, after a contract signing. They had been out drinking with a group of people who had left, one by one, until only the two of them were still there, having drunk too much, disoriented by the strobe lights, deeply tired, relaxed, happy. They had danced together, she remembered, said flattering things to one another that could barely be heard above the din. Compliments that were in that grey area between friendship and flirtation. Neither of them had been sure what, if anything, was happening. And in fact there had been nothing. They had sat very close to one another, in the taxi to the plane to catch the "red eye." There had been no possibility that there would be anything more between them that night, since they'd had to fly out. When they woke up in the plane, bleary-eyed, to drink reconstituted orange juice and fly into the bright Toronto morning, their time in the disco had seemed like a dream. Neither had ever mentioned that night to the other, and Jane had not thought of it again, until today. She knew it had to mean nothing. She had two cardinal rules, had always kept them: never with clients;

never with married men. And for the past few years it had been never, period, she thought to herself. Brian and I are tied only by a business link, she told herself, but it's still a link too strong to break.

Although it was still mid-afternoon, the sunlight was already fading, and the streetlights had come on, bathing the highway in a faint, golden iridescence. The lights of the oncoming cars were luminous tunnels in the grey mist, and the spans of the great bridges that arc over the Don Valley glimmered and were gone as Jane drove southward. Everything seemed indistinct in the fine rain, and Jane thought she would have to concentrate harder on her driving, not to miss the Bloor Street turn-off. Still, she could not help thinking about the question that Martha had raised, the question of murder.

She was intensely curious. She wanted to know what was going on at BTS. If Gary had been murdered, she wanted to know who did it. True, she was afraid. But that was a familiar feeling.

However, when it came to the other problem — would the person she sought as Levin's replacement be a target for murder? — she was more deeply involved. What should she do? How could she work to fill a position where the incumbent's life might be in danger? Was she that much indebted to Brian? I need someone to talk to, someone older and wiser to help me, she thought. But who can I talk to about this? I've signed all those confidentiality papers. I'll have to be very careful. There's really only one person, bound as I am. I guess it's clear. I'll have to talk to the boss. I'll talk to Eddie Orloff.

Eddie Orloff was a nervous man. Perhaps it was in an attempt to control this quality that he had become an obsessive runner, a marathoner. He said running had changed his life, but Jane had seen no signs of that. He had been full of energy and ambition when, at five-foot-eleven and 200 pounds, he was physically slothful. Now at 145 pounds he was gaunt, jumpy and just as driven. When he directed his energy at her, Jane found it hard not to cower.

"What do you mean you have to consider? This is your biggest deal yet. There's nothing to consider. There'll be big money on the table for Levin's replacement. Stock options, cash — we're getting a percentage, right? The bonus you'll make on this one, kiddo, could probably double your take-home this year. You have to go for it."

Jane smiled weakly. "I'm not sure you heard me, Eddie. Think about it. The new hire's predecessor died of unknown causes."

Eddie Orloff was a very bright, very quick man, but this morning he didn't seem to be at his best. They were sitting in his large corner office. Floor-to-ceiling, tinted-glass walls looked down over Toronto's financial district, many of whose denizens had passed through the office of Orloff Associates. Orloff liked antiques; maybe he wanted to hint at his white Russian ancestry. French-polished mahogany campaign-style desk, French-print-upholstered sofa. On a red leather, brass-studded chair in one corner Jane could see Eddie's Adidas bag. His thinning black hair, the silver streaks gleaming in the filtered daylight, was damp. Had he just come from a run and a shower? Jane wondered. It was eight o'clock in the morning. Orloff was rumoured to start at five, run for an hour and a half each morning, shower and be in the office by seven. But it was pouring rain that morning, dark, overcast, high winds, close to freezing.

Orloff got up and walked quickly around the office. He had a smooth grace to his step that always made Jane a little afraid; to her he resembled a hungry jungle animal, restless, looking for prey. Deep lines ran from his nose to his mouth and his skin was very white and clear, almost transparent. He was surely past sixty, but the other women in the office thought he was sexy. Jane couldn't see it.

"Well, what's the problem?" he said, sounding irritated. "I don't see the problem."

"You don't?" Jane said, her voice sounding thin and high.

"No, no problem. Looks like your classic take-the-money-and-run deal to me. You find the candidates, line 'em up. I'll put one of our legal people on this to backstop you, and have someone in finance briefed so you can consult whenever you want to. BTS will want their own best legal and accounting people as they get near to close, anyway. But you've just got to hang in for the kill; that's all there is to it." He walked past her, then turned and looked at her, intently, thoughtfully. "What's the matter? Are you saying you don't think you can handle it? Come on. Last week you said you knew everybody in the software industry. That's exactly what you said, Jane. Your very words. 'I know everybody.' With that kind of field, how can you lose?"

"It was a bit of an exaggeration," Jane said.

"Give me a break. You do know everybody who counts in management in the major software companies. That's what we pay you for. And I know everybody else. I'll tell you what I'll do. I've got a friend who practises in the criminal bar. I'll talk to him—in confidence—and see what he can find out from his friends, see if the police think there's anything to worry about. Leave that to me, okay? That make you feel any better?"

Jane said it did.

"Good." He went back and sat down behind his desk. "Then there's no problem for you right now. And since you know everybody, you just concentrate on finding some candidates for BTS who understand the software industry and will satisfy the Blumbergs — and have the money moxie Taylor needs."

Jane got up, her shoulders slumping. She had known Orloff wouldn't be sympathetic, but she hadn't dreamed he'd refuse to look at the implications of the problem altogether. Couldn't he see she was in over her head? I'm manic, that's the problem, she thought, turning to leave. Last month I told him I knew everybody. I thought I could do anything. And now the bastard is holding me to it.

"And Jane . . ." said Eddie. Jane turned toward him. He was smiling now, for the first time that morning. "Jane, if you can't stand the heat, get out of the kitchen, okay?"

Jane didn't reply. Leaving, she tried to bang the door, but it must have had a heavy, concealed spring. It resisted her, closing silently, the way it was designed to do.

THE TORONTO DAILY NEWS

Report on Business   *December 5, 1985*

BTS Stock Off As VP-Finance Search Falters

*The stock of BTS Systems Inc. fell another five points today on
the TSE, possibly in response to rumours of troubles in finding
a satisfactory replacement for Gary Levin, who, until his death
two weeks ago, was chief financial officer of the firm.*

*As well as being regarded as one of the most brilliant
financial minds in Canadian business, Levin was also seen as
protecting the interests of the Blumberg brothers who are one
of the largest outside shareholders in BTS. The Blumbergs, a
family whose closely held business interests include real estate, the Trinon chain of department stores, several insurance
companies, and widely diversified holdings in refining and
manufacturing, are known for taking a hands-on approach
in the financial management of the firms in which they have
significant holdings.*

Although neither Moise nor Leon Blumberg would comment

on the situation at BTS it appears that every effort is being made to find a replacement for Levin who is acceptable both to BTS founder Brian Taylor and to the Blumbergs.

Taylor said yesterday, "We intend to find a new VP of finance who will be satisfactory to all our shareholders, both those inside, such as myself, and other important shareholders, who include Levin's legatees and the Blumberg family of Vancouver. I will, of course, be consulting with all these people, and I don't expect any difficulty in finding someone acceptable to everybody. After all, we all have the best interests of BTS at heart."

Taylor refused to comment on whether or not BTS had hired an executive search firm to find a replacement for Levin, nor could he give a date when the position will be filled. He said the fall in the price of the stock was the natural result of uncertainty in the minds of the financial community following Levin's death. He expects to see the share price rebound as soon as a replacement is announced.

The Toronto-Dominion Centre, where Orloff Associates had their offices, consisted of two tall, black towers, designed in the sixties by Mies Van der Rohe, set back from the street so that as Jane and her friend Kersti Tamm came out of the bank tower, they walked out into a large, paved, empty plaza. The wind, channelled by the towers and the glass walkway, raced across the empty square, slapping the women's faces with hard pellets of rain.

"We should have stayed underground," Kersti complained, turning up her collar and pointing her umbrella in the direction of the rain squall.

"I hate it under there," Jane said. "It's like a Zombie world."

"I know what you mean," Kersti said. "Miles of dead bright corridors, dead bright shops and dead bright people not looking at each other."

Jane had telephoned Kersti and asked her out for lunch. It was through Kersti that Jane had first come to know Brian Taylor. Kersti's sister, Tiu, was office manager at BTS, and when Jane, starting as a research assistant at Orloff's, had been looking for a big client to help her achieve associate status, Kersti and Tiu had arranged a meeting with Brian Taylor. Brian had liked Jane, liked the fact that she had a systems background, and had hired her to find his new key people when BTS went public.

So, Jane thought, talking to Kersti would be a good way to pick up gossip about BTS. Going through Tiu, though more straightforward, might get back to Brian, so Jane thought she'd try Kersti first, and keep the idea of meeting with Tiu in reserve.

In any case, Jane was very fond of Kersti. Jane liked to talk over her problems with Kersti, then listen to her put things in perspective with a cool detachment that Jane envied. Luckily for Jane Kersti wasn't travelling, or in the studio editing, or at a story conference. Jane looked up at her friend, admiring her. Five-foot-ten inches, very thin, Kersti had long, thick, wavy blond hair and high, prominent cheek-bones. She had a cool angular look that Jane thought very beautiful. Kersti gave the impression that nothing could surprise her, that she would never be out of control.

Now, walking beside her, Jane noticed as she always did that Kersti was one of the few tall people whose height wasn't overpowering. Perhaps it was because they had been friends for so long, knew so much about one another. The time had long passed since they tried to impress one another, or compared themselves one to the other. They accepted each other, and each took pleasure in the other's success as if it were her own.

The cars on Bay Street drove by, splattered with salt,

their tires splashing dirty water. Jane's umbrella turned
inside out, and she tried to stay dry walking under Kersti's.

They were going to a little Hungarian restaurant on
Yonge Street. Once inside it was dark and quiet; there were
only ten or twelve tables, and the owner welcomed them,
with a special smile for Kersti whom he knew, and a table
by the small fireplace. Jane wanted a drink, but realized she
had a difficult afternoon ahead and ordered coffee instead.
Kersti ordered a Glenfiddich.

Jane thought she could always find out what was trendy
to drink by watching what Kersti had. She stretched out her
legs toward the fire and looked sadly at her high maroon
leather boots, which were stained with salt along the
sides.

"So what's worrying you? You seem awfully uptight,"
Kersti said.

Jane doubted that Kersti was ever really anxious about
an assignment. She certainly seemed never to be frightened. Yet Kersti denied this. Some stories, some producers,
she said, really got to her. But Jane didn't believe it. Kersti's
life always appeared to be under control. It had the glamour that Jane's life seemed to just miss. And Jane was
impressed by all the men in Kersti's life. She always had a
man around when she wanted one, yet she never got obsessed with him. Kersti told Jane these men meant nothing;
they were casual love affairs that Kersti thought of as jokes
("You wouldn't believe it, Jane, hardly anybody can get it
up anymore — you've got to see them at least twice nowa-
days before they can relax!"). And Jane envied Kersti's
elegant townhouse where there was always something to
eat in the refrigerator.

"Uptight?" Jane said. "That's putting it mildly. Actually,
this business at BTS, you know? I'm terrified."

Kersti laughed. Two men at the next table stared at her.

One took out a business card and began writing something on it.

"Did you know I went out with Gary Levin?" Kersti said. "I met him at BTS one day when I went there to see Tiu. Of course I'd already heard quite a bit about him from Tiu, and I thought he might be interesting —"

"Kersti! You're kidding! Do you mean you slept with him?"

Kersti was thoughtful. "Yes, I did. Once or twice, but it wasn't memorable. With guys like that it's always the conquest."

"Guys like that? Kersti, what was he like?"

"One of the walking wounded. The guy had a lot of problems . . . if I'm remembering him right. Yes, Levin was very, very charming and into being very sensitive. I wasn't really his type."

The waiter brought their menus, and a card from the man at the next table, which he gave to Kersti. Kersti studied it, turned it over, then looked over at the table where the two men were sitting. One waved at her. She smiled, shook her head slightly, slid her hand under the hair of the back of her neck and rubbed her neck gently. Then she made a note on the card and put it carefully in her purse.

"What did all that mean?" Jane asked.

"I collect them," Kersti said.

"Collect what?"

"Possibles' cards. You never know when you might need one of them. This guy, now. He is in the record-distribution business. Say I'm doing a story on —"

"Oh Kersti! Sometimes I think you overdo it."

"I like to have fun, too," Kersti said. "Not all of us are into work and only work." She smiled to show Jane she knew there was more to Jane's chastity than that. Jane smiled back.

"Kersti, tell me about Gary Levin — no, I don't mean what he was like in the sack."

"What do you want to know? I didn't really know him that well. I'm not surprised he had a heart attack. Type A."

Jane thought of asking Kersti if Gary had any enemies, if he were the sort of man who could cause someone to hate him so much he could get himself murdered. It didn't seem the sort of thing one could say.

Kersti ordered soup and some pickled herring and black bread. She was Estonian and had never lost her taste for sour food, for eastern-European cooking. She liked turnips and beets in the winter and would never eat a seasonable vegetable she didn't think was fresh.

Jane ordered schnitzel. Even when she was hungry, it didn't seem to matter to her what she ate. "Shall I try the *spaetzle?*" she asked Kersti.

Kersti sighed. "I've told you, Jane, don't eat things like that. They're greasy and they don't have any food value. Have the cabbage salad with the caraway seeds."

"Ugh. I'll stick with the grease. Kersti, about Gary Levin, was he the sort of man who would . . . was likely to antagonize people?"

Kersti put down her drink and stared at Jane. "I'll be damned," she said. "What's going on over there?"

Jane hesitated, not knowing what to do, what was right. Kersti was a journalist. Of course TV journalists weren't as bad as print journalists who tended to nose into everything, but still, that was her profession, to find out what was going on. Why put Kersti into the kind of conflict of interest between her professional ethics and friendship that she, Jane, was struggling with? That wasn't the right sort of thing to do to a friend.

"Oh tell me, Jane, do. It sounds absolutely delicious. You know I won't say anything until you let me."

"It isn't that," Jane said, deciding suddenly that she wanted a drink, and looking around for the waiter.

Kersti understood what Jane wanted, looked up, and the waiter appeared immediately.

"It isn't that," Jane said again, when the waiter was gone. For a moment she thought of her children and her marriage, about how she had lost her children. Perhaps it *was* all very simple. Not, as she imagined, a case of mixed motives, neither of them right or wrong. Perhaps she just didn't have what it took. It was a thought she didn't dare accept.

"It's more complicated," Jane said. "Much more complicated."

"You're always saying that, Jane," Kersti said, smiling. "You always think everything is complicated. I always think everything is simple, but maybe that's why you're so good at your job and I'm good at mine."

"Why don't you tell me about Levin?" Jane asked.

Kersti tilted back her head and stared thoughtfully at the ceiling. Then she said, "I'm probably not the right person to ask. I don't really understand men like Gary. He's the kind who goes after very young women, and usually I pick up on that sort of thing and avoid guys like that. I think there's something they didn't work out in their adolescence. Men like that are always proving things, and they're weak at the centre."

Jane took a gulp of her drink. It went down smoothly and she felt a little better. Kersti's soup came and she began to eat. She moved her spoon gracefully, and Jane liked watching her. It was soothing. "He doesn't sound like he could be a threat to anyone, the way you describe him."

"Oh, I didn't say that; I wouldn't say that. Levin was definitely what the Bay Street boys call a heavy hitter. He knew a lot of influential people, was very bright, and he hated to lose. I'd think, from what I saw of him, that when he couldn't win by fair means, he'd try to win by foul."

"I doubt that," Jane said. "Brian Taylor would never have tolerated a man like that."

"Don't be so sure. You don't build a company from nothing to forty million by being an all-round nice guy."

"No, I know all about that side of their lives," Jane said. "I know how they did business."

"You know how the industry thought they did business. Every industry has their heroes and their myths. But surely you don't take these things at face value? Jane, I'm surprised at you."

Jane was annoyed. "I know what I need to know about him as a businessman; I'm asking you about him as a person."

"You think I'm cynical, Jane. No, I know you do. You think I've got the journalistic disease. Okay, have it your way. Let's see. The fact is, I only knew one side of the man. Levin was an accomplished flirt. That's what got my attention at first, because usually I don't attract that kind, and I got a kick out of his technique. I sat back and let him do it, the whole shmear. Flowers, and notes, and phone calls at work, and expensive dinners, a weekend in New York. I thought it might be fun."

"Was it?"

"Not particularly. When you've heard one guy say his wife doesn't understand him and he just has to have you, you've heard them all, and you really don't want to hear it again — especially when the man is smart enough. If he'd only knock it off and talk about business or something, he'd be really interesting."

"So you did have an affair with him?"

"That's what I'm trying to tell you, dear heart. I didn't have an *affair* with him. I had a few dinner dates and a weekend in New York, and then decided I'd seen what there was to see, and why bother to do it again?"

"How did he take that?"

"Oh, just fine. I let him think it was his idea, and he gave me some good contact names as a going-away present. Maybe we were too much alike," Kersti went on, eyeing Jane's *spaetzle* with distaste. Jane noticed it was rather greasy. "It was the conquest that interested both of us, and after that the fun was gone. So tell me, Jane. Is it true, was Levin murdered? That's what the gossip is."

Jane fell a chill. Gossip. Not just Kersti's intuition, but gossip. How could that be?, unless the management group was already leaking. With people talking murder, how would she ever find someone good who'd be willing to take Levin's place?

She put down her fork and ran her hands through her hair, tugging it up from the roots.

"Now don't go into a dither, Jane." Kersti said. "The incumbent's being murdered won't stop the real high fly-ers." She smiled at Jane. "I wouldn't give it a moment's thought if I were you. Just load on the stock options. You know how to do it."

"Sure," said Jane, "piece of cake. No, really Kersti, the place is full of undercurrents and whirlpools. I feel like I'm getting sucked under. Have you heard any gossip from Tiu about what's going on?"

Kersti stopped smiling. "Tiu hasn't been very well these last few months," she said.

"Oh, I'm sorry, Kersti, I didn't know anything about it. What's the matter with her?"

Kersti pushed some herring around on her plate, sepa-rating it from the onions. "I guess you could say she's very depressed. She's going to take a leave of absence. Brian Taylor is very understanding, apparently."

Jane could see that Kersti didn't want to talk about Tiu, but she couldn't pass up the chance to get some insight into what was going on at BTS.

"When I was up there," Jane said, talking through a forkful of *spaetzle* and swallowing it without tasting it, "I got the impression that the happy family bit was getting a bit ravelled at the edges. Even before Gary Levin died, I mean."

"I guess it's not as nice a place to work as it used to be," Kersti said. "But I don't know the details."

"Do you think I could talk to Tiu about it? It might help me figure out what's really going on there," Jane said.

"Is it really important to you, Jane?"

Jane looked at Kersti, trying to understand her reluctance. "Yes, yes it is. It could be a big help to me. And right now I need all the help I can get."

"Well, why don't you let me talk to Tiu. Then, if I think it won't make her problems worse, I'll tell her to call you."

"Would you? That would be great, Kersti. I really appreciate it."

Kersti smiled suddenly. "Don't look so serious. After all, what are friends for, if not to collect gossip for one another? Anyway, look at the time — we've blathered on and I haven't picked up any juicy tidbits from you. And now it's too late. I have to get back to work."

She got up, pulling on her leather jacket. It was black with big shoulders and big sleeves, and a high collar that stood up, almost covering Kersti's mouth, and underlining her high smooth cheekbones. Her cool blue eyes looked down on Jane. "Do you want me to ask around? Even though you haven't said, I know some people think Levin was knocked off. He was a tough, ambitious, hard-driving man, and he probably had heaps of enemies. Why worry about it?"

She leaned down to kiss Jane, and Jane smelled leather and Madame Rochas. Kersti's touch was warm, and Jane held her hand for a minute. "I'll stop being so worried soon, I'm sure of it," Jane said.

"You always do," Kersti said, straightening up and swinging her bag over her shoulder with a flamboyant sweep. "You're not going to have any trouble at all."

When Jane came out onto Yonge Street the gusty rain had turned into a steady downpour; the rain felt cold, and the cars swept by in sheets of water.

Jane hoped she'd feel stronger soon. She had a great deal to do, and despite her friend's assurances, she wondered if she could do it.

8

"There're a few things we have to get clear," Brian was saying. Jane had the telephone in the shoulder cradle, and while she listened she leafed through the files in an open file drawer. She was listening with only part of her attention. Another part was looking for information about people filed under software/dp/services/finance. In the back of her mind, "running in background" as software people would say, she was wondering if there was any possibility at all that Kersti might have been more involved with Gary Levin and the mess at BTS than she had let on. This unpleasant idea had occurred to Jane on the way back to work, and it was nagging at her like a broken tooth.

"I don't want a high-flyer, someone who thinks I am going to give him a piece of this company, because I'm not," Brian said. "Gary helped to build BTS; that's why he had twenty percent. I want a top person, but I want him on salary. Bonuses, okay, but I'm going to buy out Gary's heirs. There'll be no shares for the new man."

"I don't think you'll find the right person thinking that way, Brian. Remember we went through this before? We've got to concentrate on finding the right person. Then we'll see what it takes to get him, or her."

"Just a minute. Didn't you ever hear of cutting your sails to fit your cloth?"

"No, and neither did you. You've got that mixed up somehow."

"You know what I mean. I don't intend to let go of a piece of my company to someone who hasn't proved himself. And, anyway, the management team won't stand for someone who hasn't paid his dues getting too sweet a deal."

"That's not what I said," Jane answered calmly. She pulled several files and laid them in a pile to her left. "I'm working for you, remember?"

"Okay, right. The person has to be very bright, that goes without saying. But the Blumbergs' suggestions are out. I don't want somebody doing an Apple on me. Someone coming in from marketing soft drinks or something who doesn't know anything about software, and tries to tell me what to do. Do you understand?"

He's really worked up, thought Jane. Where is the calm Brian Taylor, the in-control Brian Taylor?

"None of that is a problem," Jane said. "The real problem is the kind of things Martha is saying. This idea of —" she couldn't say the word "— Gary not having died a natural death."

Brian's voice was suddenly cautious. "There's no proof of that. Nobody outside of our management has even thought about it."

"I'm sorry, Brian," Jane said, "but you're wrong. I heard someone gossiping about it today at lunch."

In the pause, Jane could hear faint cross-talk, Chinese. "That's all we need right now," Brian said.

"Could you tell me what you really think?"

There was a short silence and Jane could now hear the

Chinese conversation clearly. It was more distracting than something she understood would have been. Then Brian said, "Jane, just do your job. I thought we went over this before. You are a friend of BTS. We need our friends now."

After Jane hung up she stared at her desk, trying to recover her concentration, trying to get back to work. But she couldn't stop running the conversation over in her mind. He couldn't have said it any clearer, Jane thought. He believes Gary was murdered. He wants me to ignore it. Why aren't things ever simple? I wonder where you learn about how to deal with friendship and loyalty when it interferes with doing your job in a professional way. And how do you keep from falling on your own knife when you're trying not to stab someone in the back?

Eddie Orloff poked his head in. He saw Jane poring over stacks of files, her spike full of phone messages. "About that business at BTS," he said, "I've got someone lined up in both legal and accounting to help put together the package, if you're thinking of getting creative. Just give me a shout when you're ready. And oh, no word yet from my criminal-lawyer friend."

Jane looked up. "Thanks." She was still angry with Orloff. She had decided his last crack about the kitchen was sexist. And inexcusable. And, possibly a threat. Also a good assessment of the situation.

"How's your conscience?" he asked, coming in and sitting down.

Probably decided he handled me badly, Jane thought. No point in giving him any satisfaction.

"I'm afraid it's out of condition," she said. "I haven't been giving it all that much exercise on the job."

"Okay, okay, no need to get all worked up. You'll probably have to get to the bottom of the murder, anyway. It will be impossible to get management support for any candidate under these conditions."

She was so interested in the last part of what he said that the first part didn't sink in.

"Brian Taylor doesn't think so."

"Wishful thinking," Orloff said. He stood up. She looked up at him, wishing he wouldn't loom over her. "Orloff Associates wouldn't like to be involved in setting someone up. I suggest you move very carefully. Find out as much as you can before you commit yourself. There's lot of talk around. I imagine the police will be involved soon."

"Have you heard any talk on the street?"

"Today at lunch," Orloff said, looking down at her. "You go see Martin Kaplan. Seems he has something to say. Or at least, he had too much to drink last night at the club and said more than he should. I heard about it today at lunch."

"I see you've changed your attitude since our first conversation," Jane said incautiously. "Now you believe there is reason to be concerned."

Orloff's face darkened, and Jane realized she'd put her foot in her mouth. Because she feared that Orloff didn't have confidence in her, she found it hard to be natural around him, and the result often was a tactlessness, which only made matters worse. Why, she wondered, could she not develop the easy relationship with Orloff that the others in the firm seemed to have? Or were they faking it? Impossible to tell.

"Yes, I have changed my mind since we first spoke," Orloff said. He stared past her, out the window. "I think this may get messy. Very messy. I've been wondering if it might be too much for you. After all, you're young, you haven't been around enough to know the ins and outs of something really big. I've asked myself, should I give it to one of the men? But Taylor wants you, so I guess we're both stuck with it."

"I can handle this," Jane said softly, surprising herself by the calm tone of her voice, when inside she felt the rage boiling around. She stood up abruptly feeling an overpowering sense of Orloff's height, as if he were a threatening animal ready to pounce at any minute. Her office was very small; there was room in it only for her desk, computer table, two filing cabinets and one visitor chair. Most of the other associates had larger offices, with small groupings of furniture — sofas, chairs and a coffee table at one end — where they could hold interviews. Jane always had to book a boardroom. Orloff had told her that all the larger offices were taken. She had the least seniority; she would have to wait.

Now Orloff seemed to fill the office, and Jane, coming out from behind the desk, had to shrink into herself to avoid brushing against him as she opened the door. "I'll keep you informed as things develop," she said in the same calm voice. He walked out the door, and then turned to look at her, his hostility replaced by a puzzled expression.

"You're taking all this calmly enough," he said looking down at her.

She smiled at him, and as he walked away she shut the door carefully. Then she stuck out her tongue and screwed up her face in an expression of exaggerated disgust. But nothing helped. Inside she felt sick with anger. Or fear. Often it was hard to tell one from the other.

Why didn't I tell him off? she thought. Why did I put up with his talking to me like that? Nobody should have to put up with being talked to like that. I didn't stick up for myself, I let him act as if I were a person of no significance.

She rang up Martin Kaplan and was put right through. Hearing his voice, Jane felt a little better.

"Sometimes I think I'm two coupons short of a toaster,"

he was saying. "I seem to have tied one on last night . . . and shot my mouth off, and now Brian's just been in here saying the last thing he needs is a loose cannon on deck."

"Brian said that?" Jane was laughing.

"Don't laugh. You wouldn't if you'd seen him. Look, why don't you come and hold my hand. We're all supposed to tell you what we think about Gary's replacement, anyway, right? Maybe you can do some damage control for my big mouth — tell Brian I didn't mean it. You know."

"Sure," Jane said. "I'm coming over to meet with Brian and your comptroller, Robert McDonnell, this afternoon. How about a drink after?"

"Now you're talking."

"You know a lot of people in the industry; I'd like to run some names by you, in confidence, okay?"

"Be my guest. Just talk to me very softly, love. I've got a real headache and my mouth feels like they've been running a war in it."

Jane couldn't help feeling more cheerful. Being around Kaplan always had that effect on her. Thinking about seeing him was going to make the rest of the afternoon tolerable.

Martin Kaplan looked fatter and paler than Jane remembered. It took some manoeuvring for him to get his bulk into the booth at the bar of the Prince Hotel. Jane was definitely feeling better. The quiet of the hotel, the clink of the glasses, the gentle voices of the patrons. Outside the window, rain fell mistily on the bare branches of the trees in the little garden. Jane watched it, letting it calm her, as Kaplan gave their order.

"It's looney tunes at BTS," Kaplan said. He stuck his hand into the bowl of peanuts the waiter set on their table and began tossing them in his mouth. "But what can you expect when your Mister Moneybags gets popped off? I ask you. Just the same, Brian's right. I didn't help matters by shooting my mouth off."

"Is it affecting business?"

"Are you kidding? Sometimes I think there's really only fifty people in this country, and they all know one another. Our stock is down again this morning, not that I give a bean." His drink came, and he sucked up an ice cube and crunched it loudly. "On the other hand, I deal with customers. And all they care about is whether their systems are running right, and whether we have someone ready and willing to hold their hands, d'you know what I mean? And I'm there to see that we do that thing. I do a good job on that. That's what Brian pays me for." He crunched another cube loudly.

Martin was right, Jane knew. He was good. Customers liked him. He had been a programmer once — unusual for someone in his position. He knew the software he sold, and he knew how to get the technical people at BTS to perform for the customers when it was required. In the software industry the really good techies are reputed to hate people. They don't like customers, whom they feel waste their time and get in the way of the techie's love affair with the computer. People like Martin were hard to find, and invaluable. He was a good organizer and a good motivator, too. But his job was extremely high pressure; he stood between the cranky, temperamental technical people and the cranky, anxious customers, trying to keep everyone happy. And Martha had been right about customer service. There were people in their industry — and Jane was one of them — who believed customer service was the most important element in the success of a software company. That meant Martin Kaplan was a very important man at BTS.

"What we don't need," Martin was saying, "is another

monster ego at BTS. I'm no pipsqueak in that department, and Brian, behind that laid-back manner, has more than plenty."

"But what about the joint-marketing plan? And speaking of that, tell me, Martin, is it really a joint-marketing deal BTS is trying to work out in the U.S.? I can't help thinking from the way Brian's talking that there's more to it than that."

"So you've seen through us, have you? Well, you're right, of course. Confidentially — and I'll have your first-born if you breathe a word of this — what Brian is really going for is a merger. Only the five of us know. And we are supposed to pretend to *everyone* that it's a joint-marketing deal. But now the merger—it's a real problem. We're seven months pregnant with the deal and we're either going to give birth or miscarry, I'd say. It's way too late to abort. You'll have to find someone who can deliver on this merger." He waved his hand wildly for the waiter and gestured at his empty glass. It had been a double Irish whisky.

Merger. Not joint-marketing, merger, Jane thought. "Martha seems to think the company can't handle the growth and the complexity involved in getting into the American market right now," she said.

"There's another real ego problem for you, right there," Martin said. "Martha knows shit all about it. You should excuse the expression — she doesn't have the balls for it. If we don't get into the American market fast, they'll come in here and start eating us up. It's eat-or-be-eaten time."

"That's what Brian thinks?" Jane asked.

"Right on. I wish it wasn't so. Deeply. But it is. Integrating our customer service with theirs is going to be hell on wheels, but it's something we can handle. I probably shouldn't have opened my mouth, Jane — swear you'll remember that this merger is el secret. Top el secret, right?"

"Sure, okay."

"You've got to find us someone who can handle it, without ever letting them know that's the game we're playing."

Jane sighed. "This thing's complications have complications."

"Ain't it the truth, baby, ain't it the truth. The fact is, if we don't find someone with the chutzpah to bring this thing off, we aren't going to be able to do it ourselves. There's no one at BTS now, without Gary, who can handle it. Those U.S. guys are too big-time for us."

Jane said, "So could you say that whoever killed Gary might have been thinking they were killing the merger?"

Martin put his drink down on the table, slopping a little onto the paper coaster. "Be careful, Jane! Watch what you say, watch what you even think. You're pointing the finger at Martha, and at Tom. And maybe. . ." He trailed off, and popped a handful of peanuts into his mouth. It was his second bowl, Jane noticed. She hadn't had any.

"And maybe . . .?"

"Well, look, Jane. Things are never as simple as they seem. D'you know what I mean?"

"Tell me about it."

"Where will Brian be if the merger goes through? That's the question that keeps asking itself. You know enough about these things. In a year, when the dust settles, who will control who? That's what I mean. No one knows. Gary and Brian were not getting along about that merger, how it should go. I don't know the details. Brian couldn't control Gary. You know that. Everyone knows that. Maybe things have gone further than even Brian wanted."

"No one could control Gary."

"Right, right. BTS was the tail on his tiger. He had the Blumbergs with him. He was smart as a snake. None of us are money people. Brian knows the business. He really knows it. Christ, he *is* the business. Everybody in the industry respects him. But in the money game where Gary played, that means fuck-all. If Gary did that merger, could Brian be sure he wouldn't end up pushed up — up and out? How could he be sure?"

"And if the merger didn't happen?"

"Brian's up shit creek. We all are."

"Then why does Tom Henege oppose it?"

Martin popped another handful of peanuts. The second bowl was empty. "Who knows? Who knows why marketing people do anything. They're like people from outer space. Smile, smile, ooze, ooze. You'll have to ask him."

"Do I take it you don't like Henege?"

"Actually I do. For a marketing guy he's almost human."

"Can I ask you something?" Jane said, looking directly at Martin.

"That's why I'm here, love."

"Do you really think Gary Levin was murdered? Murdered by someone in the management group?"

Martin returned Jane's look. He said, very quietly. "Gary was murdered. Take it from me, love. He was murdered. I don't know why, or by whom. We know — from the police — he died of heart failure, with cyanosis of the lungs. No one knows which came first. No sign of him being smothered, or anything. But it was sudden. Unnatural. And no sign of a heart attack. They're still looking for a natural cause. But that's because they haven't found that print-out message."

"How can you be so sure?"

"Trust me. I know what I'm talking about. And that message? Know what I think? Someone wanted to scare us. Wanted us to think one of us was a murderer. God knows why."

"So if I bring someone else in, maybe. . . ."

"Glad I'm not you, Jane. That's all I can say."

Jane was silent, thinking. Her thoughts went round and round, without getting anywhere. "About Brian, you say he wanted a merger, but was afraid Gary might work it so that he, Brian, would be pushed out?"

"Don't quote me on that, but yes, that's the way I see it."

"Why aren't you afraid of the merger? Someone could say you might be afraid you'd be forced out."

Jane noticed that Martin looked even paler and that there was a thin film of sweat on his face. As she watched him he unbuttoned the bottom two buttons of his waistcoat, which sprang open over his broad paunch. He smiled, released from confinement. "Someone wouldn't say that. The customers love my ass. Nobody in their right mind would turf me out, and if they did, I'd probably make more somewhere else. I'm so good, you see."

"Who did you say had an ego problem?"

Kaplan laughed. Jane studied his sweating face, trying to understand him, trying to decide how much of what he was telling her was true.

"My ego is not a problem, love. It's an asset. Ask anybody. I've been behind the merger from the beginning. Bigger fields to play on. I go for that, and as the saying goes I'm a team player." Martin inhaled the ice cubes from his empty glass and began chomping on them. "Well, it looks like to me there's only one way out of this for Ms Jane Tregar. D'you know what I mean?"

"Not really."

"You've got to figure out who snuffed Gary Levin. And you better do it fast too. Or you'll go down with the rest of us at BTS. Down with the ship. That's the way it is, sweetheart. Think about it." Jane heard the ice crunch. Martin was no longer smiling.

9

THE TORONTO DAILY NEWS

Report on Business   *December 8, 1985*

Police Investigating the Death of
BTS Vice-President

Fluctuations of more than $3 a share on shares trading yester-
day at a high of $12 was the response of the Toronto Stock Ex-
change to news that the police are investigating the death of
Gary Levin, chief financial officer of Brian Taylor Systems, one
of Canada's leading data-processing firms.

Martha Gruen, vice-president of human resources at BTS,
said today that Levin died in a locked computer room, and that
cause of death has not yet been determined. However, she
explained that there could be no suspicion of foul play, be-
cause the records of the card-access system showed that only
Levin had entered the computer room. She said: "I am at a loss
to explain what happened today on the TSE. I think it's be-
cause this company has always attracted so much public inter-
est — our fast growth, from 12 people to 150 in such a short

time, and the fact we've been so profitable in such a competitive industry. People have a hard time understanding the software business. We expect this will all settle down, and it will be business as usual by this time next week."

Harry Nakamura, of the Toronto firm Systems-Watch, software-industry analysts, said he agreed with Gruen's explanation. "BTS has always been fascinating to the Canadian public, and there are probably a certain number of investors who get jumpy every time something happens they don't understand. But the company is fundamentally sound. They have a very good cash position, very little debt, and have been showing a growth rate of between 50 and 75 percent a year for the past three years. They're highly respected in the industry, well-managed, with top talent both on the technical and marketing sides. This flutter on the market just means the investing public would be more comfortable if they knew who the new VP of finance was going to be."

Barbara Blaney of Thorne, Reid and Wilder, a firm which monitors the software industry for corporate clients, agrees. "There're a lot of rumours out there," she said. "When that happens the stock can swing wildly for a few days. But the real question is: what's going on with the joint-marketing agreement they're negotiating with an unnamed U.S. firm?" When asked about the delay in replacing Gary Levin, Blaney said: "I thought they would have replaced Levin before this. It could be they can't find someone satisfactory to the management team at BTS, who are known to have a great deal of input in things like this, to Taylor himself, who has strong opinions about the kind of people he wants at BTS, and to the Blumbergs, who would be very influential in the decision."

Brian Taylor, Moise Blumberg and Leon Blumberg could not be reached for comment.

Jane had always thought that Tiu gave the appearance of being a washed-out version of Kersti. Smaller, finer boned, she had the delicate colouring of a watercolour painting.

But now, Jane was shocked by the change in Tiu. Her fine pale hair, usually neatly cut to fall just to her chin, was straggly and not very clean. Although it was a cold December day she wore a cotton skirt and T-shirt under her dingy parka. Jane remembered clearly that when she had met Tiu before, even on weekends, she had been smartly dressed.

Tiu had been Christmas shopping, and had agreed to meet Jane for tea in a small café in the Eaton Centre. Beyond the glass wall of the café, which looked out into the galleria, the crowds surged in both directions, and each time the café door opened the noise of the crowds, the Christmas music and the faint burr of the ventilation system filled the room.

"I'm not asking you tell me anything confidential," Jane said, trying to set Tiu at ease. "I just thought maybe you could fill me in on what's going on at BTS. I'm working for Brian, looking for a new vice-president of finance, but you know Brian, he's so busy it's hard for him to find time to give me all the information I need — and anyway, it's the little things about the working environment that I was hoping to find out. . . ."

Her voice trailed off, as Tiu didn't seem to be listening. She had a far-off look in her eyes, as if she were thinking about something else, something that was totally absorbing her.

"I know them all so well," Tiu said in her soft, hesitant voice. "I've been with BTS since it was founded. I started as Brian Taylor's secretary, and then he promoted me to office manager. I do most of the purchasing too, except for computer equipment. But . . . I'm not sure. . . . What kind of things do you want to talk about?"

"Well, I had a meeting there last week, and there seemed to be quite a bit of tension between members of the management group. And then there is Gary Levin's death. . . . What do you think about that?"

"Tension?" Tiu said, looking down at her lap. "I don't know." She looked up at Jane. "They're all wonderful people. Truly wonderful people," she repeated, half to herself. "But I guess you know that."

Jane nodded.

The café was cafeteria style, and specialized in muffins and pastries. Tiu had chosen a giant bran muffin that puffed out above its paper, looking to Jane something like a diseased toadstool. Now Tiu broke off a piece of the crust and absently buttered it. The crust broke between her fingers, and Tiu dropped it, then began licking the butter off her fingers, obviously without realizing she was doing it. "Gary Levin was the most hard-working, energetic man," she began, speaking with more confidence. "He —"

"Did the others like him? I mean, being a giant can be pretty wearing on the people you work for."

Tiu didn't smile at Jane's attempt at humour. "Like him?" she said thoughtfully. "Like him? They seemed to."

"Did you?"

"Did I?" Tiu repeated, breaking off another chunk of muffin and smearing it more carefully this time, with the whipped butter she scooped out of a little, pleated paper cup.

"Well, I did and I didn't. For one thing, I didn't like the way he treated Martin. Martin is always so kind to me. Whenever I have trouble with the programmers — like I did when no one liked the new chairs we bought for the workstations, and there was quite a to-do — Martin helps me out. Martin pretends to be a clown, but he has an awfully good heart. Gary didn't appreciate him."

Tiu thought for a minute. "Then Tom. . . . Tom brought

in the business, and Gary always told me, 'Treat Tom with kid gloves, Tiu; whatever he wants, he gets.' When Tom wanted a special sofa, when he didn't like the one I bought, Gary told me, 'Go ahead, Tiu, get him whatever he wants. He pays our salaries. He keeps the sales reps fired up; he brings in the big accounts.' But then I'd hear them arguing about how Tom's bonus was too high and how Gary said it had to be cut back. That's hard to understand, don't you think?

"Now, on the other hand, Martha always seemed to like Gary. Martha and I are friends and I know she had a great deal of respect for Gary. It didn't seem to matter to her that he treated her like a . . . as a *woman*."

"I'm not sure I understand."

"Oh nothing — just noticing her clothes, and complimenting her if she looked pretty. He did that to all the women, though; he didn't mean anything by it. He thought we liked it."

Jane smiled. "I know what you mean." She sipped her tea, finding it bitter. "But Brian and Gary, what about them? They got along well, didn't they? They used to, anyway, when I worked with BTS last time."

"Oh yes," Tiu said, her voice more positive than anytime since the beginning of the conversation. "Oh yes," she said again, only this time, thoughtfully, as if something had just occurred to her. "They seemed to; I know that. Or, what I mean is, they *thought* they did. That's it," she repeated. "They thought they did."

"I'm not sure I follow you," Jane said, not liking what she was hearing, yet hoping to induce Tiu to say more.

"Well, you know men. . . ." Tiu trailed off. She picked up her knife and cut a large chunk off her muffin. She had forgotten to take off the paper, and Jane watched, fascinated, as she buttered muffin and paper indiscriminately and put both in her mouth. She really isn't well, Jane thought, feeling sadness both for Tiu and for Kersti. Something really is wrong with her. What about her husband and kids? It must be terrible for them to see her like this.

"At some level," Tiu went on, pulling the piece of muffin paper from her mouth, "Brian and Gary were always competing. Or that's how it looked to me. Men at the top, in business they're just so competitive. They're competitive animals, you could say, I guess. . . . Gary and Brian worked closely together, but they competed too. Then, after Gary's marriage broke up, he seemed to be trying harder, in some way, to best Brian. Take this joint-marketing thing. . . ."

She paused again, as if considering whether she ought to say more, and Jane, willing her to continue, leaned forward and said, "Yes? The joint-marketing thing?"

"They were getting along on that, and they weren't — that's all I wanted to say. Don't get me wrong," she said, suddenly looking directly, almost fiercely at Jane. "Gary and Brian would have done anything for one another. I'm sure of that. They loved one another; they truly did. But at the same time they couldn't help but try to top each other. It's only natural."

"I think you're very perceptive," Jane said.

Tiu frowned, and shook her head. Her hair swung forward, concealing her face. "No, no, not really," she said, making a gesture with her hand as if to push Jane's compliment away. "It's just I've been there for so long. I know them all so well, they're like family to me. They're all such good people. . . ."

She seemed suddenly very distressed, and Jane thought she had better direct the conversation away from Tiu herself, since it seemed it was Jane's compliment that had caused her distress.

"The management people — they're all good programmers, all computer people, that's what I hear," Jane said.

"Oh no," Tiu said. "Not at all. I mean, maybe they were once, and maybe that's what they put in their résumés. And of course they have to keep up with what BTS is doing. But Tom and Martin both came from engineering firms originally; their background is electrical engineering. And Martha, if you can believe it, is actually a biochemist. She got into computer programming doing that kind of work. No, certainly, I wouldn't call them serious programmers. Of course there's the comptroller, Robert McDonnell — we haven't talked about him. . . ."

"Yes, he seems weaker than the rest of them somehow," Jane said. "I'd forgotten him. Although maybe that's because he is the one person on the team I didn't hire for BTS."

Tiu smiled her small, unhappy smile. Jane noticed the corners of her mouth quivering, as if at any moment she could break into tears. "Yes, he's the odd man out," Tiu said. "Robert is a sweet man. *He* actually is the only one of them with a degree in computer science. Unfortunately for him, he also has a master's in business administration, and for some reason that's something Brian absolutely despises. He says it's a degree in idiocy. Robert can't help knowing that Brian doesn't respect him. It didn't matter when Gary was around. Robert reported to Gary, and Gary protected him. But now, I guess it's a problem for Robert. He doesn't have all that much self-confidence, compared to the others, anyway."

"I guess you need quite a bit of self-confidence to deal with Brian," Jane said thoughtfully.

Tiu stood up suddenly. "I have to go now," she said. "I'm sorry. I'm late." She wrapped what was left of her muffin in a paper napkin. Grease smears from the butter spread immediately to the outside, but Tiu didn't notice; she thrust the muffin into one of her shopping bags full of parcels, grabbed her purse and rushed out of the restaurant. Jane looked after her, feeling depressed. I'll have to call Kersti and tell her, Jane thought. God, poor Tiu. I wonder what's the matter with her? I wonder what's wrong?

10

They were in Brian's office, working on the description of the company and the job that Jane would use to show the potential candidates. Jane, looking surreptitiously at her watch, saw that it was seven-thirty. She felt crumpled and weary. It wasn't so much that they had been going over her drafts for two and half hours, but that Brian had been able to make them so much better. That, after all, was supposed to be *her* job.

But Brian still wasn't satisfied. He had taken their much-amended draft and was making more changes to it, when his secretary, who worked late whenever he did, buzzed him. Then her voice came through on the intercom. "It's your wife, Mr Taylor. Line one."

Brian sighed and picked up the phone. He swung his chair around so that Jane could only see the back of his head. She got up from her chair, turned her back to his desk and stretched, then walked over to the window and looked out, wanting to give him some privacy.

"Seven-thirty?" he was saying. "I'm really sorry, Dahlia, I didn't realize. . . . Oh God, was that tonight? Was she expecting us? Look, I'm going to be tied up here for an hour or more, so why don't you go yourself? I don't know how to talk to her."

He listened for a moment, then said, "She's going to ask me if I knew that Gary played around — she's asking everybody. And what am I going to say? . . . You're better at that than I am. No one ever believes me when I lie. . . . Well, you know what I mean. And I want to buy Gary's shares from her as soon as the estate's settled, so don't you think it would look kind of opportunistic if I. . . . Okay, okay."

Jane turned around and saw that Brian, while listening to his wife, was also reading over the job description, correcting words as he went along.

"Yes, right, right . . . you're right," he was saying. "But I *did* go with you to pay the condolence call, and I wrote her a note. . . . It's just that I feel so goddamned sorry for her. . . ."

He pressed the phone to his ear, smiled slightly and gestured to Jane. She walked back to the desk and he handed her the amended job description. As she read it, she couldn't keep herself from listening to his side of the conversation.

"What's that? Wait a minute, Elizabeth is your daughter too. Maybe she smart-mouthed the teacher because the teacher was out of line. . . ."

Jane forced herself to concentrate on the document in front of her, tuning out the conversation. But a change in his tone caught her and she began to listen again. "Yes, darling, I see what you mean. I'm sorry. You phone and let her know we'll be late. I'll stop and pick up some flowers."

He hung up and turned back to face Jane. "I'm supposed to be somewhere else," he said. "Visiting Linda, Gary Levin's wife. I'd forgotten. Dahlia thinks it's important that we stand by her right now. Though you'd think, with their being separated before his death, it wouldn't be so bad for Linda. Not like it would have been if they'd still been together."

"Your wife is probably right," Jane said.

Brian sighed. "I know. But visiting Linda is going to be rough, and I guess I was hoping I could get out of it. She's so wounded, and she can't stop talking about Gary, about what a bad person he was. Listening to that is hard for me. After all, he was my friend. He helped me to make BTS what it is. But then, you can see her side of it."

"I guess so," Jane said, interested in these insights into the private lives of Gary and of Brian himself.

"I have to admit," Brian went on, "from her point of view, he wasn't the greatest guy. But, maybe he had his reasons. It's not fair to judge him, when we don't know. Nobody's perfect. Look at me — still at work at seven-thirty, leaving Dahlia to deal with the kids and then forgetting our date to visit Linda. Of course Dahlia understands, but still. . . ."

Brian was slipping the sheets of paper they had worked on into an envelope, gathering up the pages of notes they had made and sliding them into a file, sweeping up scattered paperclips and dumping them into an ashtray on the credenza behind his desk.

"What's this American deal about, Brian?" Jane asked, as his secretary came in with her coat. "About its being a merger, not a joint-marketing deal?" He looked at her, waited for his secretary to leave, then shut the office door. "I don't want to talk about that, Jane." His voice was cold suddenly, his relaxed expression gone. "I don't want you to talk about it either. It's very confidential, and it has nothing to do with your job."

Jane knew she should let it go. But, perhaps because she was tired, perhaps because she was jarred by his sudden change of tone, she answered him in an equally cold voice. "Look, Brian. Either you trust me or you don't. If you have a major financial operation under way, it could be very important that I understand it; it might have an effect on the kind of person you need."

"I'll take care of that," he said. "And it's not a question of trust — of course I trust you. You're one of the people I trust most. But that doesn't have anything to do with it." They walked out of his office and across the hall to the elevator. Brian pushed the button and they both stood there, waiting, not looking at each other, feeling the hostility and suspicion that had blown up between them like a draft of cold air from a suddenly opened window.

"I don't understand," Jane pressed him. "What can be so confidential about a merger agreement. Unless —"

"Don't even speculate," Brian said.

The elevator came and they rode down in silence.

That night, as she lay in bed, waiting to fall asleep, Jane was remembering how Brian's liking for secrecy had, when they worked together in the past, both intrigued and annoyed her. Sometimes he would talk about himself, give her insights into his life and his feelings, but his ambitions and plans for his business were another matter. She had wondered if he kept things close to his chest because he liked to do so, or if he kept things to himself because their disclosure would cause actual harm to his business. Once she had asked him if he was as secretive with his wife as he seemed to be with everyone else.

"Secretive? With Dahlia?" he had said.

It was one of those nights when they were working late in his office. She remembered the greasy pizza box on the coffee table, the piles of paper, résumés, reports, their own notes. That night had been one of the few times he had talked about his marriage. Her question had seemed to open him up, and he had begun to talk about himself. He had told Jane that he loved his wife, what a good mother she was to their children, how good she was to him. Jane had found it difficult to understand how a man, seemingly so devoted to his family, could spend so little time with them. She had, of course, not said this. Certainly Brian didn't flirt with her, didn't give her the impression that there was something missing from his marriage that he was looking for elsewhere. Yet how to understand the way he spoke of his wife — distantly, almost regretfully? As if speaking about something he had lost.

"Secretive with Dahlia?" he had repeated. "Yes, she says I am. She says that often I'm very distant, but I'm not sure I know what she means. Do you?"

Jane had shaken her head.

"Let me tell you a story about me, when I was a little boy," Brian had said, his voice thoughtful, reflecting. "It's about secrets, about women and my keeping secrets. Dahlia says it explains things about me."

Brian went on to tell Jane about a summer at his family's cottage on Georgian Bay.

He wasn't sure how old had he been that summer. Eleven? Twelve? His father, a mathematician, had given him a book of Escher prints, and one of a castle that turned inside out on itself had fascinated him. Sitting on the beach he had seen the inside-out castle taking shape in his mind's eye.

At night in bed in the cottage, he had secretly made sketches of his dream castle. He'd made them with a drafting pen he bought in town, using black India ink that stained the sheets, and drawing on special, smooth, fine-grained white paper, taking care that when he wasn't at work on them, the sketches were hidden so that his mother couldn't find them. His mother, Brian had told Jane, was an unhappy woman, whose bitterness over the meagre rewards she had reaped for devoting herself suffocatingly to husband and children came out in cruel spite and mockery. Because of this, Brian had learned to keep his ambitions to himself.

When the drawing was complete, he'd said, he was ready to build the castle. He had rowed out to the small island in the old rowboat no one used. He remembered that boat, the water sloshing around with a chuckling noise between the grey splintered planks. He recalled the rough, blistered, brown paint on the oar handles, and he could still remember vividly the deserted beach on the island where, above the water line, dunes covered with long, rank, blue-green grass concealed his building site. Brian had thought that there the castle would be safe from his family if they came over in the little powerboat to picnic or gather blueberries. Safe from his mother's prying eyes, from her intense curiosity about what he was thinking and doing.

Of course she'd known he had a new interest. In a high, plaintive voice, she had pressed him, trying to find out what he was up to. "What were you doing all day at the island, so long? Why are you coming home with black under your fingernails and your hair full of sand? Why aren't you playing with your friends?"

And then, he never knew really what happened; the castle must have been about half-finished, its curving stairs and tiers geometrically perfect — or so it seemed in recollection — made from a special mixture of wet sand and gravel, which when dry grew almost as hard as cement. He remembered his hunger and suspense to know whether he was right, whether he had understood, expanded on Escher's trick, so that the three-dimensional castle would helix around upon itself as the one in the picture did. He still remembered that design, he'd told Jane, still wondered if it would have worked, doubting it at the vantage point of thirty-eight looking back on eleven, but still suspending his disbelief because of the remembered delight of his dream.

Then the devastation: trudging over the dune that one day, the sand damp and glutinous under his running shoes, to find the castle wrecked. Stomped on, dug up, completely destroyed.

He had believed that it was his mother who had wrecked the castle. Partly because he had always feared her curiosity, and partly because after that day, four or five days before the end of the summer and the closing of the cottage, she had prevented him from going off alone in the rowboat by filling his time with errands and treats she had planned for him. If it had been she, she would have known that he would have started again and tried to finish, even in the few days remaining. When he was older he had wondered if there was a more charitable explanation — that it hadn't been she, that she had seen in his face that day his shock and rage, known something bad had happened on his outing, and wanted to distract him and make his last few days at the cottage pleasant ones.

As a child, though, he had been so sure, as sure as if he had seen her stamp out the turrets, the walls, the staircases. Yet even then he had thought that she couldn't help the jealousy and rage she felt, just as he couldn't help building the castle. They both had obsessive natures, wanted things wholly and completely in their control, wanted to shape and form things to their own plans. Later he had understood even more, how the sons of mothers like his turned inward, channelled their energies, were secretive and compelled; finished what they started and were slow to trust. Dahlia had helped him see some of this in their early days together, when they had talked and talked, getting to know one another.

It was worth it, he had told Jane. The pain of the destruction of the castle was nothing when you compare it to the dreaming, designing and building.

He could still see his mother's expression, Brian had said, her eyes too sensitive, too understanding, probing as she questioned him, appropriating his, Brian's, dreams into her own. He hadn't allowed that to happen with the sand-castle dream.

She had made his school prizes, his science projects, his track-and-field records her own. She had nosed into his friendships. But the secret of the sand-castle he had kept, almost to the end. And remembering, he had felt the bitter-sweetness of that near-victory. She had, perhaps, demolished the sand-castle, but she had never known about the three-dimensional helix, about the secret recipe for sand-cement, about the dream, or about the problems he had learned to solve while building.

Did he tell all this to Dahlia? Jane had wondered at the time, not wanting to ask. And why is he telling me? She hadn't known then, and she didn't now. But perhaps what had happened tonight, after their meeting, had been somewhat the same. The same pattern, the confidences about his feelings for Gary and for his widow, followed by his tightening up. Whatever it was, she wondered if it had prompted what he had said in the parking lot, after their silent ride down in the elevator.

They had been walking toward their cars. It was very cold, and there was a high wind. Brian spoke, and the wind took his words and carried them away across the dark, empty parking lot. "The risks are high," she was sure she heard, "and I will keep secret what has to be kept secret. That way, I can do what I have to do."

Or had she just imagined it, twisted his words into a meaning that fit her own thoughts? Because she felt certain he was hiding something from her. Something she had to know, before it was too late.

11

"I have to go to New York," Kersti was saying. "Why don't we have dinner tonight before I go, and you can tell me how you're coming with the BTS business."

"Oh, Kersti, I don't know . . ." Jane said, looking at her desk and shifting the telephone to her left ear so she could shuffle through the files still remaining to be studied. "Thanks for calling, but I have so much to do tonight I don't think I should."

"Well, we'll just have a falafel or something — we won't take long. Come on, Jane. I've got some gossip for you — I talked to Tiu. Just consider it business. You have to eat anyway."

Jane looked at her watch. It was seven-thirty already, and she had at least three more hours of work that had to be done before tomorrow. If she took a break for dinner, would she have the will-power to come back?

"Well, only for half an hour, okay? And could you come by for me so I won't have to take my car out of the parking lot? That way I'm more likely to come back."

"I'll be there," said Kersti. "You stay inside the building

lobby, King Street side, and watch out for me. It's cold out. Fifteen minutes."

"Falafel is okay," Kersti said, leaning over the front seat of her fire-red Saab to open the door for Jane, "but what I really need is a drink. How about you?"

"What I really need is a way to calm my mind so I can think things through. How about a Japanese restaurant?"

Kersti didn't remind Jane that she had said half an hour was all she had to spare. Kersti was not a fan of fast food, even the Near-Eastern variety, so she was happy to agree to the change in plans. They drove up Church Street to the Maiko Gardens and were soon settled into a small rice-paper booth, soothed by the low murmur of voices, the Japanese music, which sounded like gentle rain, and the hot sake.

"Why are you so behind in your work?" Kersti asked. "It's not like you to get snowed under and be working so late."

Jane frowned, turning her little sake cup in her hands, enjoying its warmth. "This thing has turned into two jobs, that's the problem. Two research jobs."

The waitress glided up to their booth. She wore the traditional Japanese kimono, with its wide obi and its narrow skirt, which obliged her to take short, shuffling little steps in her thonged sandals. Leaning over the table to arrange their plates of sushi, she folded back her wide sleeve in a stylized gesture, so that it would not fall into the food. Jane watched her, thinking about her movements, which seemed to be almost a ballet, or a pantomime of repression. She always found it hard to believe, when she watched Japanese women in traditional dress, so graceful and studiedly passive, that this idea of feminine beauty could relate in any way to what it meant to be a woman.

Rather, to her the gestures seemed to be those of a small, cowed animal, showing submission to a larger and more aggressive one. Kersti's eyes followed Jane's glance. "I know what you're thinking," Kersti said, "but still, doesn't it make you feel kind of peaceful, everyone's place so clearly defined, everyone knowing what they have to do?"

"No," Jane said, smiling. "It makes me angry. I feel anger boiling around inside me."

"That's all the sake you've drunk on an empty stomach," Kersti said, picking up the sake jug. "We'd better order another."

They ate their sushi with their fingers, dipping it into the soya sauce and leaning over their plates.

"It's not that I can't do it," Jane said, picking up the conversation. "It's just that it's a bit overwhelming, that's all. All the research that has to be done to find the right person for Brian, and then the research on the computer system they have at BTS to try to figure out how Gary Levin was killed, and the locked-room business. . . ."

"What have you found out?" Kersti asked.

"You first. Remember the gossip you promised me."

"Well, as I said, I talked to Tiu."

"Yes, Tiu. . . . I saw what you meant when we had tea together. She really doesn't seem to be in very good shape."

Kersti pushed away the last piece of sushi. "Here, you have this, Jane. I don't want any more. No, Tiu isn't well. But it sort of waxes and wanes, you know. Sometimes she seems really . . . unstable, and other times you think she's over it. She's getting therapy, and she's on medication, but . . . I don't know . . . it's been building for years, and in a way it doesn't surprise me."

"It does me," Jane said. "When I met her five years ago when I first worked at BTS she seemed very together.

Smooth and slick and polished and almost perfect. Kind of like Martha."

"I know she gave that impression," Kersti said. "But what you couldn't see was that it was too perfect. That was the flip side of what's happening now. She's lost the ability to hold herself together like that."

"Why?"

Kersti shook her head. "I don't think I should talk about it. You understand, Jane. I'd tell you anything about me, but Tiu's private life is her own."

"Of course."

"Tiu said that she thinks Brian might give Robert Mc-Donnell, the comptroller at BTS, the sack as soon as all this stuff is over."

"She didn't tell me that," Jane said. "And how would she know? I thought she'd taken a leave of absence."

"Well, I guess Martha calls her from time to time to see how she's doing. Anyway, she said she heard it from Martha. Also, apparently having you around asking questions is making people nervous. Jane, did you ever think that what you are doing could be dangerous?"

"Oh, Kersti," Jane said, "you can't be serious. No one is going to see *me* as a threat."

Their main courses came, and they both waited silently as the waitress set out the dishes, removed the tops from the little black laquered bowls of soup, fluffed up Jane's basket of tempura and arranged Kersti's yakitori and rice in patterns on her plate. As soon as she was gone, Kersti repeated her question, but Jane brushed it aside. "You don't understand, Kersti. Maybe it's because I'm so short, but you'd be surprised how little impression I make on people."

Kersti's voice was exasperated. "Just how can you be so sure of that?"

"I *am* sure. It was the same when I worked on the newsletter. I'd ask people questions and they'd say the most indiscreet things. I don't think it was real to them, that this little blond girl would print what they said and get them in trouble."

"Jane, that happens to all journalists. It didn't just happen to you because you are a woman and little. People are always spilling their deepest secrets and then acting betrayed when they're written up. I think you're making a mistake. Sometimes I think your feminism distorts your perceptions of reality."

"Hey, just a minute. You're a feminist too."

"Yes, but when I'm working, I'm a journalist."

"Well, right now I'm a researcher. Feminism has nothing to do with it. I've been looking into the computer system and all the other systems in the computer room."

"That's interesting. What did you find out?"

"Well, first I checked out the halon fire-alarm system. I was sure that was how it was done. Everybody who works with computer systems and computer rooms knows about halon."

"So, tell. I've never heard about it."

"Halon is colourless, odourless, inert gas. Because it can't harm the equipment, it's what's usually used to put out fires in computer rooms. We're all told if ever there is a fire alarm and the halon is released, to get out of the computer room. It could kill you. So first thing, I called up one of the fire marshals who'd been on the scene and asked him if halon could kill anyone. Could it cyanose their lungs?"

"And?"

"And he said, absolutely not. It's completely harmless." She paused. "I wonder why we've all been told to evacuate computer rooms if the halon is released."

"Beats me."

"So then, I asked him was there anything else that could have been released in that room, which would leave no trace, be perfectly harmless to Martha when she opened the door early in the morning, yet kill Gary at midnight."

"So what did he say?"

"Just what you'd think." Jane took a big bite of a piece of tempura shrimp. It was delicate, and crisp, all texture and no taste. "He said nothing could do that. Nothing he'd ever heard of."

"So, where do you go from here, Jane?"

"Well, I've got an appointment with Sandy Tsu, the systems manager, to get a good look at their system and to check out the computer room. Sandy has promised not to tell anybody about my visit — I know him pretty well, because he's one of the people I found for Brian five years ago. Somehow I don't think Brian would be too thrilled that I'm taking time to snoop around checking out the system; I'm hoping he won't find out. Maybe seeing the system will give me an idea of what happened to Gary Levin."

"Watch yourself. I'm worried for you, Jane."

"Get serious, Kersti."

"I am serious, Jane. That's why I'm worried. I just wish you were."

Jane shook her head and crunched on her tempura. What she had thought was shrimp turned out to be a piece of onion, and the layers came apart in her mouth. "Oh, I'm serious enough, Kersti. The problem is, the more I want to know, the more revved up I get, and the more revved up I get, the less real any danger is to me."

"I see what you mean, but are you saying you won't be careful?"

Jane picked up a piece of tempura, checking this time to be sure she wasn't deceived by a vegetable masquerading as a shrimp. "No, but the fact that it's dangerous just doesn't seem to stop me from pushing ahead."

"Well, I think your attitude is pretty unrealistic."

Jane was touched by Kersti's concern. She reached out and pressed Kersti's arm gently, affectionately. "Believe me, Kersti, if anything happens to me, you'll be the first to know."

"Thanks a lot," Kersti said.

12

Jane was looking forward to her meeting with Sandy Tsu, the BTS systems manager, hoping that it would give her the kind of understanding of BTS's computer system that she needed. Sandy was responsible for the hardware and software systems that were used by the BTS staff. If anyone were able to figure out who had sent the threatening message, it would be Sandy. There were other technical things he would know, too, which Jane wanted to find out.

Sandy met her in the reception area of BTS. Jane signed in, pinned on her visitor badge, and Sandy led her back to his office. They walked side by side, not speaking. Sandy wore a maroon-and-white-striped rugby shirt, faded baggy jeans, and running shoes with worn patches over the toes. He wore a large watch with a calculator on it, and there was a beeper tucked into his belt. He had a pale, round, youthful-looking face, quick intelligent eyes, and a shy smile.

When she had hired him for BTS, Sandy had been what was then called a "guru." Gurus were experts in the intricacies of computer systems such as the UNIX operating system, complicated work environments which were poorly documented. Such systems could be maintained only by this fraternity of computer-obsessed young men, who communicated with one another via electronic mail networks and had a tendency to organize the systems they maintained in brilliant and complex ways that no one else could understand or maintain. They knew one another's reputations, respected one another, and hardly anybody else.

This lack of respect often extended to their bosses, which made the gurus a management problem. A common solution was to coddle them, hope they wouldn't quit, and when they did, find another who would take apart the work of his predecessor, redo it in an even more arcane way, and thus re-start the cycle.

The gurus repaid their masters by being always on hand to help all the computer-using staff (they tended to work twelve to eighteen hours a day) and by creating custom software for each staff member that would meet the most important or trivial demands.

But the age of the gurus was passing. Computer systems — even UNIX — were getting easier to use, and there were more people who knew how to use them. The gurus who could write English, communicate easily with their co-workers, and who demonstrated loyalty were becoming more traditional employees. The remainder were moving to firms involved only in research and development, firms that had no marketing targets to meet, and where team skills were not essential. And of course, a certain percentage burned out every year from overwork and the unbalanced life they led.

Sandy's office was piled high with computer tapes and magazines. He had a collection of empty New York Seltzer bottles, and a half-eaten doughnut mouldering on the corner of his desk. There was a dented file cabinet, one drawer of which was open, revealing a confused coil of cables.

He cleared off a chair for Jane, sat down himself, put his feet up on another chair, tilted his own chair so that it looked as if it might topple right over, and stared up at the ceiling.

"So how is it going, Sandy?" Jane asked. "It must be a few years since I last talked to you — just after you agreed to take the job here."

"True."

"Well? Do you like it?"

He tilted his chair back down, picked up a pen from his desk and absently twirled it in a small frayed hole in the knee of his jeans. "It's okay," he said.

"How do you find working for Brian Taylor? Do you think he's as smart as I said?"

Sandy carefully enlarged the hole in his jeans by prodding at it with his pen. When he realized Jane wasn't going to fill in the silence, he said, "He knows what he's doing, pretty much."

"And the work?"

With his blue pen Sandy carefully coloured the frayed white threads edging the hole. "It's sort of interesting," he said. "We've got lots of different systems here, and we're slowly getting them all to talk to each other."

Jane nodded.

"But most of what we do here, data processing and that kind of thing, is pretty repetitive. That's what brings in the bucks, though, so we're not supposed to complain. As long as there's enough interesting stuff at the same time I'm content."

Jane watched in fascination as Sandy began carefully drawing a pentagon on his jeans around the hole he had enlarged. "Actually," he said, "Brian is thinking about do-ing some neat projects."

"You mean the application generators?"

Sandy waved his hand dismissively. He abandoned his pen, opened up a desk drawer, took out a candy bar and began to unwrap it. "Oh, that, we did that a long time ago; it's old technology now. No, Brian is interested in artificial intelligence. Things like that. He's got some nifty ideas, and we might be getting some excellent new hardware to work on them."

"I can see expert systems for what BTS does now," Jane said. "But artificial intelligence? I thought most of that was just hype, just vaporware."

Sandy broke a small piece off his candy bar, poked it into his mouth and chewed thoughtfully. "It could be fun, that's all I'm saying. A new PSI prototype computer from Japan would perk up the techies around here. But anyway, what did you want to know?"

"Sandy, you know I'm doing some work for BTS, right?"

He nodded, crammed the rest of the candy bar into his mouth, balled up the wrapping and flung it in the direction of the wastebasket without checking to see if he was on target. He wasn't, and the wrapper nestled on the floor next to several others.

"I need to understand about why the computer crashed the night Gary Levin died, and who sent the message found after his death. And I'd just as soon that nobody knew I was asking about it. It could start gossip that would make my job harder."

Sandy didn't reply, but Jane thought he looked doubtful.

"So, what can you tell me?"

"The problem is, I don't get why you need to know," Sandy said.

"I do, Sandy, I really do," Jane said, looking directly at

him. He held her gaze for a moment, then swivelled in his chair and began tapping keys on his computer terminal. His monitor, taller than it was wide, filled with glowing lines, which scrolled by so fast that Jane, looking over the systems manager's shoulder, could not read them. She returned to her chair and waited, wondering if Sandy was going to trust her. Why should he? What could she say that would convince him that she was working for the good of BTS, rather than out of some selfish motives of her own? After all, she was hardly sure herself.

He pushed his chair back and gyrated around to face her, his expression serious. "I've been thinking about it a lot," he said slowly. "It's pretty puzzling. It's obvious that only someone with the superuser password could have sent that message. So one of the top management group must have done it. And I guess something should be done about that fact. I've been thinking about what I should do. I've talked to Brian about it."

"And?"

"He listened. He told me to find out what I could and let him know. But he didn't really focus." Sandy hesitated, then leaned forward, looking hard at Jane. "You know Brian, you know what I mean." He watched Jane's expression, then apparently satisfied, he continued. "It's like he has tunnel vision when he's working on something. It seems that when he has an important project on his mind you can't get his attention for anything else. And right now, this joint marketing thing is all he's thinking about. To tell the truth, I don't think he cares one way or the other who sent that message, or how Gary died. So he probably wouldn't care who I talked to about it."

Jane wasn't so sure, but if it eased Sandy's conscience, she certainly wasn't going to argue with him.

He turned back to his terminal and looked at it for a

moment, then typed in a few keystrokes and studied the screen again.

"I've thought about talking to McDonnell," Sandy said, without looking at Jane. "I kind of assumed he'd be taking over from Gary Levin, and that would make him the new number-two man around here."

"But?" Jane prompted.

"I decided it wasn't a good idea."

"Why not?"

"McDonnell wants to be VP of finance more than anything else in the world. How can you trust a guy like that? And he wears a tie every day, too." Sandy smiled, but Jane thought he wasn't joking.

"I don't get it," Jane said, wanting to hear more. "Why do you think McDonnell is more ambitious than any of the others? After all, he's not the only one with a tie."

"You can tell, that's all," Sandy said. "He's a suck; he won't stick up for his principles and he doesn't keep his word."

"I'm not sure I understand."

"It's not important — forget I said that. The point is, once I started thinking that McDonnell was too ambitious to trust, I decided I didn't want to talk to any of them. Once I started worrying about who to trust, I didn't know what to do."

"I see what you mean," Jane said, "but I'm different. I'm working for the well-being of the whole company. Telling me what's on your mind might be the best way to go."

Sandy picked up his pen again and carefully outlined a circle on his thigh through the hole in his jeans. Jane waited, hoping her silence would be persuasive.

He looked up at her, then past her. "The message 'That will teach the son of a bitch' came from superuser," Sandy said. "It was on the VAX computer, which runs the UNIX operating system. On that kind of system, in most companies, only one person has the superuser password. That's because it's dangerous to fool around as superuser. You can destroy things, cause a lot of damage. But Brian wanted all the key people in the management team to have the superuser password. I was against it, but . . . he's the boss."

"Against it, why?"

"Two reasons. One's technical. A person with the superuser password can read any file, look at anything, change anything. Erase anything. That's dangerous to the integrity of our systems. Disasters could happen. Things important to the running of the system could be accidentally erased."

"Has that ever happened?"

"No, but it could have. It still can. Even one accident could be pretty serious. But there's another problem. Brian said it was symbolic — that the management team should have this kind of openness and trust, and power. If you ask me, it's a bad symbol. It's got so they all think they own the company. And they don't. And here's another thing — the way that message was sent. Using the superuser password it *could* have been sent so that nobody knew it came from one of the people with the password. But it wasn't. The sender wanted us all to know it came from someone with superuser access to the system."

Jane thought about what Sandy was saying. It was an idea that she too had puzzled over. Why would the murderer want the murder known? Without the message, the death would no doubt have been regarded as a heart attack. And further, why narrow the suspicion down to just a few people? It didn't make any sense.

"It's even more Byzantine than it seems at first," Sandy said. "I've done some checking; I've looked at the back-up tapes. Someone programmed the computer to crash at

12:55 A.M. They programmed it to print out that mail message as soon as it was booted up."

"How many people have the password, are superusers?"

"Eight, but the way I see it, only six people could have sent the message. Alan Bates, the head of research and development, has the password; that is, he *had* the password, but he's in New Zealand on holiday, and the password changes from time to time. It's changed since he went away. So he's out of the picture. I could have done it, but I didn't; and you know that's true, because if I had done it, I wouldn't tell you all this."

Jane agreed. Sandy was giving her technical information she couldn't get from anyone else. He controlled access to the back-ups. He could have erased them, erased the information he was passing along to her.

"That leaves top management: Brian, Martin Kaplan, Tom Henege, Martha Gruen and Robert McDonnell. And of course Gary himself. I think it had to be one of them. And if you cross out Gary, you have a choice of five. Brian, Martin, Tom, Martha and Robert."

"The five people who were together at a meeting when he died."

"That's right. The computer crashed at 12:55. Bates was out of the country, I was at the emergency ward of Toronto General with my wife. The rest of them were together. According to what I found out, Gary died at a time when none of those who could have sent that message could have been there. What do you think of that?"

"What I can't figure out," Jane said, "is why he would go into the computer room in the first place. There's no reason for a person to go into the computer room at all."

"Except to boot up, if the system you're working on crashes."

"He knew how to boot up?"

"They all did. I'd documented it for them. They worked odd hours, sometimes late or on weekends. It was something they wanted to know how to do, and I set it up for them."

"By all, you mean the people with the superuser password?"

"That's right."

"What was Gary working on the night he died? Could you find that out?"

Sandy swung back to his terminal and keyed in a few commands. "He was working in a directory he had named Chicago, on a file he had named 1001. He was using a spreadsheet program. That doesn't do you much good, does it?"

Jane shook her head. "Sandy, how come you have all this information so easily available? All this happened a couple of weeks ago."

"The system backed itself up about an hour before it crashed. I've got records of all this on the back-up tape. I copied them the day after Gary died."

"Why did you do that, Sandy?"

He shrugged. "Seemed like a good idea at the time."

"Would anybody else — any superuser — know that all this information about why and when the computer crashed and procedures?"

"I don't think so. I organize the back-ups; different machines back up at different times. The VAX backs up Sunday nights, about ten-thirty. I found the program that crashed the computer and sent the message on the back-up tape. The program to crash the computer erased itself just as soon as the message printed out."

"How did you find it then?"

Sandy sighed. "That's what I've been telling you. The person who wrote the program to crash the computer and send the message expected his program to be erased so someone would find the printout but not the program that generated it. But he forgot about back-up. My back-up system is pretty sophisticated, and not the sort of thing most of the management thinks about."

"They just take it for granted, do they?"

"They count on it without thinking about it, that's all. Back-up is critical. Think customers would like us losing their data? Programmers don't go for having days of work wiped out either. That's why we make a copy of all the information stored on the hard disc of each computer each day. I schedule back-up. But for sure, none of the big cheeses know the back-up schedule."

Jane noticed that Sandy had a strange poster of Dr. Who. She stared at it, and the actor's face stared back at her, sardonic and amused. "Could you tell anything about the person who wrote that program, from looking at it?"

He shrugged.

"Come on, Sandy. Surely you could. Was it a good program?"

Sandy laughed.

She pushed him. "Do you think one of the more experienced people around here would write one like that, or did it look amateur?"

Again a silence. Sandy rocked back in his chair; Jane was sure it would tip over. Finally he lowered the chair, looked at her. "Whoever wrote it wasn't experienced in this kind of program. Probably. But that's just my opinion."

"Was it a hard program?"

"Trivial."

"How long would it take you to write something like that?"

"A few minutes."

"How long would your program be?"

"Just a few lines. A page maybe."

"How long was the program you found?"

"About that. But it was a pretty unsophisticated effort."

"Any idea of who wrote it, then, from the way it was written?"

He didn't answer. Jane thought, he thinks he knows but he doesn't want to say. She tried again. "It's not good for you to know something about a murderer no one else knows."

He smiled. "That's right. That's why I haven't told anybody but the police and now you that I found that program on the back-up tape. I don't have too much confidence in the police, but you understand the implications of all this. You can handle it now."

Jane thought about it. Although everyone in the management group could program, and had at one time or another done some of it, according to what Tsu had said, none of them could be considered up-to-date or truly professional except Brian. And it would take a thorough knowledge of their programming to recognize their style. Probably Sandy would not have had a chance to see examples of their programs because programming would not normally be a part of their job. "I suppose it would be a guess, in any case."

He nodded. "That's the problem, all right. If I could be sure — no problem, I'd say. I'd want to. But it's like handwriting. A neat person can write sloppy as a disguise. Someone could write kludgy code in case it was found, just to confuse things."

Jane said, "Let's see if I understand this. Because the program that crashed the system and sent the message had to be written by someone with the superuser password, only one of the management team could have done it."

"Looks that way."

"Not a question of looks that way. That's the only way it could have been."

"Right," Sandy said, not looking at her.

"So this is how it stands," Jane said. "Someone wrote that program you found. It caused the computer to crash at 12:55 A.M. That same someone knew everyone in the management group would be in a meeting, thus giving each other an alibi. They believed the death would appear natural . . . but then, why the message? It doesn't make sense."

Nothing make sense, she thought. The time of the murder gave an alibi to all the suspects. Yet the message would cause the management team to suspect one another. Did that mean something? Might it affect the negotiations with the Americans?

Sandy was looking at his terminal again. He hit the space bar and pages of type scrolled upward. He was reading his electronic mail. He didn't want to tell her any more. Jane knew. He wanted her to leave.

She didn't. "When you checked the computer room after the murder," she said, "did you find anything at all unusual?"

"No, not really."

"You must have got there just after Martha found Gary?"

"Pretty well. That's how I got to inspect the room before the police came. Martha called me before she called them. I was there in five minutes. She knew I'd want to be here."

Jane remembered Martha telling her that she knew Sandy would see anything wrong, if there was anything wrong to see.

"I know you have work to do, Sandy, but one other thing. The program you found, the one that crashed the computer, that was on the VAX, wasn't it?"

"Right."

"Because of the different back-up times, could there have been a program on the mainframe computer that you missed?"

He thought a minute. "Yes," he said. "That's possible. The mainframe backs up early in the morning. If there was another mystery program on it that erased itself before I got in, I wouldn't have found it on the back-up."

"And it would be gone? No way to find it?"

"Not that I know of. If you can figure out a way to find a file or a program that erases itself before back-up, let me know. We could rescue a lot of dumbos around here from their screw-ups."

Jane stood up. "I really appreciate all this," she said. "I know I've taken a great deal of your time. But would you mind —" she smiled at him and got a smile back "— would you mind giving me a quick tour of the computer room on the way out? I can't help wondering if something in there could have caused Gary's death."

Jane followed Sandy out of his office and down a wide hall, created by pods of sleek Steelcase workspaces defining small curved offices, set off by smoky panes of glass, and grey-and-maroon, built-in worktops and shelving. As they reached the door of the computer room, Sandy said, "I think you're wasting your time, but maybe you'll see something I missed. I checked everything right after I got here. It couldn't have been more than five minutes after Martha called me. I just zoomed over here, she was so panicked. But there was nothing unusual. Nothing out of line."

"You're probably right, but I want to see it all for myself anyway."

"No problem." Sandy opened the first door to the computer room. It was unlocked. Walking through they found themselves in a short, blank-walled corridor. At the end of it was another door with a glass panel. Inside the glass panel was wire mesh. Sandy opened the second door by inserting a plastic card into a slot.

"Why two doors?" Jane asked.

"The passcard does a good job of controlling the access of the people who work here," Sandy said. "We just let the security company know who can come in, and when. Their computer fixes it so that only those cards will let you in. And it keeps a record of who comes and goes, and when, which management would want if ever there was some kind of information leak. But at night and on weekends, the real worry is intruders. The passcard-controlled door wouldn't be much good if a burglar smashed in the whole door, right? So that locked door is steel and has an intruder alarm in it. The night watchman has one key to it; I keep a key to it; and there's always a third key in the fireproof safe that management can get at night, if they're working late and have to get in."

"So what do you think, Sandy? Could anyone have got into that room besides Gary Levin the night he died?"

"I don't see how. First, how would they get a key? Gary had the third key in his pocket. Second, the only people with night card access that night were the same people we were discussing earlier, the five at the management meeting, Gary Levin, and of course me. "I've checked the card-system log for that night; no one went in except Gary."

"But could he have let someone in?"

"Sure, but then how would they get out? You need the key to get out, too, and Gary had it in his pocket."

"A copy of the key?"

"No. This is a very expensive security system. You can't get a key blank to make a copy." He took a key ring out of his pocket and showed Jane a small key with a peculiar cylindrical shank. "See what I mean? It's not an ordinary key."

"The whole thing is completely mysterious," Jane said. She walked into the computer room, noticing that one wall, glassed-in, looked out over a large workroom. But this glass, too, had security mesh in it. Looking at the computers, Jane saw that BTS had the latest equipment. Not for them the computers with flashing lights one sees in sci-fi films. Rather, a row of staid, metal boxes, like file cabinets, a few topped with glassed-in tape drives. At one end of the computers were several consoles and printers, on which various status messages or error messages printed out from time to time.

"What are those thingamabobs along the wall there?" Jane asked.

"The first one is the telephone box. A lot of our customers are on-line to us. Lots of telephone lines coming in here. The next one is the control panel for the halon fire extinguisher. The morning after the murder, Martha switched it on, I guess because it triggers the police/fire alarm, and so it was the quickest way to raise the alarm when she found Gary's body. Actually that surprised me, because of course it released halon into the room, and I thought Martha could have been poisoned by the gas. We've always thought that if the fire alarm goes off you should get out — that the halon is dangerous."

"Apparently not," Jane said. "I checked. It seems halon is an inert gas, absolutely harmless."

"That's news to me," Sandy said. "Anyway, that last box is the PAX switching panel. We need a switch like that because we've got quite a few different computers here, and people work on different ones at different times."

Jane looked around. It all looked perfectly normal, just like any other computer room.

Sandy said, "So the way I see it there's just no way anybody could have got in here to murder Gary Levin. No way."

Jane sighed. "It sure doesn't make any sense. But I want to think about it. Do you think you could get me vendor descriptions and technical descriptions for the modems, the fire-extinguishing system, the PAX, the isolator, the electrical panel, everything electric in here?"

"Sure. Be glad to. But I can't see the point."

They walked back to the reception area in silence, Jane concentrating and committing to memory the computer room, where everything was and how all the electrical equipment worked. It seemed to her that the answer had to be there, somewhere, if she could only see it.

Five people who could have caused the computer to crash — six, if you counted Sandy — who could have sent the message. A message clearly meant to alert the BTS management group to the fact that a murder had taken place. But how did that help?

All that she had learned made the murder itself seem impossible. Gary Levin, killed in a doubly locked room at a time when all the suspects were far away. She had thought if she could only figure out *how* she might know *who*. At the moment, the how seemed impossible to figure out. Maybe the who would be easier.

Somehow she doubted it.

13

Jane drove out of the BTS parking lot thinking about what Sandy had told her, and unable to make anything of it. She had hoped she could concentrate her attention on how the murder was done. If she could get to the bottom of it, by understanding the technical aspects, figure out how the murder was done, then perhaps she wouldn't have to go over in her mind the character and motivation of the key people at BTS and imagine each of them in the role of murderer.

Somehow, doing this seemed almost like casting an evil spell on them, wishing them ill, tainting them. It was the unpleasant obverse of a fantasy, in which you imagined you were rich, or famous, or in the arms of someone you desired, knowing that by imagining it, day-dreaming it, you were in a sense willing it and helping it to come to fruition.

I ought to get back to the office, she thought, there's so much to do there. A vision of her office passed through her mind — files piled on the desk, the visitor's chair, the floor, stacks of pink telephone message slips — but she had made an appointment with Martha for later that afternoon, and there was no time for a trip downtown and back. So instead, she headed west along the 401 to the Yorkdale mall, telling herself that she had put off buying her children's Christmas presents long enough, and she would have to get it over with sooner or later.

Her heart sank as she drove into the mall's giant parking lot. In the grey winter light the ranks of cars, looking dirty and salt smeared, seemed to stretch for miles in all directions, sealed and empty, crusted with snow. I'll just drive around, she thought, and if I don't find somewhere to park in five minues I'll leave and come back early one morning when it's not so crowded.

In this case, at least, her negative thoughts had no effect on reality, because a car pulled out in front of her, very near an entrance to the shopping centre. Jane parked and walked into the mall, feeling immediately suffocated by the crowds, the noise, and the lighting, which made merchandise worthless to her glow and sparkle as if they were objects of desire. How strange, too, to see among the Christmas decorations palm trees stretching up to the skylights, and pools of still water — an oasis without a desert.

When it was built, the mall had been the height of glamour. Highly polished marble and travertine, arched roofs, rows of clerestory windows letting daylight shine on the ranks of hanging plants. One of the first large, indoor shopping malls in North America. But all the same, Jane didn't like it.

Perhaps it was the influence of her family. As early as Jane could remember, they had been very poor, though it had not always been so. Jane's parents had not been bitter about not having money; it was the reason for their downfall they complained about.

Growing up and hearing her father — who had been shunted aside in his profession as a chemist in Chicago during the McCarthy era — becoming increasingly cynical and bitter about materialism and "capitalist paranoia" as he called it, Jane had been left with a peculiar ambivalence about money. She often wondered if she had married Bernie, not because he had seemed so sure about loving her and had convinced her that their marriage was inevitable, but because he was rich. She had got confused about wealth and had come to associate it with freedom from suffering, and from feeling oneself undervalued.

Certainly she had not dared to insist upon keeping the children, when it had been made so clear that they would have a much better life with him. *He* could offer them financial security, and a two-parent family; she neither. Surely she knew better than to offer them a childhood with her, a childhood which would be a repeat of her own. And then, later, when she was earning enough money to give them a decent life, it was too late.

But then, she thought, she was deluding herself in thinking she had had a choice. Bernie had made that very clear. He was going to take the children. He would take them back to his family home in Switzerland if she tried to get them, and that would be the end of it. I didn't choose to give them up, she insisted to herself, feeling the old, familiar anger, that tight mesh that seemed to wrap around her heart and lungs, making it hard to breathe; they were taken from me.

Inside Toy World she walked up and down the aisles, appalled at the toys. There were dolls for little boys, He-men, Lords of the Universe, they were called, with exaggerated muscles like heavy metal cartoon characters. There were ranks of giant stuffed animals and shelves full of motorized toys. What would the kids want? It hurt to think she didn't know. Kerry, her oldest son, had told her that they had a special case to hold all their Lego, that they had *all* the matchbox cars, that they had more models than they could build. In other years she had bought them paint sets and clay-moulding kits. They had sent her dutiful thank-you notes. When they had stayed with her for two weeks in the summer their interests had seemed to change daily; they were easily bored, had short attention spans. And no wonder, if their father bought them everything they wanted.

Her attention was now caught by a chemistry set. She remembered, suddenly, with pleasure the chemistry lab at her high school, the shiny beakers and glass test tubes in those neat little racks with the holes, the scary hiss as the blue flame shot dangerously high from the Bunsen burner. How she had loved stirring her mixtures with a glass rod. Chemistry had seemed so real; after all, it could be dangerous. That made it more real, more exciting than any other subject; everybody knew that the year before there had been an explosion in the lab. An explosion! The high point of the school year.

A chemistry set, that would be great. She got the attention of a clerk, who carefully removed the shrink-wrapping from the box so she could look inside. The chemistry lab of her childhood dissolved as she looked at the meagre contents: a few booklets, a few packets of chemicals, a test tube. Packed in shoddy-looking, die-cut cardboard forms and coloured luridly.

Hastily she shut the box, and without thinking any more about it, bought two crystal radio sets. Jane kept looking at her watch as the clerk charged up the sale and slid the boxes into a shopping bag. As soon as she could, she rushed out of the mall. She didn't want to look into the boxes. Would the radio sets, too, have lost their magic? How horrible it was to think that her children were growing and changing from what they had been, or what she had imagined they had been, that she knew so little about them, and that there seemed to be nothing at all she could do about it.

Luckily she was due to see Martha now, and there was no more time to think about these things. She would have to think about them later.

"I have a new database management system for project control," Martha said. "Do you want to see it?"

Jane smiled and said she'd like to, although in reality her interest was lukewarm. The fact was she just wasn't that interested in computer software anymore. And that was strange, too, because once it had been her life. Jane had started out in psychology, because she had thought it would be a good idea to make her life work out of her need to understand why people were the way they were. But she had been sidetracked. A project she had been working on had needed a lot of statistical analysis. The professor had asked all the men in the class whether any of them were prepared to work on the analysis part of the project. Jane had got mad, in the way she did when someone took it for granted she couldn't do something. Because she was small. Because she was female. She had volunteered.

That had been an unhappy time for her. Married, with two little kids, trying to stay in university when her husband thought she should quit. She'd met Bernie when she was bumming around Europe, the summer between her second and third years of university. He'd been older — rich, sophisticated and protective. He seemed to offer a double measure of security, having houses and family both in Canada and in Lausanne. They'd married in Europe that same summer, after a short, glamorous, romantic and passionate courtship. He had hoped — after she quickly became pregnant, and then again only two months after the birth of the first — that she'd stay home with their children, but Jane had felt that she had to finish university. My life was a disaster then, she thought: disorder, arguments with Bernie about her going to school, kids crying at night, the house not being run as Bernie expected. But during school hours it was different. It was quiet in the computer lab. Dim light, shiny, highly waxed floors, rows of VDTs flickering. There had been something so orderly, so controllable about programming. Here was something she could master, control completely. She hadn't been great at it, but good enough. It had absorbed her. She'd often been late getting home; there had been many nights, too, when after the kids and Bernie were asleep, she'd gone back to the lab, worked all night with other hackers.

Right after she graduated, her marriage broke up. Bernie had left her for another woman, a woman who wanted to do nothing but raise kids. It had been a bad shock to Jane. Was that why she hadn't fought harder to keep them?

In any case, she hadn't had much energy to put into job hunting. And for some reason, she couldn't bear to take any money from Bernie — it was not as if she had children to support. So she'd taken the first job that came along — working on a small newsletter covering the software industry. Jane had needed a new life; she'd lost her old ones so suddenly — her family and the university and her womblike existence there. She had thrown herself into the job. It was 1975. The computer boom was at white heat. The newsletter ballooned. Jane went everywhere, met everyone. She was so small and unimportant-looking; boastful executives forgot themselves, told her too much. Jane had an instinct about when to print what they said and when to save the information, storing away the trust she gained to use another time.

Eventually she made a serious mistake. She had a love affair with the vice-president of the communications conglomerate who was responsible for the newsletter. When the affair ended, Jane knew she had to find another job. She knew before he knew, before even she knew consciously herself. It was a bitter lesson, but it ended well, because she joined a start-up computer company and found herself doing all the hiring. The company was one of those rockets, admired in the industry and a big money maker for its early investors. Jane was given a great deal of credit, particularly by her former lover, who perhaps was trying to assuage some guilt about her departure from the newsletter. Still, Jane wasn't earning very much money. She realized this and tried for more. She found she could get recognition, admiration, but she couldn't seem to get her salary above $25,000. She was young, she had a bachelor's degree in psychology and computer science, she was in personnel. So when Orloff offered a job and promised a good salary if she did well, she took him up on his offer. Orloff needed someone who knew the software industry, and Jane knew it. He needed someone who could handle people. Jane had shown that she could. Jane knew that he also needed someone with an air of authority, so that people could justify paying a percentage of some top executive's first-year salary to Orloff Associates for that person's work. Jane thought that was where she had proved a disappointment. It really didn't matter how much you knew; when a five-foot-two blonde with a small, low voice speaks up in a group of men, half don't notice, and most of the rest think she's "cute."

Jane didn't think Martha had ever had this kind of problem. Martha had a formidable look. It was as if she was covered in chip-proof nail varnish. Or perhaps, Jane thought, it was just the lighting in her office. Track lighting in the ceiling put a spotlight on her workstation, on her desk, on the painting behind the credenza. It glinted off her smooth, dark cap of hair, and flashed off the large square-cut diamond on her right hand.

"Martha," Jane said, "do you mind if I ask you some questions about Gary?"

"About Gary?" Martha said, looking quickly at the door, perhaps to see if they could be overheard, perhaps due to a momentary thought of escape. "Of course not." She got up, walked to the door, looked out, shut it, came back and sat down across from Jane in one of the visitor's chairs.

"You mean, what kind of person we should get to replace him? Well, someone more of a team player, is what I think. I've told Brian I think that. Of course Gary was the right person when we were building the company, growing. But now, when we're consolidating what we've accomplished. . . ."

"But are you consolidating?" Jane asked, recalling Martin's talk of merger. "Is that what's really going on?"

Martha smiled, a quick secret smile. "Don't get wrapped up in these internal fights, Jane. We all have our roles to play; we all know what they are. I'm the conservative. I'm supposed to keep Brian aware of how change will affect the people here, the systems, so he doesn't lose sight of these things. Brian understands that. We all do. I'm supposed to warn him if we're about to bite off more than we can chew."

"I'm not sure I understand," Jane said, hoping to draw Martha out. She was thinking that Martha seemed too confident, too sure of her power over Brian. Jane was doubtful. Perhaps Martha was trying to convince her that she had influence over Brian. That way, Jane thought, Martha believes I'll have to consult her before I recommend anyone for Gary's job.

"Well, for example, you know we've had some pretty strong disagreements about the U.S. deal, and you've heard about them. But mostly it's just noise. In the end, we'll go along with what Brian wants. We know that Brian's genius is to see into the future. That's how he built this company. None of us has that gift; we have to trust him, and in the end we always do. We just thrash around a bit, until we are sure we've figured out the best way to make what Brian wants happen."

"Did Gary see it that way?"

"Did Gary?" Martha repeated. Jane looked closely at Martha; it was her opinion that when people repeated your question they were stalling for time, trying to think of a convenient lie.

"I don't understand your question," Martha said. "It was Gary who was actually doing the work, putting together Brian's deal, negotiating. He was putting more into getting just what Brian wanted than anybody."

"So, if it's all one big happy family," Jane said, "I have trouble understanding why you are being so insistent that someone murdered Gary."

"Don't be silly, Jane," Martha said sharply. "The truth is the truth. It has nothing to do with what I want, or what anybody wants. We can't ignore the truth. That's a recipe for disaster."

"Well, then, who do you think...?"

Martha took off her glasses and rubbed her eyes. She did it carefully so as not to smudge her eye make-up. Then she walked over to her desk, opened a drawer, took out some thin, pink squares of polishing paper, came back to her chair and began shining her glasses. She did this carefully, not looking at Jane until she had polished the glasses thoroughly and put them back on. "I don't know, Jane. I just don't know." Her voice was softer now, almost frightened. "I can't believe it was one of us. People I work with so closely, have worked with for five years. People who are my friends; people whom I trust as much or more than I trust myself. They all had to know, as I know, how hurt we would be if something happened to Gary. How damaged Brian would be. He needs Gary. Needed Gary, I mean."

"Did you like one another, you and Gary?" Jane asked.

Martha smiled. "Yes," she said. "I liked him. I really did. He wasn't perfect, but underneath everything he was a nice guy, a really nice person. You know, the kind of person who, if you were upset, who, if you had a tough argument with him, would come around afterward and see if you were okay. Who noticed if you were upset."

"You surprise me," Jane said. "It's hard to imagine a person as driven as everyone said Gary was as a kind person."

"Well, he was good to me," Martha said. "I went through a rough divorce last year. . . ."

"I'm sorry, I didn't know."

"Married ten years, and things were pretty terrible when it started falling apart. I didn't talk about it, I tried to be professional and not take my troubles to work, and I guess I succeeded, because nobody seemed to notice anything different about me. But Gary found out somehow, and he was very good to me. He helped me find a lawyer, he took me out for drinks and let me cry on his shoulder — you know the kind of thing. And he never said anything to anybody about it."

"Did you and Gary . . . ? I mean, he had quite a reputation as a ladies' man. . . ."

"I know what you mean, Jane, and it's ridiculous. Only a fool gets involved with the men she works with. That only happens in books and movies. In real life, at this level, it's a sure ticket to oblivion. No, of course not."

Jane wondered whether to believe Martha. True, women who survived in business held Martha's view more often than not. But she knew, and Martha surely did too, that there *were* women who did get away with it, many who weren't strong enough not to make this particular mistake. Had Tiu been hinting at this when she said that Gary Levin complimented Martha, and "treated her like a woman"?

"I'm not the only person Gary was good to. He had a good heart. Our office manager, Tiu, hasn't been well, and Gary was always asking about her. When he saw things were getting out of hand he and I ganged up on Brian and got him to agree to a paid leave of absence for her, so she could pull herself together. Everybody else just got mad at all her screw-ups.

"No, Gary had a short temper, and he was a bad person to get into a battle with, but he was kind, and I miss him. We all miss him. I just can't understand who could have done it."

The two women sat silent for a moment. Then Martha sighed. "I guess we just have to live with not knowing — for a while, anyway. Sooner or later the police will surely get to the bottom of it. They have to, someone has to, or the company will be too seriously hurt." She shook her head. "Jane, let's not talk about it anymore. About that database, I'd like to show it to you. You can play around and see how we have the system set up to give support to management. You'll be interested, I'm sure. Go ahead, log in. I got Sandy to set up an account for you. Your password is Orloff."

Jane realized there was no way to avoid Martha's offer without being rude. She sat down at Martha's desk and typed her name and password onto the keyboard of Martha's terminal. The terminal was on a wing to the left of Martha's desk. It was in shadow, and the display glowed bright, the phosphers glimmering: "Hello, Jane. Welcome to the BTS project-management system. Which report would you like to see?"

Jane scanned the menu. There was a list of reports, and the last choice was entitled: "A special message for Jane." Jane chose the message.

Text flashed up on the screen. It read: "Keep away from the murder, Jane. This mystery is not for you. I don't want to have to kill again."

Martha, reading over Jane's shoulder, gave a little scream.

Jane's heart had taken a banging leap in her chest. "Can you save that?" she said sharply to Martha. "Please do it."

Martha leaned over Jane. She keyed in the commands to save the screen display, her fingers trembling slightly.

Jane heard the printer from a cupboard under the credenza. Martha retrieved the printout, and handed it silently to Jane.

"Any way to find out who programmed that response to my log in, Martha?"

Martha gulped. Her breath was short, and her skin looked waxen.

"Martha, are you okay?" Martha looked as if she might faint. Opening the door, Jane called out to Martha's secretary and asked her to get a glass of water.

"Sherry would be good," Martha said faintly, "there's some in the boardroom."

"Sherry," Jane said firmly. "And as quickly as you can, please. Sit down, Martha." Jane put her hand on Martha's arm. It was cold, and her skin was prickled with gooseflesh. Jane's concern for Martha dulled her own fear. She hugged Martha. "It's okay, it's okay."

"Sorry, I'm sorry," Martha said. "I don't know what's the matter with me."

The secretary came in, looking worried and carrying a decanter and two glasses. She filled one, and Martha drank it down without pausing. "Idiot, I'm an idiot. I'm sorry,

Jane. It was just seeing that message like that. It brought it all back . . . finding the body . . . everything. Oh God, I'm sorry, I'm going to cry." And she burst into tears. The secretary stood by, holding the decanter, looking helpless.

Jane knew how humiliated Martha must feel, to cry at work, in front of anyone. Her heart went out to her. "It's okay," Jane said again, gesturing for the secretary to leave. "She's just had a small shock — nothing really." She closed the door and put her arms around Martha, who was now crying quietly, the tears soaking into a wad of paper napkins she had fished out of her desk drawer.

"It's nothing, everything is all right," Jane murmured. "No one can see you. Go ahead and cry. It doesn't matter."

"Oh God, I'm crying at work. I can't believe this is happening."

"It doesn't matter, really it doesn't," Jane said. "I don't count. Go ahead. You can cry in front of me all you want."

Martha was gulping, trying to control her tears, but they kept coming. "No, you, it's almost, it's almost worst of all, you. . . ."

Jane found some Kleenex, handed a tissue to Martha, refilled her glass and then poured herself some of the sherry. "Don't say that, Martha. You have nothing to prove to me."

Martha was still crying. "You work and work to earn people's respect and then you go and blow it by doing something so utterly stupid, so utterly asinine, as crying, I can't believe it. . . ."

Earn *my* respect? Jane thought. Poor Martha. Her mouth twisted with sympathy, and her throat ached with the empathetic tears she had not shed. "It must have been awful, finding Gary—"

"Oh God, Jane, you don't know. You just couldn't ever begin to know. It was a nightmare." The tears had stopped, and Martha was patting her face with the Kleenex. Then she fished out her purse from the credenza and began to repair her make-up as she spoke.

"Gary was so important around here. You could tell when he was in the office because the atmosphere was different. He was so full of energy. Every obsession he had, we all had — I just can't explain it. Around him, compared to him, one felt so . . . colourless. And then, to come in, and. . . . That morning, it was very quiet, very still — you know how it is when you are the first one in? And ordinarily, when you open the computer-room door, all this noise just surges out: the air-conditioner, and the computer, and the console printing out. Then there're the status lights flashing, too. And that morning, when I looked in through the glass window, I couldn't see Gary, but I saw that the computers were dark, and then when I opened the door there was this awful, eerie silence. It was the loudest silence I'd ever heard. And then . . . I saw him lying there. And the silence. Just that one alarm light blinking. So I pulled the switch for the extinguisher and fire alarm, and I booted up the computer. Instinct. The computer so dark, the computer room so quiet, and Gary so . . . still. And then, to see the console come alive, and start printing that message — 'That will teach the son of a bitch!' You can't imagine, Jane. You just can't imagine!"

"Horrible," Jane said.

"Really. It was. It really was unbelievably horrible."

Martha closed her purse with a snap and put it back in the credenza. "I'm back together, now. Thanks, Jane."

"Forget it. But is it possible to find out who sent that message to me?"

"I really doubt it," Martha said. "And to try we'll have to tell someone. But I suppose it has to be done. I'll go and ask Sandy Tsu."

"Good idea," Jane said. "But before you go, could you tell me who knew you were going to show me the database?"

"Oh, everyone," Martha said. "We had our weekly lunch meeting today. I told everyone you were coming to see me this afternoon. I said I'd wow you with the database. I asked Sandy to give you an account, and told him to make your password Orloff."

"Too bad," Jane said. "For a moment there, I thought it was going to be easy."

"I'm not surprised," Martha said. "Whoever did this wasn't going to leave a trail. Why don't you go see Tom Henege? I know he wants to talk to you. I'll see if Sandy is still around. If I find out anything, I'll come and tell you."

Jane agreed. She carefully folded up the printout of the screen message, marking it with the date. "Could you initial and sign this, Martha?" she asked. "I might have to show it to someone, and I'd like to be able to prove when and where I got it."

Martha took a gold pen out of a stand on her desk and with a small flourish wrote her initials beneath Jane's. Then she went out to look for Sandy.

After Martha left, Jane sat thougtfully for a minute looking at Martha's sherry glass. The reflection of the track lighting winked and sparkled off the crystal. There was a blood-red lip print on the edge of Martha's glass. Jane shuddered. She felt, as she slowly put the printout into her purse, that by doing so she was just now really taking in the threat it contained. She set her purse down on the visitor's chair. Then she got up quickly and went out to see Tom Henege.

14

Henege looked up from his desk, and seeing Jane, smiled. It was a very attractive smile, Jane thought, but it didn't do anything for her. Tom Henege always made her feel rather stifled. She didn't know why.

"Hello, Jane. I was hoping you'd stop by." He stood up, walked around his desk and gestured toward a deep sofa at the opposite side of his office. "Have a seat. Would you like a coffee? No? Well, sit down and relax, anyway. Did Martha show you her database?"

"She showed it to me," Jane said, staring at an impressionist painting on the wall to the left of Henege's desk. It appeared to be a group of rather blurry-looking people at a picnic in a dark and ominous-looking forest.

"You don't seem impressed."

"What did you want to talk about?" Jane asked him.

Henege walked back to his desk and sat down in his swivel chair. He studied her in silence, then smiled as if he understood something. "Go ahead and sit down, Jane. You might as well. We have to talk some time."

Jane sat down. Henege looked at her.

She felt small, almost lost, sunk down in Henege's sofa.

He got up and went out of the office. He came back carrying a molded, plastic chair. "Here, sit here," he said. "Maybe we can talk better if you are more comfortable."

He knows, Jane thought with surprise. She was not accustomed to men noticing how she felt about things. Her uneasiness in his presence increased. Of course, she thought, he's in sales. It's his job to be sensitive to people. The thought made her feel better.

Behind Henege's head, through the window, Jane could see that it was getting dark. They were high up. Down below she could see the moving car lights as they swung around a cloverleaf and onto the Don Valley Parkway, joining a series of lights moving in an orderly rhythm along the roadway. The car lights sparkled and the pavement glittered in front of them. It looked distant, almost glamorous, and she felt small and lonely.

"I know Martin has been telling you how we have to find someone who can complete the merger," he said.

"Yes," Jane replied. "Everyone has been telling me that. But I hear you don't think so. Why is that?"

Henege leaned back in his chair. Then he swivelled around and looked out the window. He began speaking without turning back. Jane could see only the side of his cheek, his dark hair and his back.

"This is a very nice place to work. Do you know that, Jane?"

"I've heard that, yes."

"Part of the reason is Martha. I know she seems very hard and efficient, but there is more to Martha than that."

Jane wondered if Tom Henege and Martha were sleeping together. The thought had crossed her mind before. It wasn't likely, or she would have heard about it. But still, she wondered. For some reason, the idea bothered her.

"Martha has a special quality we all value around here.

People trust her, count on her. Because although she's tough and completely professional, she has a way of facing right at the truth, and then getting it out in the open. But she does it in a way that people don't mind, a way they respect. Do you understand?"

"I think so."

"And in the end Brian always backs her up. He knows what Martha stands for. That she cares for the people here and protects them. Almost like a shop steward. So when she expresses an idea, about how something is or isn't good for the company, Brian understands where it's coming from. It's not all ego, or fencing off her territory, or anything like that."

"All right. I see what you mean."

"Then there's Martin. If the U.S. deal goes through he could be in trouble."

"Why worry about Martin? He's not worried."

"Isn't he? Is that what he says? He should be. Gary didn't value customer service. He always said the numbers told the story; they showed that customer service was expensive, that it didn't bring in as much revenue as it should, to justify its cost. He said Martin always went over budget, gave too much service free on the maintenance contracts, so we lost money on them. He wanted Martin's division cut back. Of course I fought that, because basically what I sell is product plus service. I couldn't market one without the other."

"Well, I certainly agree with you, and I bet Brian does too."

"Yes, but the point is Gary didn't. His not wanting Martin to be a vice president was part of that power struggle — one I hope is behind us now. I don't want another Gary in here. The things that Martin and Martha believe in, I believe in too. I care about them. I think Brian does too, or I wouldn't be working for him. But Brian has a kind of weakness in him. He's dazzled by high-powered people like Gary. And he sometimes underrates the jobs Martin and Martha do."

"Did Gary underrate you too?"

Tom smiled. "Come on now, Jane. I'm not suggesting I'm a sadly misunderstood genius, or anything like that. Besides, why turn over BTS's dirty linen? Of course we all had disagreements from time to time, but ask anybody. We got along better than most management groups — that's what you'll hear."

Jane didn't want Tom to get away with not talking about Gary. She was determined to induce everyone at BTS to talk about him. Only by doing so, she thought, could she begin to get a feeling for who might have killed him.

"Well," Jane said, "I seem to have heard someone saying you and he argued over your bonus, and you said yourself you didn't agree about how much resources should go into customer service."

Tom laughed, but Jane thought his laughter was strained. "Of course we argued over my bonus. If he'd have paid me the percentage that was in my employment contract I would have earned a million two last year. Naturally he tried to get out of paying it."

"How did he do that?"

"By changing the deal. Before, my bonus was based on a percentage of the sales I made. After my bonus gets to $250,000 the percentage goes down. Gary wanted it to go down a lot further, and faster. To be fair to him, I guess he thought with the U.S. deal coming, if we didn't renegotiate my bonus, the amounts the company would have to pay would be completely out of line."

"And did you renegotiate?" Jane asked, thinking that

Tom must be earning an extraordinary amount for the company, for his bonus and commissions to be so high.

"What you probably don't realize," said Tom, who seemed to have an uncanny way of picking up on what Jane was thinking, "is that besides the sales staff's individual commissions, *all* the sales and marketing staff get varying percentages of the total the sales department brings in. The idea is to encourage co-operation and discourage us from hurting the company by competing with each other in a non-productive way. Since I'm at the top, my percentage is naturally larger. But when we first signed the deal, nobody thought I would bring in so many big customers on my own. Anyway, I'm not unreasonable, there was no problem, and we eventually cut a deal."

"So you got what you wanted, did you?" said Jane.

"No, of course not. Neither of us got what we wanted; it doesn't work that way. We worked out a compromise, we shook hands on it, and we both probably thought we'd do better the next time around. But just because I knew how to get along with Gary doesn't mean I think he was the best person for the company. It doesn't mean I think we need another person like that around here, because I don't."

"Brian hasn't told me to hire someone like Gary."

"Brian doesn't have to tell you. He's smarter than that. You watch. He'll steer you in the direction he wants you to go. That happens to everyone who works with Brian. Except, maybe, for Gary."

"Why was that, do you think?"

"Because Brian wants what he wants so strongly, I guess."

"No, I mean, why do you say Gary didn't do what Brian wanted?"

"Did I say that?" Tom avoided Jane's eyes. "That's not

what I meant. I've got no reason to think they didn't get along just fine."

Jane thought she detected a note of irony in Tom's voice. She decided she wasn't going to get any more from him, and she looked at her watch, thinking it was time for her to be checking in on Martha.

He smiled at her. "Why don't we go to the Prince Hotel for a drink? It's too late to get anything done this afternoon. We could unwind and talk some more about this, if you'd like."

"A good idea," Jane said.

They walked down the hall. Jane found herself walking quite a distance from Tom Henege. For some reason, she didn't want to be too near him.

It was five-thirty, but there were still lots of people working. From the executive offices Jane could hear voices, from the workstations in the central areas she could hear the rapid soft patter of computer terminal keys, and the muted sounds of printers. Telephones rang. There were big clocks on the wall, and Jane saw that it was only two-thirty in British Columbia and California. Lots of BTS customers might still want service, she thought. And lots of hackers were probably just settling down to work. People outside this business would never understand these people, she thought. They wouldn't know why they work eighteen hours straight to solve a problem. Or to help a customer. Why they go nights without sleep. And they wouldn't understand a Martha Gruen, a Martin Kaplan or a Tom Henege.

"Tom, I have to stop at Martha's office. Could you wait a minute?" Jane put her head in. Martha, Brian, Martin and Robert were all in the office, talking. "I'm sorry to interrupt," Jane said.

"That's okay, Jane," Martha said. "We're just reviewing some customer-maintenance contracts." There were lines of strain around her mouth, and she looked tired, but her make-up was impeccable and her voice calm.

"Did you have a chance to check with Sandy?"

"Sorry, Jane, no luck. I tried, but he left early today."

"Well then," Jane said, seeing that Martha was starting to look distressed again, "don't worry about it. I'll talk to him myself. Tom and I are going for a drink at the Prince. Do any of you want to come?"

Martha looked at Brian who said, "I don't know. We're just finishing up here. How long will you be there?"

"I'd guess about an hour," Jane said, turning to Tom who was standing just behind her in the doorway. He nodded.

"Well, we should be done before that, but then I have a few things to finish off in my office, and I imagine the others do too, since I interrupted them all for this meeting."

"We'll wait an hour for you," Jane said, "and if you're not there by then, we'll assume you're not coming, okay?"

The four of them agreed. Tom and Jane walked down the corridor together, Jane thinking again about the threatening message to her, about what it meant. In the reception area Tom went to the guest closet and found her coat. As he did so, Jane realized she had forgotten her handbag in Martha's office. She'd been carrying her briefcase, and she hadn't noticed she didn't have her bag. She started to apologize to Tom but he told her not to worry, he'd be glad to go back up to Martha's office and collect it for her. Jane let him go; she thought his absence might give her a chance to talk to the night watchman.

The reception area was very pleasant. Along one wall were large indoor trees, ficus, palm, and some she did not recognize. On the right-hand side was the reception desk, now empty, its computer terminal dark. On the other side was a small table for the night-time security guard. He was sitting there now, a large book open before him, watching a small black-and-white TV, which was showing a soundless game show.

Jane felt tired. She was tempted to sit down on one of the low chrome and plastic visitor's chairs grouped beside the trees, and enjoy a moment or two of silence. But the threatening implications of the message that had come up on Martha's terminal could not be ignored. Kersti had been right; there *was* a threat, and it was directed at her. It made her angry to think that someone at BTS thought so little of her, had so misjudged her, that they believed a threat would make any difference to her.

Jane walked over to the watchman and introduced herself.

"I guess you must have been here the night Mr Levin died," she said, smiling at him. He smiled back, straightened in his chair and smoothed his hand over his scalp. He was a man in his late sixties, overweight, and neatly dressed in a uniform of navy jacket, white shirt, navy tie.

"I was, and I remember it well, Miss Tregar. A night to remember, you could say."

"Yes," Jane said. "What I've been wondering is, everyone says no one was there late that night except Mr Levin. But how can they be that sure?"

"They can be sure because I told them, that's how. Everyone who comes in after five-thirty I sign in."

"But what about if someone came in earlier and stayed?"

"Look, Miss Tregar, we're no different from most companies in this business. We've got to control who goes in and out. Know what I mean? You'd be amazed at the number of computer terminals that can go missing, let alone the secrets we've got to protect. Can't have unauthorized people wandering around, under any circumstances. So here's what we do."

He turned around the big book that was facing him and

showed it to Jane. She had seen it before — it was the same sign-in book that was on the reception desk during office hours. It was divided into columns. The first column for the date, the second for the visitor's name, the third the visitor's firm, the fourth, the name of the host, the fifth the sign-in time, and the sixth, sign-out time.

"Nobody goes in or out without this being signed," the guard said.

"But I was about to leave without signing out," Jane said.

"You think so?" He smiled triumphantly at her, again smoothing the few remaining strands of grey hair over his scalp. "Look."

He turned the page in the book to show where she had signed in, and showed her that he had initialled her as signed out. "I recognized you when you came in with Mr Henege. I remembered you from when you were working with us before, five years ago, I guess it was. Never forget a face. Especially a pretty woman. So I signed you out. I just waved at Mr Henege and signed you both out. But then, when he went back in, I signed him in again, see? And I'll sign him out when he comes back. By the rules, that's the way I like to see it done."

"That's nice of you to remember me," Jane said. "About the night Mr Levin died?"

He turned back the book. "Look, even staff who work after six, even the most important people, they're signed out. That's the system. Here. Here's the night Mr Levin died, not a night to forget, believe me. Look, it's the same people who leave late almost every night, and here they are, all signed out around the same time." He showed her the page, and Jane read the names of Brian, Martha, Robert, Martin, Tom and Sandy, along with others she didn't recognize.

"And here, see, is Mr Levin's name. He went out around eight, and came back again at eight-forty. Probably went out for a bite to eat; he did that most nights when he was working late. And look, no one else came in until Mrs Gruen at six-thirty the next morning."

"Boy, that's early. I bet you were surprised to see her."

"Nope, she often comes in that early. She'll stop and chat a minute. Nice woman. Friendly. Says that's the only time she can work without being interrupted all the time. She has a couple hours before the rest of 'em come rolling in."

"So, is she always the first one in then?"

"Just about. Near enough. I'd say that if she comes in early, she's the earliest. I mean, there's plenty of times she'll stroll on in around eight and I'll joke with her, say, what's the matter, you oversleep this morning, and she'll say, well, nobody's perfect, or I had a breakfast meeting, or something like that. Sometimes I guess she comes in even later. I go off shift at eight-thirty when the receptionist comes on, so I wouldn't know. But like I said, if she's early, then she's the earliest."

"So it could have been anyone who found Mr Levin."

"The way I see it, it was just Mrs Gruen's bad luck that morning. She pulled the computer-room fire alarm, and that got me running, I can tell you. I took one look and called the cops. Then she called Mr Tsu, and that was damn smart too, because someone had to be here to protect those computers. So then we had the firemen and the uniforms all come running in here. And I had them all sign in too. They were nice about it. I find most folks are."

Jane took the book from the guard's hand and was studying it when Tom came up behind her and looked over her shoulder. It seemed incontrovertible that, on the night Gary Levin died, no one had come in between the departures of the members of the management group and the arrival of Martha. She said so, then added, "I just can't understand it."

"I know," said Tom, "and it's even worse than that. Here, put on your coat. Let's go get that drink, and I'll tell you all about it."

Jane put the book back on the guard's table, reached over and shook his hand. "Thanks for taking the time to answer my questions," she said.

"It was my pleasure, Miss Tregar. Anything you want, anything I can help with, just let me know."

"Nice fellow," said Jane, as they walked out into the cold.

"Yes," Tom said. "Reliable too. I think you can count on him. If he says there was no one here that night but Gary Levin, that's the truth. I believe it; there's no way around it. Gary Levin was alone, locked in the computer room, when he died."

Their table was beside a window, a black sheet of glass, which reflected Jane's fair hair and the gleam of her gold neck chain. She turned to her reflection and saw an unfamiliar blond woman, her dilated pupils glimmering ghostlike from a shiny black background. I'm distorted, thought Jane. She felt tired and discouraged.

She hoped Martha and at least some of the others would join them. She was confused, disoriented. Her back ached and she wanted to go home. But despite all this, she was thrumming with a kind of nervous excitement, caused by her talk with Sandy, Martha and Tom . . . and then there was the message.

She looked up at Tom now. "I can hardly stand it," she said. "I can't stop thinking about the murder, how it was done. Who did it, and how."

He frowned at her. "I don't think you should say things like that," he said, "at least not to one of us."

"What do you mean?"

A small smile, hardly a smile in fact, pulled tight the corners of his mouth. "It certainly looks like one of us did it, so that makes all of us pretty poor confidants."

"It's strange, but until today it just wasn't real to me," Jane admitted. "It's all very well to say someone programmed the murder. But how does a computer cause heart failure and cyanose someone's lungs? On the face of it, it seems impossible."

"I'm hungry," Tom said. "I wonder if we could get some sushi or something. Are you hungry?"

Jane found that she didn't want to share a meal with him. "No," she said. Then seeing the expression on his face, she said quickly, "You go ahead. I'll keep you company."

"I know what you mean about Gary's death," Tom said. "The only thing that makes sense is that someone programmed the computer to crash. Whoever did it knew that Gary would work late—he usually did—and that he wouldn't come to the meeting. One of us. This person also knew that when the computer crashed Gary would go into the computer room to boot it up."

"Is that what you think happened?"

"It's what the police think."

"Tell me," Jane said, giving him her best look.

"I probably shouldn't," he said, "but when you smile at me like that. . . ."

She smiled again, a wide caricature of a smile, and he laughed. "Irresistible. I will tell all."

She picked up her drink and pressed the cool glass against her lips, watching over its rim.

"The police have talked to all of us. And there're certain things you can figure out from their questions. From the evidence about when he ate his last meal, they figure he died sometime between 11 P.M. and 2 A.M. Then from what Sandy can figure out, the mini-computer went down at 12:55 A.M. When that happened, it's only logical to assume that Gary would go into the computer room to try to start it up. So he went into the room, and he died there. The night key was in his pocket. And his passcard that gave him night-time access."

"Do you think," Jane asked, "that perhaps the murderer knocked on the door and Gary let him in?"

"It's not possible, Jane. Gary had the key in his pocket when he was found. When the outer door is shut, you need the key to get out, not just in. Plus, the passcard system would have shown a record of someone going in or out. I've thought about it. Say, for example, someone was with Gary. The two of them go into the computer room. Together. The murderer kills Gary. And just suppose for a moment that the murderer has a copy of the key so he can get out through the outer door. He still has to open the inner door with his card to get out."

"But what if," Jane said, "when he was ready to leave he used Gary's passcard to open the inner door, propped the door open with a wedge or something, put the passcard back in Gary's pocket and let himself out?"

"Not bad," Tom said admiringly, "but it wouldn't work. There's a record of every entrance and exit to that room in the computer that controls the passcard system, which, by the way, belongs to an outside firm, so no one at BTS can fool with it. And that record shows Gary going in just after the computer crashed, and no one coming out again, on his card, or anybody else's card."

"So what do you conclude from all this?" Jane asked.

"That only one of the six of us, counting Sandy, could have done it because only we six could have left the nasty message. But that none of us did it, because we were all somewhere else, and because it seems absolutely undeniable that there was *nobody* in that room with Gary when he was killed. There must be an explanation, but for the life of me, I can't think what it could be."

Jane sighed, and swallowed down her drink. She was surprised to realize it was her second. "If it weren't for the threat I got this afternoon," she said, "I'd be tempted to say it's all some kind of giant mistake." She picked up her swizzle stick and bent it into an arc.

"What do you mean? What threat?"

"Oh, just a vague one," Jane said. "Forget about it." She snapped the head off the swizzle stick and put both pieces on the paper mat under her drink. Why aren't I more frightened? she thought. Is it because I still don't really believe it? How could anybody regard *me* as a threat? The idea had no reality for her.

"That doesn't seem like a very smart attitude to take," Tom said.

"You're probably right."

For a moment they were both silent, looking out of the window. It was dark now, but outside lights illuminated the Japanese garden. Rocks, raked gravel, and beyond, a fringe of trees, their bare branches glimmering wet in the light. It looked cold and forbidding.

Inside, too, the widely spaced tables, the muted sounds of conversation, the waiters stepping silently on the thick carpet. . . the whole room felt deadened to Jane, muffled in a calm ritual from which danger and threats seemed very far away.

"Let me take you out to dinner, somewhere away from here," Tom said suddenly, seeing the look she cast around her. "Then I'll follow you and see you safely home."

Jane saw the warmth in his smile, but she didn't smile

back. "Thanks, but no, I'm just too tired," she said. "I've got so much to do, to find someone for BTS, and this murder. . . . I guess it's just really starting to sink in. I just want to go home, soak in a hot bath and see if any great ideas burst through from my subconscious."

"Sure I can't convince you to change your mind?" Tom said, signalling for the bill.

Jane looked at her watch; they had been there for over an hour. Obviously Martha and the others weren't coming. "Thanks anyway," Jane said. She stood up, and as he did, their hands accidentally touched. Jane jerked hers back; his touch startled her. What's the matter with me? she thought sadly. Is this murder going to make me afraid of everybody? She looked up at him quickly, trying to decide if there were something in Tom that explained her reaction, or if it was just a general suspicion. He caught her glance for a moment, then they both looked away.

Jane walked quickly toward the hotel lobby. She found, suddenly, that she was in a great hurry to get away.

15

The Parkway wasn't very busy, and Jane's little Triumph spun around the ramp and into the middle of the lane, seeming almost to drive itself.

The streetlights' yellow glow was overwhelmed by the lights of the oncoming cars, which stabbed into Jane's eyes, causing her vision to blur. She concentrated on the taillights of the car in front of her. The lovely arc of a bridge passed over her, as the roadway swept and bent between the hills of the Don Valley. She turned off into Rosedale automatically. Driving along the curved streets flanked by tall, bare trees, the branches bending over the road, the night seemed unusually dark. Why am I so tired? she wondered. There were no other cars in the driveway behind the house. The other tenants must be out, she thought. That's not unusual.

Jane lived in the top storey of an old mansion, which had been converted into three flats. Hers had a very large room with a fireplace, which was her living-dining room, a small kitchen, renovated in the forties, two big bedrooms, one that was Jane's with a bow window shaded by a large chestnut tree. The other she had fixed up for her children, if they came to stay with her.

There was a wide entry hall to all three apartments at the front of the house, with a tiled floor, mailboxes for the tenants, and three doors. Jane stood before her own, fumbling for her key in her handbag. She couldn't find it. She fished out her car keys, dropped them into her coat pocket, and searched for the house keys, which she kept on a ring with her office keys. No success. Jane wasn't surprised. She knew there was a hole in the lining of her bag, and from time to time small objects like keys or change would work themselves through, and she'd be unable to find them. Anyway, Jane was tired, and it wasn't worth poking her fingers into the lining and risking tearing it further.

She opened her mailbox and took out the spare key she kept taped on the top of it, leaving the mail inside; she was too tired to sort through it anyhow. Tomorrow would be soon enough.

The night was windy, and when Jane walked into her darkened bedroom and threw her coat onto the chair, she could hear the boughs of the nearby chestnut tree soughing and knocking against the window panes. It was a familiar sound, one she found comforting.

She came out into the living-room and turned on the lamps. The room was very quiet, and the black rectangle of the doorway to the second bedroom was suddenly disturbing to her. She walked over to it, switched on the light and looked in.

She had fixed up the second, larger bedroom for her sons, when she'd still believed that Bernie would stick to their settlement agreement and she would have the boys for their summer holidays. There were bunk-beds, with a ladder, which she had thought the boys would like to climb, and bedspreads with red-nosed clowns. Looking at them, she realized that the boys had probably outgrown clown bedspreads, and she wondered if she should replace them. There were two desks, shelves with a single box of Lego — bought before she heard descriptions of the boys' giant collection — blocks and a teddy bear. All new, scarcely touched. The teddy bear had fallen over, and lay on his back with his short, fluffy legs sticking up in the air as if he were dead. I should keep the door to this room shut, Jane thought, even if it gets stuffy. It would be better not to look in here.

She turned off the light, and went into the kitchen, telling herself that she had to eat something. She reached for the refrigerator door.

A sharp pain, a galvanic shock, raced up her arm, which jerked suddenly. She was knocked backward as if by a blow. She cried out, and she saw, in a vivid after-image, a piece of computer paper, hanging, taped to the refrigerator door.

Jane stood for a minute, waiting for her heart to stop pounding. The pain receded, though her arm felt numb, hanging strangely limp at her side. With her left hand she fished in the drawer where she kept tools until she found pliers with thick, rubber-coated handles. With these she reached carefully back behind the refrigerator, careful not to touch it, and unplugged it. Then she went to the broom closet and, again using her left hand, found a flashlight. She checked over the refrigerator carefully, looking for leads, wiring. She found what she was looking for. A wire was wrapped around the prongs of the electrical plug. The ground prong was broken off. The wire was screwed into a bolt at the back of the refrigerator and ran around the front and wrapped around the door handle. The whole refrigerator had been live.

Jane sat down on the hard bentwood chair at the breakfast table and put her head down. She waited for her body to grow calm so she could think. She could have been killed. Why hadn't she? Electric shocks were chancy. She had been jolted severely by the charge, but she had just touched the refrigerator, not grasped the handle. Perhaps that was why she had survived. Even in her muzzy state she thought it was a strange trap. Not expert. Completely unreliable. As if whoever set it didn't care if she were killed or just badly frightened.

She knew that with the refrigerator unplugged it was safe, but it took an effort to pull the piece of paper — a computer printout — off the door. Gently she peeled away the tape and sat down at the table to look at it.

In dot-matrix printing was the message: "No merger, or no Jane."

"What I want to know is, why invite your best friend over when you never have anything to eat here?" Without waiting for an answer, Kersti began unpacking a basket she had set down on the kitchen table. There was a bottle of brandy and one of wine, a French loaf, a big chunk of cheese, a jar of pickles and a plastic container. Kersti dumped the contents of the container into a pot and turned on the gas. "I knew you wouldn't have, so don't apologize. I brought you some nutritious vegetable soup. Lots of good winter vegetables like turnips. Estonian chicken soup."

"I'm sorry," Jane said weakly.

"Oh, Jane, don't apologize. Just be quiet." Kersti poured some brandy into a thick little glass she found in the cupboard. "I recognize this," Kersti said. "It's what those loathsome, frozen-shrimp cocktails come in. Bad enough you buy them. Disgusting to save the glasses."

Kersti cut a piece of cheese, a piece of bread and put a pickle on top. "Eat this."

"I'm not hungry, really I'm not, Kersti."

"You can't have the brandy unless you eat your bread and cheese. Now be a good girl. And you can't have this beautiful Beaujolais Nouveau I've brought you either, if you don't eat your soup. And I mean it."

"I give up," Jane said. The bread and cheese tasted dry in her mouth. She seemed to have no saliva and it was difficult to chew. She was suddenly very thirsty. Too tired to get up or ask Kersti for water, she drank the brandy. The next bite of food tasted better. Jane finished the brandy. The soup was boiling now and smelled good. Kersti was watching her. Jane finished her bread and cheese. Her tongue felt thick and rough, but sensation was coming back into her right arm. She flexed her fingers.

Kersti sat down at the table opposite Jane. She watched as Jane slowly ate the hot soup with her left hand and sipped at the wine. When she finished, Kersti refilled her bowl. "Your colour is coming back," Kersti said. "You look better. When did you last eat?"

Jane couldn't remember.

"Aren't you ever hungry?" Kersti asked.

"Yes, sometimes. Sometimes I get very hungry. But not since the BTS stuff started. I seem to just want to drink."

Kersti laughed. "That's my Jane. And you are my friend. You come first, before any story, if that's what you're worrying about."

Jane nodded. "A little. I was worried about that. These secrets aren't mine. And the laws about public companies —"

"You're gibbering, Jane. We're not talking about public companies. We're talking about someone trying to kill you."

"I don't think so, Kersti. You don't kill someone and leave a note for the victim to read after they're dead. It must have been a warning." But as she spoke she thought of the death of Gary Levin. Perhaps her warning was intended for whoever found her — dead. Because the live fridge could have killed her. Stupid. Just stupid, that's what it was. She shivered.

Kersti was watching her closely. "Think out loud, Jane. Say it."

"I think it was a screw-up," she said. Her mouth didn't feel so dry. She wasn't as cold as she had been, and the intermittent twanging in her arm had stopped. Kersti's coming, the hot soup, just her friend's familiar face, the sound of her voice, was making things better. "Whoever did it couldn't have known if it would kill me or not. Maybe they didn't care. And we now know something about this murderer."

"Oh yeah? And what's that?"

"Very good with computers. But weak in electricity."

They both started to laugh. Jane couldn't stop. She laughed until the tears came to her eyes. "This person has a tiny little mind, Kersti. I can't believe it. The whole thing was incredibly amateur."

"How did they get in?" Kersti said.

"I should have realized . . ." Jane began.

"Realized what?"

"When I got home I couldn't find my key. It was missing from my bag."

"How did you get in?"

"Spare key. I keep one in my mailbox. And God, my bag was left in Martha's office for a while late this afternoon. Martha went out to talk to someone, and so did I. So, it's the same suspects, I guess. Except, I was talking to Tom Henege at the time, so he couldn't have taken it — although my bag was between us, at the bar tonight. I suppose it's just possible he could have taken it then, without my noticing.

"Same suspects?"

Jane told Kersti that the six top management people at BTS were the only ones, it seemed, who could have murdered Gary Levin.

"Great, terrific," Kersti said. "So I see why you've lost your appetite the past few days."

"And the funny thing," Jane said, "is that I trust them all. I like them all. I don't believe that any of them could have done it. There has to be another explanation."

"People always say that," Kersti said. "When friends, or people they know turn out to be crooks, or cheats, or unfaithful, or go on a shotgun-killing spree, or commit suicide, or whatever. They say they don't believe it."

"Yes, but it works the other way too," Jane said. "Often in my business I hear terrible things about people. Someone will tell me that their boss is a paranoid schizophrenic, or that their ex-employee was sleeping with everyone in the place. And it turns out not to be true. I think people exaggerate to make their lives seem more exciting."

"We work in different worlds, that's what it is," Kersti said.

"Maybe. But you are looking for stories. You journalists dramatize. You can't help it. You distort things."

"Jane, these things are real. Lies and crime and violence, they're real."

"In your world. In mine they're just. . . . Well, crime is usually a standard business practice carried to extreme, lies are just tact not well done, and violence doesn't happen."

Kersti laughed, and patted Jane. "Who are you kidding?"

"Well, it *is* like that — often it is." Jane heard a sad, pleading note in her voice. If the working world was as Kersti said it was, and that was where one lived, things seemed very bleak.

"Everyone lies — that's one thing you should realize," Kersti said. "And the sooner the better."

"You just say that because you sleep with married men."

"Smart cracks don't change the situation, and you can't make it go away by not wanting to believe it."

"God you're cynical, Kersti. I don't think you really like anyone."

"I like you, Jane."

"Well *I* don't lie."

"Yes you do, Jane. All the time. You just don't realize it yet. But don't worry. I love you just the same."

Kersti poured out the last of the soup. "Now finish your supper, all of it. And let's decide how we're going to keep you from getting killed before you find out."

"Find out what?"

"Find out who killed Gary Levin. You're going to have to now, Jane. Surely you see that. Unless you want to call in the police."

"I can't call the police, I can't do that to Brian. The repercussions at BTS would be too serious. He needs time."

"That's typical of you Jane. But what's the alternative?"

Jane sighed. "Have it your own way, Kersti."

"No, it's not my way we're talking about. I'm going to sit here until you figure out *your* way."

They smiled at one another.

16

THE TORONTO DAILY NEWS

Report on Business   *December 11, 1985*

BTS **Stock Plummets As Investigation Continues**

*There were wide fluctuations in the price of shares in Brian
Taylor Systems Inc. on the Toronto Stock Exchange yesterday.
The stock, which traded at a high of $14.75 last month closed
at $10.20, down from $12.26 at the start of the day's trading.
At one time in the early afternoon it was as low as $8.50, al-
though it rallied at mid-afternoon and was on an upswing when
the market closed.*

Industry insiders believe that the increase in activity in BTS
*in recent days is due to the mysterious death of Gary Levin, the
chief financial officer, although the market also seems to be
reacting to the much-discussed joint-marketing agreement
with an unidentified U.S. firm.*

*The situation was made murkier today when, in answer to a
question posed in the House of Commons by Jared Fullerton,
opposition member from the Ontario riding of Rainy River, the*

Minister of Industry and Small Business denied that the price was being driven down by the U.S. firm in order to facilitate a takeover.

Outside the House Mr Fullerton said: "Firms like BTS have benefitted from hundreds and thousands of dollars of tax-payers' money through tax writeoffs such as the Science Research Tax Credits and other grants. What we want to know is whether this government is prepared to let BTS be taken over by a U.S. firm."

Brian Taylor, chief executive officer and major shareholder of BTS said this morning, "I own the controlling interest in BTS and there is no chance whatsoever of a takeover. I don't understand where rumours like this come from."

Reached in Vancouver, Leon Blumberg, the largest outside investor, said he is confident there is no possibility of a takeover. "Mr Taylor works closely with us, and together we hold a substantial majority of the stock. Even if outside investors were to gain control of all the remaining shares, a takeover would be impossible." Mr Blumberg, who rarely talks to the press, agreed to comment in this case in order "to set the record straight" and because, he stated, the idea of a hostile takeover is "simply preposterous."

The last thing in the world Jane felt like doing was attending the Orloff Associates Christmas party. This year it was at the Sutton Place Hotel, and the firm's most important clients would be there. Eddie Orloff had invited the management team of BTS. There would be champagne and very expensive, rich food. Some of the clients would drink too much, and the room would be crowded and full of cigarette smoke. Jane remembered when she had liked parties, had thought them fun. It seemed a long time ago. In any case, the events of the previous day had not left her in a party mood. She had not reported the attempt on her life to the police, or to Orloff. She couldn't see how either of the two could help her, and she could think of many ways their interest in the matter would harm things. She felt time closing in on her. If only she could figure out who murdered Gary Levin, she was certain she would be able to extricate herself from what was rapidly becoming an impossible situation.

The attempt on her life hadn't changed anything. It hadn't made Jane any less determined to fulfill her obligations to Brian; it hadn't made her less determined to find out who killed Gary Levin. It only reinforced her conviction that the two were connected.

But that didn't mean she could ignore what had happened to her, or the obvious conclusion that her activities were seen as a threat by someone. She would have to act.

In the dress-up section of her closet was a long, dark-blue velvet dress without much back. Too sexy for clients, Jane thought. There was a short white wool dress with a very tight skirt. Unless she were at her thinnest, it tended to cup her bottom and she was always tugging at it. With a sigh she pulled it on and checked her back view. After all, she hadn't eaten much in the past week. She craned her neck to see her reflection in the full-length mirror. Yes, the dress clung suggestively. The side view was even worse than the back. Obviously she had drunk the calories she hadn't eaten. She pulled the dress off over her head with difficulty, and looked through the closet again. I should have thought of this, she scolded herself. Nothing to wear. As usual. The party is important to Orloff. She slid the hangers along the rod, looking for something she might have forgotten. Would the kids really want to spend Christmas with her? What would she do to entertain them? she wondered. She remembered how suffocatingly boring she had found Christmas when the kids were little, with Bernie's family who flew in from Switzerland for the occasion.

The endless eating, the children too young to care about their gifts, the tension and pressure caused by her need to live up to Bernie's expectations and those of his family. She was ashamed of herself. How could she not want her children at Christmas? It was unnatural.

Of course, her own family had never celebrated Christmas. Her mother was Jewish, her father an atheist who saw religious holidays as quaint, anachronistic rites. The family had gone south for Christmas before her father was blacklisted, after which they could no longer afford to travel. In subsequent years they spent the day together, in their apartment on the south side of Chicago, where it had been no different than any other day. Her father's rational view of such holidays had made sense to Jane once she was older and past the stage where the presents were everything. She had liked Passover, with her mother's family in Montreal. That had been interesting. Tedious, but interesting. It was the only holiday she missed celebrating.

Maybe she hated Christmas because Christmas meant family, and Bernie had taken that away. Better not to think about it. Hardly conducive to a party mood.

She found a dark-red, silk chiffon dress. It was several seasons old and no longer chic. It had a loose-draped top, and a mid-calf skirt, fitted around the hips, then wider and swirly. Jane thought it could possibly pass as a Christmas party dress. She remembered an Indian silk scarf shot with gold. It could make a sash; the dress would look less dated. And lots of jewellery. Jane liked interesting jewellery, the kind you find in flea markets. Eddie Orloff had teased her about it once, telling her he liked his women staff to "look successful." He meant rich, and that meant expensive-looking jewellery. She found a brooch that had belonged to her father's mother. It was in the shape of a butterfly with a big ruby in the centre. Rather out of fashion, she thought.

She didn't want to wear it, but it *was* expensive and would have to do. She pinned it on her shoulder.

She was late. Still, before she put on her coat she had a drink. She couldn't imagine facing the party without one. Unable to sit down, she walked around the apartment, sipping her Scotch, and shaking the glass so that the ice cubes banged up against its sides.

She told herself again that she wasn't going to sit still and be a victim of someone's plots. There were things that needed doing, and the Christmas party might give her an opportunity to put the management people at BTS off the track, while she worked it out. She couldn't risk sitting and waiting for things to happen. I can't let that failed electrocution scare me off, she told herself. I need a plan of action; I just have to focus on that.

The first move, she decided, was to give everyone at BTS the idea that she would not help the merger happen, that she would not, or could not, find a vice-president of finance who would bring it to fruition. That would buy her time. That would make whoever was threatening her think that they had scared her successfully.

The party would be helpful in another way, she thought. Whoever had tried to electrocute her would get a shock of their own when they saw her there. Perhaps she would be able to recognize that reaction when she saw it. She cheered up for a minute at the thought, then her mood darkened again. What do I think — that they'll drop their drink and cry out, "What are *you* doing here?" No, I'm not likely to know by their reaction, she told herself, realizing even as she thought this that she believed otherwise, that she believed that whoever had tried to murder her would not be able to smile at her, look her in the eyes, greet her as if nothing had happened.

The Scotch had taken effect. Jane put her shoes into a

bag, and stuck her feet into a pair of fleece-lined boots. Another Scotch seemed required before she could lock the door. She'd had the lock changed, and she put the new key carefully into the zippered inside pocket of her small evening bag, which she wore on a chain over her shoulder, turned so that the fastening was against her hip. Maybe it was the thought of the changed lock, the precautions she and Kersti had worked out, that had made the second drink seem like a good idea.

The noise was very loud, the smoke thick when Jane walked into Salon C at the Sutton Place. A long buffet on one side of the room was spread with expensive delicacies: caviar and smoked salmon, and piles of hors-d'oeuvres, plump little pockets of richness — stuffed mushrooms, artichoke hearts with cheese, chevrès tarts, sea scallops and avocado, and small, pink shrimp, speckled with fresh dill. There was so much food that Jane found it unappetizing. In the centre was a gigantic ice sculpture of a swan, glistening and melting in the light of the enormous crystal chandeliers. Near the door, Eddie Orloff was talking to Robert McDonnell. There was a very elegant woman with them, slender and straight backed, gleaming in white silk and gold chains. In her high heels she must have been five-foot-ten. When they saw Jane they all smiled. The light was artificially dimmed; their faces were blurred and their teeth glinted. Jane forced herself to walk over. Nobody started or dropped their drinks, she noticed.

"Jane!" said Robert. She could see at once that he was rather drunk. "Let me get you a drink. How beautiful you look. Merry Christmas."

"Merry Christmas," said Jane, smiling at him. Warmed by his enthusiastic greeting, she told herself that one thing she could be sure of was that the quiet, withdrawn comptroller couldn't have been the one who'd sneaked into her apartment and set that trap. The idea was absurd. Look how happy he was to see her. "Scotch on the rocks, please."

"You've forgotten, Ms Tregar," Orloff said, shaking his finger at her. "Orloff Associates celebrates the winter solstice with champagne and caviar. Like my Russian ancestors did at the winter palace." He turned to the tall woman. "Jane, meet Celia Hayd-Jones. I've invited her along so she can get a feel for how Orloff Associates operates. Celia is with Smith and Baron, the investment bankers. She specializes in high-tech firms."

Is she my replacement? thought Jane with a pang. Why has Orloff brought her here?

Robert was coming back with the champagne; he handed it to her and stood very close, looking down on her. "What a beautiful butterfly," he said. "They do not spin, neither do they — How does it go?"

Jane could smell the fruity scent of champagne on his breath. How much champagne do you have to drink to get drunk? she wondered. He must have been working at it.

"It suits you. A butterfly, small, delicate. . . ."

Jane told herself not to get annoyed. She had more serious things to focus on than her sensitivity about her height. Robert was very tall, and his glasses masked his eyes. She took the champagne from him and drank it rapidly. Robert took off his glasses and put them in his pocket. His eyes glittered. Where is the mild-mannered accountant? Jane wondered.

"I have to talk to you, Jane," he said. "Come on over here." He took her by the arm and drew her off into a corner.

Eddie Orloff smiled. "Enjoy yourself," he called after her, his tone facetious.

"Listen, beautiful," Robert said, "this is business. I know you're a smart business lady — everybody says so."

"Thank you," Jane said, thinking that now was the time to find out something, since the usually taciturn comptroller seemed to have been made loquacious with drink.

"There's something you've got to understand about this U.S. deal," Robert said.

"Oh yes? What's that?"

"We've got to control it, do you understand? Now listen Jane. You know really there's no such thing as a merger. Do you understand? What's going on here, what we've got to have, *got to have*," he repeated, stabbing her collarbone with an outstretched finger to accentuate his point, "is a takeover. A reverse takeover. We've got the cash, enough cash; they're cash short, so we can do it."

"Can *you* do it?" Jane asked coolly, not letting him see how much his comments had surprised her. A takeover. That would explain things that had been puzzling her. "Why don't *you* do it? Why do you need a new Gary Levin?"

"*I* can do it — I *can* work it out I mean. But how to convince the Americans it's a good deal . . . when the last bit of negotiating starts to get mean and dirty. For that you need a fast talker. And I know I'm no talker." He straightened a little, tucking in his chin, which was really part of his neck, Jane noticed from her vantage point. "I'm the eminence grise."

"You make the merger sound like a flim-flam game," Jane said softly.

"Flim-flam game," Robert said. He laughed loudly. "You're talking about BTS. That's not our style. It's by the book for any firm Robert McDonnell is asso . . . associated with. I've got my business principles to think of, you know."

"And this move is in Robert's book." It was Martin Kaplan who had come up behind them. He was carrying two glasses of champagne.

"I know Robert and Christmas parties," he said to Jane, "and I saw he had you in a corner, and you with an empty glass. Here."

He took her empty glass and handed her one of the full ones. "Robert telling you how he can handle the American deal without any help?"

"Not exactly," said Jane.

"Well, why not tell her you want to fly solo," Martin said. "Got to get your ducks lined up, don't you?"

"What's that supposed to mean?" Robert said, turning to look at Martin.

Martin smiled and wiped his forehead, which had begun to sweat, with a large white handkerchief. But to Jane he didn't look at all happy. "You know what it's supposed to mean."

Jane was beginning to think being late had been a bad idea. She seemed to have arrived in the middle of the party. Already she had missed her chance to see how Martin reacted to her arrival.

"So, Robert," she said. "I'm sure you could manage things, especially if the merger is postponed. Which I'm going to recommend."

"You are?" Kaplan said, looking back and forth between them, smiling. His smile, however, was fixed and without humour, a mere stretching of the lips.

"No, don't recommend that," said Robert. "I can manage everything. Yes, I know," he said as if to silence an invisible opponent. "Brian doesn't think I can handle it. But it's. . . . Oh, Martin, go away, why don't you? Can't you see I want to talk to this beautiful lady all by myself?"

Martin winked at Jane and walked away. Robert pulled

himself up very straight. Jane noticed that his jacket was unbuttoned and that his tie was hanging crookedly. She was always getting a chest-high view of people, she thought in annoyance, instead of seeing their faces. She tilted up her head to look at him. "Such beautiful eyes, so big, so blue," he said. "I guess everybody must say that to you. But really I've never seen anything like it. Never."

"Thank you," Jane said, smiling. She often thought it strange that some men thought she was beautiful, and others seemed not to notice her. Did she have beauty that came and went, or was her appearance only appealing to some? And what did it matter anyway? Although it was nice to be admired. . . . "I could do the merger, Jane, believe me," Robert said earnestly. "But Brian doesn't think so. And why doesn't he?"

"Yes, why?"

"Yes, why? That's what I ask myself. I ask myself, why doesn't he?"

"And what do you tell yourself?" Jane said patiently.

"That's what I want to ask *you*, Jane. You're a woman. You're an old friend of Brian's. What does he say to you? What does he say about me? Why does he need another Gary when he has me there?"

"What about the fast talking you said you couldn't do?"

"Oh that! I can let the numbers speak. They do, you know. The business case. I can make the business case and we will come out on top. You'll see."

"Then tell Brian what you think. Just face him and tell him what you think up front."

"But I *have* told him. Many and many a time. Well, not in so many words you understand, not in so many words. But I got the message across. He could know if he wanted to know. I had to be respectful of Gary. Brian thought the world of him. Could I come out and say, 'You're better shut of that big mouth,' could I now? Too smart by half, that was Gary Levin. Sell Brian out for a mess of pottage, then see who has the last laugh!"

"So you didn't trust him?"

"Trust him! Trust Gary Levin? That's a laugh! That's a bloody great big laugh. Trust Gary Levin? Ha, bloody ha." Robert mimed a laugh, his blue eyes blurring with moisture. "I have to go see a dog about a man. Be right back."

Jane wandered over to the buffet. She spoke to several old friends. A man she hadn't seen for several years gave her a sweet smile. Four years before, for a brief time, he had been her lover. He was a nice man, but Jane had found little pleasure in the affair. It was one she had begun before she realized that such things weren't working for her anymore.

He was married now, and she asked him about his wife. He answered in that embarrassed way that Jane read to mean he had grown restless. She saw that though he was past the age where he believed that sleeping with many different women, hunting for them through the world of semi-attached, unattached and sexual predators, would give him any real pleasure, he was finding marriage equally unsatisfactory, in a different way. "How about a drink sometime?" he asked Jane, taking her hand and leaning over her. She felt oppressed by his closeness.

She let her hand lie limply in his. His touch did not warm her. "That would be nice," she said, smiling. "You can tell me how happy you are — I'm so pleased for you."

He gave her a resentful look and turned away. Jane did not like to encourage men and then find herself obliged to hurt them. Early warning seemed better. Unfortunately, she thought, it was not a technique she was going to be able to use in her meddling into the business affairs of BTS.

Jane caught sight of Martha standing at the far end of the buffet, eating hors-d'oeuvres and talking to Brian. They were laughing, and looked cool, relaxed and elegant. Martha was wearing a long, black satin dress with a long tunic top embroidered with gold and turquoise and scarlet threads, over a long, narrow black skirt, slit at the side, and very high heels. Holding her champagne glass, she looked like an ad in a glossy magazine. She said something to Brian, who smiled and patted her awkwardly on the shoulder. His pale hair shone in the light, as if it had been waxed and polished. They both turned and caught sight of Jane, and they smiled and waved at her, as if they had been waiting for her, looking forward to her arrival. She threaded her way through the press of people, smelling of perfume or aftershave, until she came up to them.

"Merry Christmas, Jane," Brian said, leaning over and kissing the air beside her cheek.

"Merry Christmas, Brian. Merry Christmas, Martha. You're looking wonderful tonight. What a marvellous dress."

"Thank you. I got it in Japan," Martha said. "The fabric is very old — it's Chinese or something."

"Lucky you. Japan," Jane said. "I would love to go there."

Martha seemed very glad to see Jane. She leaned over and hugged her. "You're looking marvellous yourself, Jane, like a wonderful little Christmas present, all wrapped up in red and gold." No way it could have been either of these two, Jane thought. How could their natural friendliness be faked? And it was good to see that Martha hadn't taken a dislike to her because Jane had seen her cry. That happened sometimes. There were women who couldn't bear to show a sign of weakness. Jane felt good for the first time since her arrival at the party. She even decided to forgive the "little" in Martha's compliment. Her third glass of champagne, she thought, might have contributed to her more positive attitude.

Jane asked Martha about Japan, and Martha described the shopping. "Every designer is there, everyone you can name, Gucci and Dior, Tissot and Guerlain, Corréges and Hermes. It's heaven if you like to shop. You know what they say — when the going gets tough, the tough go shopping."

"But as a woman, could you work there?"

Martha laughed. She too, Jane realized, had had a lot to drink. "What can't be cured must be endured, Jane, haven't you heard? I've given up trying to change things. You don't get anywhere doing that. And it never works anyway. I learned that working for Brian." She smiled mockingly at Brian. "People are how they are. You must know that as well as anybody. You have to take them how you find them and make the best of it. So that's what I did in Japan. Brian worked. I went shopping. Brian and Tom saw the geishas and wooed the clients. I got a junket."

"We didn't plan it that way — you know that, Martha," Brian said, looking offended.

"So how's it coming?" Martha asked Jane. "Found anybody good for Gary's job?"

"I've made some progress. Brian," Jane said turning to him, "I'll have to talk to you. I've decided we need to make some changes in the job description."

"What do you mean?" Brian said, frowning.

Brian was completely sober, Jane saw. Perhaps that one time long ago was a lesson to him. She thought it would be a rare occasion when Brian had anything less than perfect control of himself.

"Let's meet on Monday and I'll explain. I'll send you a revised job description tomorrow so that you can look it over before we meet."

"I'm willing to discuss anything you want to suggest, of course," Brian said to Jane, "but at the moment I can't see any reason to change things. I know what I want done, and the kind of person I want to do it."

"I'd like to be at that meeting, Brian," said Martha. "Jane, don't forget, hiring is my job."

"Not at this level," Brian said.

"Just a minute," Martha said. "I accept that you have prerogatives, that you're the boss, that your word is law at BTS. I don't deny that, okay? But I'm the vice-president of human resources, and you shouldn't forget that either. Or why give me the job? If you don't want me in charge of the division, say so. Until you do —"

"Oh, calm down, Martha. Have some more champagne."

Martha looked at him for a minute. Then she managed to smile. But the look she gave Jane said, see, I have to fight, always, to fulfill my responsibilities. Doesn't it make you mad?

"I'm not trying to tell you how to do your job, Jane," Brian said. "But talking about changing the job description after we've gone over it with everybody and the management group have all signed off on it seems a strange thing to do."

"It's not the job so much," Jane said. "I guess I didn't make myself clear. It's the new person's responsibility in the *merger* that needs to be discussed."

"Wait a minute there . . ." Brian began.

At the same time Martha spoke. "I've said before, I think the merger should be put on ice until —"

"Not at a party, Martha," Brian said sharply.

"Yeah. Nobody's interested in business tonight," Martha said. "Look around."

It was true, Jane thought. The people certainly did give the impression that they were enjoying themselves. The room had grown hotter, smokier, the voices louder. As she looked at the faces they seemed to grow feral, the smiles predatory, the laughter raucous. The men gestured broadly and patted the women, the women stroked the rims of their champagne glasses seductively and looked sideways past their companions for more enticing company. Jane heard a man standing beyond Brian say to the woman near him, "So then I said to her, 'You forgot when you were in love with me you signed it all away, so now there's nothing to take. Do you think he's going to want you when he hears you don't even have the farm in King Township?'" And the woman laughed and said, "I knew it was a toss-up whether he wanted her for the horses or the capital gains."

Jane felt like covering her ears. Had it always been that everything came down to money, to business, that love ended up as business, and business was as confused as love? She drained her champagne glass and told herself to concentrate. *She* was working tonight, and she couldn't afford to think about anything else.

She leaned toward Brian and Martha and spoke softly. "One of the things we need to talk about is the merger itself. Don't forget you told me it was a joint-marketing scheme at those early meetings. Now I know otherwise. That makes a difference to my job, to the kind of person I find for you. Surely you can see that."

"I said we'll talk about it another time, at a more appropriate time," Brian said. His face was expressionless, but Jane could tell he was angry.

Martha, on the other hand, seemed interested only in protecting her own turf, not in whether the merger would go ahead. "I must insist on being included at that meeting," she was saying, as Jane walked away, not wanting to hear them argue.

I'll just find Tom Henege, talk to him, get that over with,

she thought, then I'll go home. She knew Orloff would notice that she had left while the party was still in full swing, and would be annoyed. I don't care, she told herself, but then she thought, who do you think you're kidding? She put Orloff out of her mind and headed back into the crowd of guests to find Tom.

17

Jane found Tom talking to a group of people, partly separated from the rest of the room by a tall, flowering tree in a big Ming pot. She stood watching him for a moment, wondering again why such an attractive man had no power over her. Once he would have excited her, she was sure of it. He was her type — medium height, a compact body, a quick, perceptive mind. His quiet manner was deceptive, she knew. Underneath he was wilful, with a desire to dominate she found challenging. Of course it was cleverly hidden. She thought that perhaps the reason Tom was such a successful salesman was that his quiet, gentle manner, appealing as it was, inspiring trust as it did, was like that of a master judo player. He gave way, gave way, as you pushed, then suddenly he stepped back and you fell exactly where he wanted you to fall. But she was certain she wasn't interested in him. After all, she thought, that feeling of shivery excitement that's always started my romances — I don't feel that.

Of course it wasn't anything to do with Tom that such feelings seemed to have been extinguished, that no one seemed to be able to re-ignite them. The men she met, who once would have attracted her, she either didn't want them to touch her at all, or their touch was as meaningless as the touch of an inanimate object. Could a person's libido vanish at thirty-four? Jane was sure it couldn't. Especially hers. She had once been obsessed with sex, constantly hungry for it. What had happened?

Tom Henege turned toward her, and his eyes widened. Jane tensed, wondering if this was the reaction she had both feared and hoped to discover, the reaction of surprise and guilt. But then she saw, unexpected as it was, that it wasn't surprise or guilt she read in Tom's expression. It was pleasure. He finished what he was saying to the others and turned to her. His smile was full of friendliness.

Why don't I trust him? she thought. At least as much as I trust the others. What has he ever done to make me freeze when he looks at me?

He came toward her and began to talk to her.

"He's some character, your Eddie Orloff," Tom said. "I think he's playing at being a Russian grand duke."

"Something like that," Jane said, smiling.

"It's those big sweeping gestures, that noblesse oblige, and all the time he's watching you and figuring out your worth to Orloff Associates."

"You're too perceptive for your own good," Jane said. "Orloff wouldn't like that description of himself."

"The way he does it with so much panache. It's entertainment. You can't hold it against him. He lets you see the con, and at the same time he lets you into the conspiracy with him."

Jane laughed.

"And all that energy. Maybe that's part of what makes him so seductive to his clients. Sometimes I think that's what sets apart the ones who get to the top, more than anything else. An extra measure of energy, and courage, too."

"I'm not so sure," Jane said, "but it's true I haven't met very many lazy people at the top."

They both turned to look at Orloff. He was walking quickly from the bar, holding two glasses of champagne, smiling, and greeting people as he walked. He moved with grace, perfectly finished from his shiny patent-leather shoes to his casually tied bow tie, just askew enough to look comfortable.

"The thing that really amazes me," Tom said, "is how you can go so far not knowing anything real. I mean, he doesn't know how to *do* anything."

"That's not fair," Jane said. "Watch how he concentrates as he talks to that man. When he focusses on someone — a client — they can't resist him."

"Do *you* find him irresistible?" Tom said, looking at her.

Orloff was talking to a tall man in an elegantly tailored dinner jacket. The man was making a point, shaking his finger at Orloff to accentuate it. A great white smile split Orloff's face, he leaned over and whispered something in the man's ear, and then burst out laughing. The man hesitated for a moment, then began laughing too. Orloff threw his arm around his companion's shoulder, whispered something else to him, and then walked away, leaving the other smiling broadly and looking pleased with himself.

"No, but he has charm," Jane said. She pressed her handbag protectively against her side, and the little clasp dug into her hip.

Orloff was now talking to a tall, beautiful woman with very long, wavy black hair. "Do you know who that is?" Jane asked.

"That's Dahlia, Brian Taylor's wife. Don't you know her? Would you like me to introduce you?"

"Maybe later. I've met too many tall, beautiful women

tonight," Jane said, sighing. "Did you see how lovely Martha looks?"

"Yes. Something's gone her way, I'd bet. Maybe she's talked Brian into postponing the U.S. deal." His tone was ironic.

"I didn't see any signs that they were getting along any better when I was talking to them," Jane said.

"That conflict between Brian and Martha is a ritual. It doesn't mean anything. Martha is completely loyal to Brian and he knows it."

"She seems very territorial to me," Jane said, thinking that Tom Henege was surprisingly perceptive. Perhaps it was all the drink she'd had, but she seemed to be warming to him after all. His conversation about people interested her. "I'm rethinking finding BTS someone who can handle this merger; I'd like it postponed," she said. She thought she had better say her piece to Tom as soon in their conversation as she could, now that she was beginning to find him attractive after all.

Tom smiled, but it was a cold smile. "Martha got to you, did she? She can be very persuasive. What happened? Did she cry for you? She does that very well."

Jane looked at him, astonished. She had thought he was Martha's friend. What had happened to *his* loyalty? All her dislike returned. In that moment the party — the noise, the colour, the movement — seemed like a sinister movie, the smiles and laughter ominous, the undercurrents inexplicable. She suddenly wanted to go home.

She turned away without saying goodbye and went to look for her coat. The coat-check woman had left, and Jane was looking through the coats in the coatroom, trying to find her own. There were several furs, and Jane, feeling slightly dizzy, dipped her forehead into the melting softness of a thick, black mink. She stood there for a minute, buried in the deep warmth of the coat, waiting for the spinning to stop. It isn't the champagne, she told herself. It's the thought of driving home, alone, the thought of standing in front of the apartment door with its new lock. Leaning into the thick darkness of the coat, her eyes closed, she smelled faintly the perfume that clung to the fur, and the peculiar comforting smell of the fur itself, dense and oily.

"I didn't mean to make you angry," a voice said behind her. She turned to see Tom standing on the other side of the coat-check counter.

"May I take you out to dinner, please?"

They walked out into the snowy darkness, not speaking. The air was full of flakes whirling lightly in all directions rather than falling. It was mild, and the flakes were large and soft; most melted as they fell. They turned like autumn leaves falling in a gentle breeze, lit by the streetlamps.

"Would you like to walk?" Tom said. "I've had too much champagne to drive, and there's a pretty good little restaurant not too far from here." He took her arm, and as her slight dizziness had still not left her, she let him. It's just because I don't want to go home, Jane thought. It's really not very nice of me since I don't like him and he likes me. She looked sideways at Tom. He was smiling slightly to himself. He put out his tongue and let a snowflake melt on it.

"You look happy," Jane said.

"I am. I like Orloff's parties, I think I met some good potential customers tonight. And now I'm going to have dinner with a very exciting, very beautiful woman. Why shouldn't I be happy?"

"You *have* had too much champagne," Jane said. She thought she should be regretting agreeing to have dinner, but surprisingly his flattery had pleased her. It was strange.

Sometimes men's compliments struck her as insults, condescending, created by lust that had nothing to do with her; compliments that would have issued from the man's mouth exactly in the same way, no matter what woman they were with at that moment. She felt their fantasy version of her, like a sticky substance they had smeared her with, one she couldn't remove. At other times, either the fantasy was particularly pleasing or she felt that it was actually she who had triggered it. She never felt the compliments were for her, herself. They were a part of a ritual of lust that was important to men. That the woman be beautiful, that she be special, that the conquest of her be a worthwhile conquest.

But in any case, she knew that such male pursuits must be turned aside in a business relationship. She knew how to do it; she had done it many times before. And now was the time, or else the compliment would stick to her. It was like accepting gifts and expensive meals from suppliers. Sooner or later you found it impossible to make a tough decision: you gave them an order they didn't deserve, or you didn't fight for the best deal.

Yet the silence lengthened. They walked east along Wellesley, passing small shops and cafés.

He was a nice height, Jane thought. About a head taller. His body didn't loom or threaten.

"Actually, I thought you didn't like me," she heard herself saying.

He smiled. "I know. You're tense around me. I could feel it. I thought it was because you sensed I was attracted to you."

This was a much stronger danger signal, and Jane reacted from habit. "I don't mix business with pleasure."

"How about friendship?" he said. He still looked happy, Jane saw, watching him out of the corner of her eye, as they walked carefully, poking their way through the slush at the curb. They turned north on St. Nicholas, stepping on a new white carpet of snow, which was now falling more heavily, covering the sidewalk with its clean, pristine softness.

"Friendship . . . friendship is possible," she said. A small warm pocket of happiness, which she had first felt when he said she was the cause of his feeling happy, expanded, suffusing her like a kind of drunkenness, her former dislike for him vanishing. She giggled. "It must be the champagne. I don't seem to be able to be businesslike tonight."

He let her arm go and took her hand. They were both wearing gloves, yet this time the contact gave her a small frisson of pleasure, and she clasped his fingers tightly. At that moment she realized that Tom Henege, despite the fact he'd had a perfect opportunity to take her key, was the one person who could not have set the trap in her apartment. Perhaps it was her dislike for him that had prevented her from seeing this before. But it was very clear now. She had been with him at the time the trap must have been set. It was a wonderful, wonderful thought, and she held his fingers more tightly in her own. "I'm kind of burned-out on romance," she said, "but friendship can be very, very nice." She laughed again, her laugh sounding like champagne.

"I think you're a bit tipsy, Jane Tregar," he said. "You're nice when you're tipsy."

They walked into the restaurant, La Bastille, which was in fact the living-room of one of the ubiquitous small worker's cottages that remain, though transformed, in so many of Toronto's city neighbourhoods, even in the downtown core. There were dark-coloured posters of Paris on the white-washed walls, about ten tables, most filled. It was noisy, but not smoky. Their coats were taken and they were seated at a corner table.

"We'll have champagne?" he asked, looking directly at her. Again Jane felt the warnings so familiar to her. I'm going to make a mistake, she thought. I'm too tired, too worried, and I've had too much to drink and too little to eat for too long. It's made me weak-willed.

The caviar and smoked salmon she had eaten at the party had not been enough to compensate for the days since she had eaten, really eaten, but they had made her thirsty. She drank down her glass of champagne without stopping. A worried expression crossed, very briefly, Tom Henege's face. "After all," he said, "what are friends for?" He called over the waiter. "My friend would like some Perrier to drink with her champagne," he said. "And bring us some of your potato soup while we think about what to order.

"I like you tipsy, Jane," he said, "but I'm not sure you'll appreciate it later."

"You are right, friend," Jane said expansively. "A man who doesn't want to see the woman he's having dinner with drink too much and lose her sense of discretion, now that's a friend. A friend indeed. A friend in need." The Perrier came. She drank two glasses quickly. It was refreshing. Tom did not refill her champagne glass, and must have given a signal to the waiter, as he did not either. The soup came. It was a thick, creamy vichyssoise. Cold and rich. Very filling. She ate it all. The dizziness was gone; she felt warm, safe and euphoric with relief. Tom could not have tried to kill her. He had, therefore, not killed Gary Levin. He could be her friend.

"You don't know," Jane said. "You couldn't imagine. Not in a million zillion years. Thank you, thank you, thank you."

"Was the soup that good?"

"I mean, you couldn't have killed Gary Levin. I can sort of trust you." She reached over and fished the champagne bottle out of the ice bucket and poured herself a glass. Her hand was very steady, and the pale golden liquid looked beautiful as it flowed into the glass, filling it right up to the brim.

Tom's face, which had been filled with humour, with his pleasure in her, darkened and tensed. "Why do you say that, Jane? You can't know. In your position, it's safer not to decide anything."

Jane didn't pay any attention. "Of course, there are many people who didn't kill Gary Levin. Lots and lots of them. And none of those guys tried to kill me." She drank deeply, then poured herself some more champagne. Surprisingly there was still a lot left. Tom seemed to have stopped drinking. She poured him a glass. "But not, if we are quite clear, quite logical —"

"Jane —"

She ignored him. "—absolutely precise, we can see that one of the following people killed Levin." She held up one hand, extended her index finger, and tapped the top of it with the index finger of her other hand, being careful to strike it exactly on the tip. "One. Brian Taylor himself. Very abtruse that, but possible. Two." She held up her middle finger. The waiter intervened. "Would Monsieur and Madame like to order now?"

"No, no, later, we're not hungry yet," Jane said. "Two." She struck this finger carelessly on the nail. "Robert McDonnell. Not that I think he has the guts for it. Three." She tried to extend her third finger, failed, and pulled it upright next to the other two. "Martin Kaplan. Would he do it as a joke? Would someone who has such an outrageous idea of a joke ever get serious enough? Tune in next week. Four." She extended her little finger and clutched it anxiously. "Martha. Not Martha you say. So say I. But she could have.

"No more fingers, you notice. That is because Tom Henege was drinking Scotch in the company of Ms Jane Tregar at the very time a trap was set in her apartment. A lethal trap."

Jane stopped talking suddenly. Tom was staring at her.

"And could there be *two* murderers at BTS? All my mystery novels say no, and I take their word for it."

"Now hold on, Jane," Tom said. "First I want to get us something to eat. I'm hungry. Then you'd better explain what you're talking about." He called over the waiter and spent some time considering. Jane gestured at the chalkboard propped up on a table near the entry. "I'll have the rabbit," she said. "Let the small eat the smaller. Though I'm small, I'm crafty."

She noticed that Tom was looking bewildered. "Listen," she said, "it's very simple." Carefully she reached up and unpinned the jewelled butterfly from her shoulder and put it in her bag.

"Someone killed Gary Levin. I am supposed to find a replacement. I find people because I know a lot of people, and because I am trusted. Can I use that knowledge and trust to find a replacement for Gary Levin when he has been murdered? When, maybe, he has been murdered so that he won't complete the merger? What if it looks like the new person will complete the merger? Will he or she be murdered too?

"Then, if this wasn't enough to drive me to drink —" she carefully lifted her champagne glass and took a very small sip — "I come home and almost get electrocuted by my refrigerator. And I get a note that says, 'No merger or no Jane.'"

"My God, Jane!"

"Not another word about it, Tom. I've taken precautions so it won't happen again. Don't go all protective on me—"

"But Jane—"

"The point is someone took my key to get in, to set the

refrigerator trap and leave the note. It was done when I was drinking with you at the Prince so I've got problems. If I don't fill the position at BTS soon, the rumours and the instability will get worse, and the stock is going to fall too far. It will be much more difficult to put together a package that'll appeal to the kind of person Brian wants and Brian's merger will be fouled up. I will have failed. And I think my boss is looking for an excuse to fire me. He'll have it. Then of course, I should tell the police everything I know. I really should. That's the right thing to do. I like doing the right thing. But how can I? Brian asked me not to. I owe a lot to Brian — he reminded me of that. Will I get another job in the industry if I goof this up, or if Brian Taylor lets it be known I can't be trusted? But then, if I don't tell, maybe the police will find out what I knew and that I didn't report it. Isn't there a crime called withholding evidence?

"What a mess. All the champagne has made it perfectly clear, perfectly clear. I'm in one hell of a mess."

"You can't just ignore an attempt to kill you, Jane. That's madness."

"I haven't. You can count on that. But I meant it when I said I didn't want to talk about it anymore. Okay?"

The waiter brought their dinner. "I hope you two aren't parked on the street," he said. "There's a snow alert. There's going to be twelve inches by morning." He served their dinner looking worried. "If you live out of town you could have a problem. They've closed the 401."

Jane wanted the waiter to go away. "Thank you, we'll let you know if there's a problem," she said. She looked into her empty champagne glass. "Maybe I'll run away to sea."

"I don't understand you," Tom said. "But I'll let it drop if you insist." He smiled at her. "When you were a little girl, what did you want to be when you grew up?"

Jane thought. "It's funny. I didn't. I didn't have any

ambition when I was a little girl. I kept wanting to make things. Things out of clay, and paper dolls. But the things I made were never good enough. They never looked as I thought they would. So I'd give up. It used to really exasperate my mother when I wouldn't stick with things."

"And are you married, or do you live with anybody?"

"No, and no," said Jane. "You?"

"I was married, but I'm not now. I was living with somebody, but we parted; we're just friends now. All the good women are taken, it seems."

"That's what the women say about the men." She knew that the conversation was unwise. He was looking at her in a way she recognized, and instead of being put off, she was beginning to respond. Feelings she had thought might be quiescent forever were rising like champagne bubbles, filling her with quick little prickles of desire. She ate all her rabbit without noticing. Sexual desire was making her hungry. She cut off every bit of meat from the bone, ate the thick rich sauce, and ate two rolls. The champagne high was dying away, but was being replaced by the euphoria of desire. Where had it come from?

"You should be afraid, Jane," Tom was saying. "I am. There's so much happening at BTS. You know, I guess, that the joint-marketing deal is really a merger. . . ."

"When we first met I thought you wanted it to happen. Then when we talked you said you didn't want it."

"That's because I wonder if it's really a merger, Jane. Or is it a takeover? You've accepted what Brian's told you about it. But what do you really know? At first I thought it just meant a much bigger customer base, more money. I'm never adverse to more money." He looked at the champagne bottle. Only a little remained. He divided it between them. "I like being able to buy a sixty-dollar bottle of champagne for Jane Tregar. I like it a lot." He smiled at her, and she could feel his desire acting upon hers. She shifted restlessly in her chair and rubbed her back against the satiny lining of her coat, divided between her desire for Tom and her worries about the implications of what he was saying. "But the more I learn about the merger the less I like it. I don't think it's a merger, Jane. I think it's a takeover bid. The Americans are going to take us over, and Brian is going to lie back and enjoy it."

"Robert McDonnell hinted it would be a takeover, too," Jane said thoughtfully.

"The foreign-investment review board in Canada is not a factor anymore, but look at the fuss there was over the British buying control of Mitel. These things have to be done very cleverly. If this is a takeover, Brian and Gary would have got very rich. Now Brian will. But what will happen to the rest of us? What will happen to BTS? I don't want to talk about this anymore. Not tonight." He smiled at her. "You've eaten all your dinner and you don't have that anxious hungry look now. Have dessert. I like to watch you eat."

Jane shivered. "No, we're friends. I want you to help me. Let's talk about what to do."

"Only if you have some dessert."

They ordered white chocolate mousse, flavoured with framboise, then cognac and coffee. Jane heated the cognac between her hands, watched it swirl, form legs, and slide glistening down the sides of the glass.

"Well, come on, tell me more," Jane said, her mind back on business, her desire like background music, only subliminally present.

"Things are happening at BTS every day, moving along," Tom said. "Don't think Brian and Robert aren't talking to the Americans, working on the deal. The lawyers were back in conference with them almost all day today. Martin, Martha and I don't know for sure what's happening."

"I should talk to Brian then; find out what *is* happening."

"Jane, be serious. What makes you think he'll tell you the truth?"

"I'll know," Jane said desperately. "Somehow I'll know. And knowing what's going on, I'll know what to do. You'll see."

She took the butterfly out of her purse and pinned it on.

"What did *you* want to be when you grew up?" she asked him.

"When I was little we lived on a farm," Tom said. "There weren't many people around. I was alone quite a bit. I read a lot and thought a lot. That's probably why, now, I want to be with people, to see what they are really like. That's how I got into sales. I like predicting what people will do, guessing what motivates them, seeing if I'm right about them. They're very interesting, endlessly interesting. To sell to people you have to understand them, what they're thinking, what they really want."

"And that's what you're good at?"

Tom smiled. "Sometimes I'm great, the best. Then there're other times when I just can't get where I want to go. It's probably not a good idea to think you can understand people. Whenever you get too carried away with yourself, you're usually in for one hell of an unpleasant surprise."

They smiled at one another. "I want to take you home," he said. "I haven't had too much to drink. You have. Let me drive you home, okay?"

The champagne was wearing off, and his conversation about people had reminded Jane of all the things she was afraid of. Even with desire fizzing inside her, so unfamiliar after such a long time, she had no inclination to yield to it. It was apart from her volition. Her will was more connected to another part of her, a part that was still wary and scarred.

"I'd like you to drive me home," she said. "But as a friend, as we agreed."

He put her coat around her shoulders and caressed the back of her neck. "As a friend, Tom. I mean it."

"I'm you're friend, if that's what you want, Jane," he said. "You can count on me."

18

There was a police car parked outside of Jane's house. They saw it as they drove up the driveway. Jane shivered. She had been expecting this. She was sorry she had drunk so much, eaten so much. "I don't want to talk to them," she said. "I'm not up to it."

"What do you think they want?" Tom Henege asked her. "It couldn't be the printout. They wouldn't come to *you* to talk about that. And how could they have heard about what happened to you? You said you didn't tell anybody except your friend."

A flashlight shone into the car window, coated inside with condensation. She rubbed a space in the window, but could see only a dark bulky shape and the aureole of the flashlight beam in the heavy snow. She opened the window. Snow blew in on her upturned face.

"Miss Tregar?"

Jane sighed. "Yes?"

"I'm Sergeant Barrodale. I'd like to talk with you."

"Okay." She rolled the window back up and turned to Tom. "Go on home, Tom. It still may be possible to keep BTS out of this."

"No, I'd like to stay. I want to help you."

She looked at him, desire, friendliness, everything forgotten. "I said I want you to leave. I meant, I want you to leave." She got out of the car.

He looked out at her with an angry set to his mouth. Then, he turned and started up the engine. His car's tires spun in the snow, then it sped backwards out of the driveway in the tracks it had made. As the car drove away, all Jane could see were its headlights, like white tunnels in the snowy darkness.

Jane mounted the stairs, the sergeant and another policeman following her, and opened the door. She felt an adrenalin surge, anger and frustration.

"Can we make this as quick as possible please? I'm very tired. Driving in this weather is horrendous. It took us forty minutes to get here from Bay and Wellesley."

"We're sorry to disturb you, ma'am. We've been waiting since ten o'clock though, and we'd like to talk to you."

"Yes, yes, what about then?"

She turned on the lights, kicked off her boots, dropped the carrier bag with her shoes in it onto the floor. She hung up her coat, and took off the butterfly pin, putting it on the coffee table where the ruby winked in the lights reflected from the ceiling chandelier. The two policemen looked at it, then back to Jane.

"I understand," said Sergeant Barrodale, "that there has been an attempt on your life." He was a tall, stolid man. Blond hair, combed over a bald spot on the top of his head, pale skin, and washed out blue eyes. He must weigh two hundred pounds, Jane thought. He hasn't any shape. He's like a tree in a suit. It was a cheap looking suit too, she thought, a shiny navy blue, with a blue-green weave in it, and he had on a red, green and navy striped tie. He was standing on the mat, holding his overcoat, and removing his rubber overshoe. "Why don't you sit down," she said. "I don't like tall people looming over me."

Sergeant Barrodale looked surprised. He removed his other rubber, lined them up neatly in the black plastic boot tray, hung his coat carefully in the small coat cupboard and sat down on the red velvet sofa that filled one corner of the living room. He sat silent for a moment, looking around him, at the large bookcase, filled with paperback books, at the stereo, at the desk piled with neat stacks of papers, at the sofa itself, Victorian looking, with a high curved back, mahogany trimmed and upholstered in worn velvet, the coffee table made from an old pine chest, the rocking chair. Jane had not really marked her character or personality on the room. She had fixed it up quickly, when she first moved there five years before, when she didn't have much money. She was comfortable there, and from time to time she thought briefly of decorating it, making it smart, or stylish, or elegant. But she wasn't sure what she wanted the place to be like; it seemed easier to leave it alone, in its slightly threadbare comfort. Especially because fixing it up for herself implied a recognition, an acceptance, that her children's needs didn't have to be considered. There were no knicknacks except for a row of brightly coloured prints with a tropical feel on the wall behind the sofa. They were a present from Kersti, bought for Jane during a time when she had been feeling very blue. She had sat and watched Kersti hang them, thinking that she would never be cheerful again, but she had been, of course, often, and the pictures reminded her of that fact whenever she felt depression or sadness pressing at the edges of her mind. Jane sat down in the wooden rocker. She curled her stockinged feet under her.

The other policeman introduced himself as Sergeant Pearkes. He too removed his overshoes and coat, and sat at the other end of the sofa. He wore a tweed jacket and brown polyester trousers. He had a small notebook in his hand, and he opened it, licked the tip of his middle finger and flipped the page.

"Your name is Jane Rose Tregar and your permanent address is 493 Rosedale Crescent, apartment three, correct?"

"You're here, you see it," Jane said.

"Is that correct, ma'am?"

"Yes, that is correct."

"And on or about eight-thirty P.M., December fourteenth you entered this apartment, which showed no sign of forced entry, to discover that an intruder or intruders had entered the premises and wired your refrigerator such that you received a severe shock upon touching it?"

"I don't know where you got that idea," Jane said. "Not a word of it is true."

Sergeant Barrodale stared at Jane. He seemed annoyed. "It's not true did you say, ma'am?"

"Not at all," Jane said airily. "Biggest load of bullshit I ever heard in my life."

"This is no laughing matter, Miss Tregar. If someone made an attempt on your life, as described, you were lucky not to be killed. You might very easily be killed the next time."

"That's true," said Sergant Pearkes, to Jane's surprise. Somehow she hadn't expected him to speak. She looked at him more carefully. He was overweight, and almost as tall as Barrodale. He shifted his weight on the sofa, and it creaked.

"I can't imagine who could have told you such a thing, or why," Jane said. "I'm not the sort of person that things like that happen to. You must be mixing me up with some other Jane Tregar." She smiled at them.

"Your landlord has stated that you requested he change

the locks on December fifteenth. You claimed there had been a break-in. No break-in has been reported."

Jane retrenched. "There was no point in reporting the break-in," she said. "Nothing was stolen. It was simply unpleasant."

She had realized that only the murderer could have reported what had happened. She knew, with absolute certainty that Kersti would not have done so. Though she couldn't be so sure of Tom Henege, she had only told him this evening, and they had not been separated from the time she told him until they arrived at the house. She had told no one else.

The murderer saw me at the party, and couldn't understand it, she thought. Perhaps he hoped to scare the truth out into the open by doing this. Or get me in trouble. I won't give him the satisfaction.

"I haven't mentioned it to anybody," she said untruthfully. "So, I'd very much like to know how you heard about it."

"An anonymous tip," said Barrodale, watching her closely for her reaction.

Jane smiled at him noncommittally, hiding the shiver of apprehension she felt at his words.

"Could you please tell us what happened?" Sergeant Barrodale said. He took a package of cigarettes out of his breast pocket and looked around for an ashtray. Seeing none, he put the package back in his breast pocket.

"No I couldn't," Jane said. "I'm not making a complaint, and as far as I know it's no crime to change the lock on your door, is it Sergeant?"

"No, no I don't believe it is."

"Then if that's all, I'm very tired. . . ."

"Not quite all," said Sergeant Barrodale, "if you don't mind . . ."

"But I do mind, that's the point," said Jane. "I'm very tired and I have nothing to say. So could you please go?"

"Just a few more questions, if you don't mind," said Sergeant Barrodale, who seemed not to have heard her.

Jane sighed loudly. The man is completely dense, she thought. Then she caught a look in his eye, a slight smile. He's putting me on, she thought in astonishment, this whole personality is a total act. She sharpened her attention and concentrated.

Sergeant Barrodale looked down at a small notebook which seemed to have materialized in his palm. "Pursuant to your employ at Orloff Associates, you are at present, conducting an employee search for the firm of Brian Taylor Systems Inc., is that correct?"

"It's correct," Jane said, "but I honestly don't see what business it is of yours. And now that we know I'm not going to complain about the break-in, could you please tell me what right you have to sit here in my apartment, after I've asked you to go, and ask me questions?"

"If you ask us to leave, we have to leave ma'am. That's the law," Sergeant Barrodale said. "But I hope you won't. We have just a few short questions. Why don't you answer them, then we'll leave and let you get to bed. I'm sorry your friend had to go."

"If that's meant as an insult, " Jane said, rising to the bait, "I'm not insulted. My friend wasn't planning on staying. But if he had been you wouldn't have scared him away."

"I'm very glad to hear that," Sergeant Barrodale said. "Now about Brian Taylor Systems Inc. . . ."

"It's time for you two to leave," Jane said. "I'm sorry. If I had anything to say which could possibly be useful to the police I would certainly say it. But I don't. So goodbye."

Barrodale rose slowly. Pearkes followed him, his notebook, in which he had been recording everything that

Jane had said, was open. She could see a line of small neat printing.

"I have to say frankly that I find your attitude very hard to understand, Miss Tregar. Why don't you want to co-operate with the police? A man died under unusual circumstances at BTS. You were hired to find his replacement. The police are looking into his death. It's your duty as a citizen to talk to us."

Jane sat down slowly. "If you put it that way . . ."

"That's very sensible, Jane. You'll be glad you co-operated with us," Pearkes said. Barrodale gave him a look of rebuke. Pearkes smiled, and sat down too. Jane saw he had a grease stain on the thigh of his trousers. She wondered if they ate doughnuts in their squad car, like on TV. Barrodale took up his position on the red velvet sofa, and consulted his pocket-sized notebook. "Did you remove anything at all from the premises of BTS in the course of your work for that firm?" he asked.

Jane understood. They had been tipped off about the attempt on her life. But hearing her denial they were wondering if, in fact, the break-in might be related to something else. To someone trying to recover some evidence she had removed.

"I've got nothing from BTS that thousands of others don't have," she said.

"Such as?" Barrodale asked.

"Oh, you know, stuff like Annual Reports, files of news-paper clippings, job descriptions, nothing confidential."

"Nothing at all confidential?"

"For heaven's sake, that's what I just said!" Jane could not recall having met a more exasperating man. Knowing he was doing it on purpose only made it worse. He put down his little notebook, which looked so absurd in his short-fingered hand, and took out his cigarette package.

He looked at Jane, who looked back at him saying nothing. He put the cigarettes down on the coffee table, picked up the little notebook and resumed his questioning.

"Can you think of any reason, any reason at all, that an employee or agent of Brian Taylor Sytems might enter your apartment unlawfully when you were not present?"

"Nope," said Jane.

"I don't think you're trying to help us, Jane," Pearkes said. "Why not be a good girl and make an effort? What if Gary Levin was murdered, eh? You're not doing any good taking this snarky attitude, now are you?"

"I'm not a girl, don't call me a girl," Jane said.

"Well you're acting like a silly little girl, if you ask me," Pearkes said.

"I'm doing the questioning, George, thank you," Sergeant Barrodale said. "If you don't mind."

I wonder if this is really the famous good cop, bad cop routine, thought Jane. If so, it's really rather clever. One can't help responding.

She turned to Pearkes. "*Was* Gary Levin murdered?"

Both men were silent. Barrodale reached for his cigarette package and took out a cigarette. He tapped the cigarette on the coffee table and put his hand in his jacket pocket, bringing out a Bic disposable lighter. Then he remembered himself, placed the lighter back in his pocket, and laid the cigarette on top of the cigarette package. He's staking out territory, taking over my place, Jane thought, interested in his technique. She too questioned people for a living. Sergeant Barrodale cleared his throat and spoke formally. "We believe at this time, that Mr. Levin was murdered. But cause of death has not been determined."

"How did he die?" asked Jane. She felt suddenly queasy. Too much champagne, or was it that hearing the stiff, uninflected voice of Sergeant Barrodale saying the things she had tried so hard not to believe made them unalterably real?

"To the best of our knowledge," Sergeant Barrodale said, "it was pulmonary edema, cyanosis of the lungs."

Jane made up her mind. There was a seriousness to this that—it seemed suddenly clear to her—overrode all other considerations. She could not imagine how she had thought otherwise for a minute. Her job, her future, her reputation, even her friendships seemed very far away. Their distance seemed to make her choice easier.

"Have you found the threatening printout yet?" she said.

Barrodale could not help looking, for an instant, at Pearkes. Jane saw that they both knew.

"What printout is that, Miss Tregar?" Barrodale said blandly.

"The printout off the console printer, the one that says 'That will teach the son of a bitch.'"

"Oh, that one," Barrodale said with a straight face. "Yes, we've seen that one. Do I understand you to say you've seen it?"

"Heard about it."

"From who?"

"Everybody at BTS knows about it," Jane said evasively.

Sergeant Barrodale took up his cigarette and lit it with the Bic lighter. It was yellow, and in the lamplight Jane could see the fluid inside. She swallowed, remembering the taste of the champagne. Her stomach was churning, and she hoped she wouldn't have to throw up before the policemen left.

"Who exactly, do you mean by 'everybody at BTS?'" Barrodale asked.

"Christ," Pearkes said. "It's like pulling teeth, Jane. Why'n't you just tell us all about it, eh? We'd all get to bed a lot sooner. At this rate we'll be here 'til New Year's."

I can play too, Jane thought. "I'm doing the best I can," she said in a girlish voice.

Barrodale smiled slightly, and seemed to relax. It was the first time he had smiled. Jane thought he was the kind of man who would be most comfortable with small frightened women, rather than aggressive ones. Making him comfortable wasn't important, but perhaps he would be easier to deal with if he were less on guard.

"We had a meeting, and someone — I don't remember who, said that they'd seen that page in the printout before they handed it over to the police," she said softly.

"That's interesting." Barrodale said.

"Especially since no one handed it over," Pearkes added. "I took it off the printer myself."

"It would be very helpful if you could remember who said they saw it," Barrodale added.

"They were all talking about it," Jane said. "They all knew about it. Maybe they just thought it was some kind of sick joke. After all, how could Levin have been murdered? The room was locked." Jane realized her legs were asleep. She shifted position. Painful pins and needles made her grimace.

"Some joke," Pearkes said. "Come on Jane. You know better."

Jane felt if she got any more tired she would fall asleep right in the middle of the conversation. What time was it? two? three? They had surely been eating dinner until well after midnight. She rested her head against the back of the rocking chair, and rocked back. "I suppose you've realized only five people could have sent that message."

Both policemen were silent.

"Oh I'm so tired I can't think. Why don't you come back tomorrow? Please?"

Barrodale leaned forward. There was a long cylinder of ash hanging off his cigarette. He got up, and reminding Jane of a lumbering bear, walked into the kitchen returning with a saucer.

"Make yourself at home, why don't you," she said.

Barrodale ignored this remark. "Miss Tregar," Barrodale said slowly, "what can you tell us? Why would anyone want to kill Mr. Levin?"

"I haven't the faintest idea," Jane said. "I told you about the message, so you can see that I'll say whatever I know. But that's it." She wanted to ask them not to tell Brian that she had mentioned the printout message, but it didn't seem like a good idea. She didn't want them to have any leverage, any power over her.

Barrodale looked down at his notebook. He began to ask Jane a series of questions about the organization of BTS. She answered slowly, carefully, exactly, feeling her lids closing as if weighted. Finally it was over. She hoped she had said nothing indiscreet, nothing she would regret. She had tried very hard. She could not remember ever being so tired. Her dinner with Tom Henege seemed to her to have taken place in another country, many years ago. She locked the door after the policemen and pulled aside her curtains to look out the window onto the street. She saw the two of them come out and begin to scrape the snow off their car, which looked like a smooth white marshmallow. In the headlights Jane saw the flakes, small and hard now, whirling with manic intensity. The car made a very careful turn and drove away slowly on its thickly ribbed snowtires, preceded by two cones of light filled with spinning white particles. She stood for a moment, her head pressed against the cold window. Then she walked into her bedroom, unzipped her dress, letting it drop around her feet, took off her underwear, put on her oldest worn flannel nightgown, one she had had since she was a teenager, and fell into bed. But before she fell asleep she set her alarm. Even half asleep she knew tomorrow was going to be a very bad day.

19

Brian Taylor Systems Inc., the high-profile data-processing firm much in the news lately, due to the unexplained death of Gary Levin, its chief financial officer, saw sharp rises in its stock yesterday. The stock, which had dropped to a low of $8.00 in the past week, began rallying yesterday, and closed today at $15.00, a record high.

Barbara Blaney, of Thorne, Reid and Wilder, a firm that monitors the performance of high-tech stocks for corporate clients, said: "The volatility is largely due to the persistent rumours that there is a takeover in the wind. But most industry observers doubt that Brian Taylor, who owns the controlling interest in BTS, will be willing to sell out. It's generally believed that Taylor would never be prepared to give up control of the firm he created and made into one of the most successful in the industry."

However, Jared Fullerton, MP for Rainy River, said today he had a reliable source inside BTS who is confident that a sale is in the offing. Fullerton believes the government should move to stop the sale.

A spokesperson in the office of the Minister of Industry and Small Business said that whether or not a takeover was being considered, the Minister would not involve himself in the private affairs of Canadian businessmen. "I believe in man's right to profit from his risk and his investment," the spokesperson said.

Taylor was unavailable for comment, but Martha Gruen, vice-president of Human Resources at BTS, denied the takeover story. "All this will settle down as soon as we have a new VP of Finance," she said. "Then we'll be able to send a strong signal to investors that this firm intends to expand vigorously into the U.S. and open up new markets. There is no one in this management group, including Brian Taylor, who wants to sell out."

Industry sources say that the management group of BTS is critical to its success. The management style practised there has been the subject of numerous articles in the press, and has been used as a case study in several books. If the management group did not support the takeover bid, the future growth of the company might be in jeopardy. This, it is believed, would substantially reduce the value of the stock.

Jane was awakened from a heavy, dreamless sleep by the telephone. She reached for her receiver, knocked it on the floor, grappled for it, her head ringing from the knocking sound the receiver made as it banged against the legs of the night table. She could hear Eddie Orloff's voice, distorted, coming from the receiver.

"Hello, hello? Hello! Goddammit, hello, Jane?"

She finally managed to get hold of the receiver and sit up. In the darkened room she could see from the illuminated clock radio that it was exactly seven o'clock. Mornings were hard for Jane. She always felt thick-headed, sluggish, weighted down with sleep as if her body were a bag of sand. She also felt very irritable.

"Jane! Jane, is that you for God's sake?"

"Yes, I'm here, what is it? It's seven o'clock."

"I know what time it is. I've been at the office for an hour. Get your ass in gear and get over here right away."

"Now? I'm not even up yet. . . ." The clock radio came on. It was a sprightly Haydn trumpet piece. Jane's head reverberated.

"Now! Goddammit. This isn't a tea party you know. You're a big girl. I don't have time to fart around. I want you over here, on the double."

Jane groaned, her head still ringing as he shouted at her. She moved the phone away from her ear and tried blinking her eyes rapidly. It didn't help. The room remained dark: it was still only seven. Her head felt pumped with air, and her stomach bloated and nauseated. She tried to turn off the trumpets, but only succeeded in knocking the radio on the floor.

"All right, all right, I hear you." Her voice was thick and creaky.

"I drank champagne until two and I was out running at five-thirty. What's your excuse, Tregar?" Orolff's voice was grating, accusatory.

Jane nodded her head. It was a mistake. She felt as if the room were turning on its axis.

"How soon will you be here, Jane? Jane!"

"An hour, maybe. I'll try —"

"An hour is no good. You better be here sooner. A half an hour. No later. I'm serious. You don't get paid for lying around in bed feeling sorry for yourself. And take the subway. They won't have ploughed the streets yet and you're likely to get stuck."

"I'll do my best," Jane said carefully.

"That's not good enough. Get over here *now*. I mean it, Jane. There's a crisis in this BTS business, and we have to talk before nine o'clock. Otherwise Orloff Associates will be twisting in the wind. And it will be your fault. And I won't forget it. Do you understand?"

"Please don't shout, Eddie. I can hear you perfectly. I understand."

"I hope so. I bloody well hope so." He hung up the phone with a crash that caused Jane to drop the receiver. She found it and tried to put it back onto its cradle. It took some fumbling before she could set it in properly. She groaned and pulled the pillow over her head. Her bedroom was very cold, and she could hear the branches of the chestnut tree banging on the window.

The telephone rang again. Jane was tempted not to answer. Orloff was at his most obnoxious. Why give him the satisfaction? On the other hand, why offend him unnecessarily? She was no doubt going to do so later. She picked up the phone.

It was Kersti. Her voice sounded thick with tears; she was crying, and Jane could hardly make out what she was saying. "Can you come, Jane? Please? It's so terrible."

"Kersti! What's the matter? I can't understand what you are saying."

"Please, Jane. Just come. Please!"

Jane dressed quickly. Warm clothes suitable for work, and heavy boots. Kersti lived in Cabbagetown, just east of downtown. Jane decided to take the subway to Wellesley first and pick up her car from the parking lot near the Sutton Place Hotel where she had left it the night before.

The streets were thick with snow, and driving was very difficult. Twice Jane's little car skidded out of control, once into the curb, another time into a U-turn, bringing her face-to-face with oncoming traffic. Luckily there was very little, as few cars had ventured out. It was still snowing heavily. There was a high wind that blew the snow against the car windows and visibility was poor. Jane's thoughts moved in thick, muddled circles; she was still not fully awake. What had happened to Kersti? What would happen to Jane, when she didn't show up at work? Orloff wouldn't forgive, wouldn't forget. It would be his chance to get rid of her once and for all. He needed a token woman, so he'd find another. Someone older, with more presence. She remembered the woman Orloff had introduced her to at the party and was sure that she was being groomed as her replacement. Orloff wouldn't want two women at BTS. He didn't like working with women. Orloff had said they had to talk before nine o'clock, so surely she could leave then. So why didn't she go to see him first, then see Kersti? What difference could an hour make to Kersti? That was obviously the best thing to do. Kersti wouldn't want Jane to lose her job. Jane knew that Kersti really cared about her.

But Jane kept going toward Kersti's house, scolding herself while she drove. This is why women don't get anywhere, why men think we aren't serious, she told herself.

Coming around the corner of Parliament and Winchester Streets, she saw the clock on the old Winchester Hotel, its glass long broken and the hands stopped at eleven-forty. The stainless steel letters over the door to the tavern were bent crazily, and Jane read the word "trance" as she skidded past and into Metcalfe Street. She wondered, as she had before, why Kersti was so fond of Cabbagetown — how she could feel comfortable in a neighbourhood that Jane found hostile.

Kersti had no driveway but Jane found a parking place at the curb almost in front of the house, right behind Kersti's red Saab. Jane drove into the snow behind it. She knew when the snow-plough came along it would wall in her car and she'd have to shovel her way out. Another delay, making her even later.

Along the street the townhouses were set back behind large verandahs, their windows hidden behind shades and nylon lace curtains. Many of the verandahs were worn with cracked and peeling paint. Others were freshly painted, and the small plots in front of them had iron railings. But the fronts of the houses were no guide to what was inside. There were many up and coming young people who had spent a great deal of money inside the houses, and left the fronts looking exactly like their neighbours. Cabbagetown was the kind of place where that was a wise thing to do. It was a rough neighbourhood in Toronto terms, although a woman could walk there safely at night.

Jane rang the bell and Kersti opened the door, letting out a rush of warm air. She was wearing a white quilted dressing-gown, carelessly tied. Her hair was pulled back with a rubber band, and her face was pale, swollen, blotchy. Jane threw her arms around her, and the two women hugged one another. Then Jane shut the door. She left her damp coat and her boots, crusted with snow, on the floor in the front hall, and then followed Kersti up the stairs and into her bedroom.

Kersti's bedroom was white and black. White walls. Black lacquered furniture — a bed, a long low dresser. A wardrobe with mirrored doors. She had white ginger-jar lamps and a white comforter with a pattern of grey-and-black bare tree branches. It was all very controlled and orderly, except for the piles of books, two and three layers deep in the black bookcase, on top of the bookcase, and stacked on the night table.

Kersti climbed into her bed. The room was oppressively hot. Kersti, still wearing the quilted dressing-gown, crawled under her comforter and pulled it up over her shoulders. She was shivering.

"It's my sister," Kersti said. "Tiu. She's killed herself. It's so horrible. My God, I can't stand it." Tears were running down Kersti's face. Jane sat down next to her on the bed and took Kersti's hands between her own. They were ice cold, and Jane rubbed them back and forth. "Will you make me some hot tea, Jane? I'm so cold, so cold. I don't think I'm ever going to be warm again."

It was three o'clock by the time Jane arrived at Orloff Associates. She had stayed with Kersti until she grew more calm, and then had driven her to Tiu's house, a couple of miles away. She had helped Kersti comfort her brother-in-law, decide what to do about the children, and had stayed with the family until she could see that they wanted her to leave. Kersti's last look was cool. Jane thought Kersti might not be too happy that Jane had seen her beyond control, overcome by grief. Kersti had had a very difficult childhood; she was proud of her strength. In their friendship Kersti had always liked to protect and mother Jane. The turnaround would be hard for Kersti. Jane thought there might be a bit of coolness between them for a while. Kersti would not want to talk about her sister, or why she had killed herself, for some time. She would regret everything she had told Jane in the first shock. It was clear, too, that Kersti felt guilty. Jane grieved for her.

Driving back to the office she kept thinking about Tiu, about the last time she had seen her, about the sense she had of Tiu being lost in some deep, flattened despair. Al, Tiu's husband, had told Jane, while Kersti was with the children, that Tiu had been saving her sleeping pills for a long time — weeks, perhaps months. She had stopped taking her antidepressants. At first, hearing of the suicide, knowing of Tiu's connection with BTS, Jane had feared that there might be some link between her death and Levin's. And possibly, it was not too far-fetched, Jane thought, that something would come to light, something that Tiu had heard about BTS, or that had happened to her there, that had deepened her despair. But there was no doubt that it was suicide. Tiu had cleaned her house, had picked up the dry cleaning and returned the library books. She had stocked the freezer and said goodbye to her children, telling them she was going on a long journey. Then she had taken a suitcase — it was found later by her bedside, empty — checked into a downtown hotel, put out a Do Not Disturb sign and swallowed two bottles of sleeping pills. She had left a note: "Tell the children I'm sorry, but they will be better off without me. Now nobody will have to worry about me any more."

Jane realized that she was not surprised. It was almost as if she had been expecting something like this, ever since having tea with Tiu. But when she thought of Kersti's ravaged face, the guilt she was left with, Jane couldn't understand. If Tiu thought her life had no meaning, how could she leave it in such a way as to hurt others so deeply?

Jane didn't want to go back to the office. The people and problems there seemed like cartoons, compared to Tiu's death. But that was probably just the shock. She stopped at the ladies' room, rubbed rouge into her dry cheeks, combed her hair, straightened her clothes. Her face looked wan and tight, but she made an effort to relax, to put her normal expression over her sadness, like a mask.

She walked into her office, smiled at her secretary and said hello brightly, as if it were eight in the morning and she were on time and fresh as a daisy. Not three in the afternoon, and her wearing clothes smelling faintly of sweat from the overheated houses, and her own discomfort and anxiety.

"Well, Jane, I hope you were in a car accident, that's all," her secretary said. "Orloff's been storming around here saying that unless you are unconscious he's going to fire your ass. His very words. Apparently you were supposed to be here no later than seven-thirty. Two policemen came here exactly at nine, and stayed with Orloff for a long time. When they left, you should have seen him! He was fit to be tied."

"And what's the bad news?" Jane said, leafing through her phone messages, pretending to be perfectly calm.

"Well, I'm glad to see *you're* not worried," her secretary said. "You've also had calls, call-back-urgently calls, from Brian Taylor, and Martin Kaplan. Also several calls from Tom Henege and Robert McDonnell. The messages are there, but all of them want me to get you to phone back as soon as you get in, okay?"

"Anything else?" Jane said.

"Yes, a reporter from the *Daily News* wants your comment on a story that he says is going to press tonight. He's on deadline. It's about BTS. I told Mr. Orloff about that one. He may have handled it for you."

"Well don't hold anything back, Barbara," Jane said. "With all this good news, surely there's something else." Then seeing her secretary's face, she added, "I'm sorry. I shouldn't be taking it out on you. Forgive me, will you?"

"Of course, but I suggest you buzz Mr. Orloff right away. He's been ringing here every half hour."

Orloff really was angry. His skin looked like wax, the lines graven in with a stick. Jane told herself she didn't respect people who couldn't control themselves. How could they manage others? The sign of a bad manager, she thought. It didn't make her feel any better.

Jane stood behind the visitor's chair, her hands clutching its back. Standing seemed to help. She looked down at Orloff who, seated at his desk, stared back at her without expression, his pale grey eyes cold and unforgiving. "Just tell me one thing," he said. "Is this a game to you? Is that the idea?"

"No, Eddie. I know it's no game."

The anger broke through his icy tone. "Then what the hell are you playing at?"

"Why don't you tell me what's been happening instead of abusing me? Then maybe we can get somewhere."

For a moment Orloff was speechless. The silence lengthened. Then suddenly he yelled, "SIT DOWN!"

Jane sat down.

"All right, all right. I'll tell you what's been happening, Ms Tregar. At nine o'clock, by appointment made by them at six-thirty this morning, two police officers were here. They questioned me for over three hours. They asked me things like: why did we conceal evidence? They asked me why someone would murder a vice-president at BTS. Could the murderer have been looking for an important document? Could *you* have removed such a document? Apparently they had a tip that someone broke into your apartment, you denied this, and that's led them to decide that you took some papers from BTS. They wanted to know, is Orloff Associates involved in withholding evidence in a homicide case? They suggested that we were behaving illegally and unethically. They threatened to get a search warrant, saying they had reasonable grounds to assume that we were concealing evidence; they asked for permission to search your office and papers. *And I didn't know what to tell them.* Do you see the problem?"

Jane remembered the expression "I wish a hole would open and swallow me up." It seemed very apropos. She forced herself to be calm, so as not to give Eddie's anger anything more to feed on.

"I am sorry I couldn't come at seven-thirty. I left my house right after you called. But a personal matter came up. I was delayed —"

"Delayed. *A personal matter!*"

"In any case, unless you have any objections, there's no problem with the police going through my files. There's nothing —"

"No problem! I don't bloody believe it! I bust my ass to earn this firm the most prestigious place in this industry, and you think there's no problem in allowing the police to go through files about our clients?"

"I didn't mean —"

"You didn't mean fuck-all, that's the problem. You've got this firm into one hell of a mess. Didn't you ever hear about keeping your options open? Well as far as I can see you've bloody well closed every single one of ours. The police are on our ass, and it will be about five minutes before everybody knows about that. We're caught up in what's going on at BTS, and I'll bet you that within the month we have the TSE investigators, the RCMP and every other royal pain in the butt subpoenaing our files. We'll be into hundreds of thousands of dollars of legal fees.

"And do you know what the worst of it is?"

Jane shook her head.

"BTS stock is up." He looked at her. "You don't understand? Shall I spell it out in words of one bloody syllable for you?"

He got up from his desk, walked to the window and looked out over Bay Street. It was so overcast that the streets looked almost like night, lit with the facades of windows and the serpentine trails of the car headlights. "Someone is trying to take over BTS. That's what it's all about. Everyone in this mess is going to be blackened. I've been around long enough. I smell it. It's a no-win situation."

"Maybe we should drop BTS then. Wouldn't that be the simplest?"

For the first time Orloff smiled, a small, mean little smile. He sat down at his desk, picked up his Mont Blanc pen, unscrewed the cap, and drew a large jagged circle on the pad in front of him.

"You've closed that option by not being here before the cops came, Tregar." He put a big X inside of the jagged circle, and then drew another circle. The teeth of the second circle meshed into the teeth of the first. "The only way out of this one is to fight it." He put a smaller jagged circle inside the second one. "I'm going to smile and smile and say everything is wonderful. You're going to tell me absolutely nothing at all about what is going on at BTS. You are going to leave absolutely no paper trace of anything whatsoever. You are going to behave in such a way that no one — and I mean no one — can find a touch of anything wrong in what you do. And you are going to replace Levin, within the next week, and then you are going to get the hell out of BTS. Do you understand what I'm getting at?"

"Yes, I do," Jane said. "But what if the replacement is killed too?"

"Aha. Now we're getting to it. Do I take it that you believe Levin was murdered because of what he was up to at BTS?"

"Some people there think so."

"Well who better than you to find out who did it? I don't see that you have any other option. You've fixed that. Let me put it to you very simply, so even you can understand. When you didn't show up this morning, I had two choices. One, to let you hang out to dry; the other, to tell the cops nothing, to say I stood behind you a hundred percent, that they would have to get a warrant before they came here, and that we would fight it.

"Now I've been around long enough to know that with the system we live under in this country, the second option is a very bad way to play it. It makes the police think we have something to hide. When it gets out, everyone will think we have something to hide. And they'll think BTS has something to hide. Right?"

Jane nodded. Her mouth was dry.

"But, Ms Tregar, either you were very, very clever, or very, very dumb, because you left me no choice. I told the cops I stood behind you, Orloff Associates stood behind you, that we would protect the business confidences of our clients to the ultimate extent the law allowed.

"But they'll be back. I've talked to our lawyers. I think we have two, three days at the most. Your window is clos-ing, Jane. There's just a tiny, tiny slit." His grin grew wider; it looked wolfish to Jane.

"You're a very small girl, Jane. Maybe you can get through it."

"I'm beginning to think . . ." Jane began. Orloff wasn't looking at her. He was shading in the smaller circle with an intricate pattern of cross-hatching.

"I'm beginning to think I might find a way out of it."

"Well that's the best news I've heard all week," Orloff said, his tone sarcastic. He drew a pyramid under the sec-ond jagged circle, so the circle balanced precariously on the tip. "I'd like to believe it."

Jane sat silent. Orloff drew another triangle under the first. Now there were two triangles doing the balancing act, holding up the jagged circle with the smaller one inside it. It all looked very precarious to Jane. "I guess we'll just have to wait and see," Orloff said. He ripped the sheet off the pad, crumpled it roughly and flung it into a wastebasket. "You'd better go and handle the press; I know they're smelling something. Say nothing to them. But say it at length, sound like you like them, and be friendly. Hint there'll be a story tomorrow. That's what I recommend."

Jane though Orloff sounded almost human as he gave this advice.

"Thanks," she said.

"I remember, you used to be a member of the fourth estate. So I can assume you won't stick your foot in it, right? And then, do me a favour. Don't do any more disappearing acts? I don't care if your mother dies, or your boyfriend runs off with your best friend. I have to know where to find you every minute of the day. If the cops need to see me again, I want you there. Do you understand?"

"Yes," Jane said.

"I hope to hell you do. Don't count on me not stabbing you in the back if I think it will help. Your act this morning took care of any feeling I might have had that I owed you. I'm doing all this for Orloff Associates."

"I am too," Jane said faintly.

"Don't make me laugh," Eddie Orloff said.

20

As Jane drove up to BTS the next morning, she wondered if it were possible for things to be worse. The highway was greasy with salt, which splashed up on her windshield. The wipers were ineffective, and the world outside looked grey and smeary.

She had called her children the night before. It was getting close to Christmas and there had been an understanding that they would spend it with her. But it seemed Bernie and his wife were taking them to Florida, to a resort on an island. There would be sailing, and snorkeling, and swimming off a reef, sand and sun and other young people. Did she mind if they went? Surely they could see her some other time?

Was this a test to see if she cared? Jane wondered. What should she say? She didn't know. What had she to offer them, what right to insist that they spend a cold, dreary Christmas with her? It had always been that way. When Bernie wanted them, had insisted on having them, he had been able to give them everything, while she . . . she had been able to offer so little. What right did she have to insist? So she had said that of course she didn't mind. The kids seemed relieved. Jane had thought she was relieved too. After all, the complications of worrying about them, when everything else was falling down around her seemed beyond her. But she had not slept well; she had had dreams that had barely started when she would awaken and lie half-asleep, half-awake, playing back fragments of scenes from the past few days. These scenes slid imperceptibly into sleep, where the anxious dreams began. And soon, with a surge of fear, she would awaken again. Her children dominated her dreams, looking not as they were now, but as they had eight years ago, when the marriage broke up. Then she had believed they needed her, but their constant demands for attention seemed somehow impersonal, endless, unsatisfiable. Had she let Bernie keep them because she feared she could not be the mother they needed? Surely that couldn't be the reason.

She wondered if her life was as messed up as it appeared, or if she were simply losing her nerve. Her work life was a shambles. Her personal life was not much better. Kersti, she knew, would call her when she was ready. But right now, Kersti didn't want to see her. She was spending all her time with her brother-in-law and his children. She was living there. Jane's other friends were involved with Christmas preparations, the very thought of which set Jane's teeth on edge.

She had bought no presents, except for the kids'. She would soon have to. She didn't want a repeat of last year, when her friends had given her carefully wrapped, thoughtful gifts, which had obviously taken time to select, and she had remembered them at the last minute with hastily chosen bottles of wine. But she could not see how she was going to marshall the time or energy required.

At one time the life she was leading had seemed desirable. Why? She had all the guilt that went with it, and none of the fun. She geared down viciously as she skidded into the BTS parking lot, barely managing to get her Triumph under control in time to avoid smashing into a row of parked cars.

Do something, do anything, she said to herself. It's the only way to get on top of these blues. It's sitting back and letting things happen that makes it so bad. In this state of mind, you'll accomplish nothing, you'll be overwhelmed.

Perhaps, after all, it wasn't totally hopeless. But if ever she could figure out who had killed Levin, that wouldn't be enough. What good would the knowledge be without proof? And without an understanding of the motive? The perfect solution would be to identify the murderer, and somehow pressure him into resigning. Then let the police take over. That would isolate BTS from the damage as much as possible. Anything short of that looked like a betrayal of somebody, a prospect that made her miserable. But it didn't seem likely that she could accomplish all that before the takeover — if a takeover was what was going on.

She pulled into the parking lot, walked across the glazed and slippery cement, keeping her eyes down to avoid slipping and feeling the familiar clammy sensation of moisture working its way through the cracks between the soles and uppers of her boots. At the reception area of BTS, she gave her name and then stood by the door, trying to stamp the snow and ice out from the ridges of her boots' rubber soles.

Jane had tried to postpone meeting Brian until she felt more in control, but he had insisted on the meeting. She was not looking forward to the interview. She had intended to think up a strategy during the drive, and now scolded herself for letting her mind wander to her personal problems, instead of concentrating on the coming meeting.

A secretary came into reception, identified Jane, and explained that Brian was not in his office. She offered to escort Jane to the "work-room" suggesting that would be quicker than trying to page him. "It's hard to get him away from there, once he's talking to his programmers," the secretary explained, giving Jane a conspiratorial smile.

Jane followed her to the elevator, up two floors, down a long corridor, and into the large work-room, an open area divided into individual workstations, where most of the programmers worked. Some tapped rapidly on the keys of their terminals, others studied long piles of printouts, and many sat, their chairs tilted back, staring at the ceiling, or reading newspapers. It was a scene familiar to Jane, and one she found comforting and ordinary. Things hadn't changed much since she was in university, she noticed — all but two of the programmers were men. At the end of a row of workstations Jane saw Brian. He waved at her, gesturing for her to come over. But as she approached, Martha came into the work-room and headed toward Brian, her face set hard in angry lines.

"What's going on in R & D anyway, Brian?" Martha was fuming. "There're at least two projects in there I don't know anything about. If you keep bringing in new projects, you're going to have more burn-outs."

"New projects had nothing to do with Bates's burning out."

"Don't tell me, Brian. I'm telling you I can't be responsible —"

"I'll be responsible, don't worry about it."

"That's your prerogative, I guess." Her voice was more subdued, as if she was calming herself by an effort of will. "But project management is my job, and if there are projects around here I know nothing about. . . ."

"This stuff is very long-term. It won't interfere with any of our contracts. You have my word on that."

Jane wandered away from the argument. Neither of them noticed her go. She had caught sight of the screen of one the programmers about whom she thought Brian and Martha were arguing. Martha had gestured several times toward him as she spoke. He seemed to be working on a separate computer crowded into his workstation. It looked like a prototype; the name PSI embossed on a small plaque on the machine, was one Jane had never heard of before Sandy had mentioned it to her. On the screen there were many windows, and sentences that looked like English. She stared at it for a moment.

"That's Prologue isn't it?" she asked the programmer.

He didn't answer. Jane wondered. Prologue wasn't a language one expected to see in a data processing company. It was used in an area of computer software concerned with much more experimental things, with expert systems and artificial intelligence. Jane had a vague memory of hearing that there were some prototype machines developed by the Japanese for their "fifth generation" experiments, machines that had been loaned out to a few chosen researchers. But why would BTS have such a machine? Perhaps it was just a perk for a temperamental programmer, one Brian had to keep happy. She'd heard of trips to Hawaii, and the latest in micro-computers being given as gifts to such programmers, so why not time on a new kind of computer? After all, BTS couldn't be doing any really serious work in the area of artificial intelligence, because in the first place it didn't fit with the kind of business they were in, and because in the second place Brian was too smart, Jane thought, to fall victim to the seductions of such an unproven area of software technology. And in any case, if BTS were working in artificial intelligence, such work would surely be secret. One would never expect to find it out in the open, where any passing visitor or staff member could see it.

Brian came over and saw her eyes fixed on the screen. "What's this about, Brian?" Jane asked.

"Just play. It's one of those new Japanese experimental artificial-intelligence machines. I let people who are interested fool around with it in their spare time."

Jane had never heard of a programmer with spare time. "I thought maybe you had a secret research project operating on the purloined-letter principle."

Brian laughed. "That's a good idea," he said. "I wish I'd thought of it." He led her out of the work-room. "Thanks for agreeing to come by this morning. We need to talk. We'll go get a cup of tea."

There weren't many people in the cafeteria, and those who were there looked up at Brian, smiled but didn't speak to him.

They went to the serving counter, got tea and Danish and sat down at an empty table. "How are you coming at finding a replacement for Gary?" Brian asked Jane.

"It's coming," Jane said.

"That's not good enough, Jane. We should be interviewing already. We go into serious negotiations next Monday. Today is Wednesday. I can't stall things anymore. I need a replacement for Gary."

"Why not let Robert replace him?"

"Robert is crucial, of course," Brian said. He was eating his Danish fastidiously. When a flake of sugary glaze caught on the side of his mouth he wiped it neatly away with his napkin. He took small precise bites. Jane watched him. "But you know as well as I do that there is a big difference between a numbers man like Robert and a brilliant deal-maker. I'm surprised you even suggest Robert. I thought we'd been all through that."

"Well, Martha said —"

"Look, Jane," Brian interrupted. His voice was very quiet, very flat. "Any more delay is unacceptable. If there is a problem, if you can't find anyone — and that doesn't make sense, by the way — then tell me. I've asked you to find me a replacement for Gary. I'm the one giving you your instructions, not Martha."

She started to speak, but he raised his hand.

"Of course it was absolutely right that you talk to the management group and hear their views. But you're too shrewd to confuse that process with what I want you to do. Unless you're deliberately stalling us. If that's the case, I think you should say so."

Jane looked down at her teacup. She could not think how to reply. Brian was right. What was there to say?

"If you have been stalling, you must stop it, all right? Either tell me you don't want the job, or get on with it. I've made compromises with you, Jane. You told me at the Christmas party you wouldn't find me someone who could complete the merger. We've agreed you'd find several different candidates with different skills and I'd do the final interview and make the final decision. There should be nothing left holding you back."

"I'll get on with it," Jane said. "I have four good candidates for you. I'll set up the interviews."

"That's good," Brian said. "It won't give us time to get the new man in on the negotiations next week. But we can string those out a little while longer. We may just make it."

Jane nodded. Then she gathered her courage. "Brian, may I ask you something? Why is your stock going up? I've heard rumours that this isn't a merger, that it's a takeover."

Brian's ears got red. Red mounted up from his neck, until his face was flushed. But his control didn't falter. It was something Jane respected. Brian was a good man to deal with. Unlike Orloff, he didn't use rage to bully people.

"I'm sure there are rumours that I would sell out the people who helped me build this company and walk away with a big chunk of money. But I hope only people who don't know me would think that."

Jane answered evasively. "There *are* people who are saying that."

"I would never do that. It's against everything I've built, everything I stand for. It's as simple as that." Brian looked directly at Jane. She felt his concern.

Jane nodded. "So why do you think the stock is going up?"

"Obviously other people have the same idea as you do. When the truth comes out the stock will go back where it belongs." He smiled a narrow, mirthless smile. "If it weren't my own company, I'd sell short."

"Don't look at me," Jane said. "Orloff Associates doesn't allow its people to trade in clients' stock while they're working for them."

"Really?" said Brian, and for the first time in the conversation his control slipped slightly. "Is that what Eddie Orloff tells his staff?"

Jane looked up at Brian, trying to read the meaning of his words in his face.

"You can't just hint, Brian, and not explain what you mean. That's not fair."

"I've got to go," he said, ignoring her last comment and wiping his mouth carefully with his napkin. He pushed back his chair. "Sorry, but I have a meeting. Set those interviews up with my secretary. And of course, you'll have the files on my desk before we confirm the interviews. I'll want to look over them. Nobody with an MBA, I hope? I can't stand those guys. Good technical backgrounds? Please keep on top of this."

Jane poured out the last of her tea. Her feeling of wretchedness returned. She turned her mind away from the problems of BTS and thought of Kersti. That puts my problem into perspective, she told herself. She decided to call Kersti and invite her over that night. Kersti should get away from her sister's family. An evening with Jane would surely be good for her, whatever she thought. Kersti couldn't wallow in guilt forever.

Kersti had at first refused Jane's invitation. But when Jane said, "What do I have to do to convince you? Offer you *food*?" Kersti had suddenly laughed. It was probably the first time since her sister's suicide that Jane had heard Kersti laugh, that loud, uninhibited, hooting laughter that was one of Kersti's most endearing traits. She'd agreed to come, but told Jane there had better be a lot of food, Jane had to cook it herself, and it had to be delicious.

Jane laughed too, but driving back downtown she thought that though they joked, Kersti was also showing her anger. She knew Jane didn't like to shop or cook. She was asking Jane to do something for her, making Jane pay a price for having seen Kersti in pieces. Jane understood. She was glad Kersti was giving her a chance to pay; she was glad to pay. Pity and compassion and understanding for Kersti were feelings she could keep at bay. Kersti would hate to be pitied.

But when Kersti arrived, the kitchen was a mess. Some of the bags of groceries were still not completely unpacked. The pots were boiling hard, their lids dancing. The table was not yet set. And half of the first bottle of chilled Chablis was gone.

"What a godawful mess," Kersti said, hanging up her coat and taking off her boots. "Why don't I not help? I'll just sit in here, at the kitchen table, watch, laugh at you, and drink the Chablis."

"Hey, have a heart. I was counting on you to figure out how to make it all come together."

"Well, what have you got?"

Jane sighed. "Here's some cream cheese. I was going to spread this caviar over it for an appetizer, with some hard-boiled egg grated on top. The eggs have been boiling half an hour, so I'm sure they're done. . . ."

"Fish roe," said Kersti, dismissively, looking at the jar.

"Whatever. Then we're going to have pasta with white clam sauce and salad. But the pasta's almost done and I haven't made the salad. I just can't for the life of me figure out how you get all these things done together at the right time. The logistics are more complicated than the landing at Normandy."

Kersti sighed. "You are really hopeless, Jane. I'm sure you do it on purpose."

"What's the point of learning when you eat alone?"

"But you were married for years."

"I had a maid," Jane said, coldly. She didn't want to talk about her married life; it was too painful.

"I bet you ate roast beef and gravy," Kersti said, smiling.

"How should I know?" Jane said. She could not imagine remembering what she ate eight years ago. Kersti remembered almost every meal of importance she'd ever eaten, including all the holiday and party meals, and most restaurant meals. You could go with Kersti to a restaurant Kersti had recommended, and she'd remember what every item on the menu was like. Jane wondered why anyone would store so much irrelevant information in her head.

"I give up, Jane," Kersti said. "With your idea of giving

me a dinner party, it looks like I'll have to rescue you. Otherwise all the expensive food will go to waste."

Kersti was cheering up. Jane could feel it. She directed Jane to make the salad. Kersti managed everything else. They ate the fish roe, cheese and the strangely darkened chopped egg, while Kersti set the table, finished the pasta and bathed it in a little olive oil while she completed the sauce. She flavoured Jane's sauce with cognac and put a lot of chopped parsley on it. Watching the enthusiasm and pleasure with which she sliced, chopped, arranged and stirred was giving Jane, for the first time since her dinner with Tom, an appetite. Best of all, she could see, as she hoped, that Kersti's taking control of the dinner, rescuing her, was righting the friendship, which had been damaged by Kersti's collapse into grief.

While they ate, Jane told Kersti all her problems — Orloff's threat, the rumours about the takeover, even Brian's insinuation that Orloff was trading BTS shares.

"You know, Kersti," Jane said, "the worst of it is, for some reason they all trust me, or say they do. They don't see how ambitious I am."

"Who else do they have to trust?" Kersti said, cutting more French bread and using it to mop up the sauce. "Not each other, that's for sure."

"But I'm bound to betray some of them," Jane said. "It stands to reason."

"I don't understand you. I really don't," Kersti said. "Your job in there is to find a replacement for Levin. Worrying about betraying people? That's the least of your troubles."

"It's not that simple," Jane said. "My job isn't that simple."

"You always say that, Jane. Maybe that way of looking at things makes you good at your job. But you know sometimes things *are* that simple. Usually they are. I never believe it when people say things are complex. Get right down to it and you see it's very simple. Baby simple."

"That's why you're a journalist and I'm not."

Kersti smiled. "No, that's not why. I can write and I can find out the truth about things; you don't believe there're any nasty truths to find out, do you?"

"Well, maybe there is this time."

Kersti's smile faded. "My sister had a view like yours. Even after everything that happened to her in her life she believed in trusting people and being trusted. I can't understand it. Growing up in our house, why wasn't she strong? Why didn't she get over it?"

Kersti had drunk a lot of wine. She was talking to herself now. Jane knew about Kersti's background. About their father who, a hero with the Estonian resistance, had never adjusted to Canadian life. He had been at the centre of a family where drinking and beatings were part of miseries that both of his daughters had taken years to overcome. Although Kersti had never said, Jane thought that their father had sexually abused Tiu. She didn't know where she had got this idea, but the suicide had strengthened it.

"She could never forgive herself for giving in to him," Kersti was saying. Her thoughts must have been running in the same track as Jane's. "And that's because I didn't give in to him. Because by the time he turned to me from her, I was fourteen. I slept with a two-by-four, Jane. If he tried to come near me I'd wallop him with it. He was too drunk to be stronger than me; and I was a big girl for fourteen. Strong too. Thank God for that, I always think. But Tiu wasn't big. And she was gentle, accepting, fearful. She was always afraid. I'd be burning with anger. Tiu would be hiding under the bed, mesmerized with fright. When I'd call the cops she'd plead with me not to. 'Daddy doesn't mean it,' she'd say. Mama would say it too. 'He's not himself. He's a good man.'"

Kersti had turned to cognac. The bottle was getting low. "Did you know Tiu was a friend of Martha Gruen's?"

"She mentioned it to me that time we had tea together."

"Tiu was really depressed after Gary Levin's murder. Martha told her all about it. That's how I knew. Tiu grieved for her friends, Jane, not for herself. She didn't believe in herself at all." Kersti's eyes were dry. "She had medicine for her depressions. But she stopped taking it. That's what her husband, Al, keeps saying. If only she had been taking her medicine.

"I talked to her almost every night, Jane. I knew she was in bad shape. All her friends did too. We were trying to do something for her."

"It's not like you to blame yourself, Kersti," Jane said.

"That's right," Kersti said, shaking her head. "It doesn't profit you to blame yourself. You don't get anywhere that way."

Jane's kitchen had been installed in the forties. The counters were inlaid with small white tiles, chipped in places. The backsplash was surmounted by a piece of grooved aluminium, dented and discoloured. The wooden cupboards had once been painted light blue, then re-painted to a cream colour. In places the powder blue paint showed through the chips. The kitchen was usually very clean because Jane hardly ever cooked in it. She had a cleaning woman who came twice monthly, who would polish the counters and taps and the cracked porcelain sink. The kettle would be gleaming. She'd throw out what-ever food Jane might have bought that was rotting in the fridge, partly eaten heads of iceberg lettuce, cans of tomato paste that Jane used to make pizzas out of pita bread, and mouldy English muffins. Bits of dried-up cheese and occasionally a leftover chop or steak.

In the centre of the room was an Ikea white laminated kitchen table, round, and rather uncomfortable matching chairs, their backs a bentwood style with Swedish-patterned bright-red cushions. On the table was a large, wooden salt-and-pepper set, also bright-red. It looked like the kind of kitchen where a cup of instant coffee and bowl of tinned soup was a big meal.

Jane's attempt at cooking for Kersti, however, had changed this pristine room completely. Along one counter were the grocery bags, still not completely unpacked, the empty wine bottles, the colander, the empty clam containers, cartons of cream, a half-pound of butter, melting, and bunches of parsley. In the sink were the vegetables Jane had washed and not used for the salad. On the counter by the sink were big flakes of crust, scattered about from when Jane had sliced the French loaf, egg shells, and a bunch of golden chrysanthemums Jane had bought but forgotten to put in water.

Her eyes passed over this disarray, without seeing it. She focussed on Kersti, whose face was pale and crêpey looking, lacking its usual glow. Kersti's hair hung straight from a centre part and was tucked behind her ears. She was wearing a bulky black turtle-neck sweater, which hid the shape of her body. She had on jeans, but they were covered with heavy leg warmers. Jane wondered if Kersti was still suffering from the feeling of coldness that had plagued her when she first learned of her sister's suicide.

"How long will you stay at your brother-in-law's?" Jane asked Kersti.

"Not much longer," Kersti said. "He's going to make a pass at me soon, even though we don't like one another. I think I've staved that off about as long as I'm able."

"You must be used to that kind of thing."

"The kids are screwed up enough, without the relationship between their father and me getting complicated. I've told him he has to find a housekeeper. He's working on it. I should be able to leave next week."

"Are the kids okay?"

Kersti shook her head. "How could they be? They seem to be, but who knows? What's for dessert?"

Jane had bought some strawberries. Taken out of the box, the berries below the top layer were whitish and hard. They ate them anyway, dipping them into brown sugar. "They're tasteless," Jane said.

"You noticed." Kersti smiled. "Don't you remember I told you not to buy out-of-season fruit? A long time ago, I told you that."

"Yes, but how do you know if it's out of season? In say, Florida, I mean?"

"I really don't believe you, Jane."

Jane wondered how Kersti could know what was in season all over the world. Maybe it was the season for strawberries in Florida or Mexico or Morocco. Could Kersti really know that?

Jane wanted to ask Kersti a question, but she wondered if she should. She felt good about the dinner. The warmth between them was back. Kersti was teasing her again, the way she usually did. She had talked about her sister. Without coming out and saying what was at the back of Tiu's despair, Jane felt Kersti had opened the door a crack, letting her in a little to the feeling between the two sisters. That had helped. But Jane wondered if Kersti realized the implications of all of her remarks. Was the door wide enough for Jane to risk stepping through a little more?

She decided she'd go one step at a time, gauging the reaction.

"Was Tiu close to Martha Gruen?"

Kersti picked up her glass of cognac and the bottle and walked into the living-room. Jane followed her. Kersti turned on a couple of the lamps, arranged some throw cushions on the sofa, then stretched out on it, resting her cognac glass on her flat stomach. Jane sat opposite in the rocking chair. Jane had stopped drinking. Her stomach felt sore and distended from all the food and drink. Having Kersti over was comforting and familiar. Drink wasn't necessary. She rocked gently back in her chair, put her feet up on the dark-red leather ottoman and waited for the answer to her question. Kersti was staring at the ceiling.

In the silence Jane could hear hard grains of snow hissing against the windowpane. Occasionally there was a gurgle in the hot-water pipes to the radiators; the refrigerator motor came on with an audible hum.

"They were in group therapy together," Kersti said finally.

Jane waited. But Kersti didn't seen to have anything to add. "And?"

"And . . . what? I don't know. Tiu liked Martha. Said she was a good person. That's all I know."

"All?"

"I knew Martha was an important friend of Tiu's. Maybe Martha's in trouble at work over this murder business? Tiu hadn't been able to function at work, you know. She'd taken a leave, but in her mind, it was virtually the same thing as being fired. From her point of view they'd forced the leave on her. Maybe having Martha — whom she'd always admired — having her apparent security rocked, maybe that didn't help Tiu. Who knows?" Kersti spoke with more passion. "Tell me, just tell me, why didn't Tiu fight back? Why was my sister always afraid, always timid, from the time we were little?"

"Weren't you afraid when you were little?"

Kersti thought. "I must have been. Of course, I must have been. But that's not what I remember. I remember thinking, they won't get me, I'll get out of here, I'll make something better. I'll get away from people kidding themselves and always pretending things are okay. Nothing will stop me."

"And nothing did," Jane said.

"Don't hero-worship me, Jane," Kersti said. "I can hear it in your voice. It's not like that. You have no idea. You can't imagine. But one thing is sure — nobody who gets out of something like that is a hero. Ever."

"I don't understand," Jane said. "You contradict yourself. What have you got to feel guilty about? It's not like you had lots of choices."

"Don't take this wrong," Kersti said, "but you have a real problem in the way you tend to hero-worship. You underrate yourself and overrate everybody else. Maybe I couldn't have helped my sister. But I ask myself, why is one person strong and one weak? How can I explain? It's like I sucked the strength out of her always. I tempered myself on her. I couldn't have got out if she hadn't been there — soft, and gentle and good. It gave me the freedom to be bad. And I've been bad. To hell with it. I'm going home now."

They kissed. Kersti said she wasn't helping with the dishes on purpose; cooking her own dinner had been more than enough. After Kersti was gone the apartment was very quiet. Jane put Jean Pierre Rampal playing Bach on the stereo, then started cleaning the kitchen. As she knelt beside the sofa to collect Kersti's cognac glass she smelled the faint scent of her friend's perfume. She thought Kersti had told her more than she realized; she thought she was now beginning to understand the meaning of relationships between the managment group at BTS. The Bach seemed to confirm Jane's view. No matter what Kersti said, there might be order, there might be pattern, but things were not simple. They were not simple at all.

21

Jane was driving a rental car along Route 95 to Commonweal Computers, on her way from the Philadelphia airport. She was not looking forward to going to Commonweal, but interviews with two other candidates in the area had convinced her that as potential vice-presidents for BTS, those two prospects were wash-outs.

Commonweal was a tough place, and the people in it thought of themselves as tough, competitive street fighters. There were no women in their top management. Jane didn't like the way Commonweal people talked. They reminded her too much of Eddie Orloff.

Greg Foisy, the man she was going to see, was one of them. Jane had met him before and thought he was a good possibility. Foisy kept her waiting in the small, sterile reception area, while visitors came, signed in for their visitor ID badges and were escorted through one of the small doors. There were two big black limos outside the front door. Jane guessed that meant the famous President of Commonweal, "Black Jack" Serota was there. Everybody would be nervous. "Black Jack came in and beat me to a pulp," they would boast to one another. On the other hand, it might be good news for her. Foisy was a financial man. He wasn't getting along with Black Jack. Few beyond Jack's sons and his inner circle did for long. It might mean Foisy could be lured away.

Forty minutes after she arrived Foisy came down for her, looking flustered. He was a tall, broad, sandy-looking man, with pale beady eyes. He was dressed in the uniform of the American financial man — a light grey suit, blue-and-grey striped tie. The suit was creased at the back vent.

Jane didn't like Greg Foisy. He moved around from job to job too fast for her taste. And neither she nor Brian were fans of Commonweal's business practices. On the other hand, he knew the software business, and he had taken two smallish Canadian companies public, very profitably, before being wooed away by Commonweal to run their acquisition division. He had a reputation for competence, which could be an asset for BTS.

"Have you had lunch?" he asked now. "No? Good, let's get out of here. It's like a hornet's nest in here today. Jack is on the warpath. Got a rented car? Good. Let's take that. Know where the Library restaurant is? In Westchester? Let's go there. Everybody will be eating in today to impress Black.

"So what kind of a peanuts Canadian outfit are you scouting for today, Jane?"

Jane told herself to behave. She looked out the window at the poor condition of the highway, the abandoned mills and rundown auto-repair shops. This area always looked to her like an undeveloped part of northern Ontario, but of course, the opposite was true. The tide of industrialization had risen and now had receded, leaving the detritus of abandoned nineteenth-century and early twentieth-century industry. To Jane, management ideas of those times — cruel, heartless and inefficient — had not, in the end, allowed these industries to survive. Now some high-tech companies like Commonweal had chosen this area for their homes. But wasn't it the same kind of thinking as that of the heartless capitalists of the past century — putting high-tech companies in places where the key people wouldn't enjoy working? The competition in the computer business was vicious: on the one side were the staid, older firms which gave no quarter and held governments and whole industries in the palm of its hand; on the other were hungry start-up firms, selling below cost, ruthless price cutting, brilliant innovators, and a technology that moved so fast today's wizard was tomorrow's old fogey. You had to stay ahead to survive, but suppose you were ahead on the wrong road? Suppose the pack you thought were following you had taken another fork? Right over the leading edge, Jane thought. These weren't the sort of thoughts she could share with Greg Foisy. He was still talking.

"All those companies are so coddled by your government it's a joke. We looked at buying a Canadian company, Plus Computer. Know why we backed out? Their machine cost more to make than what they were selling it for. Government money does that."

Jane felt like telling him what she thought of Commonweal, but she kept her feelings to herself. She knew Foisy was just starting the bargaining.

"Does that mean you wouldn't be interested in a Canadian offer? Even if it were very, very sweet?"

"Hey, who said that? A man is always willing to talk. Talk doesn't cost anything."

The Library restaurant was very pleasant. Books everywhere, and a menu that included healthy-sounding salads. Jane took out her embossed leather portfolio and her gold Cross pen. She lined these things up neatly on the table. "This company, although it's Canadian, is about to merge with a successful U.S. firm. So you could end up being VP of finance for the merged firm. Or write yourself a nice ticket."

"Hey, now you're talking. Tell me more. What business are they in?"

"The service side. Data processing. Custom software. On mainframes."

"Yech. That's a bo-or-oring business."

"Maybe to you. But this is a very exciting little firm. A hundred and fifty percent growth the last three years. Twenty percent return. Top management team of only six people. Very lean management. You'd be second after the president, who leaves the money side of the business all to the VP of finance."

"Sounds too good to be true. Let me guess. There's only two or three firms anything like that." He named them, including BTS. "Am I right?"

"Maybe. Would you be interested?"

"I think so. But this is like dancing in the dark. I gather it's a public company. Sooner or later you're going to have to tell me what it is."

It's thin ice I'm on, Jane thought. If he puts my talk of merger together with BTS, I'll have told more than I should. I'll just have to bluff it. "Yes. And you're going to have to agree, in writing, not to reveal the information I give you, and not to trade or cause to be traded any of this company's shares while we're talking and for six weeks hereafter."

Foisy ordered a Coke. Jane thought she'd need a clear head, too. She ordered a Perrier and chicken pot pie. The waitress was friendly. Too friendly. She'd told them her name was Nancy. Jane hated it when waitresses did that. It made it seem as if the waitress wanted to be her friend. Jane always found the first few days in the States hard to get used to.

"That's no problem for me," Foisy was saying. "I know too much about this business to invest in it. I have all my money in low-tech stocks."

"How about moving back to Canada? Any problem there?"

"Nope," Foisy said. "I've divorced since we talked last."

"Sorry to hear that," Jane said perfunctorily. She didn't want to talk about Foisy's personal life.

Jane outlined the compensation package, keeping it as vague as she could. "I've told them about you, without giving them your name. They're very interested. What do you think?"

"I think we should pursue this," Greg Foisy said.

"You ready to leave Commonweal, then?" Jane asked. He seemed too eager, too interested. She knew he was making slightly more at Commonweal than they'd offered. Trouble at Commonweal? she wondered. Were they in real trouble? Maybe some more fruit would fall off the tree cheaply. Foisy seemed to pick up on her thought. "You headhunters are a bit like vultures, swooping over the carcass, aren't you?"

Things must be even worse here than I thought, she told herself. Vultures, carcasses.

"Tell me what the job looks like, will you?" he said.

Jane felt her insides tighten. Here was where it was going to get rough. Sooner or later she'd have to put some of the cards on the table, or there could be lawsuits. People like Foisy sued. Americans sued very easily. Was Foisy an American? She couldn't remember. It mattered. If he were there'd be hoops to go through to get him permission to work. She'd slipped up, not checking on that. How could she have forgotten? Stupid, stupid. Now she had to ask.

"No, Canadian, born in Prince Albert, if you can believe that. No problem there. But I like doing business in the

States. It's your talk about the merger that's got me. Lots of action there. I like action."

"This merger is tricky," Jane said. "The management group is split on it."

"But the head honcho must want it, right?"

"Yes, that's right."

"Well that's S.O.P., then — standard operating procedure."

"I know what S.O.P. means," Jane said.

"Hey, no offence meant."

"Have you handled anything like that before?"

"I've handled all of Commonweal's acquisitions. Trial by fire. I know how the game is played down here. I think you'll find I'm the right man for this."

Jane knew Brian would like Foisy's aggressiveness. It's what he thought was needed to deal with the U.S. firm. But could Foisy be trusted? Would he carry out Brian's agenda or his own? Could he be controlled? Brian would put a great deal of weight on Jane's opinion, her evaluation of Foisy. Jane didn't like Foisy, but she had dealt with a lot of these high-powered types. They had their place. Overrated, Jane thought. Quiet competence was much, much better, but hard to find. Foisy was good. Look how he'd backed Commonweal off the Plus deal. She'd known Plus Computers was in trouble, and she'd thought Commonweal would snap it up at what appeared to be a bargain-basement price, then be stuck with having paid bargain basement for a sinkhole. But it looked as if Foisy had known enough not to do that, and he had what it took to kill a deal at the eleventh hour. Jane respected that. Foisy would probably be able to find BTS an alternate American partner, too, if that became necessary. But here he was, a rat leaving a ship just because it had a few holes below the waterline, long before it was sinking. Still he hadn't said anything indiscreet. Not really. That was a good sign.

She fell asleep on the plane back to Toronto. When she awoke, as the lights came on, her mouth felt thick and fuzzy. A taste she associated with guilt. Why was she feeling guilty? After thinking about it for a minute, she realized why. She'd targeted Foisy for BTS because she didn't like him; that way, if disaster struck again, she wouldn't have set up someone she cared about. It was a very unpleasant realization. By the time she reached her apartment she had a bad attack of stomach cramps. She didn't sleep that night, kept awake by diarrhea and vomiting. The adrenalin flashes kept coming, driving her to the bathroom. Between bouts she lay on a towel on the bathroom floor tasting bile. She felt very lonely and the night seemed endless. She kept telling herself that she'd had nights like this before, been afraid before. But she'd been able to handle things after all, and usually everything had worked out well. So this one, too, would pass, she thought. She couldn't even remember those things that once frightened her so much. But she still wasn't comforted.

She remembered Orloff's telling her that the blood on the floor always equalled the amount of money involved. If there's not enough blood on the floor, he said, you don't have the deal. It was a law that, in her experience, had always held true. As you moved up into the bigger money, you found yourself among people who fought harder and who stuck their knives in deeper. But then there were people like Brian Taylor. She could respect him. Kersti had to be wrong about him when she'd said he couldn't be as good as he seemed. It might be harder to do things the right way, but it had to be better in the long run. Wouldn't the heartless and the dirty fighters discredit themselves eventually? Wouldn't they leave behind a trail of people they had hurt, who would give them no quarter next time, people who wouldn't take their word, people who didn't want to do business with them? Jane hoped so. Look at Commonweal, she thought. They had pumped out thousands of shoddy game computers, forced them on their dealers. Now they were in trouble, their new products being accepted warily by retailers and consumers.

On the other hand, look at some of the big firms. No one doubted the quality of their products, but those in the business would tell one story after another of how they had crushed the life out of their competitors. Maybe you just had to be very, very, very big, Jane thought sadly. For the one indisputable fact about her own situation was that she was very, very small.

In the morning she managed to swallow some weak, green tea. Pale sun shone in on the kitchen table, lighting her glass mug and causing faint, reflective sparkles to shiver on the wall. She knew she ought to eat something, but she was already late. She always found it hard to get going in the morning. She hated mornings. Her thoughts had raced fruitlessly all night; now, in the morning, she saw that Martin Kaplan had been right. Eddie Orloff had been right. No matter how ridiculous it seemed, how unlikely, she would have to find the murderer before she signed up someone. And she had to find someone quickly. Toronto would be full of rumours; soon the rumours would reach the potential candidates, reach the police. . . . The company would be torpedoed.

There must be someone who knew more, who could help her. Not the police. That was out. The way she had behaved with Barrodale and Pearkes wouldn't give her much credibility. Surely they'd known she was lying.

Eddie Orloff wanted her to fail. He was counting on it, in fact. He'd like to justify his view that he shouldn't have made her an associate, that he'd been pressured into it against his better judgment. If I can't handle this by myself, she thought, I won't last much longer at Orloff Associates. Eddie likes presence. He likes big, strong people. Eddie would like to get rid of me, she thought. Nothing else explains his unsupportive attitude. I'm making money for the firm, I bring in business. But Eddie doesn't want me to succeed at Orloff Associates. Eddie doesn't like or respect me, Jane thought. He's looking for any excuse to get rid of me. If I go down on this one. . . .

22

"So what's the news at BTS?" Eddie Orloff was breezy, as if he had never shouted at Jane, threatened her, bullied her. Wouldn't you like to know, she thought. Especially if I picked up accurately what Brian hinted at about you, especially if you think I'm going to screw this up so badly that the takeover won't go through, and so you're selling short. Were you just trying to rattle me, scare me? Is that your idea of how to motivate me?

Jane put on a worried expression. She said defensively, "I'm doing the best I can. But these things take time. You know that."

"Yeah," Orloff said. They were in his office. He was leaning back in his leather-and-chrome, executive-size tilting chair. "Take too much time, cookie, and you'll blow the whole thing."

Jane always found it hard to get used to Orloff's abrupt changes in tone. He was an accomplished linguist. He had learned English at school, in England, as a young boy. He had been sent there from France, by his Russian émigré parents. But he had learned another English from the GIs in the war. He had a tendency to shift abruptly. To his clients he had a suave English style; for his staff he often adopted the rough persona of an American drill sergeant, or so Jane explained it to herself. She had heard he could do the same thing in several languages, switching tone to suit his purpose. It doesn't do to forget that Orloff is a very smart man, she warned herself. "I've got Greg Foisy, now at Commonweal. I've got two really good people in Chicago that Brian and I are going to see tomorrow. Maybe a third, too."

"No women? I'm surprised at you."

Jane didn't think the comment deserved an answer.

"They all have good qualifications, I suppose?"

"Brian Taylor is very particular," Jane said. "He doesn't trust anybody whose background is business or who grew up in banking or finance. The person has to know software. And has to have had experience in joint-marketing deals, mergers, things like that."

"Tough," Orloff said. "Guys like that don't grow on trees. Does he want people who have had experience with takeovers?"

"He hasn't said so," Jane said, her mind focussing sharply on the conversation. Careful, careful, she told herself. "At first they called what was going on a joint-marketing agreement. Now I'm hearing it's a merger. And Eddie, that's absolutely confidential. But that's all I've heard. I'm not sure where these takeover rumours are coming from."

Orloff picked up his pen, unscrewed the top and rolled the fat, black plastic tube back and forth under one long finger, before letting it rest on the shiny expanse of his mahogany desk-top. Jane noticed that his note paper had an extravagant monogram pressed into the top. It was only visible if the light shone on it at a certain angle. Orloff put his pen point down on the centre of the paper. From this point he began to draw a whorl, an ever-increasing connected series of concentric circles. "Let's just say they're around," he said. "Is Taylor satisfied at the speed things are going? I mean, when does he say he has to have the new man by?"

"What does it matter? Why do you ask?"

"Just trying to gauge how much pressure our little Ms Tregar is under, that's all," Orloff said. "I told you a week ago you had three days before the police came down on us to have the thing settled and get the hell out of there. Lucky for you the police have held back. I was just wondering if Taylor is feeling the heat, that's all."

"Yes," Jane said. "He seems very anxious. We've started interviewing. But I don't think I can meet your timetable. So I've been ignoring it."

"What the hell do you mean?" Orloff shouted. His Mont Blanc pen made a big blob on the outer edge of the whorl.

Jane could feel her heart bang against the wall of her chest. But she said very quietly, "I have to do what I think is best for the client. I have my own business principles to think of. And they are not being helped by the suggestion that you are selling BTS shares short."

She looked at Orloff. He looked directly back at her. He showed no anger. Only that icy, assessing look she'd seen before. This time she didn't let herself shrink under it. She hoped he couldn't hear the sound of her heart. "That is the biggest pile of B.S. I've ever heard," he said calmly. "You can forget it. But I'd like to know who said it."

"Nobody said it," Jane said. She was calmer now. I just might get away with this, she thought. "I picked up on something Brian Taylor said, that's all. I probably misunderstood."

Orloff drew a horizontal line on top of his whorl, then enclosed it in a square. He drew a door on the front, carefully sketching in the doorknob. At least Jane, looking at the drawing upside-down, thought it was a door. What else could it be?

"Of course you misunderstood," Orloff said genially, "because you know that's against company policy here."

"Yes, I know that," Jane said. "I also know it's company policy to stand behind one another, to do the best we can for a client, to put a client first."

Having diverted the conversation from the shares, Orloff apparently felt safe enough to bully her again. He banged down his pen. "Not at the expense of this firm, it's not! Don't you ever think that for one minute! Survival! That's still the name of the game around here, little lady."

Suddenly Jane found that she could not bear the conversation. Maybe it was the "little lady." She stood up abruptly and began to walk out.

"Is that all you have to say?" he called after her.

Jane said, without turning to look at him, "I'm doing my best. I'll go on doing it. I won't resign. If you decide to fire me, let me know."

As she closed the door Orloff said, his voice sarcastic, "Brava, little lady, brava."

Hateful man, Orloff, Jane thought. She was walking up Yonge Street holding the bottle of wine she had just purchased. She was to have dinner with Tom Henege at his house that night, "a friendly dinner," he had assured her. But she wasn't thinking of Tom. She turned her collar up and pulled her fur hat down over her face to keep the harsh snow from stinging her skin. I'll never understand Orloff, not as long as I live. Never. Tom's house was within walking distance of the Rosedale liquor store. She had decided to leave her car in the parking lot there and walk. His was one of the thin, rose-coloured brick townhouses on MacPherson Avenue. She felt in scale as soon as she stepped inside the door. Everything was small and narrow. She could see into the living-room from the front hall. Lots of Ontario stripped-pine furniture, baskets of dried flowers, low, soft, down-cushioned chairs, covered with chintz in muted colours — browns, beiges, creamy white.

He took her coat and brushed his cheek against hers in a sketch of a kiss; she smelled aftershave, and more faintly, food.

A fire burned in the small fireplace. The firelight glanced off the hand-painted tiles around the fireplace and the carved pine mantelpiece. "I wonder if things are getting totally reversed or what," Jane said. "Here you have this beautiful cosy place, firelight, flowers, matching furniture, and all that. And I've got a Sally Ann apartment and can't cook."

He smiled. "It's a nice thought, but all this is my ex-wife's doing — not that I don't appreciate it. I pretend I could do as well if I started from scratch. But I have this feeling that any place I fixed up would look like a suburban garage sale. And my cooking's an illusion. I've only got three dishes; after that you'll have to invite me over to your place."

Jane smiled. She sat down on the seat built into the coat-rack. It was one of those early farmhouse pieces with a mirror set into the carved back and a seat that lifted up so you could store gloves and mitts inside. Her boot stuck, and she tugged at it. Tom stood watching her. Finally she got both boots off, and sank down into one of the soft chairs in the living-room. "Why didn't your wife take some of this?"

"She wanted to start fresh. New love, new house." His tone was detached, slightly ironic. "I think she lost interest in the marriage when she finished decorating the house.

Her new place is much nicer — art deco. It cost me a small fortune, but fighting with her over money helped me to heal my broken heart, so why should I complain? Anyway, she tells me she couldn't take any of this; unpainted pine is completely passé now, apparently."

"I didn't know," said Jane, reognizing his bitterness and not wanting to hear about his marriage.

"No champagne today," he said, handing her a glass of red wine. "It doesn't go with my dinner."

Tom went into the kitchen to stir the soup, and Jane curled up in the cushions of the chair, thinking, as she had been off and on all day, about Eddie Orloff. Sometimes she thought their conversation was a subtle one, where she threatened him by hinting she *knew* he was selling BTS short, and he capitulated. Sometimes she thought she was incredibly stupid, and all that had happened was she would find that on the deadline day, she was fired. And no court would back her up, because she had said that she wouldn't even attempt to meet the conditions her boss had set out for her.

Things had seemed impossible before: she had only to deal with whether or not Gary Levin was murdered, identify the murderer, watch her back . . . but now it seemed she *had* to find out what was going on, what Brian Taylor was up to. Was it a merger or a takeover? She felt ashamed of herself, accepting Tom's warmth and hospitality, when her real purpose was business. To see what she could find out. All part of the game, she told herself.

They ate dinner in the kitchen. It had been completely remodelled with gleaming copper, red quarry tile, pine cupboards and a butcher-block table. Jane let Tom lead the conversation. He talked, in a self-deprecating way, about travel, the places he liked, the customs of the countries where he had worked. He told her about selling in Japan.

He liked to tell stories about himself; he told Jane about times he had made a fool of himself, about deals he had screwed up through stupidity.

Jane found herself talking about Eddie Orloff. She told Tom how Orloff bullied her, how he had threatened her that if she couldn't wrap things up satisfactorily at BTS he'd dump her. Tom shook his head. "Maybe you don't know how lucky you are dealing with a guy like that. Everything he is, right there on the table. You always know where you are."

"You can't be serious. Being chewed out by someone like Orloff is like being mauled by a tiger."

"Okay, but look at our situation at BTS. For years we've all believed in Brian. We've trusted him. Now we don't know what's going on. I think every kind of terrible thought."

"What do you mean?"

"Here are some of the terrible thoughts. Let's say Brian is going to sell out, maybe take Robert with him. Maybe I'd be kept on — it's possible. But Martin and Martha would be redundant. If the marketing people in the U.S. firm don't want me, or if the U.S. firm is top-heavy, I might be redundant too. Or shuttled off to something I don't like. After all, the Canadian market is barely a tenth of the American one. I imagine what Brian would think — that he'd have to offer me head of Canadian sales, that I'd report to a VP of marketing in the States. And Brian knows I wouldn't go for that.

"I don't think you have any idea how driven Brian Taylor is. When he wants something he keeps going until he gets it. I've watched him over the years. He's patient; he's like a cat stalking its prey. He'll wait a long time at the mousehole, and the mouse gets away he'll keep on chasing it. Sometimes I wonder, did he think he could get this deal through and then dump Gary? What if that was what he was planning? And Gary found out? What was Gary doing at the office when we were all in that meeting? Maybe snooping around Brian's files? Probably the safest time he could find. A good reason not to come to the meeting — or at least that's what I think when I wake up in the middle of the night and can't sleep."

"I've worked with Brian Taylor closely, really got to know him," Jane said. "He's not that kind of man. Maybe you're being a little paranoid."

"You know the old saw. . . ."

"Just because you're paranoid doesn't mean nobody's following you."

They both laughed.

"No, Tom, really," Jane said. "I think it's more like the joke about the two psychiatrists. They meet in the elevator. One says hello. The other one thinks, I wonder what he meant by that?"

They took their coffee and returned to the living-room. Jane curled up on one end of the sofa, her feet tucked under her. Tom took the other end. He stretched out, his stocking feet almost touching her thighs. Lamplight fell on his face, shadowing it, making him look blurred and indistinct. He had strong features. She admired his straight, well-shaped nose, firm lips and the nice cleft in his chin. How peculiar, Jane thought. I want him. It seemed easy, obvious. I'll just relax, see what happens. But unless he's expecting to make love, she then thought, nothing can happen. I'm not on the pill, haven't used my diaphragm for years. . . .

"I know what you're thinking," Tom was saying. "You're thinking, even if Brian Taylor is planning to dump us and sell out, it wouldn't be a motive for murder, right?"

Jane smiled. She wondered what Tom would do if he realized that she had in fact been thinking of reaching out and caressing his leg. She tucked her hands under her thighs. "What about that?" she said.

"It seems unlikely, I know. But how can we get away from the fact that one of us at BTS murdered Gary Levin? And the motive must have been related to what's going on at BTS now. Gary wasn't a hateful man. Or at least, we'd all had run-ins with him, but I just can't see that he was the sort of man who could arouse real murderous hate in anyone. I feel pretty strongly about that. So you can't help but conclude, that one of us is a bit . . . over the edge about BTS. What I mean is, I think there's enough feeling, enough passion about power and control at BTS that you could start to imagine someone killing to hold onto their perch there. But I don't believe Gary himself could arouse such feelings."

Jane was having difficulty concentrating. When she spoke her voice was husky. "You look nice in the lamplight like that," she said.

He opened his eyes wider and smiled at her. The smile was friendly. "Thanks. So how to figure Brian, what he's up to — that's got to be the key. That's why I think you're better off with Orloff. Don't you think so?"

It's all for the best, probably, Jane told herself. I'm probably just turned on because he's not. "I told you," she said, "I trust Brian Taylor, I always have."

Tom sat up suddenly. He turned to her. "You know, some people think you and Taylor were lovers years ago. Maybe it's true. But let me tell you, he's a very subtle man. Just for starters, do you know what he said about hiring you?"

Jane had a feeling something bad was coming. "No."

"Taylor laughed about it," Tom said. "He told me, 'Tregar will do whatever I want. Trust makes her loyal.

She'll keep Gary's death quiet. She's ambitious, but I know how she'll jump.' How do you like the sound of that?"

"Not much," Jane said, suppressing her hurt.

"*Were* you lovers?" Tom said suddenly, looking at her. Jane shook her head.

"You can tell me — I'm a friend," he said.

"What difference does it make? Who cares?"

"Now don't get mad. I'm sorry. I want to know, that's all. I don't know why." They looked at one another for a moment. He cleared his throat. "I think it's time for you to go home, Jane."

"What if I don't want to?"

"I want you to go home," he said. "I'll walk you to your car. You left it at the liquor store? I'll bring a shovel. It's been snowing for the last few hours."

"No need, I have a shovel in my trunk," she said trying to hide her resentment and act as if his rejection meant nothing to her.

He helped her on with her coat. He turned her face toward him and caressed her cheek. She trapped his hand and pressed it hard against her cheek and moved toward him, but he pulled his hand away, put on his coat and let her out into the snowy darkness. They didn't speak as they walked to the parking lot and as he shoveled the snow out from around the car. He watched until she had safely backed out and turned onto the road. Then he waved, and she drove slowly along the snow-bound street.

Why? Jane thought. I wanted to, and he knew it. Why? I don't understand anything. What was he telling me about Brian Taylor? Why didn't he let me stay? As she puzzled over it, her desire ebbed, and relief replaced it. Of course, he's right, it's all for the best. Things are already too complicated. This is one complication I can do without.

23

Brian and Jane were taking the 2:10 United flight from Toronto to Chicago. Jane had files she wanted to go over before the three interviews they had scheduled, and she assumed Brian, too, would want to work on the flight, because he was to meet with top executives in the firm with which BTS was negotiating. As well, she had things on her mind, things that made her feel on edge, unwilling to talk to Brian as if everything were the same as usual between them.

But Brian was in a talkative mood. First he asked Jane about Chicago, about her childhood there, about how she felt about growing up in one country and then working in another. He told her he felt at a disadvantage, being so Canadian, so knit into the Canadian way of doing business. He said he felt this most strongly in his negotiations with the Americans, which was one reason he was hoping to get a vice-president of finance with a good deal of American experience.

He had a couple of drinks, which was unusual for Brian in the middle of the day, and Jane thought that he was more anxious about the negotiations than he was admitting.

Then he told her that he'd had a bad fight with his wife the night before. "I can't understand it," he said to Jane. "I just asked her for her advice, and all of a sudden, out of nowhere, she just blew up at me."

"That can't be all there is to it," Jane said. "What did you say to her?"

"Well, I told her a little about some of the problems we're having, about what's been on my mind lately, and then I asked her what she thought. And then, boom. I didn't know what hit me. She said that I ignored her for weeks on end, then suddenly wanted her to be there, and that she couldn't turn on and off like a faucet."

He looked bewildered, and Jane felt sorry for him.

"I really don't get it," he said, staring into his glass. "Dahlia knows how much BTS means to me. She knows what it takes to build a business. She's always been behind me, never complained about anything. Where did this all come from?"

"Did you ask her to explain?"

"Of course I did. I told her that I loved her, that I'd never do anything to hurt her . . . and do you know what she said? She said she knew that, but that it wasn't the point."

"Dahlia's a writer, isn't she?"

"Yes, that's right. And that's another thing. She brought up the fact that I didn't read her last two books. But, one, she knows I don't read fiction; and two, when I did read her stuff, and commented on it, she hated that. So it seems that I can't win."

"Well," Jane said. "I'm the last one to try to give advice on marriage, having made such a mess of my own. But it sounds to me like you two need a good long talk."

"You're right," said Brian. "That's what we'll do. As soon as I'm through with all this, as soon as I bring it off. . . ." His voice trailed off, and he turned and looked out the window. They were coming in over the city, but all that could be seen were layers of grey mist, through which they now began to descend.

When the plane landed at O'Hare, they both rose, and Jane, who had the aisle seat, reached up to get their brief-cases. As she handed Brian his he looked at her in a way she found somehow troubling and said, "Thanks, Jane. It always seems to help, talking to you. Thanks for your advice."

What advice? Jane thought, as she followed the queue out of the airplane and into the terminal. She was annoyed with Brian and wished that he'd kept his private life to himself. She'd found the conversation unsettling in a way she didn't understand.

As they walked down the long corridors of the airport, Jane forgot about Brian's uncharacteristic confidences. Instead she was remembering their earlier conversation on the plane. The airport seemed both familiar and strange; it brought back a rush of feelings she associated with Chicago, feelings from ten or fifteen years earlier.

She had been born and raised on the south side of Chicago. It was not a city she had been sorry to leave. Canada had been a revelation to her: not to be afraid to walk around outside at night, not to cringe internally as one passed from a rich and glossy neighbourhood to the waste-land of slums and housing projects. She had liked the lack of ostentation, of showiness, of public displays of wealth or power that made the surface of Canadian life seem dull, but that was far preferable to her.

The taxi, unlike the taxis in Toronto, was filthy inside. There was an old newspaper and candy wrapper on the floor, a greasy salt-stained rubber mat instead of a carpet, rips in the vinyl seat.

Coming south along the Kennedy, the city skyline took

shape, unfamiliar to her, so changed was it from her child-hood. Now the giant Sears tower, and to the east of it the Hancock Building, almost as large, dominated the skyline; each was topped with its twin antennae, the aircraft warning lights blinking.

They drove along Ohio Street east to Michigan Avenue, where the glossy storefronts drew Jane's eyes — Saks and I. Magnin and Neiman-Marcus, filled with Christmas merchandise, rich furs, dresses glittering in the small display spotlights, with bugle beads and paillettes, and sequins. The bare trees that lined the street were laced with garlands of tiny lights; these she remembered. She thought those same lights must have decorated Michigan Avenue for twenty-five years. The famous landmark, the old water tower, now looked small compared to the new, white marble Water Tower skyscraper across the street and the black column of the Hancock Building. But she remembered the creamy stone of the old water tower, supposedly the only relic of the great Chicago fire, and she admired it now standing floodlit in its small plaza. Their hotel, the Park Hyatt, which flanked it, was new to her.

The Hyatt's lobby, though plush with taupe-coloured velvet wing-chairs, Chinese chests, coffee tables and pillars of travertine, did not prepare her for the large two-bedroom suite Brian had reserved.

It was enormous. There was a hallway, off which was the bedroom that she would use; it had its own bathroom and the two rooms could be completely closed off from the large sitting-room and dining-room and the second bedroom. The dining-room and sitting-room were filled with glass-topped tables, Chippendale-style side chairs, and what seemed to Jane to be Chinese antiques. The sitting-room, besides its grey, velvet-covered sofa and chairs, its antique desk with the *Wall Street Journal* neatly spread out on the leather desk blotter, had a wet bar and a refrigerator filled with full-size bottles of white wine, as well as the usual miniatures. On a glass tea trolley were crystal decanters of Scotch, bourbon and brandy. The rooms Brian would use off the sitting-room, and had two televisions, one in the bedroom and one in the bathroom, where there was also a sunken bathtub with a marble surround, two telephones and a stock of expensive toiletries.

Back in her own room Jane opened the curtains and looked out. Michigan Avenue stretched beneath her, the hard little lights glittering on the trees like icicles. She had forty-five minutes before her first appointment, not enough time to go shopping, she thought. Business travel never felt like real travel — one seemed only to see the insides of hotels and restaurants — but she found it glamorous just the same. Today, however, she felt surprisingly lonely. Brian had not even come up to the suite; he had gone directly to a meeting at the Chicago firm with which BTS was negotiating. So Jane was alone in the suite, waiting for her first interview, which she had decided to do without Brian. She thought it was strange how the sterile lushness of the hotel made her think of sexual adventure. She imagined herself going down to the bar and picking up some interesting man, and bringing him back to this suite. She went into her bathroom and studied her face in the mirror. Her skin was still smooth, marred only by lines of strain under her eyes. In the artful make-up lights her hair looked blond, glinting with silvery lights. Jane looked closer at the silvery lights and saw with astonishment that they were grey hairs. She tugged angrily at one until it came out. She turned it over, looking at it. It had a dull gleam and looked slightly kinky. She studied herself, found others, and pulled them out too. Her life hadn't really started yet; she was just getting warmed up, getting the hang of it. She had no security and she didn't understand how things worked yet. How could she be getting grey hairs?

She knew she would never have gone down to the bar and picked up a man, not when she was younger, because she would have been too frightened to do it. And not now, because that free-floating lust that had once animated her seemed to have completely chilled. But soon, perhaps, it wouldn't be possible. She would never know what it was like to sleep with a man she didn't really know. She wanted to find out, but not enough.

The telephone rang, and a gravelly voice announced Ernest Lochinsky. She told him to come up, giving him the number of the sitting-room. How much easier it would be if Ernest Lochinsky were a woman. A whole class of problems, of difficulties in communications, of signals one had to avoid giving inadvertently, would go away. But there were very few women in the software business. And at the higher levels of business finance in Canada, Jane didn't think she knew of any. Besides, it would be naïve to think that the Blumbergs would accept a woman in the position. It will come, Jane told herself, using the future as reassurance.

Lochinsky was a very big man, massively overweight. Jane had met him seven years ago when he had piloted several new issues onto the Toronto Stock Exchange, and made a lot of money for himself and others doing it. She had interviewed him for her magazine. Then he had been in his early thirties, slender, with theatrical good looks, wavy auburn hair and a moustache beautifully trimmed, an elegantly cut pin-striped suit, and buffed fingernails. His walk had been almost a run, his telephone voice implied someone more important was waiting on hold, and his briefcase had a gleam that suggested that inside were contracts worth millions.

Now Lochinsky weighed close to three hundred pounds.

His hair was sparse and poorly cut; in the back it wisped over his collar. His blue eyes were washed out and full, and his suit jacket strained slightly as he sat down on the sofa opposite Jane. She offered him a drink and he accepted eagerly.

He wore a big gold ring, with a large, dull-looking diamond on one finger, and a Piaget gold watch. He opened his briefcase, which was covered with scratches and a large stain of the kind one gets when one uses one's briefcase for a foot-rest on airplanes, and took out a gold Cross pen and a Lucite clipboard.

"You wouldn't believe how cold it is out there," he said to Jane, as he arranged some papers on the coffee table. "It's unreal."

Jane nodded. "Have you had a chance to look over the papers I sent you?"

"Just glanced at them," Lochinsky said. "We've been incredibly busy." He shifted on to one hip and took a gold card-case out of his pocket. Extending it toward Jane, he pressed a lever, and an embossed card popped out.

Jane took the card. Ernest Lochinsky and Associates, Venture Capital, it said. Jane turned it over, running her finger over the type. The card had a small, gold-embossed crest above Lochinsky's name, and was larger than most cards. "We're getting ready to take Biochip public. Have you heard about Biochip? No? They were written up in *Forbes* last month. I'll send you a tearsheet. That's where the action is now, in the biology companies . . . very little going on in software. D'you see where I'm coming from?"

"Well, if you're involved in your own business . . ." Jane began.

"Always on the lookout for new challenges," Lochinsky said. He leaned back on the sofa and put his shoes on the coffee table. Jane saw that the soles were worn, scratched and salt-stained. The heels were rundown. "I bet I know who you're acting for. Mind if I guess?"

"I'd rather you didn't," Jane said. "I can't comment until we've gone a little further into this."

Lochinsky grimaced. Jane noticed his face was tense and anxious. "I'm not sure it will be productive for us to talk unless we get some cards out on the table. I know the Toronto business scene pretty well, and — I don't mean to put you down, but most of it is pretty Mickey Mouse compared to the action here in the States."

"Is that so?" Jane said.

Lochinsky steepled his hands together and held their edges over his mouth. His words were mumbled. "Thinking about what you told me on the telephone, seems to me the key here is the compensation package. I mean, I have to know what the firm is before I can put a dollar value on the stocks and options. . . ."

"I think we're getting a little ahead of ourselves," Jane said. "I'd like to talk to you first about your experience in the kind of situation I described, so I can get an understanding of how you'd fit in." Lochinsky leaned forward and drank greedily from his glass. Jane wondered if the obvious deterioration in Lochinsky was caused by a drinking problem, and feeling rather disgusted with herself, she refilled his glass from the decanter. Lochinsky watched her as she sat down, and Jane realized that his eyes were focussed on her breasts. "I was saying . . ." she began.

"Listen, Jane," Lochinsky said, picking up his drink, and holding it so that the diamond in his ring flashed in the lamplight, "unless you are talking really major conglomerate merger, then I have to say, frankly, that anything *you* represent would be pretty small potatoes for me. Don't forget, even when you knew me I was handling deals in the 50- to 100-million dollar range. Do you hear me?"

"There are some very significant amounts involved," Jane said.

Lochinsky's eyes glittered. "Then I would say I could be a real help to your client. With my knowledge of the TSE and all the top financial people in Canada, and my experience in the States — frankly, there're just not too many people with my qualifications. To be perfectly honest with you, I think the question we've got to get on the table is, can these people afford me?"

"Let's just back up a minute," Jane said. "My client needs to be satisfied about *your* qualifications first. They've put knowledge of the industry as the first priority for this position."

Lochinsky leaned forward and waved his hand, holding the now-empty whisky glass, at Jane. "Then that's where your client is wrong. Completely. Out to lunch. Typically Canadian. If you're talking joint venture or merger, you're talking business. It could be consumer, it could be resources, it could be communications, it could be high-tech. It's how you structure the deal that counts. D'you think Philbro-Salomon or J. Boone Pickens are good because they know their industries? Be serious. It's street smarts you need to deal with the Americans. That's why Canadians always get taken to the cleaners.

"And Jane," he said, crossing his feet one over the other on the coffee table, "I don't say that because I don't know software. Because I do. I was senior systems analyst for B.C. Systems; we put the place together, and we organized the entire data-processing infrastructure of the province of New Brunswick. That was long before you knew me in Toronto, when I was just in my late twenties. Let's be honest, Jane, that stuff is child's play. When we put together the deal between Tamen, who are the biggest German-Italian mass consumer merchandiser, and Archibold Foods, I didn't need to know bugger all about mass merchandising food. It was putting together the package and selling it. And you know Gerard St. Michel? He's the top arbitrager in New York. He was on the cover of *The New York Times Magazine* last week? He said to me the other day that the Tamen-Archibold deal was one of the smartest things he'd seen in the business in a long time. D'you see where I'm coming from?"

For a moment Jane wondered if it were true. Could there be a level of financial manoeuvring where the fact that a man was — as Lochinsky so obviously was — an insensitive boor who had an incredible ego, would be immaterial? Or was she suffering from culture shock at his aggressive, boastful style, something that, perhaps, would not elicit any surprise or distate in U.S. circles? Did BTS really want to consider such a man?

But then she thought of the people at BTS. She knew that none of them could get along with a man who boosted himself at the expense of the person he was talking to, and put down his own country and his own industry.

She knew from some industry gossip that Lochinsky had made a lot of money with his venture-capital firm, but had been caught unawares by the downturn and disappointing performance of some of the most highly touted computer-software companies. Now he needed a high-profile job to lever himself back up again. She had thought he might be suitable, but listening to his conversation, which showed almost every quality she disliked and distrusted, she was sure he would not do.

But Jane reminded herself that things could turn around. The man who was unsuitable, or vulnerable, today, could be in a pivotal position tomorrow. So she managed to smile, and said, "Well, how about I get you another drink, and you can fill me in on what you've been doing for the past five years."

Three drinks later as Lochinsky continued his boasting, Jane, drinking Perrier, could hardly keep her eyes open. She was wearying of everything about him, from the slurping sound he made as he swallowed the last drops of his drink, sieving them up from the ice cubes, to his referring constantly to himself as "we."

Her attention sharpened, however, when she realized that his speech was becoming slurred, and he was asking her out for dinner.

"Alone in Chicago," he was saying, "I could take you to some really sensational clubs. You wouldn't believe what has happened to the north side. What say we forget business for a few hours, have dinner, and then really have some fun?"

"Thank you," Jane said, "but I have a lot of work to do tonight, and my client is joining me this evening." She stood up, gathered together his coat and scarf and started walking toward the door. He came after her and pinned her to the wall in the anteroom with his large stomach, leaning over to give her the ritual kiss on the cheek. But his hand stroked her side and his fingers brushed her breast. Jane shivered with distate and slipped away from him, under his arm, and opened the door to the corridor.

"I'll get in touch with you after I've conferred with my client. . ." she began.

"No, don't bother," Lochinsky said. His mouth turned down in a mean grimace, and Jane could smell whisky on his breath. "To tell you the truth, I don't know why I wasted my time with this interview. From the start, I could see you weren't serious when you wouldn't talk dollars or give the name of your client. And now you're acting like a scared bunny when I come near you. Frankly, Jane, I think you're out of your league, d'you hear what I'm saying?"

Jane stood by the open door. She knew she shouldn't have given him so much to drink, but she had thought it would be a quick way to confirm her opinion of him. Now she had to get rid of him before he really turned ugly. Stifling the desire to defend herself, she said, "I'm sorry if you feel your time was wasted." She took a few steps out into the hall, holding the door open, and he followed her reflexively. She held on to his coat and scarf, and now she handed them to him, at the same time quickly stepping back into the room. "Good night and thanks," she said, shutting the door quickly.

As it closed she heard him mumble, "Waste of time. Dumb broad."

Sighing with relief, she walked back through the dining-room, the sitting-room and into her large bedroom, where she picked up the room-service menu. She didn't think she would have the courage, after Lochinsky, to leave her room and face a dining-room of unfamiliar men. "You've got a lot to learn, Lochinsky," she said aloud. "But nothing can help the fact that you are a complete turd." Feeling better, she turned on the bedroom television and picked up the phone to call room service.

24

Jane was tense. Sitting across from Brian at the breakfast table in the Park Hyatt dining-room, she felt as if both she and Brian were actors in a glamorous play, and she might at any time forget her lines.

Behind Brian on a large plinth was an antique wooden horse, rearing up on its hind legs, looking both graceful and unstable. Beyond, the diners, lit by small ceiling spots, heads tilted toward their morning papers or their business colleagues, were part of the same drama as Brian and Jane, but they, unlike Jane, seemed to be acting their parts with the assurance that the play would never close.

"I'll take your word for it, that I don't have to see Lochinsky," Brian was saying, "although his résumé certainly looked promising. But a drinking problem. . . ."

"Believe me," Jane said, "he wouldn't do at all. You would hate him."

"Okay, if you say so. I'll consider him scratched. Tell me about the two candidates you have lined up for today — Saywell and Craig. They both look good."

Jane's breakfast was croissants and coffee. She had broken the croissants into several pieces and was now restlessly pushing the large flakes of crust into heaps around her plate.

"Saywell is very smooth," she said. "He's bright, and he's driven. Beyond that, I won't say anything until you've met him. I'd like to get your impression." She took a bite of a croissant and carefully wiped the butter from her mouth. She saw that Brian was watching her mouth with a small, almost hungry smile, and when she caught his eye he looked away embarrassed. These moments of attraction, ephemeral, meaningless, were bound to happen when they travelled together, she thought. Best to ignore them. "Craig is less slick — or so it seems," she went on, avoiding his eye, reaching for the jam and spreading it on a crois-sant. "But I'm not sure if that's just another kind of slickness, only more sophisticated. He's very quiet, very understated. He'd get along well at BTS because his manner inspires respect."

"But?" said Brian. "I hear a but in your voice."

"It's not up to me to assess the financial mind of some-one at the level of these two," Jane said. She was choosing her words carefully. This was where she began putting her own plan into action, becoming, she hoped, not only actor, but producer. Seeing how Brian played the part she had cast him in might tell her what she wanted to know, what she had to know. "So that's what you'll have to do. Both of them have pretty impressive records. Craig in particular. Right now he's working for Behrens, the Chicago invest-ment banking firm, and he's put together some of the most sophisticated municipal-bond fundings ever seen around here. Apparently he's known for coming up with new and innovative ways of doing things, so everybody gets what they want. He has a reputation for fair dealing and integ-rity." She put down her coffee and looked right at Brian, letting him see her conviction.

"So where are your doubts coming from?" Brian said, putting down his fork and looking at Jane questioningly.

This time, despite herself, despite all her intentions not to alert him to her concerns, Jane didn't meet his eyes. She stared down at her plate and spoke very softly, almost sadly. Her desire that Brian not disappoint her, not turn out to be what she feared he was, drew out from her words she had not intended to speak. "I don't know, Brian. I don't know what you really want with this. I've got this idea that you have a plan that no one else knows." She smiled, but her mouth had a tight, ironic twist. "I guess there's nothing so unusual in that; in fact it happens more than it doesn't with my clients. But in this case there's so much at stake, and so many people involved — and then there's the murder. Your secrecy makes it almost impossible for me."

"Don't worry, Jane," Brian said, smiling warmly at her. "I'll tell you everything you have to know. So far you're doing just fine."

Jane smiled back at him, and they looked at one another for a moment.

"Why don't we interview the two of them first," Brian said. "I'll lead the interviews. You listen. Then afterward, I'll tell you more, and we can decide where to go from there."

"That's okay with me," Jane said, smiling back at him.

She had given him a chance to confide in her, and he hadn't taken it. So let's see what happens now, she thought, her worry lessened. We'll play it out, and I'll find out what I have to know.

Mark Saywell was a big man, with fine brown hair growing in what looked almost like a tonsure, and a stomach that sloped sleekly out from his chest. Under his well-cut, navy pinstripe he carried his paunch proudly before him like the bow of an ocean liner.

He had a warm smile, a firm handshake and a rich, sincere voice. Brian asked him questions about his interests, his past, his business dealings, and he answered them clearly, concisely, and to the point, but he showed himself always to advantage, and always as the lead player.

They were in the sitting-room of their suite. Jane had ordered up coffee, and Saywell was smoking. He smoked the same small cigars that Gary Levin had smoked, and Jane could see that Brian felt comfortable with him. Perhaps, she thought, those cigars reminded him of the camaraderie he had shared with Gary when things were going well. Saywell had some of the same brashness as Gary, and that same hunger, or greed, or whatever it was for more and bigger, just barely held in check under the polite business clichés. Remembering how Brian had described Gary and how well the two of them had worked together, Jane thought Brian must be drawn to this type of man, no doubt feeling that he supplied some of the qualities that he, Brian, lacked.

Saywell was sitting on the sofa, in an easy, upright position, leaning forward from time to time to tap the ash off his cigar into the big crystal ashtray on the coffee table. Brian sat opposite. Jane sat slightly off to one side, watching both men. Brian seemed scarcely aware of her, he was concentrating on Saywell.

Now the dynamics shifted. Saywell began asking questions, dominating the interview. Brian let him do it. Jane knew that Brian wanted to see this side of the man, see him taking control of a situation, see how he did it. He answered Saywell's questions about the company, about the job, and he even put some numbers on the table. But they were ranges, and when Saywell pressed him for specifics, Brian took back control of the interview.

"Before we get any more specific — and I'll come back to that," Brian said, "I want to try another line of questions. You've told us about your successes, and they sound very good to us. Now, tell us about some of your failures. The roughest ones you've had, the ones that went sour, or almost."

"Failures?" Saywell said musingly. He had a smooth, round, pink face, with small opaque amber eyes and almost colourless lashes and brows. His smile was gentle and warm, matching his tone, but not those hard, determined eyes.

"That's unpleasant — failures. I like to look on the positive side. . . ." His smile broadened, and he turned his cigar around, watching the ash burning. "This isn't really an answer to your question . . . because I couldn't exactly call any of the deals I've worked on *failures*, though of course some went better than others. But once, in England —" he gestured with his cigar "— once we were bidding on a big contract, an electronics contract over there for the PTT, the British post office. I was the financial officer for a new American company. And we were bankrupt, virtually bankrupt. We couldn't even meet our next payroll. It was a twenty-million-dollar contract, I think. And we had to get it. We picked those guys up in a chauffeured limousine, with a driver in white gloves, and took them to lunch at the Savoy, and told them what our company could do for them.

"I got one of the biggest banks in the U.K. to take a seat on our board. It was tough. We had to jump through some pretty slippery hoops. But we got the deal, and then we sold that company for twenty-seven million pounds six months later."

"Where is it now?" Brian asked.

Saywell smiled with pleasure. "It's just been resold for fifteen, but we're out, and we got our major investors out clean. A lot of people said we screwed up that company. They called it a failure. I say we brought it back from the brink. Maybe you heard about it, and that's where your question was coming from?"

Brian looked at Jane who, with an effort, kept her face expressionless.

"We did something similar in the way we used the big names in our start-up of Bio-gen in California two years ago. We were having trouble coming up with the venture capital we needed in the States. But then we got Satsumi, the big Japanese trading company, to pay two million for a seat on the board," Saywell went on, watching Brian to see if he was convinced that any rumours he might have heard about failures could be discounted. "They never said much, language problems I guess, but they were in to learn, and they got their learning experience. And we raised a good chunk of capital based on their being in the game. Maybe they didn't get the inside look at bio-technology they expected, but then it wasn't our business to protect Japan Inc. *Caveat emptor* with the big boys is fair game in my view. We turned that almost-failure around.

"So, I'd have to say, if you're looking for true failures, I'd have trouble coming up with one." He gestured with his free hand. "I guess that's just about the best I can do. Most of the people I work with don't expect failures from me, so I just keep at it until I turn it around. Fair enough? How about now we get back to talking about this position you're trying to fill — and more specifically, the compensation. The cards you've put on the table are interesting enough, but I think we need to shuffle them up a bit and try laying out a few more hands and looking at them again to see what we can come up with, okay?"

The interview with Saywell went on half an hour beyond the time scheduled, and Brian used the short time between that interview, and the one with Craig, to make notes. He seemed not to want to talk to Jane, and she was content with that, knowing that sooner or later he would have to tell her what he thought.

John Craig was very different from Saywell. Slender, dark Mediterranean-looking skin, with thick wavy hair, he must have been an extremely handsome man when young. But now, in his mid-forties, there were deep lines carved from nose to mouth, and frown creases on his forehead. His skin looked rather worn, as if faintly pitted by old acne, or just by the strains of life.

He had a quiet, calm voice, and in the stories he told of his past he always described himself as part of a group. He inspired trust, but there was a suggestion of fanaticism or rigidity in the dark, hard face, in the driven set of the mouth, in the infrequent smile.

Brian had asked both the candidates financial questions, to see how fast they were at mental arithmetic. It was an important skill in bargaining, and though it stood to reason that anybody who had reached this stage in Jane's selection process could sift, re-sift and calculate complex financial calculations mentally, Craig was truly remarkable. He seemed to have almost a multi-plan running in his head, and gave answers far beyond those of Saywell or Foisy. Jane could see that Brian was impressed.

The question about failure brought an interesting response from Craig.

"That's a good question," Craig said. "I like that. Sometimes I think you learn more from failures than from successes. It's almost as if you can build a whole string of successes out of each failure, from what you learn, but it's only chance that allows you to repeat a success you didn't completely understand.

"Yes, I've had my share of failures. Some weren't my fault. Sometimes, for example, in the municipal-bond business, our competitors offered things we couldn't, or competed in a way we wouldn't." He waved his hand dismissively. "You know, women, payoffs to cronies, like giving the legal contract or the accounting contract to certain firms. Not to say we wouldn't do that sort of thing if we could — I mean the contracts not the women — but sometimes there was just no way we could do it ethically." He smiled at Jane and the smile was slightly mischievous. "And other times it was my fault. The other guy was just smarter than I was. The other firm thought of solutions for clients that were better than mine, or they sold themselves better.

"I try to see new ways of doing things, not only on the financial side, but on the people side, and in putting together all the components of a deal so it will go on working well long after I'm gone. Then I have to sell that — not only what the client thinks he wants, but what he really wants, and even better if you can get it, what he needs. And sometimes, a competitor just does it better. If I'm lucky, I can figure out what was better about it and not get outsmarted that way again. I try very hard not to make the same mistake twice." Again the wry smile. "And sometimes I succeed.

"And now, if that answers your question —" he looked at Brian who nodded "— I'd like to hear more about the people at BTS and how they feel about the proposed merger. And if you are seriously considering me for the position, before I let you know if I'm interested, I'd have to go to Toronto and meet them. As I've said, to make something like this work, I need to know all the people involved. And in your company, from what I've heard about it, the management team will have to support any initiative that you and I take. So I'd like to meet them and see how we get along together before we go too much further. Does that make sense to you?"

Brian nodded and made the usual statements about when they would be getting back to Craig. All three shook hands, and then Jane and Brian were alone in the sitting-room, looking at one another over the cold cups of coffee and the faint stale smell of tobacco.

Now we'll see, Brian Taylor, Jane thought. Now speak the lines and show me what you've tried to hide. "Well, what did you think of them?" she asked.

Brian didn't meet her eyes. "The best, by far the best yet," he said. "You've done well, Jane."

Jane gathered up the coffee cups and ashtray, put them on the tray and put the tray on the bar. She dumped the ashes into the sink and rinsed the ashtray. Then she tried to open a window, to let out the smell of cigar smoke. Brian was watching Jane. She felt his gaze, felt it shift so that for a moment she felt exposed. She turned to look at him and saw his expression change, become thoughtful, tense.

She sat down in her chair again, curled her feet up under her, smoothing her skirt down and tucking it under her calves like a blanket. She folded her arms under her breasts and pressed them tightly to her rib-cage, tense, waiting. The silence between them lengthened. Finally Brian said, "I'm leaning toward Saywell."

"You *are*? Why?"

"Two reasons," Brian said slowly. "One, I think his experience is more relevant than Craig's. And that counts for a lot. I think the U.S. people will recognize the type of man he is; it's a type they're used to. We'll do better in the kind of negotiations I have in mind. And two, I think I can motivate and control him with money, so he'd do what *I* want, not what he wants."

Jane exhaled suddenly, and the sound filled the room, almost like a gasp. She realized she had been holding her breath. Now her tension, her anxiety, her curiosity turned to anger, but it was an anger filled with the exhilaration that winning, outwitting an opponent can bring.

"I understand now," Jane said. "It's a takeover, not a merger. A takeover you want to happen. That's the only possible explanation for what you just said. You're going to sell out BTS to the American company. And you can see that Craig has too much integrity to go along with you when you try to slide it by the management group."

Brian stared at her, his face reddening with anger. And she looked back, daring him to challenge her, to lie to her again. He opened his mouth to speak, closed it, then burst out, "You set it all up. I'll be damned. You set this up to smoke me out, and I walked right into it."

Jane said, "It's the artificial-intelligence work, isn't it Brian? That's why you want to sell out. You want to go into a new business. You're bored with this one, and you need money for the research and development in something new and experimental. So you're going to spin off your AI research into a new company and sell out the rest of BTS to get the money you need."

This time Brian was unable to speak. He just stared at her, his face now pale, completely astonished.

"But you're in a bind," she went on, "because the value of BTS is so tied up with keeping that management group that you have to keep them onside until the sale is consummated, or you won't get your money out. And they'd never go along with it willingly. At least that's what you've decided."

"What's got into you, Jane? Where did you get these ideas?"

"I want to talk to you calmly about this," Jane said. "It's time you told me the truth; it's time you trusted me. Fix yourself a drink, sit down, and I'll tell you what I know."

For a moment she thought he would just walk out, keeping his secrets, risking the harm she could do him. But faced with her knowledge, how could he take the risk? She watched as he took off his jacket, loosened his tie, poured them both drinks. When he was settled into the sofa across from her, she smiled at him, lifted her glass and toasted him. "To the truth," she said.

Brian lifted his glass as if to salute her. But Jane, watching him over the rim of her own, saw that he touched it to his lips without drinking, saw that his eyes were cold, thoughtful and withdrawn.

25

"When I did my first interview with Saywell and heard that story about what he did in England, I knew it was a story he'd get into every interview," Jane said.

They were seated across from each other, the decanter of Scotch between them, their bodies stiff with tension. Outside the light was failing, but they had not turned on the lamps, and the dusky greyness in the room made it seem to Jane as if they were in a kind of timeless limbo. She ignored the sensation and focussed in on what she had to say.

"You could tell from Saywell's expression when he came out with that anecdote," she said, "how proud he was of what he had done. He'd tricked a lot of people. That was the kind of thing I knew you hated. It used to worry you, because you thought people like that would screw you in the end, remember? You and I discussed that years ago when we first worked together.

"So I thought, if it's true, if Brian is trying to put something over on the management team at BTS, Gary would have gone along with it. And now Brian needs someone else who will go along. So I'll offer him someone who will play those kind of games and someone who won't, and I'll see what happens."

"I didn't trick you or betray you, Jane," Brian said. "I thought all this, the takeover aspect, had nothing to do with what I asked you to do."

"I can't believe you could think that! You asked me to find someone to do a job for you. How could I, unless I knew what the job was?"

"How do you feel now?"

"I don't know how I feel, because I don't understand. Why don't you tell me your side of it?" She leaned toward him, anxious for the answer, hoping that despite her conviction that she understood only too well what he was up to, he could explain and make it right. That there was a way to justify his deceit and his betrayal of the people who trusted him.

"I'll tell you," he said, looking distressed, pushing his fingers down between the sofa cushions, as if to hide something he was holding. "But I don't know if I can explain it so that you'll understand.

"When I started BTS I was interested in application generators. That was a very new technology. Hardly anyone was involved with it. So we built a data-processing company, and by stretching ourselves, and with Gary's help, we got enough money in to do the research and development we needed to develop those generators. Now fourth-generation languages are everywhere, and it's easy to see I was right. But back then, nobody could have raised money on my idea."

"But things are different now," Jane said. "After what you've done with BTS you'd have no trouble raising money for a new company, or getting research-and-development money for the one you have now, for BTS. Or why not just sell your shares in the company?"

Brian sighed. "It even bores me to explain it — how much more would it bore me to do it? If you only knew. . . . Look. To finance BTS's growth, Gary got the Blumbergs involved. Now they're always looking over my shoulder. They're smart, and Gary had to make certain promises to them. The long and the short of it is, they won't give me what I need to expand into artificial intelligence. The advice they get is that most of it is hot air, and we could lose a lot of money. At best, it will be several years before it pays off. They're not prepared to risk a lot of new money for a future payback when we are doing so well now. So I can't do what I want inside BTS. They won't stand for it. The plan I'm working on now was the only one the Blumbergs would accept, and I thought it would give me what I want.

"As for raising money for a new company, yes, I could do that. But then I wouldn't control it. I never want to be in that position again. I've hated doing the R & D on artificial intelligence by stealth. I've hated concealing it from everybody. Why should I have to do that? I've hidden the work so that everyone thinks we're developing a new kind of application generator, but that can't go on much longer." He smiled at her. "You were right on, Jane, that time you teased me about doing my research on the purloined-letter principle. Remember? I guess that's how you figured this out, seeing the Prologue work in the lab. I never thought anybody would put it all together.

"But as for selling my shares —" his expression grew sober again "— as soon as I hinted that I was going to do that, the price would drop; I just wouldn't get enough.

"BTS is no fun anymore. Do you know what I mean, Jane? Do you know that feeling of suffocation, almost, that you get when you're deeply, deeply bored? Bored isn't even the right word to describe how I feel when I hate something and want to get out of it."

Jane nodded, not liking what she was hearing, but understanding, and softening toward him because she did.

"They say there are people who like to start things, and others who like to build things, and then others who like to make them grow and flourish," Brian went on. "I like to start things. New and risky things. . . . If I could only tell you what I'm dreaming about, make you understand. . . ." He gestured helplessly. "How it feels to go to work, to solve the problem you solved before, to do more and probably better, though the same thing fundamentally, that you did yesterday. It gives me this kind of grey, achy feeling, as if I'm in a colourless tunnel, and I'm condemned to walk along it, never getting out. But the artificial-intelligence work, it's a different world. It's risky, it's scary, but I love it. Of course things go wrong, but that's what makes it real.

"Okay, Alan Bates, the head of R & D, burned out, maybe because our first AI prototype was a disaster. I can deal with that; I don't mind it. I had plenty of disasters along the way when BTS was getting started. But I know, even if nobody else would believe me — and they won't — that I learned what I needed to know from that first prototype. Now I know what we have to do next — how to get where I want to go."

"AI is such a big field," Jane said. "You must be working on something specific."

"Yes, yes, of course I am. And if I get where I'm going. . . ." He paused, and Jane could see he was wondering whether to trust her.

"I know, Brian, I've figured it out. It's the only thing that makes sense of all this, of all this secrecy."

He smiled, and this time his smile was full of joy. "You see, I don't care. I don't care even if what I'm planning eventually hurts BTS. Because they've had a chance at it, and they haven't got the courage. If I take the risk I'll reap the rewards. And what I'm planning will be a terrific risk, there's no doubt about that. At first, I'll just start up a little R & D company. Nobody will be threatened by that."

"Then slowly you'll take away little bits of BTS business," Jane said, her voice flat, "announce new products, make what they have look obsolete. You'll wound them and bleed them until you have them where you want them. It'll be easy for you, knowing everything about both the American and the Canadian companies, their strategy, their pricing, their customer base, everything. Maybe you'll even try to buy them out; by that time their marketing clout, with the Canadian and American market position, will be just what you need."

He shook his head, but his denial was half-hearted. She could see he was having trouble taking in the fact that she had understood so much.

"If I'm successful," Brian said, "what I develop won't be easy to understand. People won't be beating down my doors — you know that. It will be a long time before this new way of handling large data-processing applications makes any headway. Most of BTS's big customers won't be interested. They like to play it safe. I won't be any threat to BTS."

"Maybe," Jane said. "I agree, the effects of what you're planning won't be immediate. But even if the customers don't see the significance of what you're doing right away, BTS is going to be very vulnerable. You'll be in a position to pick off their most profitable business. Maybe you're hoping they'll come to you, offer to buy you out, and you can go after a true reverse takeover. This time, you'd be in control, not Gary and the Blumbergs, and you might be able to bring it off. I'm sure you're planning something like that. After watching the way you're orchestrating this one, I can't believe we're seeing the last act here."

He waved his arm, waving away the implications of what she was saying. "I didn't think you would understand. Everything you're saying, sure, I've thought about it. But that's not the point."

"No? Then what is the point?"

Now he was leaning toward her, willing her to understand. She knew he was thinking that if she did not keep his secret, his plan was endangered. Why was she taking this risk? Letting him see how much she knew. Why did she want to give him an opportunity to justify himself to her? Maybe it was the suppressed — perhaps imagined — attraction between them. Was that the reason she didn't fear Brian, couldn't imagine him as Gary's murderer? Because surely, if Gary had decided to thwart Brian's plan, Brian would have had a motive. Brian's plan could never have been carried out without Gary's knowledge. Almost as if he heard her unspoken question, Brian said, "The point is *time*, Jane. That's the point.

"I have to finance my research and development well, and I have to do it right away. Because a lot of people are working in this area. I have special advantages: knowledge that I've gained from BTS's huge database, understanding of the market. But without money to get and keep a headstart, those things may not be enough. No one knows better than I do that having the technology is one thing, but timing, timing is everything. I've got to do what I want to do *now*."

"Okay, okay," she said, moved by his passion, feeling the urgency that was driving him. "But how can you justify what you are doing to Martin, Robert, Martha and Tom?"

That's what I can't understand, Jane thought. That's what's hardest to accept. I so much want to understand and I can't. She got up and walked around the room, behind the sofa where Brian sat, then back to her seat, sitting back, waiting for him to prove to her that her worst fears about his ability to betray were groundless. But his answer, when it came, she found self-serving, thin.

"It's true, I need them to stay there at BTS. I have to keep them onside until the sale is consummated. Because there's a perception in the market that without that team the company is worthless, that those people *are* the company. But that cuts both ways. They belong there, their skills belong in a company the size of BTS. You can't expect them to take the kind of risk I'm talking about, to understand it. And you can't expect that they would want to follow me into a little fifteen- or twenty-person R & D company. We've made something strong — BTS — and I'm leaving it to them. Don't you see?"

She did see. It was as if he had captained a large sailing ship, which now, under full sail, was running with the wind into a safe harbour. If he, taking the people who had plotted the course into that harbour with him, the key R & D people, quietly went over the side in a small boat and rowed off, what was the harm in that? And wasn't that a thousand times better than trying to turn the ship, sail back into the wind, out into the open sea, to a new destination that only he had confidence in? They, after all, wanted to work for a successful profitable company. He wanted something else.

How do people convince themselves that what they want is the right thing? Jane wondered sadly. Here is a man I thought incredibly rational. But he is driven by his ambitions. And then, with a chill, she thought, how far have they driven him, those passions, that desire to get where he wants to go? "But Brian," Jane said at last, "you've lied to them. You've promised them you won't sell them out."

"I don't see it as a lie. Not fundamentally," Brian said. "I'll keep the company together, and keep their role in it for them. I'm not sure how to explain it, but in spirit I've already left; what BTS is now isn't my company anymore. It's theirs."

"I don't understand you," Jane said, unable to keep the anger and disillusionment out of her voice. "What they are all afraid of is that if the U.S. company takes over, everything will change. Some of them, maybe all of them, will lose their jobs."

Brian stared at her for a moment. Then he laughed. "That's absurd. *They* are most of what we'll be selling. The U.S. company wouldn't cut them loose, especially once I'm gone. Not with the expertise in their heads and the customer loyalty they command."

"Let's look at it, Brian, not as you want it to be, but just coldly, for a moment, okay?"

"What do you mean?"

"What you're saying is that if you were in the shoes of the American company *you* wouldn't fire any of them. But it's very naïve, and not like you, to imagine that's what will happen."

"Well . . . maybe Martha would get the push," Brian said unwillingly.

"Martha for sure, I'd say," said Jane. "And probably Robert."

"Definitely not Martin and Tom, though," Brian said. "But after all, it's not the end of the world if you're fired. It's not *that* big a deal. There are other jobs."

"With the profit sharing they get they are all making over $150,000 a year plus stock options, isn't that right?"

"I'd guess about that. It varies."

"That kind of money, in a job they enjoy, they're unlikely to find elsewhere. They could end up heading divisions in branch plants. They'd hate that."

Brian shrugged. "Maybe, maybe. I hadn't thought about it like that. If you're right, then that's bad. But it's beyond my control, what happens to them after the take-over. After all, they're grown-ups; they can look after themselves. As you said yourself, they haven't done badly at BTS."

"Brian, you have to do something for them. At the very least you can see they get golden parachutes."

Brian nodded. "I accept that. I should have seen that they were protected financially."

"You know, Brian," Jane said, "the truth is that I don't want to understand what you're doing, because I think it's wrong. But I do understand." She tried to keep the sadness and the fear out of her voice, not wanting him to know how she really felt about what he was telling her.

He reached out and turned on the lamp on the table beside him, and his face sprang clearly into view, his eyes full of life, warming to her sympathy, seeming to forget that a few minutes ago she had been cold and judgmental, and he resentful and defensive.

"This is probably the most exciting opportunity I'll ever have, Jane. I can feel it, taste it, touch it. It's a time for us in this field. It's what the physicists must have felt when they were on the edge of nuclear fission.

"The power of these new computers, the new chips, the potential of the new software tools, the new database technologies — you put that all together and we are going to have machines that people can talk to, that help people think, that make us really smarter.

"What I want to do is just one step on that road. But it's a step I know I can make. I'd never forgive myself if I weren't on that road, if I held back, because I didn't have what it took to get out there and get moving on that journey."

Jane looked down at her hands. They were clenched tightly in her lap. She spoke, but so softly Brian couldn't hear her.

"What was that, Jane?"

"I said, Gary's death. Don't you see, Brian, all this, it connects to Gary's death."

"I think that's pretty far-fetched."

"It isn't. It's true. It's obvious. Gary was working on all this, on selling BTS for you. And someone on your management team didn't want it to happen."

"But was Gary working on selling BTS?" Brian said. "That's what I thought too. But after he died I went through his papers. Because I had been getting the feeling, those last few weeks, that he was up to something.

"Oh, he seemed to be enthusiastic about the strategy. The plan for the merger that would, as the other company saw how incredibly liquid BTS is, become a takeover. The U.S. company would make a takeover bid for us. I would seem to be unwilling, and Gary would talk me into it and arrange for me to be bought out at the price I needed. Gary was keeping the Blumbergs onside. At least that's what I thought. But in those last few weeks . . . he wouldn't look me in the eye. At the time I wondered why he was acting like that. Was it because he didn't like deception? I even thought, maybe he doesn't mind leading a double life at home, because he can play it straight at work. And now, to play the management group, maybe it's getting to him and that explains his attitude."

"So you were worried about him before his death?"

"Right. I wondered, was he losing his nerve, was that what it was? Then after he died and I went through his files, I found out. And in a way it didn't surprise me. Can you guess, Jane? You've figured everything else out."

"I think Gary had his own strategy," Jane said. "You thought he was a piece on your chessboard, but it turned out that he and the Blumbergs were moving you around."

Brian got up suddenly. "Dead on! Very good. Of course

it's easy to see now. Hindsight. Gary had his own strategy, bigger and more complex than mine. It stands to reason. Games like this were Gary's life, what he was best at. And he had his plan well hidden. But after he died, what I put together was this: Gary and the Blumberg brothers were going for one large U.S. company, with Gary fully entrenched. One company. I would have been out all right, but not with cash. I'd have had shares in the new company, but it would have been set up so I couldn't cash out right away. They'd have had me locked in." He sat back down on the sofa and stretched out his legs. His eyes were closed, he seemed to be far away, and Jane couldn't read his expression.

"But to be fair to Gary," Jane said, "you didn't tell him you had to have cash. That you wanted to be out clean so that you could walk away with most of BTS's R & D and start up your own company. I bet you just told him you wanted to get out, and how much money you needed."

"There's that about it," Brian said, and Jane realized he didn't care that much anymore. Didn't care that Gary had almost outsmarted him. To Brian, the financial side of things wasn't the real game. He didn't have to out-do anybody, or prove he was the smartest. He just had to win what he wanted. Gary's death had removed one obstacle, so Brian could afford to take Gary's manoeuvring in his stride.

"We outsmarted each other — that's what happened," Brian said. "Let's you and I not do that." When Jane didn't reply Brian went on, "Probably Gary believed his plan was better than mine, and that I would accept it in the long run. I didn't know. I trusted him, and I see now he no longer trusted me. But then, I'd asked him to deceive people on my behalf, and that always leads to betrayal."

"And what are you asking me to do, Brian?"

"That's not fair, Jane. Don't forget, all this business

strategy doesn't have a lot to do with what I hired you to do. You were to find me a vice-president of finance. You've found me two very good candidates. I'm satisfied. You've done what I asked."

For a moment, Jane was happy, enjoying a small sense of success, but the feeling faded rapidly.

"It's not good enough," she said. "It can't end here, like this. You keep evading the point. I didn't force all this out in the open just to make things difficult for both of us. It's Gary's murder."

There was a long silence, and the word murder seemed to reverberate in the air. Speaking it, alone like this, with Brian, took all of Jane's courage. Why did she, after everything he had said, still trust him enough to take this chance? Why did it seem so important to get everything out in the open with him?

"Murder. . . ." He repeated the word as if he could barely get it out of his mouth. "I know it sounds foolish, but I've tried so hard not to believe that Gary was murdered. It just doesn't make sense. The room was locked. A heart attack — that's what I think. He had a heart attack and then someone left that message as a prank."

"A prank? A joke by one of the six of you? No, Brian. You know better and so do I. And so do the police. Gary was murdered to stop the takeover."

"No. That can't be right." His voice was pleading.

"Brian."

He sat up and spoke to her as if to a child, his tone angry, chiding. "I'm not responsible if someone goes off the rails. It's Martha who's put all these ideas in your head. She can be a trouble-maker. That's always been a problem of hers."

"Responsible!" Jane said. "Trouble-maker! You're changing the subject again. Why won't you face the fact,

Brian? You have to. You just have to." She saw from his expression that she had given herself away, that he heard the fear in her voice.

"Jane!" He walked over to her, and circled her hands between his. "Don't think that about me. Don't. It hurts, and it's not true." Her hands lay between his, cold, limp, unresponsive. "It's just that . . . it's impossible for me to believe that anyone, especially people I know, would be so desperate to hold on to his job that he would kill for it."

Jane was silent for a moment. Then she smiled, and her cold hands turned in his and grasped his fingers. "I know you don't understand it, Brian. But other people are afraid, afraid of losing things they've spent a long time earning, afraid of falling down from the high places they struggled to climb to."

His fingers tightened painfully on hers. "I can't believe you could suspect me. I thought . . . we were . . . friends. That between us there was a kind of understanding. That you could even think —"

"You bring these suspicions on yourself! You won't face up to what's happening! You won't let me deal with it!"

Brian released her hand, walked to the window and looked out. Jane followed him. Night had fallen. Below them was Chicago Avenue. From this height the street looked like a tunnel. The cars moved in a line, glistening in the streetlights, held in their single pathway.

He turned toward her, touching her arm with a tense, unnatural gesture. "How can I get your confidence back, Jane? What can I say that will convince you that I haven't done what you fear?"

She shook her head.

He took her hands again and looked at her steadily, his voice calm and compelling. "I promise you, Jane, I give you my word. I didn't kill Gary Levin. And I didn't really believe, until now when you forced it on me, that he was murdered."

They looked at one another in silence. Finally he said, "Do you believe me?"

Jane sighed. She wrenched her gaze from his and stared beyond him, at the window and the dark night beyond. "I want to," she said gently. "I want to. But I guess right now I don't believe anybody." She turned to face him, kissed him gently on the forehead and walked through the foyer of the suite and into her room. There was a sharp sound as she shot the bolt in the communicating door.

26

WALL STREET JOURNAL

December 21, 1985

. . . and in other technology news, Brian Taylor Systems Inc. of Toronto, Canada, initiated a takeover bid for Oriono Data-systems of Chicago yesterday.

Oriono has been regarded as a likely takeover target by insiders in the industry, because although it has lost money for the past two years, rapid expansion has given it a major market position in the data-processing industry.

The directors of Oriono seem to have been taken by surprise by the BTS takeover play. In his statement to the press Stephen Burns, chief executive officer, said only that Oriono had been in negotiations with BTS for a joint-marketing deal, with a view to getting access to BTS products and an entry into the Canadian market, when the takeover offer "came in out of the blue."

BTS has referred all questions to its new vice-president of finance, Mark Saywell, who has just come onboard and was unavailable for comment.

Industry insiders say Oriono regards the offer as a hostile

takeover and is looking for a "white knight," another firm to whom the board is sympathetic, who will make a more attractive offer. Others have suggested that since the financial power behind BTS is the Blumberg brothers of Vancouver, the BTS offer is "greenmail." Greenmail occurs when one company makes an offer for another without intending to complete it, in the hopes of reselling the shares of its target company at a profit. This opinion may be based on the fact that Oriono had a loss of $200,000 on revenues of $300 million, while BTS had profits of $10.5 million on revenues of $45 million.

Burns said, "We feel the offer is at least $3.00 too low and will be recommending to our shareholders that they not accept it. The Blumbergs' reputation in matters like this is a key factor in our decision."

"They're buzzing around at BTS like a bunch of hornets when you poke a broomstick into their nest," Tom Henege shouted at Jane.

"How about this one?" Jane shouted back.

They were in Harry Rosen, a men's clothing store. Tom had asked Jane to help him with his Christmas shopping, and she had agreed, thinking that otherwise she might never do her own. He said he was a total gull in the stores, spending too much money and regretting it when he got home. They were looking at woollen scarves for Tom's father, whom he had described as a conservative Albertan who rarely liked any present Tom gave him, though Tom said his father always was polite about his gifts, and Tom kept trying.

"No, no, no!" Tom shouted back, as other shoppers milled and eddied between them. "Can't you see that's imitation Burberry?" Coming closer, he showed her one he had found. "Nobody can believe it, nobody. That creep Saywell and a takeover bid by us. . . . What does it mean?"

"How much is that one?" Jane said, taking the scarf from

him. "Cashmere? Are you a millionaire, or what? This is a hundred and fifty dollars!"

Tom took it out of her hand and picked up another, twisting it around his neck. "Maybe I'm going to be VP of marketing for a big multi-national, eh? Maybe I'll be wearing hundred-dollar cashmere scarves and taking you to Il Pelicano for New Year's Eve."

"You don't wear cashmere scarves for New Year's Eve in southern Italy," said Jane, unwrapping the scarf from around his neck and gently caressing his cheek with it.

"Let's try it on you," Tom said. He put the scarf around her, smoothed her hair and then looked at her. They smiled at one another. "That blue-green makes your skin look like wildflower honey," he said.

"Okay, but how will it look on your father?" She picked up the fringe and turned it over. "Forty dollars more like it?"

He unwrapped the scarf, found another, then a clerk. "I'll take two of these," he said, "and the lady will wear one."

"Hey, no you don't," said Jane, laughing.

"You've already bought me a Mickey Mouse watch."

"Well, that's different. I was making a comment on the role of the BTS staff in the takeover," Jane said, ruffling his hair.

Out on the street he took her gloved hand in his and tucked it into his pocket.

"I should be worried sick about this takeover business," Tom said. "But I'm not. I'm enjoying being with you too much."

Jane felt a qualm. But she pushed it aside. Why think about business, about all she knew, when this was personal time? Her work at BTS was over. What went on there was none of her business. She was in the clear. Brian had hired

Saywell against her advice; she had put that in writing. But she had found him, and BTS was paying her what she had earned.

She had confounded Eddie Orloff, who had been caught short, she was sure, and lost a lot of money. Teach him not to gamble on my failing, she thought with satisfaction.

But could anything change the fact that she knew what was going on at BTS, knew the takeover was greenmail, knew BTS had no intention of buying Oriono Datasystems, knew Brian was just waiting to be taken over himself, to get out with enough money to start up a new company that would eventually undermine BTS, knew that he was throwing Tom and his colleagues to the wolves?

It's not my business, Jane said to herself again. She wondered why the look Tom gave her as he turned to smile at her, a look of happiness, and desire, and friendship, gave her a feeling of both joy and anxiety. Whatever happens between us, she thought, he'll never know I knew. I can't tell him. Legally, I can't. Morally I can't, and besides it would mess up how good we feel about each other. I can't. I just can't.

They put their packages in the car, got out their skates and walked the short distance to City Hall. The ice rink was thick with skaters, but Tom helped Jane lace up her skates, then each wrapped an arm around the other's waist and pushed off, sliding smoothly over the ice between the other skaters.

It felt wonderful to Jane to be in the circle of Tom's arm. The cold air bit her face, and the blue-green scarf blew out behind her, then across his face, blinding him for a moment, so she guided him until he pushed it away and regained control.

"I'd like to go skating round and round here forever,"

she said, "just like this, with your arm around me, and my new scarf blowing in your eyes."

"I'd like to take you home," he said in her ear, "and go round and round there."

"I thought you didn't want to," she said. "When I was at your house, you turned me down."

"I wanted to. You didn't. That's why."

They skated for a while in silence, Jane trying to understand what he meant. "I thought I did," she said softly. He bent his head toward her, pulling her closer so that the power of his strides now carried both of them along, and she scarcely needed to push off at all.

"I know you thought that," Tom said, "but you seemed scared to me, and I thought it would be a mistake. I think you told me the truth that night after Orloff's party. We have to be friends first, really good friends."

"So you're not actually inviting me now, either?"

He kissed the top of her head. "That's right."

"I don't understand."

He laughed, letting go of her waist and taking her hands in the traditional cross-over skater's handclasp. They regulated their strokes, so that each push-off and glide was perfectly matched, and they skated in and out between the other skaters, in what seemed almost a magical pattern. "I'm old enough to wait for what I want; we'll both know when it's the right time. When you're not scared of hurting me, when I'm not scared of hurting you. When we feel safe enough."

How generous he is, Jane thought, her mind clogging slightly with desire. But then she thought, is it that he knows, or suspects, he can't trust me? That I know more than I'm saying? She remembered Tom's asking her, angry and suspicious, if she'd had an affair with Brian. Then there was her trip to Chicago with Brian; Tom knew about that. People always gossiped, always wondered. She remembered Kersti's telling her that men had no morals or compunctions when they wanted a woman badly enough. Did Tom not want her badly enough? Or was he maybe impotent? Why was nothing ever simple? Other people just fell into bed together; in books they never worried about contraception, or what he meant when he said that you said that he said. . . . She sighed.

"Why the frown?" asked Tom. "You know I'm right. Didn't you tell me you were burned out on sex? Why should I make the same mistake those other men made? You're tired," he said, feeling her flag. "Let's go back to your place. I'll make you some of that Dutch chocolate we bought, and then I'll tuck you in."

Jane felt her weariness ebb into comforting tiredness. They had eaten bread and cheese and cold ham for dinner, then Tom had made them hot chocolate, and now she was lying on the sofa, drinking hers, admiring him, the way he looked as he moved around her kitchen, straightening up, washing the plates, putting away the remains of the meal.

He came and sat across from her, watching her drink her chocolate, looking thoughtful.

"There's lots I'm afraid of," Jane said. "It's because I know too much about BTS, about Brian. It gets in the way. That's what you feel."

"That, among other things," he said. "Can I tell you a secret?"

"Better not," she said drowsily. The skating, the physical tiredness, the relaxation from strain, now the hot chocolate. . . . She was almost asleep.

"I'm looking for another job."

Jane sat up and stared at him. Why was he trusting her

with this? What if she told Brian? Brian regarded loyalty as the single most important thing. He'd fire Tom if he knew. Or maybe, Jane thought, Tom is sending a message through her to Brian not to fool around. Maybe he wants an assurance; he wants Brian to know he can't take Tom for granted.

"Why are you telling me?" Her voice was loud, harsh.

He stared at her, not understanding. "I know you're close to Brian, but —"

"Oh, go home, go home," she said spitefully. "I don't want your secrets or your messages. I'm not your errand girl. I didn't sleep with Brian. I can't help you. Get off my case."

Tom slammed his cup down on the little table. "Well, to hell with you, Jane Tregar." He banged the door behind him.

He answered on the first ring.

"Tom? I'm sorry. I'm really sorry," Jane said.

"Sure."

"You trusted me, but I'm not brave enough to trust you. I was wrong."

"Okay."

"Am I forgiven?"

"You're forgiven. I'm tired. Good night."

Jane heard the phone click. She hung up sadly, rolled up in a ball, and tried to go to sleep. But there were too many doubts, too many uncertainties. A draft blew in around the window and the bedroom door creaked. She got up out of bed and closed it. But it went on rattling worse than ever, and Jane found she was too tired and too unhappy to get up and open it again. She finally drifted off to sleep, and all night her dreams were troubled by the sounds of the door banging against the frame.

27

"I don't know what Martha had to do with it," Al said. Kersti's brother-in-law was a tall, once-handsome man, now so thin as to appear anorexic. The lines radiating out and downward from his tired dark eyes, stood out against the tightly pulled skin like blood vessels. "I don't know what it was that happened between the two of them, but something did. Make no mistake about that."

"Let's not get into that again," Kersti said. They were sitting around the table over the wreck of Christmas dinner. The children could be heard in the next room, squabbling over their new toys, while Kersti, Jane and Al, stuffed and irritable from too much rich food and drink, tried to keep the conversation alive. Around them were the remains of the plum pudding and mince pie, the crackers, the bowls of walnuts, the heaps of nutshells, the chocolates and brandy.

"You don't know what you're talking about," Kersti said to Al. "Just because they were friends for a few years doesn't make Martha an accomplice in Tiu's death."

Al looked as if he were about to respond angrily, so Jane tried to deflect him. "About Martha," Jane said. "What did Tiu think of her?"

"She liked her a lot," Kersti said.

"That surprises me," Jane said. "Somehow I always thought of your sister as being kind of hypersensitive and fragile. Martha seems so tough and driven. You get the idea Martha wouldn't have much time for the delicate nuances you needed for a friendship with someone like Tiu."

"Oh, I don't know about that," Kersti said.

She was showing her usual disinclination to analyse people, Jane thought. She searched her mind for another topic of conservation but none occurred to her. She felt the first twinges of indigestion from having eaten too much, and she asked herself again, as she had been doing off and on for the past hour, why she had thought that having Christmas dinner with Kersti and Al would be a good idea. Had she thought it would keep her from thinking of her own children, living it up in Florida? She decided to press Kersti on the subject of Tiu and Martha. After all, there were things about Martha she wanted to understand. "Kersti, what do you mean, you don't know?"

Kersti stretched out her arm and plucked a shiny, red Macintosh apple from the fruit bowl in the centre of the table. She turned the apple in her long fingers, pressing it gently as if to test how hard it was, then put it back in the bowl. "I wouldn't say Tiu was fragile. And I never think of Martha as hard. Driven, yes. But she puts on that tough air to hide what she really feels. She isn't at ease with herself, so she doesn't show her true feelings. No, she's not really tough; at least I don't think so. Not tough like you are, Jane. When I met Martha, I got the feeling she was covered by a thin shell that could crack at any minute."

"That's not my reading," Jane said.

"Well, of course I don't know her all that well," Kersti said. "I've only met her a couple of times. I could be wrong. But I think I formed my impressions more from what Tiu told me than from my own observations. And Tiu had that really sharp insight that some neurotic and disturbed people have, do you know what I mean?"

Jane nodded.

"The thing that surprised me the most was hearing Tiu talking about Martha's health problems. When you see Martha she looks like one very together lady, but according to Tiu she had back problems, and neck problems, and migraines, and was in pain a lot of the time. I think that's why she joined Tiu's therapy group. They both decided that all those things could be stress related, and they thought the group might be able to help."

"That really does surprise me," Jane said. "I never would have expected Martha to have health problems and go into group therapy. I guess I don't understand her very well."

"Funny you should say that," Al said, staring at Jane. His eyes under their colourless lashes were red rimmed, as if he hadn't been sleeping well. "Because that is exactly what Tiu said the day before she died." He rubbed his eyes. "The day before she killed herself," he repeated, looking at Kersti as if to challenge her.

Kersti responded with a small spurt of energy. "For Christ's sake, Al."

"Why do you think Tiu said that, said she didn't understand Martha?" Jane asked.

"I don't *think* — I *know* why she said it," Al said.

The children's voices rose, and there was the sound of a slap and a wail. "Kersti, could you?" Al asked. "I've just about had it. . . . "

Kersti got up and went into the living-room. Through the doorway Jane could see the tree, its green and red lights winking off and on like demented traffic signals, and the tinsel shivering like broken glass. Jane watched Kersti kneel between the two children, separating them as they fought and taking the smallest one into her arms.

"She's good with them, you know," Al said in a confiding voice. "Better than Tiu. That hurt Tiu, but hell, everything hurt Tiu." He took a big walnut from the bowl, placed it between the jaws of the nutcracker, and rended it in two. "Kersti will talk to you about Martha, if you push it," he said, "but she hates for *me* to talk about Martha. That's because she knows Martha was a surrogate sister for Tiu. And when Tiu got disillusioned with Martha, well, maybe that was what pushed her over the edge. Kersti can't stand that idea." He reached for a nut pick and pressed the sharp point of it into the walnut meat.

"But why would Tiu need a surrogate sister? Kersti would have done anything for her. She loved her."

"Kersti's idea of love is pretty strange, if you ask me," Al said. "Kersti didn't want Tiu to hero-worship her or be dependent on her. It was cruel the way Kersti would tell Tiu the worst stuff about herself." His eyes seemed to glisten. "Kersti is a very sexy woman, you know; she made Tiu feel cold and timid with all her talk about her wild sex life." He held up the walnut meat on the end of the pick for a moment, then poked it into his mouth. "It backfired, that's what I think."

"But Martha?"

"Well, what Tiu told me was, in that last therapy session, Martha suddenly started talking about how she had been sexually abused as a child. It really upset Tiu; she was a basket case that night." He dug his nutpick into the convolutions of the walnut half still in the shell. "Tiu should have taken her pills. I told her to take her pills."

"Bullshit," said Kersti, coming back into the dining-room and taking a deep draught of her brandy. "What makes you think hearing that Martha was abused as a kid would upset Tiu? Tiu knew Martha had plenty of troubles."

"*You* know why," Al said, looking meaningfully at Kersti. Kersti returned his gaze, and a look of dislike passed between them. Jane remembered Kersti's fear that Al would make a pass at her and that she would have to turn him down. Maybe it had happened, and no doubt, believing in Kersti's promiscuity, Al had been humiliated by her refusal. Maybe that explained the bitterness, Jane thought.

"If you mean that Tiu was upset because of her own problems, then forget it," Kersti said. "Half the women in that therapy group had been abused by a relative and Tiu knew that. She told me all about it. Why would one more make any difference to her? And anyway, Tiu thought Martha was the healthiest person in the group."

"Well, bully for Martha," Al said. He picked out another nut and positioned it between the claws of the nutcracker. "Being the healthiest was being a failure in that therapy group. The way I see it, they competed to see who could be the sickest."

"Well, Martha hates to lose, I know that," Jane said. "If they were competing to be the sickest, attract the most attention by the tragedy of their experiences, maybe that's why Martha told that story about being abused."

"Yeah, maybe Martha was lying," Kersti said.

"Was that it?" Jane asked Al. "Was that what upset Tiu?"

Al closed his eyes, holding the nut and the nutcracker for a moment, then he split the nut suddenly, so hard that a crack appeared around its entire circumference, the shell broke apart, and the meat fell out in four even pieces. "Yes," he said. "Could be that was it. Of course —" he hesitated "—I've been thinking about other things, when I look back on Tiu's last days. Thinking about what *I* did or didn't do, but now that you mention it, it comes back to me. It was at the therapy group. Martha came out with all this stuff about her childhood, but Tiu knew it wasn't true. Tiu said it was horrifying to her because, even though none of it was true, Martha must have believed it while she was telling it. Tiu told me Martha was crying and pale and sweating when she suddenly came out with this story."

"If Tiu thought the story was a lie, then it was a lie," Kersti said softly. "When she was most troubled she was most sensitive. Her pain made her incredibly perceptive; she could look right into you."

"I loved her," Al said suddenly. A tear trickled down his face, while his jaw moved up and down, processing the walnut.

Jane looked down, not wanting to see him cry.

"Let's do the dishes,"Kersti said. "We're getting ridiculous. Whatever Martha said or did, she can't be held responsible for Tiu's death. We know how depressed Tiu had been for months. We know that she felt she would never stop being afraid, never stop feeling dread and guilt and despair. Tiu simply couldn't stand it anymore. Martha's lies — if they were lies — were just a side issue."

Jane got up and started stacking the plates. Al wiped his tear away and scooped up the walnut shells, adding them to the pile in the bowl in front of him. "God help me to forgive her," he said suddenly, "because I don't think I can do it on my own."

Jane, carrying the dishes into the kitchen, wondered if he meant Martha. She was convinced that she now knew who murdered Gary Levin. The conversation seemed to confirm this view, making it clear that death went on reverberating until it was understood. Tiu's death, unexplained and unaccepted, was eating away at Kersti and Al. The explanation of Gary Levin's death, however, was in her power. It was time to do something about it.

28

This time Sergeant Barrodale didn't wait before lighting up. But as they were in *his* office, Jane thought, perhaps it was too much to expect that he would remember that she didn't smoke and didn't like it when others did.

He sat behind his grey steel desk and looked at her without speaking. At the end of the office, through the partly open, cream-coloured, loosely woven curtains, Jane saw that it was already dark. The narrow room, with the large desk set at an angle like a street barricade, the file cabinet and metal shelving, felt to her like a military barracks — where order was everything, and complexity and subtlety could be squeezed out like juice from a lemon.

"I want to tell you some things," Jane said. "I think it's time."

"That's good. That's very good." He puffed on his cigarette and watched her. His body was very relaxed; he seemed to have all the time, all the interest in the world. Outside the office Jane could hear telephones ringing, muffled voices, time moving. Inside, Barrodale's stolidity made it seem there was time for careful thought and measured words.

"You haven't come to Orloff's yet with your search warrant," she said.

"It's too close to Christmas," Barrodale said. "The judges we like to work with on things like that are away; I've decided to wait until after the New Year. Now especially after your call, I thought maybe we could do it the easy way."

Jane knew Orloff was an influential man; no doubt Barrodale knew it too, or maybe he wanted them all to sweat. Maybe making them wait was just another one of his tactics.

Jane smiled slightly at Barrodale. "Don't get your hopes up," she said, "that you're going to get any great revelations from me. I've got a lot of half-baked ideas, that's all."

"We'll see."

"Have you followed up the computer side of things?"

He nodded.

"What do you think?"

"Why don't you tell me what you know, and then I'll tell you what I think."

"Okay," Jane said. "Here goes. First, of course, I believe Gary Levin was murdered."

Barrodale nodded. "No doubt about that."

"Someone wrote a computer program that caused the computer to crash at 12:55 A.M. Then when Gary went into the computer room to boot it up, some other mechanism, some mechanical device, was timed to do something to cause his death."

"Do you know what that other mechanism was?"

"I'll get to that. Anyway, the point is, once I started to think about that and to check into the computer system there, lots of things seemed obvious to me. In the first place, there were only five people who could be quite certain that Gary would be there that night and who also had the password to write the program that crashed the computer."

"You know there was such a program?"

Jane nodded, and Barrodale made a note on the pad in front of him. But he didn't ask any more questions, and Jane went on.

"The five people are, of course, Brian Taylor, Martin Kaplan, Robert McDonnell, Tom Henege and Martha Gruen.

"But more than that, think how chancy it was. If Gary hadn't been working that late, if when the computer crashed he decided just to go home instead of booting it up, there would have been no murder. I'm sure that the mechanical device, whatever it was, was timed to go off based on the time of the crash, not triggered by the re-booting of the computer. Because if it had been triggered by the re-booting, Martha would have been endangered, maybe killed, when she re-booted in the morning. And in fact, Gary never completed the re-booting cycle. He died first."

She told Barrodale about the attempt on her life, about the trap in her apartment. "That, too, was chancy. It was as if the murderer were saying: I'll plan this, I'll set the plan in motion, and then I'll let fate make the final move. Do you see what I mean?"

Barrodale nodded, and gestured with his cigarette for her to continue. Jane waved away the smoke, but he didn't seem to notice.

"There's something else about the way the murder was committed. Did you know that Gary Levin smoked those little cigars of his nonstop? That he smoked even in the computer room?"

Again Barrodale nodded without speaking.

"I've got an idea how the murder was done, and I think

the mechanism is tied up with that — with his smoking. The only person who would have been endangered by the trap was someone who was smoking in the computer room. *Nobody* smokes in computer rooms. Gary, the number-two man, an arrogant man, a man who rarely, if ever, dealt with the computers in a technical way, considered himself above the rules. The murderer knew that; he or she could count on Gary being the only person endangered by the trap.

"I think I know how it was done, but it's impossible to prove, impossible to test. I've researched every piece of equipment in that computer room, and I've thought and thought about it, and I can only think of one thing. Before I explain it to you, before I can be sure myself, I need to understand the motive."

"Let us worry about the motive, you just —"

"No. These people are my friends. Some are very close friends. It's not that easy.

"The motive is in this takeover," Jane continued, now looking away from Barrodale, and at the dark window, in which she saw reflected the hard fluorescent light and the pebbly pane of white glass in the door behind her. "One of the five feared that the merger, or takeover, was going wrong, and that Gary was the cause of that. It's hard to explain — money's part of it — but there's much more at stake. When those people built up that company, they put themselves into it in a way that's pretty unusual. It's been noticed and commented on by a lot of people in the industry. All of us are always going on about teamwork and company culture, but you have to wonder, has anybody stopped and thought what it must be like to devote yourself to something, to put all your creativity and energies into it, to identify with it as something *you* built, and then to see it taken away from you? To lose your job, or be demoted, or have all your power taken away? And money — the five managers made a great deal of money. Much more than they were likely to make elsewhere. And in terms of money and power, Brian, of course, had the most to lose if the merger went sour and the company was taken over. Or so I thought.

"So that was the situation. Everybody, except Gary, was threatened by the merger. And even Brian risked getting pushed out if Gary Levin's plans for a takeover came to fruition."

Barrodale was writing again. He wrote left-handed, with a ballpoint, and his hand curled over the lines of writing, concealing them from Jane.

"My problem was that I was hired to find a replacement for Gary Levin. I worried myself sick about the possibility that the replacement, too, might be murdered, if he were seen to be doing exactly what Gary had been doing.

"So for a while I stalled. My boss was on my back, and eventually Brian figured out what I was doing and leaned on me. I didn't dare find someone for the job, to carry through on the merger, or takeover, until I was sure exactly what was going on. So I had to find out.

"And having found out, I decided it was safe to put someone in, because I understood that the next step in the complicated manoeuvring going on would be for BTS to make an offer for the U.S. company, and for everybody to think it was greenmail. Greenmail would not worry the murderer, and there would be time —"

"Greenmail?" Barrodale interrupted for the first time.

"Greenmail is where one company makes an offer for another company with no real intention of buying it. What they want is to be, sort of, paid off to drop their offer. They buy some stock in the target company, and eventually the target company buys it back, or somebody else does, for more money. The greenmailing company makes a big profit for doing virtually nothing except scaring the target company. Of course, it only works if the greenmailer acts as if it really wants to buy the target company, and there is some reason to believe that this time it just might do it. The Blumbergs, who own part of BTS, are famous for successful greenmail.

"While the greenmail scenario is playing itself out, which is right now, there is no danger to the financial vice-president at BTS. The greenmail stage is part of Brian's plan, and from the point of view of the other four it's a no-lose situation. Either BTS ends up owning the American company, which would be fine, or BTS comes out of all this a richer company."

Jane's mouth was getting dry. She asked Barrodale for a glass of water, and he brought her one, cold and stale tasting, in a coffee mug.

"But the next stage — and nobody knows this but Brian, the new vice-president of finance and the Blumbergs — is for the U.S. company to launch their own takeover and eat up BTS."

"How could Brian Taylor know that will happen?" Barrodale asked, looking confused.

"Of course he can't *know*. But look, he has nothing to lose. If his plan fails he ends up richer and stronger and BTS can try again. But he is counting on the fact that it is highly unlikely that a company twice the size of BTS, and an American company at that, is going to sit back and let itself be bought with shares of a smaller Canadian company. That kind of thing happens sometimes, but it could only happen if Oriono Datasystems were willing. And Brian knows they're not. So Oriono will find a white knight who will help them buy BTS."

"Is that what usually happens?"

Jane sighed. "Well, not usually. Usually in this kind of takeover play, Oriono would find a white knight who would buy them. That is, it's a white knight because it's someone Oriono likes, someone they call in to help them. But Oriono's CEO is as determined to keep control of his company as Brian Taylor seems to be. So Taylor is betting that Oriono will try to take over BTS and get rid of him. And that's what he really wants. He's going to let it happen. He's going to do it so cleverly everyone will think it happened against his will. And it's all going to go very quickly. It will be over before anybody even knows what happened." Having trouble articulating her words she said softly, "If the murderer is Brian Taylor, the new vice-president of finance is safe; if it is one of the other four, it will be all over before he or she realizes what is happening, so I'm pretty sure the VP is safe from now on."

"You think!"

Jane sighed. "That, of course, is the nub of the problem. What if I'm wrong?"

"So what do you intend to do?"

"I wanted to tell you this much. Then I have an idea I want to try out on you. If you don't think it's good, maybe you have a better one. I got my idea from TV police shows and murder mysteries, so you'll probably laugh at me."

"So what's your idea?"

"I'll tell you, but one thing you have to understand. I owe these people, especially Brian Taylor, a debt, and it has to be paid. It's going to be paid. And in a strange way, I trust them all, even the murderer. There's a right way to deal with them, and that's the way they have to be dealt with, all of them. It's the only thing I can accept."

"Fine, but what we need is evidence."

"You're not going to get any. There isn't any. But if I'm right about how it was done, you should be able to make a very strong case."

"Why don't you tell me what you want to do?"

Jane did.

29

New Year's interfered with Jane's and Sergeant Barrodale's plans. They decided to wait until it was past, and Jane, in suspense, and looking for escape from her worries about what might happen, turned her attention to her private life.

Before their fight, Jane and Tom had planned to spend New Year's Eve together. Jane didn't know if it were still on.

She had called him at work, the day after Boxing Day, and he had not returned her call. Now, two days before New Year's Eve, she got up her nerve and called him at home.

Hearing his voice gave her such a strong feeling of longing to see him that she was surprised, and perhaps he was feeling somewhat the same, because after the first cold hellos his voice softened.

"I just wanted to know if New Year's was on or off," she said, trying to sound matter-of-fact.

"On, of course," he said. "Why wouldn't it be?"

"Well, as the last words you said to me were 'Go to hell, Jane Tregar,' I did have the idea you might not want to see me again."

"Not at all. The last words I said to you were, 'You're forgiven.'"

"But you didn't sound like you meant it."

"I know. I'm having trouble forgiving you, but hearing your voice. . . . I want to see you again. Very much. What do you want to do for New Year's?"

"Sit around at home and drink. But my friend Kersti is having a party. Would you like to go? Or would you rather go out dancing or something?"

"I'm not in a dancing mood this year. How about we sit around your place and drink and just drop in at the party for a little while?" His voice had softened completely now, the coolness gone, and he managed to invest the phrase "sit around and drink" with the flirtatiousness Jane so much enjoyed.

"I'm looking forward to seeing you," she said, and she wiggled her bare toes happily as she put the phone back in its cradle.

Despite the heat and the smoke, everyone was gathered around the narrow white fireplace at Kersti's, waiting for the first small chunk of melted lead to be retrieved and dropped into the basin. The melting of the lead was an Estonian tradition, a traditional part of Kersti's New Year's parties. Kersti had given Jane the honour of being the first to pick out a chunk of molten lead from the fire with an iron ladle, and drip it into the cold water. Jane watched with pleasure, heightened by the strong brandy eggnog, as the lead hardened and took shape, forming tendrils and knobs.

She plunged her hand into the water and pulled out the little shining object, holding it up for everyone to see.

"Jane!" someone said. "It's a head. Perfect for a head-hunter."

"No," said someone else, laughing. "It's a little mouse, absolutely wrong for Jane."

Tom looked at it. "I think it's a bird, a beautiful bird, maybe a swan. Look at this long, curved piece — that's its neck and beak."

Kersti leaned over and took the piece of lead from Tom, turning it over and over in her hand. Then she said in her throaty voice, looking at Jane, "No, it's a flower. A perfect iris, and this long tendril is its stem, bending in the wind."

Jane was happy. She hugged them both, first Tom, giving him a gentle kiss on the ear, then Kersti, holding her tight and feeling pleasure in her warmth and the return of their friendship. "Come into the kitchen and help me get more eggnog ready," Kersti said. "You can manage the stirring at least."

Jane followed her into the kitchen, which was also full of people. Kersti shooed them away, and taking the milk from the fridge, she began adding the brandy, rum, sugar and nutmeg.

"I like Tom Henege," Kersti said. "I like him a lot."

"I think I do too," Jane said.

"But be careful," Kersti went on, handing Jane a whisk. "He's in love with you."

"Oh Kersti, be serious. We just like one another. We're friends."

"He doesn't look at you like a friend, Jane. He looks at you like a lover. And you look at him the same way."

"We're not lovers. He says we're not ready to be."

"You just proved my point. He is in love with you." Kersti got a bowl of egg whites out of the refrigerator and began beating them with a hand-held electric beater.

"Strange way to show it."

"You know better. You're very lucky. I'm jealous. I

wonder why I never meet anyone with an attention span of longer than five minutes."

Kersti took the milk mixture back from Jane and began folding in the beaten egg whites.

"Do you think you can be in love with someone you've known a month?" Jane said. "At our age?"

Kersti stopped stirring, holding the white rubber spatula in the air so that a crescent of egg white curved down and hung suspended over the bowl. "Maybe not," she said thoughtfully. "I think I see what you mean." She resumed her stirring, more slowly and more carefully, watching to be sure that she didn't lose the air of the egg white. "It's all very delicate," she said.

"He's teaching me something," Jane said, "and I'm trying to learn. It's a surprise, because I never think of men as having anything to teach women about love, or about friendship."

"Me either," said Kersti, gently scooping up some of the eggnog on her spatula and tasting it. She poured some into a small mug for Jane.

"But I'm not a good student," Jane said sadly. "I find it too hard to trust him."

"What are you afraid of?" Kersti said.

Jane didn't answer. Kersti lifted up the bowl of eggnog, and Jane followed her back to the living-room with a tray of clean glasses. Then she went to find Tom. "How are you doing?" she asked him. "Want to stay longer? Ready to go?"

He smiled at her. "I'm ready to go. I feel hot and stuffy and I've drunk too much of that heavy eggnog. Why don't we walk part way and then take a taxi?"

Jane agreed. They had left Tom's car at her place and taken the subway and the streetcar to the party, so now

Jane had only to find her coat, mixed in among the others piled high on Kersti's bed. When she was ready she met Tom at the door, and as he took her hand the door opened letting in a group of people and a draught of icy winter air, mixed with small flakes of snow. "Leaving? It's not even midnight yet," someone said.

Jane pushed past them, out the door, and Tom followed. The sky was thick and black and in the streetlamps she could see a few small snowflakes, like feathers, drifting slowly downward in the cold air.

"It's just ten minutes before the new year," Tom said. "Perhaps you'd rather have stayed and spent it with your friend."

"I don't feel as if the new year is starting tonight," Jane said. "I don't think it will start until I do something about Gary Levin, until there's a resolution."

"What are you going to do?"

They walked in silence for a few minutes.

She turned toward him, looking up at him, feeling, to her surprise, close to tears. "I'm going to trust," she said. "It seems to be the only thing I can do.

"And I am sorry," she went on, looking up at him, "that when you trusted me, I doubted you. But I couldn't help it."

"I asked too much," he said. "It's a problem of mine. You don't owe me anything."

Jane nodded, agreeing.

"I want to get to know you so well that maybe—" he hesitated, searching for the words — "we would be really safe with one another."

"Is that possible, ever?" Jane said.

"When I look at you, I'm sure it is," Tom said. "Sure of it. Absolutely sure of it." He put his arms around her, and they kissed, gently. Then he pulled her closer and they kissed until their mouths felt bruised and painful, and Jane's skin stung from the harshness of the bristles just beneath his skin. When they came apart, they began to walk again, without speaking.

Suddenly Jane said, "My husband took my children away from me, you know. He said he could give them a better life, with money and travel and everything. And with me they would have nothing but daycare, poverty, and a working mother. And I believed him."

"But couldn't you have got them, and money to support them?"

"Yes," she said. She was crying, and the tears ran down her face without her noticing. "Now maybe I think that. Then he convinced me that he would win if we went to court. He had money, power; he was twenty-five years older than I was. He said I'd have other children. He married me to get those children, I can see that now. Then he took them, and I didn't fight back. I must have known from the beginning that he married me to get children and that he would let nothing stop him from keeping them. He'd have taken them to Switzerland, and I'd never have seen them again. He said so. He threatened me that if he didn't get custody I'd lose them completely. But I deserted them. I gave them up. He was bigger and stronger and richer. I never want to be in the power of a man who is bigger and stronger and richer ever again. Do you understand?"

Tom didn't answer.

Jane went on. "When he saw that I was going to graduate, that I was ambitious, that I was going to learn to control a part of my life, he took the children before I could do it, and then married a woman his own age with a tradition of dependence. Clever, wasn't it?"

"Are you sure, Jane? Most men aren't that way about children."

Jane was still crying. "He is very, very rich, and family is incredibly important to him. I was too young to understand things like that when I married him. With him it's not children as it is for a mother, for a woman; no, it's some male thing I don't understand. Oh, it's terrible to be so young and so stupid that you can make a mistake that you never get over. Then it was so easy to trust, to give someone power over you, power to hurt you. But now?"

"I'm in love with you, Jane," Tom said. Jane felt his love and his trust lying on her, like a burden. She thought that he wanted her to say that she loved him too, and knew it was beyond her.

But he went on, "Don't say you love me. Don't think I want you to say it. What you've told me tonight is more than enough for you to say. Just let me be your friend, and we'll both wait and see what happens." Jane took his hand and held it tight. Through their gloves, the warmth of his touch seemed to soften the hard kernel of grief and guilt that lay like a stone, always, just beneath her heart.

30

Jane had thought a long time about what she would say and what she would keep secret when she had them all together.

She had decided that, despite her growing affection for Tom, despite her fondness for the others, she would say nothing about Brian's plans. It was true that they all felt safe now, with the greenmail scenario working its way toward a conclusion they believed they understood and could accept. But Jane was bound by a contract, a legal and a moral contract with Brian to keep silent about what was really happening. It was this loyalty that had shaped so much that had happened, and even now she could not let go of it. Brian's business strategy was not her secret, and she was not going to tell it.

Now, looking at them sitting around her in the living-room, she knew that what she was going to tell them would be a shock — if they believed it. She thought she could predict what they would do, and she hoped she was right. In any case, once this part of things was over, it wouldn't matter anymore what she did; her part would be played out, and the rest would be up to them — and to the police.

Martin and Martha were sitting on the sofa. Brian had

chosen Jane's rocking chair, and was facing them, looking, as usual, cool and contained. Robert McDonnell was sitting stiffly in a wicker chair brought in from the bedroom. On the floor, Tom was leaning his back against one of the hassocks. Jane, perched on the edge of a kitchen chair, checked anxiously that they all had full glasses. She patted her ribcage self-consciously.

"Now that my work for BTS is done," Jane said, "I want to say goodbye to you all, and that's one of the reasons I invited you over. But there's another. I think I know who murdered Gary Levin and I want to tell you about it first, before I tell anybody else."

They all looked back at her, silent, surprised. Finally Martha said with a tense little laugh, "Why tell us? Why not the police?"

"A tad bizarre," Martin said.

"I know," Jane said. "But this is something I want to do, so bear with me, okay?"

"You should have discussed this with me, first," Brian said, his voice cold, angry.

"I don't agree," Jane said.

Robert McDonnell looked very pale. Tom had told Jane that the comptroller had been happier since Saywell was hired, had given up his ambitions to be the top financial person, almost with relief. But he didn't seem happy to Jane. He had the anxious look of a man trying to convince himself of something without success. "Is this necessary, Jane?" he said.

"Here is what happened," Jane said, ignoring him. "The night Gary died you five had a meeting to thrash out the way the plans were going for what all of you — except Gary and Brian — thought was a merger. At least one of you knew Gary wouldn't come to such a meeting —"

"We all should have known," Tom interrupted. He

looked very unhappy. "You could tell, when Martha asked for the meeting, that he wouldn't deign to come —"

"That's right," Martha said.

At the same time Robert said, "*I* didn't know —"

"I'm sure Brian knew," Jane continued as if they hadn't spoken, her voice riding over theirs and silencing them. "He had more complicated plans than any of you realized. Gary knew those plans, and so it would have been a waste of Gary's time to come to hear all of you arguing over things that were irrelevant."

"Gary was not a man for wasting time," Martin Kaplan said. He got up, went into the kitchen and poured himself another drink. As he returned to his seat, his face was red. "This is a mistake, Jane. By doing this, you prove you are no friend to us."

Jane felt his anxiety, and the fears of the others, pressing on her, like powerful hands pushing against her chest. Their sense of their own rightness was like a wall, and for a moment, a sense of futility and helplessness washed over her. It seemed a sick joke to imagine that any words of hers could affect a large and powerful business, large and powerful people.

She went on. "The murderer was a person who desperately wanted to stop the merger, but shrank from taking the responsibility, the complete responsibility, for murder. I think the murderer wanted there to be an element of chance in the murder, a possibility that it might not happen. That same attitude was evident when there was an attempt on my life that was set up in the same risky way as Gary's murder. Both were planned so that the last card was played by chance. I think that the murderer was a person who was deceiving himself or herself, imagining that his or her acts were not actually murders, that fate would strike the final blow.

"What the hell are you talking about?" Martin said irritably.

"The murderer programmed the computer to crash at 12:55 A.M. The murderer also rigged up a gadget that was timed to set off the halon fire extinguisher a few minutes after the computer crashed. Then, when Gary went in to boot up, he was puffing on one of those little cigars of his. When you do that in a room full of halon — which is, as you all know, colourless, odourless, inert, harmless—the halon, taken up through the cigar is burned and turned into cyanide. That was what killed Gary. Halon is only dangerous when it's burned. That's why computer people are taught to get out of the computer room if a fire triggers the release of the halon."

"My God!" Brian said.

"Think how chancy it was," Jane said. "And think also, it couldn't have killed anybody but Gary. Only a smoker would have been endangered."

"But that's wrong, Jane," Martha said. "If the fire alarm had been triggered and the halon released, I would have seen that on the fire alarm system the moment I came in the room. The alarm light would have been flashing, showing the halon was depleted."

"You saw it," Jane said, her voice gentle, "but nobody else did — because you pulled the fire alarm as soon as you saw Gary's body. So when other people arrived on the scene, when you were calmer, of course the halon had been released and the alarm light was flashing. There was no way to know if it had happened when you came into the computer room, or when Gary died."

"My God! My God!" Brian said. "That means it was you, Martha. Who else could it have been? It had to be you, the first person into the computer room the next morning. So that you could remove whatever you rigged up to set off the halon fire system, so that you could pull the fire alarm and no one would know that the halon had been released hours before."

Everyone was looking at Martha, who sat still, her face pale and frozen, her eyes fixed on Jane. "He killed himself," Martha said, her voice cold and hard. "Jane said it. If Gary had come to that meeting, if Gary had been part of the team, he'd be alive today. But he was trying to destroy us, all of us, even Brian. What was he doing, working night after night, alone? I ran his histories; I checked the files he worked on. I knew he was going to sell us out — all of us — even you, Brian."

Brian was staring at her, his fists balled up, his shoulders hunched as if he expected to be attacked. "But to kill him. . . ." He stood up suddenly, as if he could not bear to sit across from Martha, and walked restlessly around the room, coming at the end of his circuit to stand behind Jane's chair.

Martha's face was no longer pale and frozen, Jane saw. It was now flushed with rage. "You men, you're all so passive. You play the game, but the rules are made by you and fixed by you. What did you all think? When BTS went sour you would just say, well, we have to take our lumps? We're up to our ass in alligators? Win some, lose some? There're a hundred people there counting on us to get it right. If we screw up and have to cut our expenses, that's not just numbers — that's people and jobs!

"Why didn't any of you *do* something? Money people play with numbers, but this game was our lives!" She struck the arm of the sofa with her palm, her face mottled so that Jane hardly recognized it.

"Don't give me that!" Martin, too, was in a rage. "Who do you think you're kidding? Now we can all see what you're really about. Boy, you had us fooled. You don't give a shit about anybody else and you never have. You just care about *your* life, *your* job. It's all been an act, a damn good act. But all along, you've just been looking after number one!"

Martha stood up so suddenly that Jane started. "Oh, to hell with you! To hell with all of you!" she said. Then, looking straight at Jane she said, "I thought you, you of all people would understand. But you didn't. I wish to God the electric shock had killed you, before you butted in with your little mealy-mouthed virtue. You're the worst, the worst of them all!" She turned, the door banged, and she was gone.

"Martha! Martha!" Jane called. The main door at the bottom of the stairs slammed, and Jane ran down the stairs, shrugging on her coat. Outside the night air was bitterly cold. Jane saw that Martha's car was in the driveway, boxed in by the others, Martha saw this too, turned, looked at Jane and began walking rapidly away along the dark street. Jane ran up to her, calling her name. A car moved along the street, parallel to them.

Martha stopped, turning suddenly, "You'll never prove it."

"You admitted it Martha. And I know."

"You know whatever you pretend to know," Martha spat out. "But think about what I said back there. I admitted nothing. That's because I did nothing. Ingenuity did it, skill did it, forward planning did it, machines did it — they're all guilty, but I'm not."

"Stop, Martha! Stop it!" They both were standing close together now, facing one another. Martha had rushed off without her coat, and was shivering in the cold. Jane took off hers and put it around Martha. "You're strong, very strong," Jane said. "Look at it, Martha. Look right at it. You killed Gary Levin and tried to kill me. *You* did those things. Nobody else." For a long time the two women looked at one another. Then Martha began to cry. Not as she had when she had played out the scene for Jane in her office, but awkwardly, with great, racking dry sobs that shook her body. Jane put her arms around her, and as she comforted Martha she felt the transponder the police had taped to her body press into her ribs. She waved dismissively at Sergeant Barrodale in the car following them along the street, and he nodded at her.

The two women walked slowly back the way they had come.

31

"The police were listening when I accused Martha," Jane said to Tom, "because I thought, I really thought, she might confess. And they wouldn't let me confront her unless I agreed to be wired."

"You were right about a lot of things," Tom said, "but wrong about that. She still hasn't admitted what she did. I don't think now, with lawyers and everything, she ever will."

"After they arrested her they searched her apartment," Jane said. "Sergeant Barrodale told me. They were hoping to find signs of the electrical equipment she built to trigger the halon fire-extinguishing system. But they didn't find anything. He says it doesn't matter, though. He says that the circumstantial evidence about the cause of the death, with the medical evidence, the fact that she was first on the scene and pulled the fire alarm, will be enough. Of course, her being a biochemist, she was most likely to know about the halon, and that will tell against her too."

They were in Tom's house, sitting close together on the sofa, and Tom was smoothing Jane's hair. They took every excuse they could to touch one another; they were being drawn closer and closer by both friendship and desire, but the space between them was still too great for them to bridge.

"Why did you do that, Jane? Why did you tell all of us what you thought had happened, instead of the police or Brian?"

Jane didn't answer. She was thinking of Brian. BTS stock was up substantially, and she thought that in the next day or so, the U.S. company and its white knight would make an offer that Brian would accept. The company that Brian had built was changing to something else. Tom had given his notice; Martha, of course, was no longer working there. Brian was close to realizing his ambitions. Was he happy? Did he feel vindicated? He seemed, to Jane, despite the events around Gary's murder, to be a man who had everything. A good marriage, a successful business, money, and now he was on the verge of being able to start again. And there was plenty of business for her, too, if she wanted it. Filling in the vacant positions at BTS, finding a few management people for Brian's new company. Would she take it? She hadn't decided.

She knew she had done the best she could, and so it was hard to understand the profound feeling of dissatisfaction she felt; perhaps it was the recognition that there had been no right solution. Was that why her throat ached so that it was difficult to swallow?

"Don't be angry with me, Jane," Tom was saying, "but somehow I think you did it all for Brian, so that Martha would step out before the police were involved, so that his strategy wouldn't be undermined."

"Maybe . . . I don't know," Jane said.

"I always feel as if there's something between you two, something I don't understand."

"Yes," Jane said.

"He uses you with his trust," Tom said, his voice sounding almost desperate.

"Does he? Is that what it is? Or was it, this time, the other way around?"

They were silent for a moment.

Then Tom said, slowly, almost unwillingly, "Yes, maybe this last time, it was the other way around."

"I want to see my children," Jane said, suddenly, turning to him. "I want to see them, be with them."

"Yes, I understand." He pulled her closer.

"And I'm falling in love with you."

"I understand that too," he said.

"But I might not get there."

"You've opened the door, anyway," he said. "That's a beginning."

"I'll do the best I can," Jane said. "That's all I can offer. Will that be good enough?"

"Yes," he said. "That will be good enough."

"Happy New Year," Jane said.

32

Oriono Gains Control of BTS Systems
U.S. firm wins battle for leading Canadian-owned software firm

*Oriono Datasystems of Chicago announced today it had ob-
tained a controlling interest in Brian Taylor Systems Inc. of
Toronto. After the close of trading today on the Toronto Stock
Exchange, Oriono had 57 percent of the shares in the Toronto-
based software company.*

*This announcement brings to a conclusion a hard-fought
battle for control of the highly profitable Canadian company.
Previously it was thought that BTS would succeed in its bid to
take over the larger U.S. firm. However, Oriono, with the help
of Arcon, a "white knight," succeeded in stopping the BTS
takeover bid and gaining control of its would-be aquisitor.*

*Oriono has announced its desire to keep the current
management team in place at BTS, but it appears that, well*

317

protected by "golden parachutes," all but Martin Kaplan, the vice-president of customer support, and Robert McDonnell, comptroller, will leave the firm.

Brian Taylor, founder and CEO of BTS, announced his resignation today after trading ceased on the TSE. He said that his shares have been purchased by Oriono for a sum estimated to be between $20- and $25-million (Canadian). Taylor has refused Oriono's offer of a seat on the board of directors. He has also said he will not be available to act in an advisory role during the transition phase.

In Ottawa, a spokesperson for the Minister of Industry and Small Business said that under the new foreign investment regulations there would be no problem whatsoever with the Oriono takeover.

Shares of Oriono Datasystems were up $2.00 at the close of trading on the NYSE today.

MAJOR NEW CRIME TITLES FROM VIRAGO

THE DOG COLLAR MURDERS

Barbara Wilson

**'Someone screamed, very loudly,
"You've *all* killed her!" '**

Loie Marsh, prominent anti-pornography activist, is found
strangled by a dog collar at a Seattle conference on
sexuality. The clues point to any number of suspects and
it's up to Pam Nilsen, the printer-sleuth of Barbara Wilson's
earlier mysteries, *Murder in the Collective* and *Sisters of the
Road*, to find the killer. Was it someone who wanted to
prevent Loie from speaking on her panel? The local lesbian
sadomasochists? Feminist activists opposed to censorship,
or Loie's ex-lover and former research collaborator? Or
someone from Loie's distant past? In investigating Loie's
death, Pam begins to come to terms with some of her own
fears and desires. Meanwhile the murderer is still at large
and strikes again . . .

MAJOR NEW CRIME TITLES FROM VIRAGO

BEYOND HOPE

Eve Zaremba

'A fast-paced thriller, featuring a female detective who's a cross between Philip Marlowe and Lily Tomlin. The one-liners alone are worth the trip' — Margaret Atwood.

A sixties revolutionary, Sara Ann Raymond, the daughter of a right-wing US presidential candidate, has been missing for ten years. She has recently been spotted working on a road-gang in the interior of British Columbia. What seems at first like a simple chore in vacation-land for Helen Keremos, lesbian detective, turns out to be her most complicated and terrifying case. Tracking down Sara Ann through the beautiful and remote mountains and valleys, Helen encounters an unlikely crew of people: an ex-draft resister, radical feminists, Doukhobor farmers and construction workers, a lumberjack . . . plus assorted agents, spies, arms smugglers, mobsters, cops . . . not to mention a dog. All are involved one way or another in a deadly game of multinational terrorism, murder and intrigue just forty miles from the Canadian-US border.

MAJOR NEW CRIME TITLES FROM VIRAGO

THE JAMES JOYCE MURDER

Amanda Cross

'If by some cruel oversight you haven't yet
discovered Amanda Cross, you have an
uncommon pleasure in store for you' — *New
York Times Book Review*

What could be more idyllic for Kate Fansler, Professor of
Literature, than a summer in the country sorting through
James Joyce's letters to his publisher. But with a
rumbustious young nephew and two graduate students in
residence, life is less peaceful than Kate might have hoped.
Then total chaos breaks out when a next-door neighbour is
murdered. Although the murder appears not to have the
remotest connection with literature, even the very
unliterary police inspector, Stratton, has a strong hunch
that the killing is somehow linked with James Joyce.
Amateur sleuth Kate, finding herself and her house guests
as prime suspects, sets out to solve the mystery. The
solution is as extraordinary as the murder itself.

MAJOR NEW CRIME TITLES FROM VIRAGO

THE QUESTION OF MAX

Amanda Cross

'Kate Fansler is the most appealing detective since Lord Peter Wimsey. She is the treasure at the centre of all Cross's cerebal puzzles, intelligent and self-doubting' — *Newsweek*

The exquisite Max Reston is the least likely person Kate Fansler would expect to invade her rural retreat — and, as things turn out, he is nearly the last. The two of them become deeply involved in the death of one of Kate's students, Geraldine, found drowned in a rock pool. Is it murder or simply a tragic accident? Kate cannot leave the matter alone and the teasingly elusive investigation leads her to Oxford, and to Somerville library, where she immerses herself in the past, unearthing clues she thinks lie hidden in the tangled lives of England's leading women novelists and feminists during the war years and the twenties.

This is Amanda Cross at her civilised and audacious best, with a highly original puzzle which will intrigue the most exacting reader.